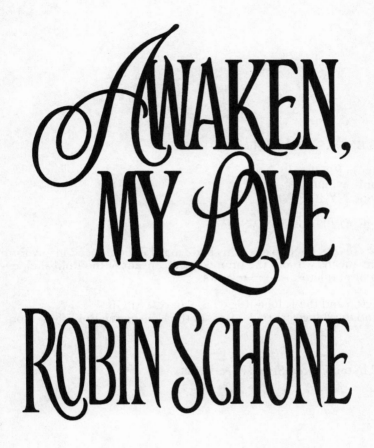

AWAKEN, MY LOVE

ROBIN SCHONE

BRAVA

KENSINGTON PUBLISHING CORP.

BRAVA BOOKS are published by

Kensington Publishing Corp.
850 Third Avenue
New York, NY 10022

Kensington and the K logo Reg. U.S. Pat. & TM Off.
Brava and the B logo are trademarks of the Kensington Publishing Corp.

ISBN 0-7394-1774-6

Printed in the United States of America

I dedicate this special edition of *Awaken, My Love*
to you, my readers.
It would not have been possible without you.
Thank you.

ACKNOWLEDGMENTS

Druidism is an ancient religion of magic and ritual. *The Magic Arts in Celtic Britain* by Lewis Spence (Dorset Press, 1992) helped me to unravel a few of its mysteries. I am particularly indebted to Mr. Spence for the two *fith-fath* spells that appear in my manuscript, the first a spell of transformation, the second a spell of invisibility.

Love, also, is a matter of magic and ritual. *The Encyclopedia of Erotic Wisdom* by Rufus C. Camphausen (Inner Traditions International, 1991) is an invaluable reference book for anyone interested in exploring Eastern and Western sexuality, both past and present. Thank you, Mr. Camphausen, for sharing your extensive research on Tantric traditions and terminology.

HER

Hot.
Wet.

Her flesh wept for release.

Matthew slept beside her in their Chicago condominium, as he had slept through seventeen years of emotional incontinence, forcing her to slake the very passions he inspired. Had used to inspire. Time and again he had turned her aside: "Go to sleep, honey; we'll make time tomorrow night," or, "Go to sleep, hon; we have a busy day tomorrow," or simply, "go to sleep; I'm bushed."

Her hips arched, fingers slippery with desire. For her husband. For someone. Somewhere. *Oh, God, what a waste.* It wasn't his fault, not Matthew's. All these years, forever, she had wanted that which could never be, would never be, wanted more than self-indulgence, fleeting, furtive pleasure—wanted, *wanted*—

Her breath caught in climax, loneliness a physical implosion. She was never more aware of just how alone she was than at these moments. She gratefully surrendered to the oblivion of solitary gratification.

HIM

Cold.

Dry.

Her flesh repelled his.

Morrigan turned her head aside, biting her lips to endure that which she had refused for the duration of their marriage, one year today—tonight. He gritted his teeth. Though reputed to be one of the most licentious men in England, he could not in good conscience seek another, forced to slake his passion on a woman who would be happy for him to do the very thing that his fickle nature would not allow.

His back arched, manhood flexing deep within his wife. Tension pooled at the base of his spine. *God, what a waste.* It wasn't her fault, not Morrigan's. He hadn't known, hadn't been able to see beyond his own desires. His own wants. But he did want; he did desire. More. More than this, more than duty, *more*—

His breath caught in climax. He had never known what aloneness was until this moment, knowing he would always be alone at moments like this. He gratefully surrendered to the oblivion of solitary gratification.

Chapter

1

Dorset England, 1883

The quirt fell and rose—once, twice, beating a silent rhythm. A
dark maze of geometrical patterns studded the chamber, the
four-poster bed an achromatic cube, the bedside table a dense cylin-
der, a chair a dusky quadrilateral. Within the four-poster bed the
woman lay deathly still, her patrician features a pale blur. A stark
white cap shrouded her head, unfrivolous, unfeminine, ungiving.

Charles Lucien Villiers Mortimer, twelfth Baron of Arlcotte,
clenched his hand about the descending quirt.

He was thirty-three years old. He had married this sleeping
beauty on her twentieth birthday. She had remained a virgin until
last night, her twenty-first birthday. And he . . . he had remained
celibate for one long, useless year, hoping against hope that he could
spark life into that cold, cold body.

A glimmer of gold shone in the shadows.

He had given Morrigan a ring of the purest gold to celebrate their
union, to replace the wedding band she had lost almost as soon as he
had slipped it onto her finger a year ago. A symbol of new beginnings, he had assured her, sliding the wide band onto her finger.
There was no shame in what a husband and wife did, he had reas-
sured her, gently kissing her lips.

She had turned her head aside, rejecting his kisses. Her body had
remained stiff and unresponsive, rejecting his seed.

And there was his ring on the bedside table.

Cold anger swelled over him. She must be awake; the report of the parting bed hangings had been pistol-sharp in the early morning silence.

The woman, his child bride, now his wife in body if not soul, remained effigy-still beneath his perusal. As if last night had never been—as if *he* had never been—which he himself would doubt if he had not washed her blood off of his male member, testimony of his virgin bride's unwilling sacrifice.

For one mad moment Charles wanted to rip the bedcovers away and see if she had pulled her gown down from around her hips, but of course she would have.

He was tired of expending unnecessary energy on lost causes. And Morrigan, he realized, was a lost cause.

When he had happened upon her in the forest thirteen months earlier, she had danced a fairy dance around a circle of worn stones, oddly graceful, beguiling as Eve. Her black hair had tumbled down her back. She had tossed handfuls of spring flowers into the air so that they rained down upon her head.

Watching her, he had thought that at last he had found that rarest of gems: a woman of passion.

Charles's fingers tightened around the riding crop.

His parents had lived together in placid harmony, as so many of the *ton* did, bartering wealth and titles for a marriage of comfort and convenience. He had sworn to avoid that particular hell. Now, having thumbed convention, he found himself wed with neither comfort nor convenience.

He had been so certain that she was the one, this child bride recently turned wife. So certain that he could unleash the needs that must surely be inside her, raised as she had been with hate and rejection and scorn. There must be emotion within her. Where was it, that she would be his soul mate, spirit to his spirit, sex to his sex. *Where was it?*

He forced his fingers to loosen, to give up that which he held.

Time and again she had turned him aside—his gifts, his person, denying her very station. All those long months, a lifetime, he had hoped against hope that he would reach her.

He could not.

The passion he had glimpsed in the forest had been a mirage, created by his own desires rather than hers.

Charles sighed, warm breath a stream of gray vapor in the chill room.

Would that he could have warmed her, that she had come hot and moist into his keeping, his care. He would have honored her until the day he died, loved her each night until she cried her pleasure.

Now . . .

Now it didn't matter.

If he could not have her passion, then he would have what he must: he would have an heir.

But not yet.

The thought of lying with her now, repeating the mating rite that she in her righteousness had turned into an act of self-gratification, made his stomach churn.

Last night he had been filled with regret for what should have been but never would be. Anger ruled this morning for what was and forever would be.

In his current frame of mind it would indeed be rape if he should press in his suit for an heir. Not the taking of a sanctimonious virgin bride, but an act of aggression with no other purpose than to inflict pain, as she had hurt him over the course of a year.

As he would continue hurting over the course of a lifetime.

A man alone.

A ray of sunlight blazed through the French doors behind Charles.

The indistinct blur of his wife's face, trapped between the starched nightcap and the silk sheet, sprang into focus.

Her eyelids twitched. Beneath the delicate skin he could see the pulsing network of tiny blue veins.

Without warning, Morrigan's lips—more red and swollen than usual from biting them to endure his caresses—gaped open. She audibly inhaled, a gagging sound that echoed in the dark corners of the chamber.

The hair on the back of Charles's neck stiffened.

He had heard that sound before from soldiers on the battlefield struggling to draw in one last breath: it was the sound of death.

The beam of light that illuminated his wife's face divided, what had been one becoming two. The bedside table leaped into clarity; on top of the ebony surface a gold ring glinted with red fire.

Endless seconds passed before suddenly the forked beam of light dimmed and the band of gold shrank to a dull gleam.

Muted red dawn infiltrated the chamber, infusing Morrigan's pale cheeks with the radiance of a new day. The bedcovers over her chest shimmered with velvety yellow highlights, rhythmically rising, falling.

Charles expelled his breath, not even aware he had been holding it until new air expanded deep inside his lungs—chill, damp, musky with the stench of stale sweat and white ginger–scented sheets.

Anger roiled anew.

She still played the game, sleep to his wake, ice to his fire, death to his dreams.

He snatched the ring off the night table. "It will not fadge, Morrigan. I know you're awake."

Morrigan remained silent, still, righteously aloof.

Charles ripped the covers down to her waist and grabbed her left hand.

Her eyes popped open at the unexpected contact, showing the lie: that she had been awake all along, certain in her power over him and their travesty of a marriage.

He pressed the ring into the palm of her hand and forced her fingers around it.

They were stiff, unyielding. Her blank stare mocked his efforts.

He could not force her to accept the ring, her gaze said. Any more than he had been able to woo her with gifts and kindness.

Charles stepped back.

Immediately her hand plopped down onto the mattress. The gold band spilled from her palm and rolled between the sheets.

Morrigan made no move to retrieve it, impervious to the end.

He gritted his teeth. "You are my wife. Whether you choose to wear my ring or not is immaterial. Think about this, *wife*. I will be gone a fortnight. When I return, willing or not, ring or not, you will be mare to my stud, for I have a stable to fill, and by God, madam, you *will* fill it."

Viciously he pulled shut the bed hangings, a sharp clang in the stillness of dawn. Smooth silk momentarily clung to his fingertips before falling in a curtain of gleaming yellow.

The Oriental carpet that he had taken great expense and trouble to purchase for a wife who cared naught for him or his home muffled his retreating footsteps. Bleakly he wondered if two weeks would be enough time to work out the anger of a lifetime of disillusionment.

Outside Morrigan's room the house was subtly alive. A distant clang of pots and pans heralded breakfast for some fifty-odd servants. The muffled tread of an army of shuffling footsteps descended from the attic bedchambers, traipsing like carpenter ants through the various corridors hidden behind the elegant walls.

A narrow door opened near the end of the carpeted hallway.

Charles smirked, espying the familiar figure. Pausing, standing well back from the open door and the openly bristling woman, he gave her a mock bow. "My round, Mistress Hattie."

Chapter

2

Elaine blinked at the abrupt darkness. What a strange dream. The culminating sharp clang echoed in her mind.

It was so cold—Matthew must have turned the thermostat down. There was a tightness about her head and underneath her chin—the pillow or sheet had somehow wrapped around her. She dislodged the constricting material and pulled the covers up over her face.

Elaine stirred restlessly. It was too quiet. And the sheets were scented. She must have picked up the wrong fabric softener last week.

She slid her left hand out and away from her body, simultaneously flexing her left leg; yes, that was nice—the slight realignment of body and sheets afforded a wealth of deliciously cool comfort. The realignment also brought home the awareness of a burning, stinging sensation between her legs.

Elaine frowned, the slight pull of facial muscles adding to her unwanted wakefulness. Shifting her legs, she felt a cold, viscous fluid.

Surely it had not come from her. Certainly it had not come from Matthew. Matthew made love only on Wednesday evenings; this was Monday morning.

Oh, no. Elaine remembered that her secretary started vacation today. She would be stuck with a moron temp who didn't know her head from her parallel interface port.

Without warning, the silence exploded in an earsplitting clang. The bedcovers were ripped away in a rush of frigid air.

Elaine's eyes and mouth and body jerked open and upward.

"Ach, that filthy *Sassenach* couldna keep 'is 'ands off ye, could 'e? M' puir little lamb, look at ye, co'ered wi' 'is filth!"

Elaine lowered her eyes against the pale flood of light where but moments before there had been unmitigated darkness. The startled surge of adrenaline was arrested at the sight of a white cotton nightgown. It was bunched up around her waist. Something dark crusted her inner thighs—thighs which were surprisingly shapely beneath a patch of thick black pubic hair.

Elaine's shrinking pupils dilated.

A liver-spotted hand jerked the hem of the nightgown down over the bushy black hair and splotched thighs. "There, there, m' dear, ol' Hattie'll take care o' m' little lamb; ne'er ye fear."

Fine black hair covered the slender legs protruding from the more modestly arranged gown. The left calf was covered with puckered white scars.

Elaine forced her eyes up and away from the scarred, hairy leg.

Pale light aureoled the old woman leaning over the bed. She wore a dark, bell-shaped dress and an Aunt Jemima–type apron. A puffy white cap covered her head and ears. She looked like a character out of a movie adaptation of a Charles Dickens novel.

Elaine was having a waking dream.

She lay back and closed her eyes. *Damn.* She really could use a few more hours of sleep. She felt as if she had walked all the way from Chicago to New York and back to Chicago again, but judging by the light streaming through her eyelids it was almost time to get up. Just as well. First there had been a man with a whip, and now this. She was afraid of what her dreams would conjure up next.

"Git up; it's temptin' th' de'il, ye are! I willna be lettin' ye git idears in yer 'ead now 'e's 'ad ye!"

Elaine was physically hauled out of bed. A heavy black braid spilled over her left shoulder; at the same time a sticky glob of fluid oozed from between her thighs.

She dug her toes into a wool carpet and stared down at the old woman's puffed cap. It was flat on top. Warmth emanated from the scarecrow body—along with a body odor strong enough to fell a football player at twenty yards.

Elaine's heart skipped a beat before wildly racing. This was no dream. She could not ever recall smelling anything in a dream. Yet it had to be a dream. This wasn't her and Matthew's bedroom. She wasn't wearing her tricot nylon pajamas. Those slender, hairy legs did not belong to her, not plump Elaine who religiously shaved. Her pubic hair was the color of her other hair, mousy brown threaded with gray. Her left calf was not scarred. Matthew did not speak with a bastardized Scottish accent, nor was he in the habit of masquerading as a nineteenth-century bag lady.

She took a deep, calming breath. She was thirty-nine years old. This was not the first dream she had had in which she dreamed she was dreaming. There was nothing to panic about. Now that she knew she was dreaming she would wake up. That always happened in sex dreams, right on the precipice of a tremendous climax. There was a faint pressure in her lower abdomen. She needed to pee. Didn't that prove it was a dream?

"What ails ye, girl?"

Upon closer inspection the old woman looked more than ever like a character out of a Charles Dickens movie adaptation. Scrooge's twin sister, perhaps. Played by Bela Lugosi.

"Ye look as if ye'd ne'er a'seen yer ol' Hattie!" The sexagenarian's words were punctuated by white plumes of vapor, rendering the scene even more dreamlike. "Ach, I tol' ye t' wear th' garlic, tol' ye it'd keep 'is lordship from mountin' m' puir little girl! Ne'er ye fear. 'E's gone, th' *Sassenach;* 'e willna be dirtyin' ye wi' 'is dirty *Sassenach* 'ands agin. Ye're a good girl; I willna let ye be else. Sit o'er 'ere; 'tis shamin' th' Lord, ye are, standin' in yer night rail wi' yer 'air 'angin' down about."

Elaine found herself being turned and marched across a bedroom easily the combined size of her and Matthew's living room, dining room, and kitchen. The large, rectangular bed blocked most of the light. Elaine stumbled—righted herself—only to stumble again. She felt like Cinderella after the ball, with one shoe on and one shoe off.

She collapsed onto a curved wooden bench with bright yellow silk upholstering. A dull ache shot up through her pelvis. She stared into the shadowy depths of the dressing table mirror. The hair ruthlessly released from the braid was black as night. Eyes like great dark gapes in a fluorescent ceiling returned her perusal. The waist-length hair was anchored in a tight bun by hundreds of needle-sharp hairpins. Reflexive tears pricked Elaine's eyes.

"Git up now. Ye'll pray fer yer breakfas', aye, an' pray th' *Sassenach* dinna soil yer soul."

A gnarled hand grabbed the girl in the mirror by the nape of the neck. A stumbling, clumsy Elaine was pushed to the opposite side of the room. A massive black screen monopolized the corner. It winked.

Elaine was jerked to a halt in front of a plain, unlacquered table. Pressure accrued on the back of her neck. She dropped like a steel beam, knees cracking, half-on, half-off, of the carpet and cold, hard wood. A large, moldy-looking crucifix was attached to the wall above the table. Fingers every bit as hard as the wooden floor bordering the carpet forced Elaine's head forward.

"Ye pray now, lovey; ye git all th' dirt an' filth out o' yer soul. Ye pray real 'ard now, or ol' Hattie willna take th' blame, canna now, cause yer nae ol' Hattie's girl anymore; 'e did that, that filthy *Sassenach*, took away m' puir little girl."

The old woman knelt suffocatingly close, her voice alternately rising and falling in a didactic blend of admonition and prayer. The greens, blacks, and yellows of the woven carpet mishmashed with the sharp pains running up and down Elaine's knees. The fullness in her lower abdomen increased to the point of bursting.

The wailing and praying abruptly ceased. There was a swish of skirts interspersed with the creak of bones. The peculiar body odor dispersed; Elaine gratefully gulped fresh air. The smart closure of a door echoed behind her.

Elaine jumped up. This wasn't a dream; it was a nightmare. The old woman was crazy. This whole nightmare was crazy. Fortunately the end was in sight.

She stumbled toward the ebony screen. A life-size geisha girl was carved into each of the three panels; the kimono-clad beauties coyly wielded jewel-encrusted fans. It was their jewels that winked and blinked in the chill gloom. A large, fluted bathtub resided behind the screen, and not the door she had hoped to find.

Elaine pivoted. Bathroom, bathroom, she must find a bathroom; only then would she be released from this nightmare. Finding one, she would awaken, go to the john, and hope like hell there were a few more minutes before the alarm went off.

Elaine discovered a small door between the "praying" table and the dressing table, but it was locked. There was another door opposite the yellow silk–lined bed, larger than the first. Elaine could not bring herself to try it for fear the old crone in the bell-hoop skirt would pop up like a macabre jack-in-the-box. A sudden inspiration sent her down onto her knees beside the enormous boxed bed.

Porcelain glinted in the cavernous depths. Quickly Elaine dragged the chamber pot clear of the bed and hurried to the Japanese screen. Dream or no dream, she would not risk exposing herself.

The porcelain was cold. It bit into her buttocks. Her left leg cramped and protested the ungainly position. Near-orgasmic relief was brutally terminated by a splatter of hot liquid. Elaine jumped. She gritted her teeth and finished, automatically reaching for a roll of toilet paper, but there was none, nor, upon reflection, could she ever remember having had that commodity in previous bathroom dreams.

She stood, grimacing. Neither could she ever remember residue urine dribbling down the inside of her thighs.

Well, it would soon be over now, she consoled herself. In another second she would again be perched on that god-awful pot peeing her brains out. The scene would repeat itself several times and then she would wake up to seek the real McCoy.

No sooner did Elaine straighten up than she heard the echo of the door opening and closing. Leaving the chamber pot lid on the floor, she braced herself and stepped out from behind the Japanese screen.

"Ye need t' be eatin' a little somethin'; ye got a lot o' prayin' t' do. I willna let that *Sassenach* undo all our good work, me an' th' Lord's. I pledged th' rev'ren', so I did, an' I willna let th' de'il take yer soul like 'e took yer leg. Come o'er 'ere; I ain't got time fer yer fags."

Elaine ran her hand over her stomach. There was no renewal of pressure inside. Forcing down a surge of panic, she limped across the Oriental carpet, holding the gown well out from beneath her feet. It did no good. She still stumbled.

It was warmer near the French doors. Dust motes danced in the bright morning sunlight. Elaine sat down in front of a small ebony table, where a silver tray had been deposited.

With a flourish, the old woman balanced the hollow cover on the edge of the table. Clicking her tongue, she then hurried toward the bed. The yellow drapes flew back with a grating clang of metal hooks on a metal rail.

Elaine stared down at the silver tray, through force of habit shaking out the accompanying napkin and spreading it over her lap. The most unappetizing dish she had ever seen lay congealed in a dainty rose-and-green-painted china bowl. It was gray, like mortar. Smooth, like mortar. She picked up a heavy silver soupspoon.

It tasted far, far worse than mortar.

She put down the spoon, using her tongue to pry the oatmeal-based foodstuff off the roof of her mouth. Reaching, then, for the single cup of liquid, she washed down the food with the weakest cup of tea she had ever had the misfortune of drinking.

A scratching sound came from behind her. Elaine turned, wide-eyed with curiosity; at the same time the old woman called out, "Come in, ye fagged *Sassenach;* th' door dinna be locked!"

The door that Elaine had been afraid to try opened. A white cap bounced above a load of folded laundry; a black skirt belled out beneath. The faceless figure turned to Elaine and bobbed a curtsy.

"Begging yer pardon, yer ladyship, I brung yer linen." The girlish voice behind the laundry was pleasantly musical, purely English. "I'll just be a minute, marm, or I can come later, if ye'd rather. His lordship, he left orders fer ye to have a bath, marm; the water's all heated, it be just a bit more—"

"An' since when is 'is lordship gi'in' ye orders fer m'lady, ye fagged *Sassenach*? Change th' linens, an' mind ye hasten. I willna 'ave ye a'sullyin' 'er ladyship's ears wi' yer drivel. An' dinna mind that bath. Bah! Ye *Sassenach*! Ye'd warsh th' skin right off a body. 'Tis indecent, doin' all that bathin'. If th' good Lord wanted us t' bathe, why, 'e woulda made us wi' scales, now wouldna 'e? Hsch! Dinna ye tarry, girl! There's work t' be done!"

Elaine's eyes darted from the young English maid to the old Scottish harridan. A secret smile played about the corners of her mouth. Bath. Water. A dream symbol as potent as a bathroom. The nightmare would be over very soon now.

The maid changed the sheets on the bed. The old woman kept up a vituperative monologue, berating the maid, the *Sassenach*, the maid, always coming back to the *Sassenach*. Elaine intercepted more than one sympathetic glance from the young maid, who was just a child, really, no more than seventeen.

Another scratch, more timid than the first, sounded from the door. An even smaller maid entered, nothing but a child—a *child* child—only six or seven years old. She carried a shiny clean chamber pot. Head bowed so that only the stark white cap was visible, she dropped a curtsy before scampering toward the bed. The child pushed the chamber pot underneath; her little black-clad backside wriggled for several seconds. She suddenly straightened and turned frightened eyes toward the old woman, then to Elaine, then back to the old woman, who was busy upbraiding the adolescent maid, then back to Elaine.

Obviously the little maid wanted the chamber pot that Elaine had used.

Elaine wondered at the symbolism of this. She supposed that in this dream, instead of running from one bathroom to the next, she would be running from one chamber pot to the next. She pointed toward the far corner.

The child broke out into a wide grin, displaying two missing front teeth, before scuttling over to the Japanese screen. She disappeared, then immediately reappeared clutching the used chamber pot to her chest, no doubt still warm, Elaine thought, her cheeks burning.

"An' dinna ye be a'spillin' that, ye little *Sassenach*!"

The child maid stumbled; a yellow stain blossomed on her white apron above the chamber pot. "Yeath, marm," she lisped softly. "I mean no, marm."

Bobbing a curtsy, the little maid escaped through the door, only to return minus the chamber pot and urine-doused apron. Her little shoulders drooped over the weight of a copper bucket. She set the bucket down beside a black-and-yellow-lacquered chest and stretched to reach the green pitcher and matching bowl centered atop.

Elaine watched the child maid labor with satisfaction. More water. The little girl used the balcony outside the French doors for a sink, another signal to Elaine's subconscious.

"I found yer ring, marm—here it be; it wus lying between the sheets."

The adolescent maid stood in front of Elaine, her body bobbing in a curtsy, her right arm extended. Elaine instinctively reached out her hand.

"What d' ye think ye're doin', ye fagged *Sassenach*? Ye gi' that t' me, ye 'ear. I willna let 'er ladyship be spoiled by fancy gewgaws!"

Out of the corner of her eye Elaine saw a flurry of black and white. Instantaneously a warm weight dropped into her palm. She closed her fingers around a circular object.

"Ach, look what ye did, ye clumsy *Sassenach*!

The adolescent maid skipped out of range just as a black-clad arm slapped outward. Deprived of prey, the old woman thrust her hand toward Elaine in a no-nonsense, you'll-be-sorry-if-you-don't-comply type of manner.

"Gi' it t' me, Morrigan, girl, or I willna be responsible fer it."

The adolescent maid gathered up the soiled linens. She and the child maid carrying the copper water bucket made a hasty exit.

"I sed gi' it t' me. I've put up wi' enough o' yer nonsense fer one day."

Elaine studied the circular object. It was surprisingly heavy. The smooth surface gleamed with a rich red hue.

"Gi' it t' me!"

Elaine raised her hand to comply, but instead of handing the ring over, her right hand slipped it onto the ring finger of her left hand. Without volition. As if the ring had a mind of its own.

Elaine stared in horrified fascination at the ring, at the long white finger that wore it, then at the long white fingers that adjoined it. Piano fingers. She had dreamed of having fingers like these when she was a child, instead of the short, sturdy fingers that had belonged to the short, sturdy systems analyst–type person Elaine had become and not the concert pianist that she had wanted to become more than anything on earth. The soft gold seemed almost to mold itself around her flesh, pulsing in time with that place between her thighs.

"I willna 'ave ye gainsayin' me doin's, girl. Yer ol' Hattie knows what's best fer ye. Now gi' me that ring!"

Elaine slowly raised her head, dream complaisance turning to anger. If there was one thing she could not abide, it was a bully.

"I sed gi' it t' me!"

Two things happened simultaneously. Elaine watched the old woman's hand pull back; at the same time she realized that the forthcoming blow was not the product of a nightmare. The pistol-sharp crack elicited upon impact supported the theory. The stinging imprint of five fingers irrevocably proved it.

Being the logical, systems analyst–type person that Elaine was, one conclusion rapidly followed the next.

This was no dream, and she was in deep—trouble.

Chapter

3

"Ach!" Hattie picked up the breakfast-laden table and pigeon-walked it backward. "Git up. I see ye willna eat yer haggis. Enjoyin' yer sulks, aye, that ye do, a sure sign o' th' de'il."

The dream anger that had consumed Elaine just moments before burgeoned into very real panic.

"That *Sassenach*, 'e willna be 'ere t'night nor fer a full fortnight. 'Eard that pulin' manservant o' 'is say so 'imself."

She, Elaine, was in Morrigan's body.

"Dinna ye worry, I'll git th' de'il out o' ye, and when 'e comes back, ye willna furgit t' wear the garlic, now, will ye?"

Her pupils—Elaine's? Morrigan's?—dilated to the point where they felt as if they would explode. The five fingerprints emblazoned on her cheek pounded in time to her heartbeat.

"Ach, it be e'il, what men do t' us womenfolk, but ne'er ye fear, ye puir little lamb; I'll save ye from th' likes o' 'im."

Puir? Hysteria bubbled on the top of Elaine's tongue. Was she being called poor, as in financially indigent, or pure, as in morally intact? Hattie claimed she was going to save Morrigan. Who, she wondered, was going to save Elaine?

The old woman frowned. She bore an uncanny resemblance to a bulldog. "Ye ain't said a word all mornin'. Ye ain't th' only girl t' 'ave 'er 'ymen burst. Th' good Lord, 'e made us women t' suffer fer the pleasurin' o' man. Spread yer legs, then, an' let ol' Hattie see what th' lord did wi' 'is pillagin'.''

Hattie stepped around the ebony table.

Elaine clamped her legs together, her mouth opening to tell the old woman exactly who and what she could see. Her jaws audibly snapped shut.

The maid had spoken with an English accent, but Hattie spoke with a Scottish one.

What was Morrigan? English . . . or Scottish?

It was a sure bet she wasn't American.

"Pshaw!" Hattie stomped off to an ebony armoire the size of a garden shed. She retrieved a drab gray dress and threw it over her shoulder. "Ye're goin' t' 'ave yer sulk, I see." She bustled toward the lacquered black-and-yellow chest. Her voice was muffled. "Dinna think 'is *Sassenach* lordship'll be keepin' ye 'ere in Dorset. 'E's 'ad ye now; 'e willna 'ave ye agin—I willna let 'im." She turned with an armful of material. "Stand up. I canna dress ye when ye're sittin' on yer arse!"

Elaine took a deep breath, forcing down the scream that hovered behind her tonsils. So. She was in Dorset. That didn't solve the mystery of Morrigan's accent, but at least it told her where she was. Dorset was in England.

Bedlam had been in England.

Oh, God.

She was in Charles Dickens's country and era, a place and time when women had yet to gain the right to vote. When women and orphans could be impounded as easily as a stray cat or dog.

Elaine gritted her teeth and stood up. Hattie tossed the armful of clothes onto the chair. Without hesitation she reached for the long row of buttons lining the front of Elaine's nightgown.

Icy air invaded the broadening neckline of the cotton gown.

Elaine had not been dressed since she was five years old. She found it a thoroughly distasteful process thirty-four years later. The old woman performed the service so perfunctorily that it was obvious it was a morning ritual, something Morrigan would not have

blinked an eye at, however much Elaine herself objected to exposing cold, pebbled nipples.

Elaine stared down at the small round breasts. The nipples were
dark brown, disproportionately long and swollen-looking.

The white gown dropped around Elaine's feet.

"Git yer 'ead up; what d'ye think ye're lookin' at?"

A stinging red suffused the too-white skin. Elaine jerked her chin
up. Almost simultaneously a calf-length slip was forced over her
head and arms.

She reluctantly thrust her hands through what looked like a
sleeveless straitjacket.

"'Old in yer ribs, girl; I willna 'ave ye showin' what's 'tween ye
an' th' Lord."

Elaine's lungs collapsed like an accordion. The straitjacket was a
corset. Elaine had never worn anything more constrictive than
control-top panty hose. She remembered reading that the constant
wearing of corsets had actually broken and misaligned women's rib
bones. Surreptitiously she ran a hand over the slender, elongated
waist. How many ribs had been broken to achieve it?

Hattie tossed a canvas-stiff, long half-slip over Elaine's head and
tied it around her waist; two others followed in rapid succession. A
heavy drape of gray wool next settled over her head. The skirt of the
dress flared in a bell shape, like those of Hattie's and the two maids'.
Once buttoned, the high-necked, long-sleeved bodice fit her upper
abdomen tighter than her own skin had in the twentieth century.

A hand pressed down on her shoulder. Hard. Elaine toppled back
into the chair.

"'Old yer feet out. 'Ow d'ye expect me t' put yer shoes on?"

Elaine extended her feet. They were long and narrow with high
arches, a far cry from her own square, flat feet. The multitude of
skirts and slips were impatiently pushed up into her lap.

The old woman's hands were warmer than the air. They crawled
up the thin, hairy legs like giant, wrinkled, liver-spotted slugs, first
smoothing a pair of coarse wool stockings, then tying the thigh-
length tops with corded strings. Hard black leather shoes were

squeezed onto the narrow feet, their only claim to comfort being in the rounded toes.

"There." The white slips and gray wool skirt were jerked down. Hattie sprang up from the floor, a scrawny black-and-white phoenix. "Ye know what t' do, girl. Scriptin' keeps th' de'il away; that be what th' rev'ren' say."

Hattie turned and bent over the breakfast table. The astoundingly broad backside barked.

Elaine bit back an incredulous laugh. All sense of humor fled when the old woman's pervasive body odor was immediately overridden by an even stronger one.

Hattie swung around. She balanced the silver tray in one hand; the other she shook in Elaine's face, as if the charge and not the keeper had committed a gross impropriety. "Mind yer penship, now!"

Seconds later the door slammed shut behind Hattie.

Elaine scrambled to her feet. The action, combined with the binding of the corset, left her slightly dizzy. She ignored the too-tight shoes and the dark specks that danced in front of her eyes. She needed answers, and she needed them now.

She bolted for the black-and-yellow-lacquered chest. The wool carpet rose to meet her.

Elaine caught herself on the ebony table just before she catapulted facedown. *Damn.* The limp was not a result of a Cinderella syndrome, one shoe on and one shoe off, but rather of a shorter left leg. Inestimable time lapsed, forced to move at a snail's pace while her heart raced at the speed of a Pentium processor.

The top chest drawer was filled with towels and washcloths. She unearthed a bar of harsh-smelling soap, discarded it. The second drawer contained underclothes identical to the ones she now wore, and four nightgowns. The third drawer was filled with a totally different type of underclothes, silks and laces that at any other time would have thrilled her all the way down to her feminine toes. Satin corsets were neatly stacked in the fourth drawer, with cups—unlike the torture device that now flattened her size A breasts into double

A. She picked up a pair of lace-tiered drawers; her fingers slid through the seamless crotch.

A large blue marble was buried beneath an assortment of peeka-boo lace and flimsy gauze nightgowns in the bottom drawer. Elaine dug more deeply. A familiar scent wafted upward. She lifted a box of soaps and powders, recognizing the scent now: white ginger, the scent that was on the sheets. Setting the box aside, she picked up the piece of white silk that it had been sitting on.

There was something inside.

Elaine carefully unfolded the slippery material. A small dried leaf broke off. Morrigan had saved a bough of mistletoe. Hurriedly Elaine folded the silk cloth and tucked it back inside the drawer.

The massive armoire was filled with rows and rows of dresses in every conceivable color and material. Elaine fanned out the skirt of a yellow satin gown. It resembled drapery more than a dress, complete with valance, cords, braids, and tassels, definitely not the style worn in Charles Dickens's time. The discovery was of less immediate concern—no time to panic at its significance. She hastily drew her hand back from a large wire cage buried behind the dresses.

Did Hattie hang Morrigan from the ceiling if the girl misbehaved?

Wriggling backside-first out of the wardrobe, she straightened the matching assortment of shoes underneath the clothes. The base of the armoire was lined with myriad drawers. They contained all the accessories a nineteenth-century lady could possibly want—hand-kerchiefs, gloves, scarves, small baglike purses, silk stockings, elasticized garters—and absolutely nothing of benefit to a twentieth-century woman seeking answers.

Elaine wildly glanced about. She hurried to the other side of the room, lurching side to side like a run-down top.

The large black Bible centered on the ebony desk was devoid of family history or even of proof of ownership, as blank and impersonal as a Gideon Bible in a hotel room. The top drawer contained bottles of ink and what Elaine assumed was a precursor to the modern-day fountain pen, little more than a steel quill tip screwed onto a tapering wooden handle like the kind used on an artist's paintbrush. The stack of blank stationery she immediately assigned for toilet paper.

Elaine opened a second drawer, and almost laughed with triumph. She picked up the sheaf of papers and quickly thumbed through the stack. And almost cried with dismay.

Painstakingly copied, verse after verse, were whole books of the Bible: Hosea, Daniel, Ezekiel, Lamentations, Jeremiah, Isaiah. The script was the same, small and awkward, sharply slanted to the left.

She carefully put back the finished papers and opened the bottom drawer. It was filled to overflowing, the script the same—Morrigan's—pages and pages, the work of months, perhaps years, of laborious Bible transcriptions.

Elaine braced herself against the hysteria straining to burst free. She determinedly pictured Morrigan's pale, thin face with its swollen red lips and dark, haunted eyes that had earlier stared at her from the depths of the mirror. The girl was only what—eighteen? Nineteen? Even Elaine at the ripe old age of thirty-nine had secrets, special hiding places where she stashed those things better left for her eyes alone. There had to be letters, books, something that would give her a clue as to who Morrigan was, English or Scottish, there had to be, damn it!

She stood up, blindly stumbled toward an occasional table topped with a heavy candelabra that looked as if it had never been lit.

"An' just what d'ye think yer doin', pray tell?"

Elaine's heart slammed against the boned corset. She swiveled toward the door, grabbing the occasional table to retain her balance. The candelabra rocked dangerously close to the edge.

Hattie wielded the silver tray that had earlier held breakfast. Behind the old woman Elaine could make out a shadowy hallway, visible proof that there was life beyond the four walls of this bedroom.

Suspicion glimmered in the old woman's rheumy eyes. "I tol' ye t' do yer penship. It's scriptin' th' Lord's words that keeps ye from e'il."

Hattie closed the door. "Ye've been a bad puss, but ol' Hattie'll feed ye. Ye go an' kneel an pray t' th' good Lord. I willna let th' de'il 'ave yer soul."

Elaine limped to the plain table and lowered herself to her knees. The tarnished crucifix monitored her clumsy movements.

Dear God . . .

Prayer refused to come. Elaine licked her lips.

"Yer t' pray, little girl; dinna I say ye was t' pray?"

Hattie set the tray down on the table. Elaine was surrounded in a flurry of black and white. Her head was yanked back, chin anchored against a bony white bosom.

"Yer ol' Hattie's girl." Elaine willed herself not to move at the vent of halitosis, concentrating instead on a sliver of dried meat that adhered to the old woman's stained apron. "Ol' Hattie willna let ye 'urt yerself."

Elaine was abruptly released.

"Now bend yer 'ead and close yer eyes."

Darkness.

Coldness.

Elaine shook with it.

Without warning, hot liquid spilled onto her lips and chin. She jerked back, eyes instinctively opening.

"Nae, little girl, close yer eyes. It's prayin' ye need, an' prayin' ye'll do. Now open yer mouth. I willna leave yer side till the de'il's cleansed out'a yer body. T'morrow ye'll be ol' Hattie's girl agin. I willna let th' lord take ye away from me."

Tomorrow.

Electric hope surged through Elaine.

She closed her eyes and opened her mouth.

Tomorrow morning she would awaken between permanent-press sheets. She and Matthew would laugh over Sara Lee croissants and gulp strong, hot coffee. They would catch the bus and be jostled in the morning rush.

Scalding broth filled her mouth; Elaine automatically swallowed.

Matthew would get off at Michigan Avenue; Elaine would get off at Randolph, there to fight more people and cars to cross the street.

A wad of bread was stuffed between her teeth.

All of it mad.

She and Matthew had often joked about moving to the suburbs to escape the hustle of the city.

The brittle edge of china pressed against Elaine's lips. A gush of tepid tea followed.

All of it quite, quite sane in its utter madness.

Chapter
4

Elaine's backside exploded in pain.

"Ach, ye be sleepin' th' day away, girl! Ye dinna draw th' curtain t' yer bed; ye'll catch yer death! And jus' what d' ye think ye were doin', ruinin' yer puir nightcap an' sleepin' like a *Sassenach* 'eathen? Git up now. I willna 'ave ye temptin' th' de'il wi' yer laziness!"

Elaine fought a tangle of slippery sheets to sit upright.

Pale gray light streamed through French doors. Bela Lugosi in a bell-hoop skirt stood over the bed, nursing a rumpled white cloth.

Elaine blinked. Just a second earlier she had been telling Matthew about the mad nineteenth-century dream she had had when all of a sudden the bottom of her chair had detonated. She could still smell their shared breakfast—strong, hot coffee and freshly baked Sara Lee croissants. Tears filled her eyes, realizing the first had been a dream and the latter reality.

Hattie raised her right hand as if to issue another wallop. "Git up, I say!"

Elaine's dismay at not finding herself in her own familiar time dissipated in a surge of anger. Yesterday she had been too disoriented to defend herself against the old woman's tyranny. Not so today. Absolutely she would not tolerate any more physical abuse.

Hattie's grim-lipped snarl sagged. The liver-spotted hand lowered; she took a half step backward. A crafty gleam suddenly appeared in the rheumy eyes.

"Ye be bright-eyed t' be sleepin' s' late. Mayhap ye ain't been a'sleepin' a'tall. Mayhap ye been doin' other things, things ye ain't s'pose t' be doin'. Ye been doin' dirty, sinful things? Playin' wi' yerself, mayhap? Now 'is *Sassenach* lordship 'as 'ad ye, ye got a 'ankerin' fer it, ain't ye, girl?"

Elaine's glare turned to puzzlement. Doing other things, things she wasn't supposed to be doing? Doing dirty things, playing with—

Herself!

Blistering heat rose to Elaine's chest, neck, and face.

Playing with herself!

Why, that old biddy! Elaine opened her mouth, forgetting the need for silence, forgetting that this was an era where Bedlam was a place and not just a word. Forgetting that although she had somehow been transported into Morrigan's body she, Elaine, spoke with a Midwestern Yankee drawl and not with the Scottish or English accent that Morrigan was bound to possess.

"Ach, ye be a good girl. Aye, I'll see t' it, m' puir little lamb; ye willna suffer th' *Sassenach* agin. Pray, that's what ye'll do, pray fer th' almighty Lord t' forgive ye." With a twist of an arthritic hand the sexagenarian pulled down the bedcovers. "Git up now; git up an' pray."

Elaine's bared thighs erupted into a solid mass of goose bumps, while at the opposite end her ears burned and throbbed. Grabbing hold of the gown that was twisted up around her waist, she pulled, but it was firmly entrenched beneath her buttocks. She leaped off the bed, the force of her body catapulting Hattie back and away, and jerked the nightgown down around her hips.

Elaine hated gowns. They always did this. That was why she wore pajamas, to prevent herself from being strangled.

She gritted her teeth against the knowing smirk on the old harridan's face. *Damn, damn, and double damn!*

Hattie reached out a proprietary hand and commenced unfastening the long row of buttons lining the front of Elaine's nightgown. "Ye've been o'erly cosseted, that ye 'ave, an' look where it's got ye, sinnin' wi' yer own 'and. It's puir t' see, Morrigan, m' girl, ye take a mile when gi'en an inch, an' I willna let ye be lollin' 'bout in yer undress agin. Th' *Sassenach* can diddle ye till ye canna walk, an' I willna be goin' soft wi' ye!"

Elaine found the process of being dressed as thoroughly distasteful today as it had been yesterday, surrounded by Hattie's foul odor and jabbing fingers. A heavy drape of gray wool settled over her head. It was the same dress she had worn yesterday—there was the circle of soup Hattie had dribbled onto the front of it. Her nostrils flared, discerning one of yesterday's odors that had nothing to do with Hattie.

So much for *Up the Down Staircase*. The maid, even Hattie, had addressed Morrigan as *m'lady*, yet here she was dressed in the same wool gown she had worn yesterday, and which, judging by the smell and appearance, had been worn for quite some time before that. But then Elaine would never have thought being a "lady" included pissing all over oneself while straddling an icy chamber pot or eating fare a twentieth-century dog-food factory would be sued over, either.

Hattie herded Elaine toward the vanity and set about adding baldness to Morrigan's other infirmities. Carefully averting her attention from the pale oval face in the mirror with the great dark eyes and swollen red lips, Elaine dispassionately noted that for all of its curly thickness, the blue gloss of Morrigan's hair was as much from grease as from its black coloring.

Instantly her scalp felt as if it were crawling with several dozen species of little live things. And her mouth . . . it tasted like something she had left in the refrigerator for a week.

Or two.

She ran her tongue over her teeth; the tongue was coated, the teeth slimy. Bile pushed up past the corset.

"Now, turn aroun' an' put yer feet out. 'Ow d'ye expect me t' put yer shoes on if ye dinna turn aroun'?"

Elaine pushed back the bench. She dug her fingers into the carved arms as the shoes were laced from a B width to an A.

Hattie scrambled up off of her knees. "Ye willna break yer fast this mornin' wi' good ol' haggis. Tea ye'll git, girl, an' that be all, till ye learn 'ow decent folk goes on. Now ye git o'er there an' pray fer th' good Lord t' guide ye!"

Without checking to see if Elaine followed her orders—as if Morrigan were nothing more than a well-trained dog, Elaine thought resentfully—Hattie exited the room in a flurry of black and white.

Elaine made good use of Hattie's departure, with keen distaste using the dangerously filled facilities hidden behind the Japanese screen. A nightgown lay in a sodden heap by the bathtub, a casualty of a late-night encounter with no light for guidance. After relieving herself, she loosened the shoelaces. After that, she extracted a washcloth and the bar of lye soap from the top chest drawer. She scrubbed her teeth. Sipping directly from the heavy green pitcher filled with water, she defiantly spat a mouthful of bubbles into the matching bowl.

Bare necessities satisfied, Elaine continued the exploration that had been interrupted yesterday and that she had been unable to return to with Hattie breathing down her neck the remainder of the day. The occasional table with the candelabra contained a small, empty drawer. She ran her hand up the chimney above the fireplace that looked as if it, like the candelabra, had never been used, and—deducing from her experiences thus far—probably had not. There were no loose bricks, no sign of a cache.

Elaine had debugged computer systems for million-dollar corporations. She refused to be stymied by a girl young enough to be her daughter.

She eyed the desk with the giant black Bible. What better place to hide secret papers than inside the reams of Bible transcriptions?

"Dinna I tell ye ye was t' pray whilst I was gone?" Hattie thumped the silver tray down onto the ebony table that apparently served as Morrigan's dinette set. "Ye wouldna mind yer penship yest'rday; it be too late t' try an' git in m' good graces t'day. Come o'er 'ere an' sit yerself down."

She took a deep, calming breath. Elaine tucked the stack of papers back inside the drawer before standing and limping across the room. She sat down on the designated bamboo chair. Hattie, with a malicious flourish, uncovered the tray.

A cup sat in solitary splendor, the dainty red-and-green-painted china filled with a watery, brownish yellow fluid. Not one little vapor of steam rose from it.

Elaine wistfully remembered the steaming-hot coffee in her dream. This looked more like it belonged in the chill chamber pot than in a china cup.

She looked up, her eyes meeting those of Hattie. Mad lights glittered in the sunken, pale depths.

Lifting the cup to her lips, she discreetly sniffed . . . tea. Impossibly weaker than yesterday's, but still only tea, she thought thankfully.

The two maids came while Elaine sipped her breakfast with every evidence of enjoyment. After a moment's hesitation, the child maid went beyond the Japanese screen. She emerged with the nightgown furtively tucked beneath the chamber pot.

Hattie viciously decimated *Sassenach* ancestry while the adolescent maid straightened the bed. The child maid returned with fresh water; she rinsed out the green bowl in a matter-of-course manner. Once the two maids left, Hattie turned her vituperation full-force upon Elaine.

"Fer yer sin ye'll pray wi' me, little girl, an' I willna put up wi' yer sulks anymore, ye ken? Git up now an' kneel in th' place o' th' Lord; I willna bide yer laziness." More sharply when Elaine did not immediately do as she was commanded, she added, "Git up, I say, an' repent!"

An extremely satisfying four-letter response rose to the tip of Elaine's tongue. Only by biting down on Morrigan's already swollen lips was she able to restrain herself from saying it, wondering even as she mentally shouted the expletive if the word existed in this world, in this time. Or was it a product of the twentieth century, like hamburgers and AIDS?

Hattie crossed the room with mean intent. "Ye will git off yer arse an' git yerself o'er t' th' Lord's place an' pray t' God t' forgive ye. Now!"

Elaine stiffened her back, though heaven knew it was impossible to slouch strapped inside the corset as she was. She tilted her head, retaining eye contact with those colorless orbs, matching glare for stare.

Hattie leaned down over the silver tray. Raising a gnarled hand, she deliberately swung it wide.

Elaine caught the descending hand a hairbreadth away from her cheek, the slap so nearly making contact she could feel the rush of air. Heat emanated from the age-spotted skin. She held Hattie's hand there in midair where it had been caught, by her cheek, the palm and fingers smaller than Elaine's own, the skin dry and callused.

The air crackled with tension as the two struggled in their power, Hattie to obtain release that she might regain dominion and, perhaps—considering her awkward position—balance; Elaine to contain, that the old woman's power be curtailed and that she be made to suffer the pains of her unwieldy position.

Morrigan's muscles cried in protest. Hattie was ridiculously stronger than the young woman's body despite her imbalance, but Elaine's thirty-nine-year-old will superseded. She held the older woman's struggling hand steady. Sweat crested on her forehead and pooled beneath her arms, managing, somehow, to trickle down the insides of the corset. It felt like an army of stinging, itching ants had invaded her clothes, along with the sharp knives that had invaded her muscles.

The militant gleam in Hattie's eyes was replaced with confusion, then finally defeat. Elaine cautiously released her hand.

The old woman jerked backward. She tripped on the crow-black dress and catapulted forward against the ebony table. The silver tray and empty china cup tumbled to the floor, the first a muffled clatter, the second a silent roll.

Hattie immediately snapped upright; she slowly backed away. "Ye'll be sorry, aye, that ye'll be, sorry as a breech-born babe! Ye'll strangle on yer e'il ways!" The door slammed shut behind her. A key grated in the lock.

"An' dinna ye be thinkin' 'is *Sassenach* lordship'll be savin' ye from disgrace." Hattie's tyranny resumed full-force behind the safety of a locked door. " 'E's gone, I tell ye. Gone fer a fortnight or more! There'll be no food fer ye, Morrigan Gayle, nae, nor drink neither, till ye mend yer wicked ways!"

Elaine stared down at the overturned tray and cup.

Had Hattie said Morrigan, *girl*, or Morrigan *Gayle*?

There was something on the bottom of the cup. Elaine picked it up. *Spode* was impressed in the china.

Outside, a ray of sunlight broached the gray bank of clouds; inside, it pierced the translucent yellow curtains. The silver tray captured the sunbeam. Blinding light danced on the ceiling.

Elaine clutched the cup between both hands. A cold trembling commenced in the pit of her stomach.

What was happening to her? She had used physical force on an old lady, a woman almost twice her age. Elaine had never used physical force on anyone in her life, had deplored the use of violence as much as she had deplored cowardliness.

In the mere hour or two it had taken to be dressed and have her room straightened, she had gone from despair to anger, humiliation to rage, victim to victor, mistress to prisoner. If she didn't get back to her own time soon she would go stark, raving mad. A proper candidate for Bedlam.

And on top of everything else, she was ravenously hungry.

Chapter

5

E laine sat in front of the open French doors, intent upon the progress of the quill tip grating across bonded stationery. Forgery, like being a lady, was not all it was cracked up to be. Morrigan's handwriting had neither rhyme nor reason. The pronounced leftward slant was practically impossible to achieve without breaking her wrist. Elaine had looped and curlicued until blisters throbbed on the second and middle fingers of her—Morrigan's—hand. To make matters worse, the steel-tipped quill pen leaked, smeared, and ran perpetually dry.

Warm sun streamed through the French doors. A pleasantly cool breeze blew the hair that refused to stay in place across Elaine's eyes. She shoved it behind her ears, almost wishing she had left it pinned to her scalp.

Outside, newly leafed trees jutted upward beyond the wrought-iron balcony. The sky was a postcard blue.

She closed her eyes against the impossibly bright sunlight. Her stomach—Morrigan's stomach; it didn't matter, the effect was still the same—did a somersault, then seemed to swallow itself, emitting a dry, belching gurgle. Elaine had never been this hungry in her entire life, not even when she had joined Jenny Craig. Or thirsty. Unable to bear the ceaseless itching any longer, she had foolishly used the lone pitcher of water yesterday to wash away the sweat of her and Morrigan's trials.

Did Hattie intend to let her *die*?

The seam of the crotchless drawers had worked open. Elaine squirmed. The valance and tassels padding the yellow skirt—another mystery that would never be solved if she did not establish a means of communication—poked and prodded at her thighs and bottom.

She grabbed a clean sheet and fit it over the page of Bible transcription. Every line, every dot of Morrigan's script was visible through the overlying paper. She would forge that writing, she thought grimly, or die trying.

If Hattie didn't kill her first.

Her body, framed between the French doors, made a sundial. Elaine practiced until her shadow made half a revolution on the Oriental carpet. Sighing, she sat back in the bamboo chair.

The bonded stationery looked as if a flock of pigeons had waddled across it. Exactly like the Bible transcription underneath it.

A quiet click invaded the silence.

Images of Hattie sneaking in to strangle her as if she were a breech-born babe instantly leaped to mind. Mouth dry, Elaine sprang to her feet.

"Marm?"

Elaine whirled around. *Damn!* Flailing, she grabbed the back of the chair to keep from toppling over.

A maid stood in front of the main door. Elaine sagged in relief, recognizing the adolescent girl who cleaned the room.

"M' lady!" The maid's dark eyebrows shot up to the edge of her white cap. She surveyed Elaine from the top of her unbound hair to the hem of her yellow skirt.

Elaine self-consciously tugged the matching jacket down over the waistband of the skirt. She wondered how long it would take to get back via the servant grapevine that the "puir little lamb" had dressed in non-Hattie-approved clothing. Not that she had had much choice. The tight gray dress had not come off last night without a struggle.

"Oh, m' lady! We wus afeared . . . But ye look . . . That is . . . Well, we brung yer dinner, we did." Anxiously, she asked, "Be that all right, m' lady?"

Elaine's lips stretched in a thin smile. *Be that all right!* She hadn't had anything to eat in over twenty-four hours, and the maid asked if it was all right to bring her food!

The faint aroma of roast pork wafted toward the French doors. Elaine's stomach emitted a growl of consensus.

The maid giggled, then looked as if someone had kicked her in the solar plexus. She freed a hand to cover her mouth. The large tray tilted. A discordant rattle of cutlery and dishes echoed through the room.

The maid promptly balanced the tray. "Oh, marm, I be that sorry, I am!"

She bounded toward the ebony desk on the opposite side of the room. The cutlery and dishes rattled in time with her bouncing steps. Elaine hurriedly limped around the foot of the bed, the back-heavy skirt trailing behind. Her hair, an equally heavy weight, swayed to and fro about her shoulders, silk and grease a slippery combination.

The maid elbowed aside the large black Bible and plunked the tray down onto the desk. She lifted the cover with a flourish. "Here ye be, m' lady!"

Saliva flooded Elaine's mouth. The tray contained more food than she had had in the entire three days she had been here. Steam rose from the pot of tea.

The maid set the upturned lid on top of the Bible and bobbed a curtsy. "If that be all, m' lady, I'll be back about me duties, if it please ye, marm. I'll come and git the tray later, so I—so ye'll not git in trouble." The maid bobbed again. "Marm."

Elaine reluctantly tore her eyes away from the food-laden tray. And felt the sickening flow of adrenaline.

Taking a deep breath, she lightly touched the bobbing girl's arm.

"M' lady!" the maid shrieked.

Elaine jerked her hand back, her heart racing, racing. At this rate she wouldn't live long enough to be sent to Bedlam. She would die of cardiac arrest.

The maid dropped down to her knees. "M' lady, ye lost a button!" She held up the article for Elaine's inspection, "Look!" then crawled on the floor. "There's another one! And there's another one there!"

Elaine eyed the buttons. A reflexive ache settled between her shoulders; it was followed by a glimmer of satisfaction. She had no doubt that Hattie had thought to compound the pains of hunger with the additional discomfort of spending the day and night strapped inside the restrictive wool dress and corset. It had not taken an elaborate flowchart for her to figure out how to undo the tiny buttons down the back of the dress. She had merely applied the basic concept of physics—mass meets force—and had worked her spine against the door frame until the buttons had popped off one by one like miniature cannonballs.

The maid stood. Elaine determinedly grabbed her arm.

Startled brown eyes looked up.

Elaine stared down, momentarily distracted. The serving girl was several inches shorter than herself. Elaine had looked down at Hattie, but one expected that when dealing with the elderly. This girl, however, was nearly the same age as Morrigan. Did that mean that Hattie and the maid were uncommonly short, or that Morrigan was uncommonly tall?

"Marm? Be there something ye be wanting?"

Elaine smiled wryly. Oh, yes, there were a whole host of things that she wanted. She wanted to know why she had been transmigrated into Morrigan's body. She wanted to know what had happened to her own body. She wanted to know why Morrigan, a lady of the realm, was treated worse than a slave and could be confined by a crazy old woman who had other servants sneaking about behind her back to serve their rightful mistress. Most of all, Elaine wanted to return to her normal, placid life where combating rush-hour traffic had been her most dangerous challenge.

The maid's black-belled skirt contrasted sharply against the yellow silk skirt crinkled around Elaine's feet. She wondered what the girl would do if she asked her what year this was. Or what accent her mistress spoke with—Scottish like Hattie or English like herself?

Instead she crooked her finger to indicate that the maid was to follow her to the French doors.

Dipping the steel-tipped pen into a bottle of ink there on the small ebony table, she proceeded to scribble in the awkward left slant that she had spent the last day and a half mastering.

The maid stared blankly at the note.

Taking a stab in the dark, Elaine slashed through the intricate longhand and printed, careful to maintain the wrist-breaking slant, the sharpened corners, the descending loops:

Can you read?

The maid pocketed the buttons before gingerly accepting the piece of paper. She squinted in such a way that Elaine didn't know if she was nearsighted or preparing to cry . . . fraud.

"Aye," the maid finally said. "That is, I can read some, marm, but it ain't much, just what the cook taught me when she had the time. Begging yer pardon, but be ye all right, m' lady? Why're ye writing me a note when I'm standing right here in front of ye? That don't make no sense now, does it, marm?"

Elaine gasped. Her hand flew to her throat, choking off a scream of vexation. This was the maid who twice now had braved Hattie's anger, who must surely, Elaine had thought, be a champion. Didn't Morrigan command respect from anyone?

Comprehension bloomed on the maid's face. "Oh, marm, ye should of said something!" She blushed. "I mean, Cook makes a right good tonic fer the throat. Me da got the putrid throat real bad; he couldn't talk fer a whole week! Took Cook's tonic, and sure as rain, he was talking a blue streak, he wus."

Elaine's ire evaporated. She stared in wide-eyed wonder at the reprieve the maid had unwittingly supplied. The dilemma of Morrigan's accent had been summarily allayed. Scottish, English, it no longer mattered—she, Elaine, would not have to speak. By the time speech became necessary, she would be back in the twentieth century.

Success rushed to Elaine's head. Remembering the bath that

Hattie had denied her, she snatched the piece of paper from between the maid's fingers.

Yes, I have a putrid throat. I would like a bath. Can you read that?

The maid's forehead crinkled with concentration. Suddenly her whole face lit up. "Bath, m' lady! Is that what ye be wanting?"

Elaine shared the girl's exuberance. She bobbed her head up and down. The maid practically jumped up and down in her enthusiasm. Elaine had to restrain herself from joining. It felt so good to communicate after three days of silence, even if her side of the conversation was performed with pen and ink.

The maid abruptly frowned. "Bath, m' lady! But yer throat! Ye'll sicken fer the worst!"

Elaine scowled, all of her previous irritation returning.

The maid's face brightened. "But Mr. Fritz, he did say as how the lord sed ye wus to have a bath, now, didn't he? Like as not the lord wouldn't be too pleased if I didn't do as he said. I'll git it fer ye, marm. Cook, she always keeps hot water. I'll bring it meself, marm, see if I don't!"

The maid's enthusiasm lasted all the way to the door. There she turned, her expression guarded. Her white cap seemed to lose some of its starch. She reached into her apron pocket and extracted a large skeleton key.

"Marm, I . . . I . . . What if *she* finds out about the bath? I got to lock the door; if I don't she'll—"

Elaine greedily stared at the slender piece of metal. Holding out her hand, she limped toward the maid, barely conscious of the awkward gait necessitated by the short left leg.

"But marm, if I don't—"

Elaine's mouth tightened; she jerked her outstretched hand, silently demanding the key, she who had never demanded anything in her life. Dimly she wondered what she would do if the maid refused to relinquish it—wrestle her to the floor?

Endless seconds passed. The maid reluctantly placed the key in Elaine's hand. Long white piano fingers curled around the body warmed metal. Relief and triumph merged in dizzying combination. Elaine rewarded the girl with a brilliant smile, all twenty-eight teeth—she had counted them last night while trying to go to sleep—coming into play.

After the maid left, Elaine stood by the door, tossing the key from one hand to the other, triumph a fleeting thing, changing hands as quickly as the key.

The battle lines had been drawn. The refusal to talk, the physical restraint in preventing Hattie's slap, they could be excused as the acts of a rebellious child. But the key gave her independence, the right to go as she should choose, the ability to keep out those she would choose.

Elaine slid the key into the lock.

Hattie's "puir" little girl had just proclaimed her adulthood. And Hattie did not strike Elaine as the type of person to allow a bird to fly free of its cage.

Elaine calmly ate the roast pork and stuffing dinner. No, that was not correct, she thought, sitting back and delicately patting her mouth with the dinner napkin. She had ravished her dinner. Demolished her dinner. Gobbled her dinner. And now she contemplated with equal pleasure the steam rising above the Japanese screen.

"Marm?" It had taken the adolescent maid four trips—three with twin steaming buckets and one trip with what Elaine assumed was cold water, as it did not steam—to fill the tub behind the Japanese screen. She looked decidedly winded. Elaine felt a twinge of guilt, then quickly pushed it aside. The filching of the buttons had not been lost on her.

"Marm, ye'll be needing a lady's maid. If ye'd like . . ."

Elaine waved the adolescent girl away with a heartfelt smile. And nearly danced with glee when *she* locked the door behind the maid.

Food, a bath, and privacy! Elaine felt as though she had died and gone to heaven.

She surreptitiously surveyed the bedroom, the printed green silk wallpaper, the japanned furniture, the gleaming yellow accents.

Well, perhaps hell, then. Surely heaven would not be so decadently beautiful.

Elaine checked the door to make sure the key was securely positioned in the lock. Feeling all of a sudden quite wonderfully decadent herself, she searched in the chest for a bar of the scented soaps she had found that first day, then added to it a washcloth and large bath towel, also occupants of the chest.

She draped her outer clothes and slip over the top of the Japanese screen. The drawers she left lying where they dropped. Grimacing, she tugged the white silk stockings down her legs and neatly paired them with her shoes. She wondered how the maid would have responded to a request for a razor. Somehow she didn't think Lady Remington had as yet made its debut.

Shivering, she grabbed the bundle of bathing materials and stepped behind the screen. The air was misty warm. She put the towel on the far side of the bathtub next to the wall, as far away from the chamber pot as she could get, and stepped into the hot water.

Steam curled up around her body. A good six inches separated her hips from the sloping metal sides. There was enough room to accommodate another person.

She grinned, remembering a certain fantasy.

Or two.

The water stung her blistered fingers. Elaine clutched the washcloth in her left hand and brought it up over her chest, allowing the hot water to trickle over her flesh. The gold ring gleamed and pulsed. She remembered the bundle of dried mistletoe in the bottom chest drawer, Morrigan's memento of a Christmas past. Had the poor girl received her first kiss underneath it? Did she have secret fantasies that Hattie had been unable to destroy?

Elaine raised her left leg out of the water. The scars were very old, the ridges sunken and white. She recalled a movie in which the hero, a little boy, had broken his leg and the bad drunken doctor had improperly set it, so the bone did not grow at the same rate as the uninjured leg. Had Morrigan suffered from a set of similar circumstances? Of course, in the movie, everything had ended happily ever after, and a surgical procedure had miraculously cured the deficit, bone shortage and all. But that was the movies, and the twentieth century, whereas this was . . . Well, it wasn't a movie, and it certainly wasn't the twentieth century.

She turned the ridged, slightly twisted leg this way and that. Hattie had babbled that she wouldn't let the devil take her soul like he took her leg. Had she been with Morrigan at the time of the accident?

Elaine's lips tightened in a spurt of protective anger, imagining the injured little girl with only Hattie to take care of her. Had the old woman summoned a doctor to set Morrigan's leg, or had it been left to be miraculously healed through divine intervention?

Thank heaven Elaine lived in the twentieth century, where rational thought ruled.

She lowered her leg and sank deeper within the water. Long hair clung like seaweed to her back and shoulders. Most peculiar. Sexy, almost.

But the heat would not last forever. Unlike its twentieth-century counterpart, once the bath turned cold, she could not simply turn on the hot-water faucet to reheat it.

Elaine ducked her head beneath the water, then, surfacing, ruthlessly applied the bar of soap to it. She repeated the process twice more, each time able to work up a larger lather as the dirt and grease dissipated. Next she lathered the washcloth and vigorously scrubbed her body, applying less stringent pressure there underneath the water. Stationery did not compare to Charmin.

Finished, Elaine stood up and reached for the towel. The air was doubly cool against her bath-warmed skin. She rested her dripping left foot on the edge of the tub and patted it dry, then carefully stepped to the floor. Proceeding with the next foot and leg, she idly wondered how the bathtub would be emptied. She smiled, envisioning the little chamber-pot maid tipping it over the balcony.

Elaine suddenly visualized the master bathroom in her and Matthew's condominium. The white-enameled tub had sliding glass shower doors. The toilet beside it had an air-cushioned seat.

The vanity had double sinks. A heating vent was built into the bottom of the wall beneath the toilet paper dispenser.

Was Morrigan in Elaine's body, there in the twentieth century? Was she even now immersed in the enameled tub, watching a strip of toilet paper leap and dance in a gust of ventilated heat?

Elaine froze, fingers digging into the damp towel. If Morrigan was in Elaine's body, then it would require dual cooperation to return to their rightful places. Given the choice between twentieth-century convenience and nineteenth-century primitiveness, which would Morrigan choose?

Given the choice between Matthew and Hattie . . .

"Ye let me in, Morrigan, girl, or I willna be responsible fer it, ye ken?"

Elaine jumped. The old woman's shriek was punctuated by thunderous pounding.

"I know what ye're doin', an' I willna be a part o' it. Ye unlock this 'ere door an' let me in or I'll tell th' rev'ren', aye, that I will!"

With superhuman effort Elaine unclenched her muscles. If Hattie could have gotten in, she would not now be shouting outside the door. Wise move, that, leaving the key in the lock to prevent the insertion of another key from the opposite side. Amazing what one learned from the movies. She had picked up that particular trick from one of those special presentations for children. Come to think of it, that was where she had seen the one about the little boy with the improperly set leg.

She had never thought she would live to see the day when she would be grateful for Matthew's PG tastes.

"Ye let me in, ye 'ear? Open this door, Morrigan Gayle!"

Elaine expected the door to shatter underneath the frenzied pounding that followed. She bit her lips to hold back a scream. Her legs had started trembling again. Along with her stomach. She hated being afraid. Why wouldn't the old bitch just go away?

There was an ominous pause. Elaine dried her hair; it fluffed out like an unpruned evergreen. She worked the towel underneath it and briskly dried her back.

"I'm warnin' ye, Morrigan Gayle, I willna let ye turn t' th' de'il; aye, ye'll know yer duty an' open this door like a good girl! Open the door, ye sinful 'ussy!"

There, Hattie had said it again. Morrigan Gayle. Elaine tucked the piece of information into her brain while she wrapped the towel around her body. Taking a deep breath, she stepped out from behind the shelter of the Japanese screen.

And dropped the towel.

And squeaked.

"Very fetching, my dear. You should greet your husband thus more often."

Chapter

6

Charles's anger, once he was away from Morrigan, had died a quick death. Very well, he had made a fool of himself, playing the lovesick swain for the past year to a female who like most of her sex cared nothing for the passions of men. So be it. The fact remained that he needed an heir. She had cost him too much time as it was; he would not allow her to continue to cheat him of that precious commodity.

So Charles had cut short his property inspections and returned to the source of his real problem. The land would benefit as he would—through being fertilized, and, in his case, in fertilizing. That the seeds might multiply and grow. And there would be something to represent his labors instead of the interminable gray bleakness that was like carrion, weighting and fouling his every waking moment.

Charles was intrigued to learn from his valet, however, scarcely before he had time to slap the dust from his clothes, that Hattie had locked Morrigan in her room without food or water the day before. And that Morrigan was reputed to have the putrid throat and could not speak. And that she had never looked so well, dressed in yellow silk with her black hair hanging all loose and curly down her back. And that she had demanded the key to her room, and then demanded a bath.

Interesting, that. That she could demand and yet be unable to utter a single word.

"Nonsense, Fritz." Charles idly assessed his travel damage in the mirror above the fireplace. "The maid is merely stringing a tale. You should not encourage the servants to gossip about your mistress."

"I do no such thing, my lord. Gossip is for lower servants. But how, might I ask, may I avoid listening to it when you ride off for days and days and leave me behind so that I have nothing to do *but* to listen?"

Fritz, very much on his upper stiffs, appeared in the mirror behind Charles.

"And it is not gossip. I myself heard Hattie sending away the maid this morning. Ka—the maid said the mistress communicated with pen and ink."

Charles gently swirled the swallow of brandy left in his glass. A knowing smile played about his mouth as he surveyed the valet's reflection.

"And when, pray tell, did this Ka-maid learn to read?" Charles asked, fully aware of the brown-eyed maid in question. "Was that before her duties or after your pleasure?"

The valet's sharp, thin face turned cherry red. It never ceased amazing Charles that Fritz could still blush after having served with him in India.

"I do not fraternize with the lower servants, my lord." Fritz sniffed haughtily. "It is the cook; she teaches the young girls to read so that they will have less time to socialize with the men."

"Commendable," Charles commented dryly, refraining from stating the obvious: that in Katie's case the practice was patently unsuccessful. He returned his attention to his own image. A fine film of gray covered his cotton shirt. His brown hair was as dull as Fritz's sense of humor. "I am waiting for that bath, by the by."

Fritz held up the riding coat he had been attempting to brush clean for the last fifteen minutes. "I told you the baroness used up all the hot water," he complained, his attitude mutating from hauteur to that of long-suffering grievance without so much as a flick of an eyelash. "It will be brought up first thing once it is heated."

The valet sighted the collar and neckcloth Charles had carelessly consigned to the floor. He swooped down on them. From that position he located his master's waistcoat, which had been kicked underneath the bed.

"Really, my lord, you would save the both of us—"

"Ye let me in, Morrigan, girl, or I willna be responsible fer it, ye ken?"

The shrieking voice erupted the afternoon's serenity, clearly audible despite the obstruction of plaster and wood. Immediately following the verbal invasion, the walls shook and reverberated.

Charles pivoted. "Good Lord, what is that racket?" He knew the answer before the words had left his mouth. There was no mistaking Hattie's voice. It was just that he had never heard it quite so . . . elevated. And certainly she had not evidenced such robust behavior before, though he had no doubt of her capability.

"I know what ye're doin', an' I willna be a part o' it. Ye unlock this 'ere door an' let me in or I'll tell the rev'ren', aye, that I will!"

Charles looked speculatively at Fritz. Could it be possible . . . ? Instantly he derided himself for even considering that the icy maid had been thawed.

Hattie punctuated her threat with more pounding.

Charles set his glass of brandy onto the black marble top of a Louis XVI side table. Leisurely, pounding heart belying his outward calm, he ambled across the room to a *semainier* chest and took from the top drawer a key. In mere seconds he closed the distance to the connecting door between his and Morrigan's room. The key slid in quietly, easily, though it had been used only once in the course of their marriage, and before that not for nearly two decades. Charles's mother had died when he was a mere boy, and his father never remarried. But, like his father before him, Charles did not tolerate laziness among the servants; everything was meticulously maintained on his estate.

Charles stepped inside the connecting bedroom, curiosity and wariness warring. There was a faint aroma of roast pork. The Bible atop the desk had been pushed aside; a silver cover balanced on top of it. Beside it, the matching tray held an assortment of empty dishes—they looked as if they had been licked clean. Beyond the desk, Morrigan's door visibly shook beneath the onslaught of Hattie's fists. A key shimmied and danced in the lock.

"Ye let me in, ye 'ear? Open this door, Morrigan Gayle!"

The old harridan's voice shrilled even more loudly inside Morrigan's room than it had in his, but of Morrigan there was no immediate sign.

A frenzied pounding commenced, as if by sheer dint of strength Hattie could force the lock.

Charles closed the connecting door and stepped farther inside Morrigan's bedchamber.

The French doors were open; a slight breeze ruffled the yellow curtains, cool but not as cold as the room usually was. Most of the time Morrigan and that Scottish bitch kept it as cold as the ice cellar. Upon reflection, Charles had never known the doors to be open, for fear some demon might visit on the wind.

Half expecting to hear a shriek of a different sort, Charles ambled toward the four-poster bed. He grinned, a sarcastic pull of the lips, imagining his beloved wife crouched over the chamber pot on the other side. But she was not. Nor was she out on the balcony that his wife's keeper had deemed frivolous and *Sassenach,* following therefore that his wife also deemed it frivolous and *Sassenach,* tit for tat, a Rowland for an Oliver.

The pounding abruptly ceased. A faint sound emanated from behind Charles, to his right—a rubbing sound—the brisk application of cloth on skin. He swung toward the Japanese screen and froze to the spot.

A yellow skirt lay draped over the black-lacquered screen, by its side a matching yellow bodice and white chemise, the gleam of silk unmistakable. In front of the screen lay a pair of silk drawers, one leg curled out, edged in tantalizing rows of pink ribbon and lace, the crotchless bottom a seductive dark slit. Beside the drawers rested a pair of yellow silk slippers; atop those a blue ribbon and lace garter encircled each of the pair of white silk stockings, shaped still to the curve of a calf and thigh.

Charles's eyebrows rose as he surveyed the clothes he had purchased for Morrigan's bridal trousseau and which Hattie and Morrigan had thrown away. Or so he had assumed, as he had never seen them again after their purchase.

Until now.

The air was misty above the Japanese screen.

Charles's eyebrows rose higher. It would appear Fritz's little maid had not lied. His wife *had* requested a bath. She who had not fully bathed during their entire year of marriage.

Curiouser and curiouser.

Hattie's caterwauling shattered the silence. "I'm warnin' ye, Morrigan Gayle, I willna let ye turn t' the de'il; aye, ye'll know yer duty an' open this door like a good girl! Open th' door, ye sinful 'ussy!"

Morrigan stepped out from behind the screen wrapped in a thick white bath towel, black hair hanging free and wild in tangled wet profusion about her shoulders. Her face was flushed and dewy from the heat of the bath. She saw him instantly. The thick white bath towel slithered to the floor, providing Charles with a sight he had never thought to see without a major battle the likes of which he had fought in India: a butt-naked Morrigan.

A sight almost worth waiting for.

Her body, though too thin, was creamy white and perfectly proportioned, her breasts high and round, her waist long, her legs slender, longer still, with well-rounded thighs.

Voluptuously well-rounded thighs . . .

Reluctantly he forced his gaze downward from that temptingly plump anatomy. He had never seen the scars on her left leg. They did not detract from her nude appeal, but perhaps that was his military experience at work, having learned very early in his career to judge a man not by the wound, but by the fortitude of the character bearing such a wound. Morrigan had survived pain and suffering, she could stand upright, she could walk. Charles found that rather surprising, now that he saw the extent of the corded white ridges and the difference in leg length. Her feet were long and elegantly narrow, the left one twisted slightly outward.

Leisurely he reversed the visual tour. The hair between

Morrigan's legs was as lush and dark and curly as that on top of her head. A drop of water glistened there among the curls. Mocha lips peeped below it, moist and ripe with a woman's promise. Charles was utterly fascinated.

Morrigan squeaked. There was no other word to describe the sound.

Charles's eyes crinkled in amused appreciation, slowly traveling up her body, lingering on the high, round breasts. Her nipples were also the rich color of mocha, a shade lighter than the tantalizing lips peeking from beneath the curls at her thighs. Budded from the cold, they fairly begged to be pinched and suckled.

His wife, without doubt, had the most erotic nipples he had ever seen.

He raised his gaze to her face, amused afresh at her full mouth shaped into a red, round O as if frozen while holding a note in a Christmas carol.

"Very fetching, my dear. You should greet your husband thus more often."

Charles had fought on many a battlefield, yet he could in all honesty say he had never seen a soldier move as quickly as Morrigan moved then in retrieving the towel that lay in a semicircle about her feet.

She squeaked again, holding the towel draped in front of her as if holding a lifeline. Her eyes were enormous pools of black shock. That was a positive sign, surely. Morrigan had never displayed anything other than cold acceptance, reluctant acceptance, befitting that of a cold, reluctant wife.

Charles's eyes narrowed. But then again, maybe his reluctant wife had been so glad to be rid of him, the carnal, irksomely demanding husband, so certain of her freedom if just for a fortnight—and so dismayed as its rescindment—that she had been unable to temper her feelings.

"Perhaps you would care to extend that greeting," Charles said. "A welcome-home kiss is surely in order, do you not think so?"

The dark pools of shock narrowed to dismay.

Charles stepped forward.

" 'E's in there wi' ye, ain't 'e? Answer me, ye sinful 'ussy, ye! I willna let ye play 'arlot t' a *Sassenach*!"

Charles's lips twitched. "That woman never ceases to amaze me. Does that mean she would allow you to play harlot to a clansman, I wonder?"

For a moment something flickered within the dark depths: laughter—he would almost swear there was laughter in his wife's eyes. As quickly as whatever it was had flared, it was extinguished. Her dark eyes stared unblinkingly; once again she was the Morrigan of old, eyes void of emotion, a soul without depth.

The advantage, or disadvantage, depending upon whose perspective, of surprise had been short-lived. Something spurred Charles on, enticing him to force from this wife of his a response, any response.

"Well, Morrigan, I am waiting. Come give your husband a welcome-home kiss."

"Ach, I willna let it 'appen! M' puir little lamb, ye leave 'er be, m' lord!"

Morrigan's eyes remained locked with his, cold and blank, her towel-shielded body stiff and unyielding. A lie, it had been a lie, that brief flare of emotion. She was cold through and through.

"Ye dinna need t' put up wi' 'is pawin', Morrigan, m' girl, I'll—"

"Shut up and leave, you old tabby," Charles roared, never once breaking contact with those unfathomable eyes. "The game is over! Morrigan is mine. I'll not brook your interference any longer."

Morrigan's face neither softened nor hardened; she was indifferent to the death.

The pain took Charles by surprise. And with the pain came a renewal of anger, hot, consuming, seeking to inflict that which it received.

With interest.

He should have stayed away the full two weeks as he had planned.

Too late. One year too late. He would no longer be denied. She was his wife.

Charles took another step toward Morrigan. "Very well, madam, if you will not extend the honors, I see that I must."

"Pray, Morrigan, girl, git down on yer knees an' pray t' God! God'll save ye!"

Charles turned and spewed his rage onto the voice coming from behind the door. "I said shut up and leave, damn you! One more word from you and you're out of here!"

"Ye canna—"

"Fritz!" The single word echoed in the high-ceilinged room. Charles turned back toward his wife, staring so still and cold, the queen bitch, never a care, never a feeling for anything outside of her own small, sick world.

The door connecting Morrigan's and Charles's bedchambers immediately flew open. Fritz hurried into the room. Another squeak escaped Morrigan, completely ignored by the two men. Fritz trained his eyes on Charles, his carriage stiffly erect, painfully correct in this most incorrect situation.

"Yes, my lord?"

"Escort Hattie to her room."

"But my lord—"

Charles gave Fritz a look that would have had a lesser man bowing and scraping. "Get a footman if you must, I don't care, just get that frigging woman out of my presence!"

"Very good, my lord!"

Fritz hurried through the interconnecting door, soundlessly shutting it behind him. Within seconds the bedchamber was filled with the strident expletives of a gracelessly protesting Hattie and the voluble murmurings of an adamant Fritz. Hattie's voice grew dimmer as she was forcibly led down the corridor by the valet, then faded altogether.

In the silence Charles could hear his own breathing, slightly harsh, his own heartbeat, slightly accelerated, but from his wife he heard nothing, felt nothing, saw not the slightest trembling of her hands, clutched to her breast over the towel like a virgin Madonna, the right hand overlapping the left.

Charles took another step toward his wife, the distance nearly closed. A faint scent of white ginger wafted through the air. Her face, he noted with satisfaction as he stepped closer, looked distinctly white around the gills. She nibbled on her bottom lip, luscious, red, full. He had tried to nibble on that lip three nights ago, only to have her turn her head away as if he were the most dire perversion that had ever stalked the dark of night.

"Let us start over, shall we?" he said silkily, stepping closer still, so close he could feel her heat, wet and moist from the bath, smell her scent commingled with the essence of white ginger. So close he could see himself reflected in the mute black irises, the pupils a thin band, slightly lighter, dusk as to night. "I believe we started here."

Charles reached out and yanked the towel from Morrigan's hands.

Chapter

7

Elaine gasped. Another one of the squeaking pips escaped her throat. *Good Lord,* she thought in a rush of insanity. *Hinges* squeak; *mice* squeak—*women* do not squeak!

The large, brown-haired, brown-skinned, scar-faced man claiming to be her husband stepped closer, so close she breathed the not-unpleasant smell of sweat and leather, the scent of some kind of animal, familiar yet not familiar, and something else, a faint, musky scent that seemed to exude in waves of heat from his skin and clothes. She tilted her head back. He was so close she could see Morrigan's pale face reflected in the black of his pupils. So close she could feel the soft brush of his shirt against her breasts.

Elaine glanced down. The brown nipples were distended with cold.

She squeaked. And brought her hands up to cover her breasts. And stepped back. All at once.

The man followed, the heels on his dusty knee-high boots as silent as her bare feet.

Her *naked* feet.

Weren't men supposed to be shorter in historical times? Elaine wondered, perilously close to hysteria. If Morrigan, as she suspected, was above average height, then this man had to be well over six feet tall. He loomed over her, dark, menacing. Just like—

Elaine's eyes widened. He was the man in the dream, the one who had stood over her with a whip.

Without warning, her wrists were chained in callused fingers.

Elaine jerked backward—too late.

He stared at her splayed hands—at her left hand—as if he had never seen it before.

She wondered if Morrigan's husband was as crazy as her old Scottish maid.

His dark lashes slowly swept upward. Elaine found herself staring into the bluest, coldest eyes she had ever seen.

A tug of will ensued, he to reveal, she to conceal. The large, brown-haired, brown-skinned, scar-faced man separated her arms and pulled them down to her sides as easily as if he were bending disposable pipe cleaners. Elaine's breath escaped in a rush; she was unwittingly mesmerized by his sheer physical power. She had never before realized how utterly vulnerable a woman could be rendered.

The man's lips slanted in a slow smile. He released his bruising grip on her wrists. One hard hand curved around her buttocks; his other hand slid up and about her shoulders.

Heat. Pure, unadulterated heat enveloped Elaine. Pure, unadulterated sensation. Flesh on flesh, callused hands gripping her back and buttocks. Cloth on flesh, the slight scratch of cotton chafing her nipples. Leather on flesh, butter-soft breeches meshing into her thighs. Her feet were pinioned between hard, gritty boots.

Elaine stared up at the descending face, at the skin deeply tanned, at the white ridge of flesh extending from the man's right cheekbone to just above the corner of his mouth. The dilated blue eyes glittered a challenge.

He wanted to hurt Morrigan.

Elaine's heart skipped a beat, raced to regain the missed rhythm.

He wanted to hurt *her.*

The harsh features swooped down. His lips covered hers, hot, so hot Elaine felt as though she were being burned alive. Something wet and hotter still pushed against her lips.

My God, she thought, instinctively compressing her mouth, he was trying to French-kiss her, something Matthew had never done, would never do.

The slick prodding ceased. Relief instantly turned to dismay when her bottom lip was sucked inside a vacuum of hot, moist flesh. Sharp teeth sank into the tender skin. It hurt. Involuntary protest rose at the unexpected assault: "Don't—sto—"

Wet, scalding heat invaded her mouth. The taste of Morrigan's husband was part brandy, part salt, purely *male*. And all of it alien. Invasive. Nothing in Elaine's twentieth-century life had prepared her for the raw sexuality of this moment, not her sex manuals, not her fantasies, certainly not her seventeen years of marriage with dear, gentle, fastidious Matthew.

The man pushed in with his right hand. Morrigan would have bruises on her fanny, Elaine thought, thought immediately suspended as she felt the rasp of her pubic hair against the bulging leather of his breeches, felt the buttery soft/hard grain rubbing against the lips of her sex. His tongue withdrew only to force itself back in. *Out*. Rub. *In*. Rub. *Out*. Rub. *In*.

Deep.

Hard.

Hot.

Filling.

Like the thrust of a man.

A jolt of electricity ran from her mouth to her breast to the flesh between her legs.

Elaine froze, suffused with shock at the surge of sensation. She had never dreamed it was possible to feel such heat, such lust. And with just a kiss. It was demeaning, a reduction of hard-won civilization to pure animal instinct. Having just experienced what she had secretly fantasized about all her life, Elaine was shocked all the way to her toes.

The rotation of her hips ceased. Simultaneously, the hot, wet tongue retreated and the hard, gripping hands withdrew. Elaine opened her eyes, not aware until that moment that she had closed them.

The man's pupils had dilated to the point that she could not even make out the blue band of his irises. Even as she stared, the dilated pupils contracted. The corner of his right lip kicked upward, curling toward the thin white scar. He stepped back.

"You will dress for dinner, madam, and when the dinner gong sounds you will join me downstairs. If you wear that stinking gray dress I will rip it off you in front of the servants. And if you do not join me I will carry you down the stairs and tie you in a chair and force-feed you. Do we understand each other?"

The voice was deep, resonant, the words clipped yet perfectly enunciated. Elaine had had an emeritus college professor once who had spoken like that. He, too, had been English.

His eyes narrowed to blue shards.

"I have been informed that you have the putrid throat, and though I personally am inclined to think that the only thing putrid with your person is your soul, I am willing to give you the benefit of the doubt. Therefore I will overlook your reticence—this time. However, that does not mean I will overlook a sullen and ill-mannered disposition. If you cannot speak, you may nod. I repeat, do we understand each other?"

Elaine nodded. Oh, yes, she understood him. Loud and clear. It was quite evident that he would go out of his way to make Morrigan's life a hell on Earth.

"Excellent. We will discuss future arrangements over dinner. You will wear your hair down like that around your shoulders until I say otherwise. God knows you have little else worth looking at."

An icy chill started at Elaine's ears and descended to her toes. She had not been ridiculed since she had been an overly plump high school student in the late sixties and early seventies. The nakedness that had become a natural extension of the kiss now became a self-consciousness so acute that it was an actual pain. The fine black hairs on her legs felt as though they were charged with static. She fought this alien body of hers to stand tall and straight, digging her nails into the palms of her hands so that they would not independently reach down and grab the towel to shield Morrigan's flaws— her flaws by default.

He turned in a dismissive manner, as if what he saw was not worth viewing, and walked to the door that had previously been locked. Elaine had never seen such poised, erect carriage. He paused on the threshold.

"If you ever attempt to lock *me* out of your bedroom, I will tie you spread-eagled to your bed. Naked. So that I may enjoy your scrawny arse at my leisure. Do we understand each other?

"By the by, if you are going to bathe, I suggest you apply equal attention to all of your body parts. You have an ugly black spot beneath your left ear."

The door closed softly. Not once had the *dirty, filthy Sassenach lord* and devil incarnate turned around to verify Elaine's compliance. He and Hattie were a matched pair. Both seemed to think Morrigan had graduated from canine school.

Elaine gritted her teeth. Hattie had gloated that " 'is lordship" was gone for a fortnight or more. A fortnight was fourteen days. Only three days had elapsed. There were eleven more to go.

She was not prepared for this eventuality. It wasn't fair that, having obtained the key to lock out Hattie, the lord should appear through the other door. She needed those eleven days. She needed that privacy.

She needed to be back in her own time.

A black wave swept over Elaine. The floor swayed. For a moment she thought she was going to pass out—she *hoped* she was going to pass out; perhaps then she would return to where she belonged— but like most things, the vertigo passed, leaving the excess adrenaline inside her stomach to churn and roll.

Conversely, Elaine was consumed with anger. She leaned down and grabbed the bath towel.

How dare he expect her to have dinner with him when she had the putrid throat? She did not, true, but she could have; all kinds of diseases lurked about waiting for discovery in the nineteenth century.

She ruthlessly tucked the end of the towel between her breasts. How dare he expect her to be civil to him when with just a few words he had annihilated every shred of self-esteem she had ever possessed?

Elaine closed the French doors with unrestrained violence. And what did he mean, she had an ugly black spot beneath her left ear? Just who did he think he was, implying that she had not thoroughly washed herself? If she had scrubbed any harder, there would be no skin left.

She marched to the mirror. She was almost used to seeing the pale oval face with the too-large eyes and too-red lips. A splotch of ink marred the skin beneath her ear where she had rammed it with the steel-tipped quill pen while practicing her forgery.

Elaine was sorry that she had popped the buttons off the gray dress. Who did he think he was, telling her what she could or could not wear? If he disliked it so much, he should not allow Hattie to dress Morrigan. In fact, if he had any regard for his wife whatsoever, which he obviously did not, he would not allow Hattie within a ten-mile radius.

Well, Elaine was not some poor, dumb, naive kid to be reduced to a quivering mass by a great bully of a man. Even if that man had seen her all and dismissed it like stale bread.

She gingerly prodded the inside of her bottom lip: the slick flesh was tender. The lips in the mirror were swollen. Like the morning she had awakened in Morrigan's body, filled with the lord's semen, more keenly conscious of that fact now than she had been then.

Morrigan's husband hadn't been real then.

He was all too real now.

His taste lingered in her mouth.

Had he bitten Morrigan's lips?

She thought of her—Morrigan's—nipples. Had he bitten her there, too? Was that why they appeared so . . . swollen, so *carnal*? Marching to the chest, Elaine grabbed a washcloth and the bar of lye soap. She scrubbed the ink spot; then she scrubbed her mouth.

She was sick and tired of nineteenth-century bullies.

He wanted her to join him for dinner?

Fine, she would join him for dinner. Putrid throat and all!

* * *

A gonging sound vibrated through the walls. Immediately a low scratch came from the main door. Elaine's heartbeat accelerated to a painful thud.

Was it Hattie?

But Hattie did not scratch.

Was it Morrigan's husband?

Elaine could not imagine *him* scratching for entry. The places that she could imagine him scratching brought a wave of hot blood to her face.

"M' lady? M' lady, m' lord bade me to escort you downstairs. M' lady?"

Elaine licked impossibly dry lips.

Maybe the male servant would go away if she didn't answer, Maybe the lord would think she really was sick and leave her be.

And maybe a cow would jump over the crescent-moon riding on the sky beyond the balcony.

Elaine opened her mouth to answer, caught herself just in time. She carefully picked her way through the darkness. The swish of silk on silk accompanied her slightest movement. She tugged the lavender silk jacket that buttoned in front, similar in style to the yellow one she had worn earlier. It felt strange not wearing a bra. The slick friction teased and caressed her nipples into a state of near-painful hardness. Her thighs were engorged with blood above the elastic constriction of the garter belts.

She turned the key. The hallway was lit with flickering coach lanterns. A man, about her own height, stood stiffly at attention.

If the maids dressed like characters out of a Charles Dickens novel, this man could only be described as a character out of *Dangerous Liaisons*. He wore a black jacket with red lapels, a black waistcoat, and a white . . . cravat? That was what the neckcloths had been called then, wasn't it? And he sported the largest, sausage-rolled white wig she had ever seen.

Elaine recoiled. What year *was* she in?

The man stepped back from the door and bowed.

And stayed bowed.

Elaine fought down the urge to shout, *What are you waiting for—confession?*

The bewigged head finally rose the tiniest bit. She gestured for him to precede her. With a frown of disapproval, the man straightened and marched down the corridor. Elaine hastily shut the door and followed.

Their footsteps were muffled by an Oriental runner. She blindly passed heavy, gilt-framed pictures, dainty tables with clawed feet, an occasional high-backed chair, all of it as old as Queen Elizabeth the First or as new as a twentieth-century furniture store.

What if the lord deliberately served dishes Morrigan couldn't stand? What if Morrigan was allergic to, say, carrots? What if she ate something that would kill her? *He* certainly wouldn't stop her; he'd probably laugh while she lay writhing and dying.

The servant held open a door and bowed.

The corridor opened up to what Elaine imagined was the center of the house, if a structure of this magnitude could be labeled such. Bright red carpeting lined a wide hallway. To her right, the highly polished gleam of wooden banisters and the expanse of open space was lit by a ten-foot-tall crystal chandelier. The banister gradually curved the length of the wide staircase, also carpeted in red, reminiscent of the one Rhett Butler had carried Scarlett up, that he might have his wicked husbandly way.

As the lord would endeavor to have his way with her, if Elaine was forced to remain in this time. Providing, of course, he could get it up, confronted with her "scrawny arse."

The servant gracefully descended the staircase to the black-veined marble floor below them. Elaine haltingly followed, gripping the handrail to aid the crippled leg.

Would the silverware be recognizable? she wondered frantically. What if she used the wrong fork? Perhaps Morrigan was an uncivilized brat who didn't know a dinner fork from a salad fork, and by correctly choosing, she, Elaine, would be damning herself more surely than if she had misbehaved.

The servant waited impassively by the foot of the stairs. No sooner did she place both trembling feet onto the marble than he pivoted and strode to the left.

Elaine received a fleeting impression of sparkling space and elegant japanned tables adorned with tall jade figurines before hurrying after the servant. A naked female was tucked in the alcove made by the base of the stairs. The curvaceous statue did not wear a fig leaf. Nor did she need to. She was flawless.

The three half-slips Elaine had donned to cover her "scrawny arse" dragged at her feet. She glanced up. The ceiling had to be at least fifty feet high. The marble was hard and cold through her thin slippers. The stairs looked very tall, the second floor landing very far away. Elaine was seized with a sense of agoraphobia.

The servant stopped in front of a pair of wide double doors; he flung them open. Elaine reluctantly stepped over the threshold.

The room inside was large, with the typical high ceiling. One entire wall was comprised of windows. Red velvet drapes with gold cords and tassels—Morrigan's next dress, perhaps?—were drawn against the night. A fireplace comprised the diagonal wall. Inside it, residing on a grate large enough to roast a good-size man, a quartered tree trunk snapped and popped. The center of the room was monopolized by a thirty-foot-long dining room table. It was covered by a white tablecloth. An elaborate flower centerpiece was flanked on either side by large candelabras. Two places at the far end, well away from the hazardous fireplace, were set with plates, an assortment of glasses, and silverware.

The double doors closed with an almost imperceptible swish. Elaine swung around, immediately seized with a sense of claustrophobia.

A liveried servant materialized behind her. Elaine bit her lips to contain a scream. She turned back toward the table. A male servant, dressed identically to the one who escorted her, bowed and gestured toward the far end of the table.

Elaine allowed the servant to seat her. No sooner did she free the hem of the skirt from beneath the chair leg than a steaming bowl of soup appeared near her ear. She jumped back in the chair; the male servant, perhaps the same one who had seated her—they all looked alike in their sausage wigs—set the soup down in front of her.

Elaine instinctively reached for the white silk napkin folded like a tulip on the plate. She draped it across her lap and hoisted the soup-spoon.

The flavor of the clear bouillon was overridden by that of the lye soap she had used earlier to scrub her mouth. While she sipped the broth, hoping she was doing it right by dipping the spoon down the front side of the bowl, tilting it, then righting it back up—hoping Morrigan also did it right—the servant filled one of the myriad stemmed glasses with white wine. She promptly abandoned the soup.

Dish after dish was offered her. Elaine indiscriminately gulped the wine and picked at the food placed on her plate. And still the lord did not come. Alcohol gradually shed the fear of discovery that was like a second skin.

He had done this deliberately, she fumed—set her up for something he must know she would be terrified of, and purposely did not show, thereby taking away from her the opportunity to demonstrate her fearlessness. Now she would never be able to avenge herself for her humiliation.

For *Morrigan's* humiliation.

It was so confusing sometimes, keeping the two separate. Elaine, Morrigan. Morrigan, Elaine. Why did she bother? It was her body as long as she was in it, wasn't it? Graciously she acceded Morrigan the same rights to her body in the twentieth century, sealing the bargain by finishing her sixth glass of wine.

Would this endless parade of food never cease? At Elaine's plumpest she would not have been able to do justice to one-fourth of the dishes presented to her as if they were sacrificial offerings. Or perhaps *she* was the sacrificial offering, a lamb to be fattened before the slaughter.

Elaine fortified herself with another sip of wine, looking at the glass then with some surprise, not having seen the servant refill it. Truly her cup runneth over. She made a small, mocking salute to the centerpiece. Well, by God, his "arse holiness" might eat her, but he would come away with a hangover for his efforts.

The absurdity hit Elaine midswallow. Air gushed up in a giggle;

the sip of wine spewed over the white silk, a red wine now, creating great red blotches. When had red wine taken the place of white?

The servant daubed at the stained tablecloth with a napkin and refilled her glass, as if spitting diners were an everyday experience. Deftly he removed her untouched beef and set before her a dessert plate.

Elaine studied the pudding-filled tart. It looked very tempting, something the thirty-pounds-overweight Elaine would have gobbled in a second. Well, not gobble, exactly, not like she had the roast beef earlier, but she would certainly have had only one glass of wine and devoted the rest of her attention to her food.

A smile played about the corners of her lips. Well, she was *not* fat Elaine, and she didn't have to worry about shocking a sedate husband. She didn't have to worry about *any* husband, since the other one had not shown, and this was the first time in her life she had ever had too much to drink, and, by God, she *liked* it.

She held her glass of wine to the light of the candelabra. Ruby lights sparkled. Elaine brought the glass up to her lips and inhaled the bouquet, letting the fumes of alcohol stimulate her nostrils. Daintily she took a small sip, letting the wine slowly roll over her tongue as she had been instructed to do during a tedious wine-tasting party in that other life. Her lids half closed as she analyzed the taste. Dry, light, with just a hint of redness. Excellent. She took a large gulp.

The servant removed her untouched dessert. He placed a bowl of fruit and nuts on the table, but did not refill the wine. Elaine scowled at him. His face remained as expressionless as a sphinx.

Damn waiters. Damn *servant* waiters.

Too hell with them. Elaine didn't need them.

Elaine didn't need anyone.

A surge of nausea rose to Elaine's throat. She clapped her hand over her mouth.

Elaine didn't need any more *wine*.

The black and red and white livery receded, then slammed into her face. She gratefully accepted the servant's assistance in pulling back the chair and helping her to her feet.

"Are you all right, m' lady? Shall I ring for a maid?"

Elaine opened her mouth, closed it, as much from the threat of regurgitation as Bedlam. She shook her head, then held very still, the movement having sent the entire room into a whirlwind. The servant took her arm and led her to a pair of doors.

Elaine stepped out into the Taj Mahal, everything black and white and gold and jade.

Where was she?

The waiter-servant handed Elaine over to another servant. All men, it seemed, dressed alike, as the women dressed the same in their white Jiffy Pop caps and crow dresses and Aunt Jemima aprons.

Why was she lurching around like a crab?

Oh, yesss, she was crippled. *Crippled whippled, crippled nippled. Crippled diddled.* She giggled. *Crippled giggled.*

Elaine glided up the back stairs, crippled leg belonging to someone else, the black, red, and white-liveried man, perhaps. Suddenly she was in her room. At least it looked like her room. It had the same yellow silk-curtained bed, the same Oriental rug. But there were candles everywhere. Lighted candles. And there were flames popping and crackling in the fireplace.

Elaine stumbled to the bed. Her stomach somersaulted. She swiveled mid-recline and darted to the Japanese screen.

A hint of sobriety surfaced.

The chamber pot was gone!

She hiccuped. Bitter gall flooded her mouth.

Elaine dove for the bed, dove *beneath* the bed. The hard, cool porcelain was as welcome as had been the bath earlier that day. She drug the lid off and heaved, remembering in some minute corner unstupored by wine to hold back the curtain of black enveloping her face.

Elaine heaved and heaved. Small chunks of undigested food swam in an ocean of white and red wine. At last she stood, lurched to the left—*damn,* must have lost one of her shoes, all his fault, that damn lord's—and fell with a thunk face down onto one of the three turned-down beds.

Funny, the bed hadn't felt this hard the other nights she had slept on it. Or so close to the floor. The silk sheets and velvet bedspread felt more like wool. She curled her hand beneath her cheek.

Unconsciousness was not without conscience. Just as a dark wave rolled over her head, she remembered: she was Elaine in Morrigan's body. And Matthew's kisses had never, *ever* made her feel the way the lord's had.

Chapter

8

"'In Edinburgh town they've made a law, / In Edinburgh town at the Court o' Session; / That standing pricks are fauteors a', / And guilty of high transgression.'"

Charles tugged at his boot. A nasty grin curled his lips. Bet the Scottish hag that guarded his wife's virtue like a fetid dragon didn't know Robert Burns had written *that* song.

"'Act Sederunt o' the Session'—Shit!"

His boot shot across the room; Charles sprawled back onto the bed, one boot on, one boot off. He closed his eyes, succumbing to the lull of several bottles of rotgut whiskey that he had imbibed at a nearby tavern.

Pale dawn lit the sky behind the drawn curtains. The gleam of gold circling Morrigan's finger shone behind Charles's lids. He felt again the sense of homecoming, the surge of hope that at last something could be made of this marriage that should never had taken place. Immediately he felt his flesh shrivel beneath the cold void of her eyes and the cold brittleness of her body.

Damn her soul to hell and back again! She *must* have known what that ring meant. She must have known that by wearing it he would take the gesture as a sign of reconciliation. As a sign that she wanted to be his wife in more than name.

Putrid throat.

Her throat hadn't been putrid when he had kissed her earlier this evening—yesterday evening. "*Sto*—" vibrated on his lips still.

She had not tasted cold, this child-bride grudgingly turned wife of his who now showed propensities of becoming a sadistic tease. She had tasted hot, woman with a subtle flavor of roast pork and lye soap.

The bed whirled beneath him.

Charles frowned.

It had been many years since his mouth had been washed out with lye soap, but the flavor was unforgettable.

Morrigan had tasted of lye soap.

Her body had smelled of white ginger.

He wondered what those delectable mocha lips and nipples tasted of: the passionless lye or the promising white ginger? The enigma followed Charles all the way down the spiraling tunnel.

Metal grated across metal. Sunlight slapped Charles in the face. He was immediately enveloped in chill, damp air.

Charles threw an arm across his eyes. He did not need to ascertain who the harbinger of such a chill awakening was. Only one person entered his room while he was still in it. And it wasn't his wife, he thought sourly.

"What in bloody hell do you think you're doing?" Charles asked softly.

"This room smells like a pigsty," Fritz said, not at all intimidated by his lord's tone. "Since you deemed it necessary to take yourself off for *days*, you really must be up and about to see what mischief that steward of yours has gotten us into. The sun has been up these past few hours. Your bath is getting cold. Really, sir, the time and effort it will take to get the wrinkles out of that coat could be better spent. What will the servants think, their master stumbling home singing in his cups at all hours of the morning and passing out fully clothed?"

Charles's lips, visible below his coatsleeve, compressed into a thin line. "I do not pay my servants to think, Fritz," he said in a dangerously soft voice, "any more than I pay you to deliver homilies. If you are so concerned about my image"—his voice suddenly whipped out sharp as a cat-o'-nine-tails—"then pull my frigging boot off and be gone!"

Fritz grabbed Charles's booted foot and pulled.

Charles clutched the covers to prevent himself from being dragged to the floor. "Oh, for Chrissake!" He sat up and glared at his valet.

Fritz held the boot aloft as if it were a piece of dried camel dung. Sighting its mate halfway across the room, he swooped down onto it and neatly slammed the pair onto the wooden border surrounding the Oriental carpet. The resulting thud echoed inside Charles's head.

A spark of amusement lit Charles's bloodshot eyes. It would appear he was not going to be forgiven anytime soon for leaving Fritz behind four days ago. He undressed, deriving a grim sense of pleasure from watching Fritz wildly jump for the discarded garments.

A fire crackled in the anteroom that had been converted into a bathroom, Charles's first project upon inheriting the title three years past. Steam fogged the air, a welcome departure after the chill morning breeze circulating about in the bedchamber. He lay back in the tub with a sigh and prepared to resume the sleep so precipitously interrupted.

Scalding water poured over his submerged feet. Charles sat up, yelping. "What the—"

Fritz vigorously applied a soapy cloth to Charles's back. "I assigned my lady a maid just as you ordered before you left and got yourself glorious."

Charles rolled his eyes upward. Fritz was thirty years old; his vocabulary was seventy-five.

"When you failed to present yourself at dinner, she consoled herself by *drinking* her dinner. The maid, when she entered the chamber to bank the fire, found her passed out cold on the floor by the bed. Not knowing what to do, the maid roused me."

It was obvious by now why Fritz had awoken him. He would

surely have burst had he held all this information inside him one second longer. The man had not shown this degree of animation when surrounded by a group of renegade Maratha.

"Was that the same maid who supplied you with yesterday's gossip?" Charles caustically interrupted. "What the hell are you jabbering about? I have the devil of a head, so make it quick. And any skin that comes off my back will come out of your wage."

"Humph!" Fritz ceased his scouring and rinsed the soap off of Charles's back. "As I was saying, the maid roused me from my rooms. I was immediately alerted to the problem from the smell in my lady's bedchamber. Her ladyship had, ah, cascaded. Feeling it my duty in your lordship's absence, I lifted the baroness to her bed, then summoned another maid to assist the first maid in . . ."

Fritz cleared his throat. Charles could feel the heat emanating from the valet's face.

"In preparing her ladyship for bed. The footman said her ladyship imbibed two whole bottles of wine—"

The gist of Fritz's gossip finally sank into Charles's sleep- and drink-muddled brain.

"What did you say?" Charles interrupted.

Fritz adopted his aggrieved valet tone. "If you would but listen, my lord. I said her ladyship imbibed two whole bottles of wine—"

Morrigan? *Drunk?*

"—and hardly touched her food at all. He said—"

"That will be all, Fritz."

Morrigan's aunt and uncle were strict Methodists. As far as he was aware, his wife had never touched a drop of alcohol in her entire life.

What the hell was going on?

Charles stood up. Water streamed down his body.

"Have your Katie prepare milady for breakfast."

"She's not *my* Katie!" Fritz protested indignantly.

Charles ignored the valet's cherry-red coloring. He reached for the towel folded on top of the basin.

"Since milady was distressed by my absence from the dinner table, she may join me in the morning room."

Chapter
9

"Morning, m' lady. His lordship, he sent me to fetch ye fer breakfast, he did."

The grating sound of the curtains being drawn sliced through the morning calm. Immediately, searing white sunshine flooded the room.

Elaine groaned. Where was she? She must be in the hospital. Only a nurse would be that insensitive. And a body that felt like hers could only *be* in a hospital. Or in a morgue. Undergoing an autopsy.

"Rise 'n' shine, m' lady! I put out a dress fer ye and all yer underthings. If ye don't like the dress, I'll git another one fer ye. His lordship, he said as how I was supposed to help ye, he did. And that I should hurry ye up fer breakfast."

Elaine cracked open an eyelid. A body was tucked under the covers, the exposed upper torso clad in a white nightgown. She immediately closed the eye against the searing white light. A trembling hand groped up and down from beneath the covers, encountered a nightcap perched on top of a tangled mass of hair. She would never get the tangles out.

Memory staggered into consciousness.

This was Morrigan's body, Morrigan's head, Morrigan's hair, and Morrigan's husband occupied the adjoining room.

Oh, God, how could a head ache this much and not split in half?

Elaine slid the nightcap off over her face and crushed it into a ball in the palm of her hand.

The wine. The killer wine.

She ran her tongue over her lips. Her mouth tasted rancid, as though it and not the wine had fermented.

How much had she drunk?

How had she gotten into the nightgown? The last thing she remembered was jumping for one of three beds.

And landing with a thunk.

She moaned.

Triple vision. Elaine had heard coworkers joke about getting triple vision, but she had thought it was a joke. Never for one minute had she actually believed a person could drink so much they would see three images.

Remembering the bottomless wineglasses, she was only surprised she had seen merely three. She was only surprised she wasn't dead from alcohol poisoning. She was only *sorry* she wasn't dead from alcohol poisoning.

Elaine's whole body was one giant ache. The sun throbbed with energy, very noisy, very *nauseating*.

"I have just the thing to make ye feel better."

Surprisingly strong hands lifted her shoulders. The canopy bucked and whirled. Elaine squeezed her eyelids tightly together. She was laid back on a pile of plumped pillows. The balled nightcap was pried from between her fingers.

"Here's a nice cup of hot chocolate, just the thing to make ye feel better."

Elaine's hand was shaped around the contours of a hot cup and brought to her mouth. Chocolate vapors curled around her nose, moist, thick, *clogging*.

Elaine gagged, eyes bulging open. Recognition flashed through the painful red haze. It was the juvenile-delinquent maid. She thrust the cup of hot chocolate back toward the serving girl.

"But marm, ye'll feel ever so much better if ye drink it! Cook, she says—"

Elaine jiggled the outthrust cup, not in the least interested in what *Cook* or anyone else in this barbaric time said. Hot chocolate slopped dangerously around the rim. The maid reluctantly accepted the cup.

"I was only trying to help ye feel better, m' lady. Jamie, that be the footman, he says as how ye tied one on in a bad way last night, and I says to meself, 'Katie, me girl, I sure wouldn't want to be in her ladyship's shoes this morning,' no, marm, and what could I do to make ye feel better? So Cook says as how nothing's better than a nice cup of chocolate to git ye over a boozy."

Elaine closed her eyes against the daggers of light streaming through the French doors. The girl's voice seemed to be echoing over and over in her head, as if it were hollow—her head, that is—but there was no way it could be hollow and hurt that badly. *Shut up!* she wanted to scream at the maid. *And shut those curtains, too, while you're at it!* The force of her emotions only increased the pulsing headache.

The bedcovers slid off her lap.

Elaine's eyes snapped open. She glared at the maid.

"We'll just git yer ladyship dressed all nice and pretty fer his lordship."

Elaine grabbed the covers and jerked them over her lap. Her lips folded into a mutinous line. She was too sick to be afraid. If "his lordship" wanted her to breakfast with him, then he could have it in her bedroom. At which point she would puke all over him.

"Marm—"

Elaine flattened her left palm and made a frenzied scribbling motion on it with her right hand.

The maid scampered to the desk and returned with the quill-tipped pen, ink, and paper. She gave the writing materials to Elaine, then stood uncertainly for a second, her weight shifting from first one foot then the other. A look of supreme enlightenment suddenly inundated the mobcapped features. Katie skipped back over to the desk and returned with the Bible for a writing top.

Elaine adjusted the heavy Bible on her lap for the umpteenth time. She studied the paper, the pen, the paper, the elongated bead of ink on the end of the nib. How should she address the note? She didn't know his name, that brown-haired, brown-skinned, scar-faced monster.

Ha, that was a joke. She didn't know the name of her supposed husband, knew him only as *my lord*, or *his lordship*. She didn't even know how to spell Morrigan! Was it spelled with one *r* or two, an *i* or an *e*, an *a* or an *e?*

Oh, well, that at least she could get around. It was the salutation that presented the most trouble. Should she start out, "My dear lord"? No, that sounded blasphemous, at the very least a plagiarism of a George Harrison tune. "Dear my lord"? Bad grammar. Finally she wrote:

> *Dear Lord,*
>   *Not only do I have the putrid throat, but I have the putrid stomach. I regret to inform you I will not be able to join you for breakfast.*
>   *Sincerely,*
>   *Your Wife*

Elaine sat back against the pillows. The words danced and skated across the paper. Something was wrong. She squinted and held the paper up in front of her face. The dots over the *i*'s looked like donut holes, and the crosses on the *t*'s resembled skid marks. No, it was something else. The longer she looked at the note the more the words moved, until the bed itself seemed to be writhing.

Folding the note, Elaine hurriedly thrust it out to the maid—what had she called herself during the interminable monologue that would have done Hattie herself justice?—Katie.

The maid gingerly took the letter.

"Who's it going to, m' lady? His lordship—"

Elaine's glare turned vicious.

"Ye want me to give it to his lordship?"

Elaine nodded, the glare firmly in place.

The maid departed.

Elaine relaxed her facial muscles. It hurt too much to be angry. It hurt too much to think, period. She carefully slid out of bed. A piercing thud resounded. Cringing at the reverberating sound, she stepped over the fallen Bible, crept to the door, and softly turned the key in the lock. Shutting her eyes against the daggers of light, she eased the curtains over the French doors. She then removed the extra pillows from her bed, crawled beneath the shifting covers, pulled them over her head, and promptly went back to sleep.

Charles glared at the maid. "What is it? You were told, my good girl, to prepare your mistress for breakfast. Promptly."

Katie dropped into a curtsy, bowed head presenting him with an expansive view of the top of her mobcap. A black-sleeved arm extended; a folded piece of paper rattled.

"Her ladyship, she bade me to give this to ye, m' lord."

Charles took the piece of paper, unfolded it, and perused its contents. Immediately the frown on his face cleared. His lips quirked upward.

Dear lord?

Morrigan had directed the maid to the wrong floor: the note should have gone up, not down.

A *putrid stomach?*

Charles would not have credited Morrigan with a sense of humor, and though he was quite certain she had not intended her note to amuse him, it did. Vastly.

What better way to describe a hangover than as having a *putrid* stomach?

He lingered over the closing. *Your wife.* What game was she playing? First she wore his ring, and now this address from the woman who had spent the last year ignoring her wedding vows.

"Was Hattie with your mistress?"

The girl remained sunk in a curtsy. "No, m' lord, she's kept to her room this morning. I did what ye told me to, m' lord, but m' lady, she was feeling ever so poorly, m' lord."

Charles restrained a grin. "You may go about your duties, Katie. Allow her ladyship to sleep off, ah, to sleep for a few more hours, then serve her luncheon. Food will no doubt settle her stomach. Prepare her a bath then."

The maid rose awkwardly. "Yes, m' lord." She silently backed toward the door.

"Katie?"

The maid sank into another curtsy. "M' lord?"

"Was milady still afflicted with the putrid throat when you woke her this morning?"

"Yes, m' lord, leastways, she didn't speak none, m' lord."

"Very good. You may go."

It had been part deviltry, part curiosity that had inspired Charles to summon Morrigan for breakfast. And now this note.

She had not disappointed him.

For once.

Charles took his plate to the buffet and heaped it with bacon, sausage and mushrooms, fried eggs, deviled kidneys, a slab of ham, and toast. He eyed a plump hot cross bun, heavy with raisins. It joined the pile of food.

Charles ate with single-minded concentration, almost feeling the food absorb the remaining alcohol inside his body. He wondered how Morrigan was getting along—and grinned around his toast. Obviously not well. Too bad she hadn't come down for breakfast. He would have enjoyed his food all the more knowing every bite would only add to her "putrid stomach." He forked a large kidney, paused with the utensil halfway to his lips.

Something was wrong.

Her note. Something about Morrigan's note did not sit well.

He lowered the fork back down to his plate and picked up the note. The writing was sloppy, but that was to be expected. The actual content—well, perhaps Morrigan possessed unplumbed depths. No, it was—

"Ye canna see 'er; she's doin' 'er penship!"

"Let me by, damn you. Morrigan is my wife. I will see her whenever I please."

"Nae, I willna let ye go a'botherin' 'er; 'tis sinful, it is, 'usbands a'botherin' wives in th' light o' day!"

Charles firmly pushed Hattie out of the doorway and stepped into

Morrigan's room. His "wife" was seated at the desk. A large Bible lay open beside the sheet of paper she was carefully writing upon.

"Morrigan, my dear, I've come to take you riding. It's not healthy to sit in this room day after day. Come, it's a beautiful morning. The rain has stopped; the sun is shining."

Morrigan continued writing as if he were not there, as if she were deaf and dumb as well as crippled. He tamped down the spark of anger.

"What are you writing?" Charles strolled toward the desk, Hattie's foul odor following behind him. He restrained an impulse to pivot around and catalyze a head-on collision. "May I see it?"

Without waiting for permission, Charles leaned over Morrigan's shoulder. She was copying text from the Bible. Her writing was ponderously slow, due, he saw, to the extreme left-hand slant. Even the fact that she wrote with her left hand did not explain the extremity of the slant.

"Do you do this often, Morrigan? Copy text from the Bible?"

Morrigan looked up at him with those black eyes that should have been attractive but more and more were starting to resemble bottomless pits, empty save for space.

"Yes, of course, my lord." She opened a drawer, pulled out a sheaf of papers, and handed them to him.

Charles glanced at the sheaf of papers in an abstract manner, then looked back down into those pitlike eyes. Snake eyes. He had seen that look in the eyes of a cobra before it struck.

Suddenly the image his retina had hastily captured upon accepting the sheaf of papers registered in his brain. His gaze leaped to the heavy pile of papers in his hands. Slowly he flipped through them, more than a hundred, two hundred, three hundred, maybe four. The exaggerated left hand was almost hypnotic, rather like a yantra in its repetition.

Charles focused again on Morrigan's note.

"M' lord?"

He looked up at the footman standing in the door. It was open wide enough for his body only; his right hand behind him held the doorknob as if preventing someone from wresting it from him. Even as Charles stared, the man and the door jerked.

"Begging yer pardon, m' lord, but—"

"Git outta m' way, ye fagged *Sassenach!* Th' lord, 'e'll speak t' me when 'e 'ears what I got t' say, aye, that 'e will!"

The door and footman jerked again, the two parting, the door to slam open and hit the outside wall, the footman to go sailing across the marble floor in the hallway. Hattie stood in the doorway in all her dingy, dirty glory, looking more like a bulldog than ever with her gloating, malevolent eyes and upside-down snarl. The footman scrambled to his feet and lunged toward the female harridan.

"That will be all, Roddie." Charles contemplated this Hattie who for so long had ignored him at every turn, yet who now deliberately sought him out. "You may go," he added, referring to the red-faced footman.

Hattie glared at the footman, then at Charles, her face filled with malevolence—the pugnacious features jutted with triumph, like a dog with a coveted bone clamped between its jowls, strutting its conquest before the losing mutts of the world.

"Please, won't you come in?" Charles asked in his most courteous voice. "Close the door. Now. I believe you have something you wish to discuss?"

Hattie closed the door. "Aye, I jus' bet ye wouldna want anyone t' hear what I 'ave t' say, now, would ye, yer *lordship?*"

Hattie stared down at the heathenishly brown-skinned baron, his chair scooted out from the table, dressed in a faded green morning coat and skintight leather breeches with boots so shiny they reflected the sunshine pouring in from the open windows of the breakfast room. So pristine he came across, him and his Adam appetites. She crossed her arms over her shrunken chest.

"I 'ave somethin' t' say t' ye, all right. An' ye willna be wantin' t' diddle that wife o' yers agin, not when I git through tellin' ye what I know; nae, ye'll let 'er go back t' the rev'ren' where she can git th' de'il purged from 'er soul an' live th' life o' a decent, God-fearin' woman like she was doin' 'fore ye started yer interferin'. She's e'il, that one is, e'il an' steeped in th' wickedness o' Jezebel an' Lucifer. She needs watchin', aye, that she does."

Chapter

10

Dear Lady,

I trust that your putrid throat and stomach have recovered suffi-
ciently to join me for dinner. I have requested that special dishes be
prepared in your honor. I feel certain you will not disappoint either
myself or my chef. As you are no doubt aware, there still remain cer-
tain arrangements to be made.

Your Servant, and, always,
Your Husband

Elaine studied the note, the bold, clipped handwriting, the words
leaden with sarcasm. Why had he not addressed Morrigan by name?
Why had he not signed his own?

"M' lady, it be time to ready ye fer dinner. I know just the dress.
It'll make ye look ever so pretty."

Elaine irritably scribbled a note, wanting nothing more than to be
left alone.

Katie read the note and promptly burst into tears. "Mr. Fritz, he
told me I was to take care of ye, that I could be yer lady's maid till
the lord finds someone else. I can help buy shoes fer the little ones
with the extra shillings. Oh, marm, please don't send me away! I already told the other servants. If ye don't want me now, they'll think
I lied, and the lord, he'll think I didn't please ye, and he'll let me

and me sis go and . . . and I'll not be able to see Mr. Fritz anymore, and . . . oh, please, marm, please, ye got to give me a chance!"

Elaine wasn't sure if it was the thought of thwarted ambition, shoeless children, maligned reputation, or displaced lovers that brought the deluge of tears. Whichever it was, it was easier to submit than to endure the maid's bawling. Besides, if she sent Katie away the lord might reassign Hattie. She put her foot down only when the maid insisted upon lacing "m'lady" into a corset.

Katie finally left her in peace and quiet. Elaine's thoughts returned to the lord's note, to her note that had preceded it. Why had he addressed his exactly as she had addressed hers, substituting the appropriate gender, but otherwise exactly the same?

She had known something was wrong when she had written that note earlier. But what? Why, oh, why couldn't she remember? The entire morning was a haze of pain and nausea. She remembered Katie pulling the drapes and jabbering endlessly about dressing her to join "his lordship" for breakfast; then the girl had added insult to injury by thrusting that revolting cup of hot chocolate in her face. She had written the note in desperation, claiming . . .

She had claimed a putrid stomach.

That was why he had phrased his note thus. Little wonder the reference conveyed sarcasm. If he only took her for a class-A fool, she would consider herself lucky.

But there had been something else. *God!* Why couldn't she remember? Something he must have caught, too. Why else would he have imitated her form of address? Her mastery of Morrigan's handwriting was good enough to pass inspection if it was not placed directly by an original. *So what . . . ?*

The dinner gong sounded—funny that it gonged only when the lord was in residence—followed by a scratch. Elaine hesitated for the merest second. Hattie would not be so servile; neither would "his lordship." Besides, scratching was almost as personal as, say, a voice or a signature, she was discovering. Katie scratched one way; the chamber pot maid another; the male servant another way still. And this definitely sounded like the male servant. She opened the door.

The black and red and white–liveried servant of last night bowed low. "M' lord bade me to fetch you for dinner, m' lady."

Elaine looked down at the rows and rows of fat sausage curls, mildly affronted. *Fetch* her? Surely the lord trusted his wife to make her own way to the dining room?

She didn't make the servant suffer long minutes of contortion this time. Firmly closing the door, she preceded the servant, fully cognizant of the dining room's direction.

The hallway flickered with ominous shadow. On each alternating step Elaine thought, *He knows that I'm not Morrigan.* Left foot. *How could he?* Right foot. *He knows.* Left foot. *How could he?*

The crystal chandelier glared with hundreds of faceted lights. She continued the foot-damning repetition on the stairs, stepping onto the black-veined marble on *He knows.*

Elaine slowed her steps, allowing the servant to catch up. He opened the double doors and bowed. She took a fortifying breath and entered the dining room.

It was empty save for the waiter-servant. Elaine wondered if the excruciatingly blank-faced man avoided her eyes because he was a servant and she a lady, or because he was embarrassed by her drunken behavior of the night before.

The servant held out a chair. Elaine sat down, remembering to pull her skirt out of the way before it caught beneath the legs when he scooted the chair forward. For the span of a heartbeat her hair hung forward like a dark blanket—or like blinders.

Suddenly the twin streamers of hair were caught and pulled away from her face. Elaine sat back against the chair. Surely the servant, emboldened by her drunken behavior last night, wasn't making a pass?

Gentle hands draped her hair over the back of the chair. Before Elaine could muster a form of protest, the hands slid to her shoulders, a hot, cupping weight. Callused thumbs lightly rasped back and forth over the smooth silk of her dress, paused to investigate the hollows below her shoulders, smoothing to measure the protuberant collarbones.

This was no crude servant. Elaine braced herself against a slow creep of lethargy. A thin line of electricity radiated from the heat of those hands, spreading through her shoulders to the tips of her breasts and the nipples that he had seen, had probably suckled. Bitten.

With superhuman effort, Elaine remained rigid beneath the onslaught of unwanted sensation.

No, it wasn't a servant who caressed her. Elaine would recognize the lord's touch anywhere, anytime.

The marauding thumbs joined the rest of his fingers; he lightly pressed down on her shoulders, then slid a finger around the front of the armhole seam, coming perilously close to an unconfined breast.

"Really, my dear, there is no need to flaunt your . . . charms. I thought we had already established the fact that they are few and far between."

Heat flooded Elaine's face and chest. Why had she not allowed Katie to lace her up into one of those blasted corsets? Surely he did not think she was attempting to seduce him?

The hard, hot hands tightened, loosened. A light pressure stirred the hair on the top of her head—a kiss?—then she was free of that enervating touch. He seated himself directly to her left at the head of the table.

Elaine stared.

The lord's "brown" hair glowed a rich, burnished chestnut. Her yuppie contemporaries in Chicago would kill for the healthy, golden tan of his brown skin, strikingly set off by a stark white shirt. The black tuxedo he wore could have come from a Gingiss Formalwear showcase, the clothes as different from the liveries of the male servants as the dresses in the armoire were from the maids' uniforms. Only minor variations set the suit apart from the twentieth century: the lapels were rounded, the cut was tighter, more formfitting, displaying an excellent pair of shoulders. The vest stretched tautly across his flat stomach, riding a pair of dinner pants that left nothing to the imagination. She inspected the bulge in his lap.

"My dear."

Elaine hastily looked up. Diamond studs held together the pleated white shirt. Above those his glittering blue eyes were every bit as cold and hard.

"Is there something amiss with my person?" he asked. He looked down as he draped his napkin over his lap, briefly perusing the bulge in his crotch before covering it with a flow of white silk, resulting, then, in a bulge of white silk.

Elaine followed his deliberately provocative movements before, catching herself, she quickly brought her eyes back up to his face. He was waiting for her. That long mouth with the full lower lip stretched in a taunting smile, gelid eyes bright with a knowing gleam. He looked as if he had hidden beneath her bed and witnessed things no man—or woman, for that matter—had a right to witness.

Elaine felt a rush of blood start at her chest and crawl to the tips of her ears.

His smile broadened.

A black arm snaked down and around. Elaine caught her breath in alarm. A bowl of soup was neatly placed in front of her.

Elaine's stomach growled in anticipation. Katie had brought her lunch earlier, banging on the locked door loudly enough to wake the dead, but between a blinding headache and stomach-churning nausea, Elaine had not been able to eat. Ignoring the knowing, glinting blue of the lord's eyes, Elaine draped her napkin across her lap and picked up the soupspoon.

Her hand halted mid-descent. She stared at the soup in dismay. Great yellow balls rolled about in the bottom of the bowl. The soup itself, a murky, yellow broth, was filled with oily globules. Elaine looked up in time to see the servant place an identical bowl in front of the lord, the contents, however, far different.

The lord picked up his spoon and openly grinned, displaying two rows of sharp, white teeth. "Egg soup, my dear. Eat hearty. The country folk here hold great faith in the fertility of eggs. Cook prepared that particular confection just for you." His smile faded. "Eat."

Elaine delicately arched the spoon into the soup, careful not to disturb the great yellow balls in the bottom of the bowl. It was very rich, the globular, yellow confection nothing more sinister than fatty chicken broth. Not bad. Perhaps with a touch of pepper . . .

"The servants think it most peculiar that we have been married now for a year—"

Broth spilled from Elaine's spoon.

"—with no visible results. Hence the special dishes. They are determined that all wagers be covered, you see. They will provide the eggs, and I"—the lord delicately sipped clear beef bouillon from his spoon—"will provide the sperm. What's wrong with your left hand?" His voice switched from silk to steel mid-swallow. "Is this putrid thing spreading?"

Elaine choked. The spoon dropped into the bowl, splattering the front of her silk dress with chicken broth. The yellow yolks rolled back and forth.

She could feel the blood drain from her head.

No wonder Morrigan's fingers had been as tender as Elaine's own in the twentieth century, used to typing as opposed to longhand. Morrigan, she belatedly realized, had a perfectly legitimate reason for writing with a leftward slant so extreme it nearly broke Elaine's wrist when reproducing it.

Morrigan was left-handed.

Elaine was right-handed.

A black-clad arm reached for her bosom just as Elaine reached for her wineglass with her right hand—no, *left* hand. She held the glass between clenched fingers while the servant patted the front of her gown with a towel.

Patted her *breasts* with a towel.

While *he* watched, damn his eyes. Didn't he care that a servant was touching his wife's person?

"I really would have thought that after your experience last night you would prefer something with less putrid effects, my dear," the lord commented lightly. He gracefully dipped his spoon into his soup. "Jamie, bring her ladyship a glass of fresh milk."

Elaine glared at the blank-faced servant. Jamie, the footman, had apparently apprised not only the entire staff of m' lady's "booziness," but the lord as well.

The footman folded the white cloth with which he had been manhandling Elaine over his arm. He deftly pried the wineglass from between her fingers. "Very good, my lord."

Elaine transferred her glare to "my lord." She hated milk, a carry-over from a disastrous fourth-grade outing in which she had been bitten by a pony. In addition to the carnivorous horse, there had been a cow with great, bloated udders. Each child had been encouraged (in her case forced) to squeeze a hot, nubby udder to draw forth nature's preferred beverage (the teacher's words, not hers)—milk! And having drawn forth the excretory substance, to sample it. Hot, fresh, straight from inside the cow who stood and chewed and chewed on an all-day cud. One might as well drink cow saliva, nine-year-old Elaine had deduced. Or urine. The cow had a nasty habit of twitching its tail and hitting one square in the face, a constant reminder of the udders' proximity to less savory body parts.

His lordship smiled. He was enjoying this. As if he *knew*. But how could he? Unless Morrigan also disliked milk.

He and Morrigan had been married for a year.

What else did Elaine and Morrigan have in common? Or not have in common?

The lord sedately finished his soup. Elaine wished with all her might that he might choke, or that she had the balls to toss the remainder of her soup in his face.

She looked down at the hard-boiled egg yolks. A grin tugged at the corners of her mouth. Well, she had the *balls*, if she only dared use them.

A black-sleeved arm reached out in front of Elaine and set down a glass beside the soup bowl. The substance inside the tumbler was white and frothy, like the saliva of a rabid dog. A great yellow eye peered out through the bottom of the glass.

A raw egg.

Elaine understood how a chameleon must feel. First she had burned red with embarrassment, then white with shock. She felt sure she must now be green with bile.

A raw egg!

Drawing a deep breath, she raised defiant eyes.

"Morrigan, if you do not drink that, I will take it as a sign that you, er, do not need assistance in gaining fertility. Now, I had been prepared to give you a day or so to recover from your putrid state. But if you feel you are ready . . .

Elaine drank the warm milk. Once the egg got started, it slid down without mishap, fairly tasteless, in fact. The footman took the empty glass. Elaine suppressed a burp of satisfaction, feeling like Rocky in training.

His lordship smiled with genuine amusement. He was really quite handsome when he was not being cold and nasty. Gold and copper highlights glinted in his chestnut hair. He raised his hand, then balled in his fist the white silk napkin that had covered his crotch.

Elaine drew back, the fear and uncertainty returning. What if it had been a test? What if Morrigan despised—not milk, perhaps, but eggs—as much as she herself despised milk? What if she despised eggs so much she would have thrown up?

The lord gently wiped Elaine's mouth with his napkin, the silk smooth against her lips. Beneath the silk was a touch of roughness, callused fingertips.

Had he been gentle with Morrigan four nights ago? Or had he treated her as he had treated Elaine yesterday, using tongue and teeth and implacable strength?

The footman took their soup bowls. Round after round of food followed, egg a predominant factor. The lord himself served her, selecting from the myriad plates and bowls the servant presented and placing a few spoonfuls of each of the dishes upon her plate. Elaine ate what was placed before her, carefully manipulating the fork in her left hand. She was afraid of accepting, afraid of rejecting, almost numb with the knowledge that he knew something was wrong, that she had failed the test before she had even picked up that dratted soupspoon.

The lord tossed his napkin on the table. "Bring the port, Jamie. There's no need to go, Morrigan. I assure you I can get as drunk with you as without you. Well, what did you think of your special meal?"

The servant removed Elaine's dishes. Her thoughts tumbled over one another in their haste to be answered.

Would Morrigan have left him to his port? Did he frequently get drunk after dinner? How could he not already be drunk after all the wine he had consumed *with* dinner?

Good God. Morrigan was left-handed. How was Elaine supposed to communicate now?

She studied a painting on the wall facing her. A group of men dressed in red coats riding lathered horses surrounded a panic-stricken fox.

What else did she still not know about Morrigan?

"Morrigan, you do remember what I said about not abiding an ill-tempered disposition, do you not?"

Elaine tore her gaze away from the trapped animal. The lord's eyes were blue shards again.

She nodded.

"So did you enjoy your special meal?"

Anger flared, quickly died, was followed by despair. That note. *Damn him.* What did he want?

She curtly nodded, once.

"And do you feel more fertile now?"

There was no need to hesitate over that question. Elaine vigorously shook her head.

The amusement was back on the lord's face. He leaned back to allow the footman to remove his dishes.

"Then perhaps we should make a pilgrimage to the Cerne giant. I understand it is very beneficial for women to sleep within the outlines of the giant's penis. And it *is* giant. It has a penis eighteen feet long. Quite puts that of a mortal man to shame."

The footman filled a glass with a dark red wine. The lord waved his left hand toward the crystal decanter. The servant set the port down on the table and retreated. Somewhere behind Elaine a door softly opened and closed.

The lord took a sip of wine, staring at Elaine over the rim. He took a heartier swig before lowering the glass. "Though I assure you I will strive to do my best with these mere mortal dimensions of mine." He toyed with the stem of his glass. "The local folk still perform maypole dances on Beltain, there at the heart of the giant. Or perhaps not the heart. How would you like to ride a maypole, my dear? In private, of course."

Elaine stared at her water goblet. Reflected flame danced in the crystal.

The lord drank glass after glass of port. His eyes remained riveted on Elaine as if she were the most intriguing thing he had ever seen. Or as if she were an unknown species of insect.

Elaine's bladder expanded to the point of bursting. Finally even a strong will could no longer keep the dictates of nature at bay. She stood with as much dignity as a shortened leg would allow and walked toward the door.

A crash originated from the table, the sound of a toppling chair. Elaine made a dash to reach the door. Her left shoulder was grabbed from behind; she was whirled around.

Elaine stumbled. The lord steadied Morrigan's traitorous body with his right hand, his left hand rising, both hands holding her firmly by the shoulders.

A hot, live current ran from his flesh into hers.

He studied her, intense, tense.

"Hattie came to me today. She said you did unspeakable things when you were alone in your bed. She said you 'played' with yourself. Said you sinned against God and man. Against me. Do you, Morrigan?" Callused thumbs brushed against her neck. "Do you prefer your own touch to that of a man? To mine? I could give you so much, if you would just . . ."

Elaine died a thousand deaths, looking up into those blue eyes. It had been bad enough to have Hattie smirk at her, but to have told *him* such a thing! No matter that a survey she had heard over the radio assured the world that 99 percent of the population did, and the remaining 1 percent lied. No matter that as far as she knew

Morrigan did not, only Elaine, and as Morrigan she had not touched herself there, would never touch another's body there. No matter that the look on his face was not one of condemnation. It was worse. He looked at her pityingly, as if he knew that what she did in her own time to her own body was a poor substitute. As if by denying him she was ignorantly, childishly denying herself.

Elaine wanted to melt into the floor. She wanted to howl with mortification. Instead she returned his perusal with wide, unblinking eyes, hiding the embarrassment, the tingling lethargy that she felt even through her embarrassment, lips pressed tight against her teeth, body still and cold, like marble, like the statue by the stairs. Yes, that was it; she would emulate the statue, become the statue, feeling nothing, thinking nothing.

The air rushed around Elaine, cold, the candlelit table receding at what would have been an alarming rate if there had only been time to sort through the multitude of jumbled perceptions. Her back crashed against the door, breath whooshing from her lungs at the force of the impact. Her left foot twisted. Elaine caught herself on the door handle, her legs amazingly like jelly, or like the raw egg she had consumed in the name of fertility.

"Get out of here! Just get out of here!"

Elaine got out of there. She rested her back against the opposite side of the door, impervious to servants, to the wrath of the lord on the other side. She felt as if she had run a mile, as if she had leaped a mountain. As if she had single-handedly wrested majority stock from Hewlett Packard, IBM, and all the other moguls of the computer world.

As if she had lost something incredibly precious.

The explosion of glass on wood jarred the door. Elaine felt each splinter of glass, each splatter of liquid. Something cold and wet trickled down her cheek. She wiped it away with the back of her hand.

Mad. She was utterly, utterly mad.

Like this world.

Like the lord.

By degrees Elaine became aware of a human presence other than hers and the lord's on the other side of the door. Out of the corner of her eye she assayed the black, red, and white–liveried footman who stood rigidly to the side of the double doors. He was the one who had been her guide, the one, no doubt, who had also helped her up the stairs the night before.

And now he had witnessed this.

She squared her shoulders and walked toward the staircase.

As if *this* held any significance whatsoever.

Charles stared at the wine-splattered door, then at his empty hand, at the shards of glass sparkling on the hardwood floor in an ever-expanding pool of red, then at his empty hand again. A steady stream of port drip-dripped from the bottom of the door, inexorably adding to the circle of wasted wine.

He was going mad. Stark, staring mad, he thought, his gaze traveling up the door. The flow of wine divided; the seceding branch oozed slowly down the fine wooden grain while the main stream surged ahead to join the growing puddle.

That cursed gold band had flashed a promise all through dinner every time she lifted her fork, her water goblet. Wasted, empty promises.

All night he had attempted to evoke a reponse from his wife, hoping to find a hint of the passion that her naked body promised. But there was none. Her eyes looking into his had been dull, lifeless, like the port puddling on the floor.

That could be her blood beginning to seep beneath the door. For a brief moment he had wanted it to be her blood. He had wanted the door to be her head. He had wanted to make her be the woman he needed.

Ah, God. He should have stayed away. He *would* stay away this time. Stay away before he destroyed both of them.

Ignoring the crunch of shattered crystal beneath his feet, Charles threw open the dining room door.

"Have a groom saddle my horse, John."

"Very good, my lord." The footman bowed, his face carefully expressionless, though the lord did not turn to appreciate his efforts. The baron left a trail of red on the marble floor, curiously thick for port. Shrugging, John straightened. It was not his business that the master destroyed valuable property, even though that property be his aristocratic self. Any more than it was his business to dry the tears of stupid, childish baronesses.

Chapter

11

The pillow pounded around Elaine's ears. She moaned a protest. The pounding increased.

"Ye let me in, girl! Th' lord, 'e's away now; 'e willna be interferin' wi' what's right anymore. Ye open this door, Morrigan Gayle!"

Pound, *pound*.

"Ye open it now!"

Elaine sat up in bed, morning disorientation immediately dispersed by that voice. By that *woman*. A trickle of fear ran up her spine.

" I tol' ye once, m' girl; th' lord ain't 'ere t' interfere wi' yer punishment, an' punishment ye'll git. I'll nae let th' de'il 'ave yer soul!"

The lord was gone.

Relief dispelled the trickle of fear that had defied gravity and traveled up Elaine's spine at Hattie's morning intrusion. She wouldn't have to worry about being interrupted at inopportune times, such as when taking a bath. She wouldn't have to worry about him taking unwanted liberties, thinking her his wife instead of the strangers they were. She wouldn't have to face him after what he had said to her yesterday evening, the thought of which had kept her awake most of the night. Nor would she have to wonder what further acts of violence he might engage in. Now she would truly be free to concentrate on returning to her own world.

"Ye let me in Morrigan, girl, or I willna be responsible fer th' consequences!"

Dismay instantly replaced the giddiness of reprieve.

He was gone!

That meant Hattie would have full reign without fear of retribution. Which meant, in essence, that Elaine was right back to square one. In a foreign body in a foreign time with a crazy old woman for a keeper.

"I 'ear ye in there, ye 'orin' 'ussy, ye! I know ye're awake, lyin' all hours o' th' day in bed like Godless 'eathen. I'll nae let ye be slidin' further in yer sinful ways. Ye open this door!"

Elaine slid out of bed, half afraid that at any moment the door would splinter beneath the pounding of Hattie's fists. But the vibrating wood did not spilt, and the key, though it shook and bounced, showed no signs of being dislodged. Hattie would tire soon, Elaine thought. The lord would return.

But Hattie did not tire. And it could be days, or even weeks, Elaine was finally forced to admit as the dim morning rays turned bright and golden and the pounding on the door did not cease, before the lord returned. They had not, after all, been on the best of terms yesterday evening. He had thrown his wine at her. Leaving her with Hattie could very well be his method of punishing her. Or breaking her of bad habits.

"I'm warnin' ye! I'll nae put up wi' yer e'il ways, Morrigan! Repent! Unlock this door an' gi' me th' key!"

Elaine sighed. She really could not allow that old crow to bully Elaine—Morrigan, that is—for the rest of her life. And she would be damned if she allowed either herself or Morrigan to hide away from that shriveled-up hag like some poor little gray mouse.

Elaine closed the distance between herself and the vibrating door. Her head throbbed in time to the beating of the fists. Taking a deep breath, she turned the key.

Elaine stepped backward just in time to avoid being flattened. The door bounced against the wall. Hattie whirled through the opening, a rank cyclone of flapping black skirts. Pain exploded in the left side of Elaine's face, the result of a swinging fist. All of it happening at once, or so it seemed to Elaine. The room and her body slowly spun around, for once in perfect harmony.

"That be jus' th' first o' it, ye sinful 'ussy. Ye'll be thankin' yer ol' Hattie come th' morrow, aye, prayin' t' th' good Lord, 'cause Hattie looks after 'is little lamb. I willna let ye stray, girl. Nae, yer ol' Hattie'll take care o' ye now."

Hattie wiped her hands together, all as it should be, the Lord in his heaven, Hattie in hers, bullying Morrigan. A gnarled fist reached out. The bedroom door slammed shut. The gnarled fist again reached out. The finely wrought skeleton key disappeared from the lock.

Elaine stared at the liver-spotted hand, then at the protruding key that at the moment of its rescindment became the gateway to the twentieth century and all it entailed. The jagged white stars circling her head consolidated, becoming one giant hot light. Elaine looked at Hattie's smug, sanctimonious face and forgot everything she had ever been taught. Respect for one's elders. Respect for those physically smaller. Respect for self-survival. Respect for respect.

She threw herself at Hattie, screaming every invective, every filthy word she had ever heard or seen written on bathroom walls. Words that, judging by the variety that spewed out of her mouth, she had apparently paid meticulous attention to throughout the years.

"All right, Chas, out with it. I have mended your foot and anesthetized your soul, and you have said hardly more than a mouthful of words since you woke the household this morning at a most decidedly inconvenient moment. If you don't like my company, then leave—I didn't invite you here in the first place—but for God's sake, quit swilling that brandy like it was water! It happens to be French. As in costing a third leg, old boy."

Charles stared up from a half-empty snifter of brandy. Words buzzed around in his brain like so many pesky flies. He shook his head in an attempt to clear it, dimly realizing that the fuzzy fellow who was leaning against the mantel was Damon, his friend, and that it was he who was making those buzzing sounds, and that Charles should at least make an attempt to decipher the cacophony. And he would. If only his brain weren't smothered in a haze of alcohol.

He contented himself with bringing his friend's body into focus. Damon was a large man, every bit as tall as Charles, every bit as muscled. His hair was black, black as midnight, black as Morrigan's—Charles remembered the hidden red highlights in his wife's hair that had shone in the candlelight over dinner, brought out by that single application of soap and water. No, Morrigan's hair was not as black as Damon's hair, he thought sourly, but her heart sure as hell was.

Charles gulped the brandy. A Westminster clock somewhere outside the library chimed the quarter hour.

"How is . . ." He found his tongue. "How's Bainbridge doing?"

"Really, Charles. Hie yourself up to London and you can find out for yourself."

"He never should have married that bitch of a wife of his," Charles muttered viciously into the nearly empty depths of the brandy snifter. Almost as an afterthought he downed the remaining liquid. "The Fates were smiling on you the day that bitch jilted you, Dam." He saluted his friend with the empty glass. "Would that Bain and I had been as lucky."

"Would that Bain were lucky enough to commiserate with you himself. I take it this binge of self-pity has something to do with the joys of holy wedlock."

"She's frigid, Dam. Cold as a witch's teat. Colder. The devil himself couldn't get anything out of that sanct—sanctimonious virgin."

Damon pushed himself away from the mantel as if it had suddenly burned him. His damnable black eyes, black as Morrigan's eyes, black like Morrigan's heart, were wide open, as was his mouth.

Charles's lips twitched.

After all those years whoring at Cambridge—the three of them, Charles, Damon, and Bainbridge—he had finally managed to shock Dr. Damon Schyler, not-so-gentlemanly scholar and physician. Charles couldn't remember what he had said to provoke it—he didn't really care—the idea of shocking Damon Schyler was suddenly of more importance than anything else in the world. He burst into laughter, vaguely wondering who the hell was making those silly, idiotic giggles.

"Your wife is a virgin, Charles? You have been married for over a year, and your wife is still a *virgin?*"

Charles sobered instantly. He sulkily stared into his empty brandy snifter. "What is virginity? A piece of skin that is more often than not not there? An emotional barrier that women use to barter for jewels and titles?"

"I can't believe I am hearing this," Damon said lightly, black eyes alight with unholy glee. "Charles, renowned for his knowledge of the Tantrics—Charles, with whom I have had both whores and ladies alike to beg for a setup—this is the same Charles who cannot bed his own wife?"

"I didn't say that," Charles snapped. He sighed. His head felt hot and heavy. He should be in alcoholic oblivion, bottled nirvana, not hearing the echo of Morrigan's silent disdain. He closed his eyes against Damon's laughing black eyes, just like Morrigan's—God he had made a fool of himself—and allowed his head to drop back against the cool leather of the chair. "Be a good fellow and fill me up."

"Why not? In fact, I think I'll join you."

The empty brandy snifter slid from between Charles's fingers, sensation immediately followed by the clink of glass on glass, a splash of liquid, another clink, another splash.

"Yes. This definitely calls for a celebration."

The snifter was returned to Charles's hand.

"'Charles the Tantric he did wed, a virgin bride who spurned his bed.' Not bad, what? Bottoms up, old boy."

Charles ignored the toast and proceeded to down the half glass of brandy as if it were indeed water. Water from the Thames, Charles thought sourly. On the other side of the bridge where the sewer lines emptied. He opened his eyes to find Damon laughing at him over the rim of his snifter.

"That hell-hen, she tol' me Morrigan mas—masturbated."

"The devil, Charles!"

Damon wasn't laughing anymore. Charles had shocked him again. Twice in one day. Charles laughed and laughed, wrapping his arms around his stomach it hurt so, his knees a necessary rest for his spinning head.

Damon sighed. Or at least it sounded like an emission of air. A fart was an emission of air, too. One of those fice kind that old ladies blamed on innocent lap pugs. Tears streamed down Charles's cheeks. His whole body shook and quivered. It felt good to laugh, to really laugh. He hadn't laughed in over a year. Ever since he had married.

Charles jerked free of the restricting chair arms and sat up straight. Damon loomed over him like one of those Greek choruses.

"Chorus, old boy. I am singular, not the several that you probably perceive at the moment. I am going to ring for coffee, and you are going to drink it, and then we can get down to the bottom of whatever it is that is driving you to this before you cause yourself and your wife further embarrassment. *Comprendez?*"

Charles glared at Damon, but Damon had disappeared. Shrugging, he leaned his head back and closed his eyes. The next thing he comprehended was that he was being drowned with a cup of scalding coffee.

"Drink, or I'll use a funnel."

Charles drank. After a few more cups of the scalding liquid he informed his lifelong friend that he would use a funnel on Damon if he did not cease—in that orifice opposite the tonsils.

"All right, Charles. If you think you can manage that, then I think you can manage a few explanations. What is this bloody nonsense about Morrigan still being a virgin?"

Charles ran his hands over his face and through his hair. They trembled as if he had been on a weeklong binge instead of the six or seven hours that he remembered drinking. *Jesus.* What had he said? He had only wanted some companionship, to be in the presence of someone who cared whether he lived or died. Hence the impromptu visit to Damon, whose estate was thirty miles north of his.

He winced, remembering the lathered, heaving sides of his

horse. The ignominy of Damon removing the pieces of the decanter from his foot. The echoes of drunken giggles.

Madness. All madness.

He sighed. "I didn't say that. Did I?"

"And what the hell do you mean telling me that your wife masturbates?"

Charles smiled. He did remember that. "If you could have seen your face, Dam, you wouldn't be prosing on so."

"Charles, you're talking about your wife, for God's sake! Not some twopence whore!"

"Then let us hope that you hold your friends' secrets as confidential as you do those of your patients," Charles said coldly.

Damon's saturnine face suddenly lit with mischief. "My patients, being for the most part of the so-called upper ten thousand, wouldn't dare confess what you disclosed for fear of meeting me over some dinner table. Alas, now I'm afraid of meeting your wife over some dinner table."

Charles remembered the stilted explanations, his endless humiliation when Morrigan had refused to join his friends for the wedding breakfast, her steadfast refusal to leave the sanctity of her bedroom upon removal to his estate in Dorset afterward. The right side of his mouth drew upward, a habit he had developed in India when his injury was healing, to relieve the pull of slashed muscles. "I sincerely doubt that ever taking place, so don't make plans to leave the country yet."

"Charles, you knew when you married Morrigan that she was not quite your normal . . . debutante."

Charles restlessly moved his hand; coffee sloshed over the rim of the cup. "I know that," he said, staring at the spill of dark liquid. "I wanted . . . I wanted—"

His fingers tightened around the delicate bone china. "Hell, it doesn't make any difference what I wanted, does it? I'm trapped, just like Bain, and contrary to your impressions the marriage has been consummated, so there is not even hope of an annulment."

He laughed, a bitter, hollow sound of self-derision. "What can you prescribe for that, Dr. Damon? A purgative? Leeching? A cold bath? I've had enough of those, I can tell you."

"I would prescribe a medicinal dose of brandy. . . ."

Charles looked at his friend hopefully.

Damon grinned. "But you've already depleted my stock. Chin up, Charles. At least it's not you. For a while there I was afraid you had gone impotent on us."

And he would have, Charles thought, frowning over a sip of coffee, if he had followed his original plan to impregnate that pious ice bitch he had married.

Charles and Damon sat in a companionable silence. Charles felt he should be embarrassed—after all, a gentleman was expected to retain a stiff upper lip and, like Atlas, stoically bear the weight of the world—but he wasn't. At least, not yet. Perhaps there was still too much alcohol floating around inside his veins. Or perhaps it had been more than the need of sanctuary that had driven him from his home last night, more than a little drunk, bleeding, in pain though he had been. Perhaps he had needed to talk. Friend to friend. Man to man.

"I thought she might change," Charles said. "The strange thing is, I could have sworn, for a couple of days there, that she had. Do you know that in our entire year of marriage Morrigan never once took a bath?"

"More secrets, Chas? You'll have me bursting with so much confidential information. Besides, not bathing is more common than bathing here in these our enlightened times. You probably scared the hell out of her, you know, by taking so many baths. Many of my learned colleagues to this day claim that frequent bathing leads to lunacy."

Charles grinned. "Then perhaps Morrigan has finally succumbed to my madness. She bathed. Right after—no, no, I'm not going to shock you again—right after I consummated the marriage last week. Made quite a homecoming, I can tell you, going into her bedchamber and finding her in nothing but a drape of towel." Bitterness crept into his voice. "I was married for a year, yet I had never seen my wife's body."

"Don't feel badly. Bain has not seen his wife, let alone her body, in well nigh ten years. That is rather interesting, though. So Morrigan had not taken a bath until you—consummated—her. Of course," Damon said, talking more to himself than to Charles, "it could be that she just wanted to well and thoroughly rid herself of your scent."

Charles scowled.

"Have you noticed any other irregularities in her behavior? Such as fainting, hysterics? I knew a girl once who went completely berserk when she started her menses. Or that was the diagnosis her parents and the local physician chose. She was eighteen. A late age to be starting, to be sure, but the medical books are filled with cases of women who start their menses far later. Has Morrigan—?"

"Morrigan is twenty-one, for God's sake," Charles interrupted irritably. "Of course she has her menses. And I would be delighted if she would have hysterics. At least there would be real feeling then instead of that holier-art-I-than-thou sheep's face she wears like a horsehair shift."

Damon shrugged. "Just a thought. Guess she didn't like you, old boy, and you can expect a bath whenever you practice your conjugal rights." He envisioned all those unwashed bodies that he had in the past and would in the future examine. "A not unpleasant benefit, to be sure," he added with an irrepressible depth of feeling.

The muffled echo of the Westminster chimes announced the eleventh hour.

"There are a few other . . . irregularities."

Damon topped their coffee cups.

"She dressed in the clothes I purchased for her trousseau."

Damon laughed. "I didn't realize your taste was so atrocious that you considered it odd for a woman to wear a dress of your choosing."

Charles smiled, albeit reluctantly. "Very clever. What I meant was that she dressed in her trousseau *after* the consummation. For an entire year I never saw her in anything but a gray wool dress. Then a day or so afterward, she took it upon herself to dress in a yellow silk dress, or so one of the maids claims, and since I saw proof, I have no reason to believe she lied. Also, Morrigan claims to have a putrid throat, so she won't talk, not even to the servants. Not that she ever talked much before, but still . . ."

Damon raised a dark brow. "She won't talk, but she claims to?"

Charles chuckled. "My initial response exactly. She writes notes. And that is another thing. . . ."

Morrigan's note had had a decided rightward slant. He suddenly remembered that singular occurrence when she had used her right hand to sample her soup. The memory was diluted by several bottles of wine and brandy. Had she actually *used* her right hand, or had she merely been transferring the spoon to her left?

"Hysteria," Damon promptly said. A faraway look appeared in his eyes, as if he were mentally turning the pages of some esoteric tome. They took on a familiar glow. "D'you know, there is a theory . . . I've never yet met anyone I cared to test it on, but there is a theory. . . . I wonder, did, ah, this keeper you refer to, did she tell you when Morrigan first started masturbating?"

"Really, Dam, *I* might have to meet her over the dinner table."

Damon grinned. "No, really, you see, if she started masturbating *after* you made love to her, then it would absolutely support this theory. The theory being—and it's not a recent one, mind you; it's been around for eighteen hundred years—in fact, some texts have recommended this form of treatment from the time of Galen and all the way up to the last century. . . ."

Damon brought his coffee cup to his lips, then held it there, immobilized by the trek of his thoughts.

Charles set on the edge of his chair, intrigued despite himself, despite the innate hopelessness of his marital situation.

Damon sat his coffee cup down untouched. He continued staring off into space.

Charles sighed, remembering a similar situation at Cambridge. He and Bain had slipped a live insect into Damon's tea and watched as the young boy had sat lost in thought, then had continued to watch in horrified fascination as their friend had drunk his tepid tea without noticing the squirming addition. Until the cup was nearly empty, that is, and the insect, an impressively large beetle, Charles recalled, had grabbed hold of Damon's lip between outraged pincers. Damon had gotten his revenge, of course, with interest, but had unfortunately never learned from the experience.

Irritation surged. "What? Speak up, man. I hated it when you did this in school, starting up and then going off on some mental exodus, and I don't like it any better now!"

"Don't exercise yourself so, Charles; it's bad for the spleen. As I was saying, the preferred treatment for hysteria—and excess piety and frigidity is a recognized form of female hysteria—was the excitation of the clitoris. Maybe—just a possibility, of course—but maybe when you, ah, had coitus you provided the necessary stimulation to start her onto the road to recovery. And now all she needs is more stimulation to bring her completely around. Preferably by your hand, of course."

Charles stared at his friend as if he had grown two heads. In his nether regions.

Damon shrugged. "It's just a theory—one, as I said, I myself have yet to try. I suggest you read what my medical texts have to offer on the subject, and then . . ."

It was pure lunacy, of course, to think that one could be cured by the very thing one disdained. And it was the height of male presumptuousness to think that sex could cure anything at all, save a stiff prick. Yet . . .

Yet.

Facts were facts. And the facts were that Morrigan had not changed, not one single strand of unwashed hair, until *after* the marriage had been consummated.

My God. It did fit, Charles thought incredulously. Nothing had changed, not her personal habits, her mode of dress, or the slant of her writing, until *after* that disastrous night of consummation.

Only perhaps not so disastrous.

If what Damon said was true—and he had no reason to doubt either Damon's personal veracity or professional expertise—then . . .

Then . . .

Charles grinned, a slow, purely masculine grin, the grin of a hungry male predator sighting tender, unsuspecting prey.

Then he had been wasting an entire year. And there was one thing Charles hated more than anything: waste.

A condition soon to be rectified.

No, he did not need to study ancient tomes in archaic Greek and Latin. Morrigan's cure lay in the East, not the West. What she needed was locked away in the bottom of his desk drawer. What he needed was to be there with her.

And he would be. Just as soon as he allayed a few physical necessities.

"Don't you have any food in this cottage you call a house, Dam, old fellow? And after that, by God, even a straw bed would feel good. I haven't slept in days. Hell of a host. You need a woman to hone up your social skills."

"I was having a woman, Chas, when you forced me out of my bed this morning," Damon said in a slightly aggrieved voice. "Why do you think I've been doing my damnedest to get rid of you?"

Chapter

12

Katie washed Elaine as tenderly as if she were a sick infant. "Everything'll be all right," she crooned over and over. "Everything'll be all right; bad old Hattie's gone back to Cornwall, where she and the likes belong. Heathenish place, that, good Christians praying side by side with no-good Droods. Everything'll be just fine now. Just fine . . ."

Steam beaded on Katie's face. Shadow and light rippled on the ceiling above the maid's white mobcap.

Elaine repressed a groan of shame. Fritz had had to pull her off of Hattie. A footman had dragged away the screaming, straining sexagenarian. Elaine had promptly rewarded Fritz for his interference by being sick all over him.

Katie brought up the washcloth and gently touched Elaine's bruised cheek.

Elaine flinched.

"Never ye worry, m' lady. Ye gave better'n ye got. That old Hattie, she was sporting 'bout the biggest shiner I ever seen."

Elaine squeezed her eyes shut. How could she have done that, beat up on a woman old enough to be her grandmother?

"It be a good omen, marm, ye gitting yer voice back and that old Hattie sneaking out of the house like the snake she be. We'll all be sleeping the better fer it, that we will. She was always creeping around, could hear her snooping in the attics, gave a body the creeps, it did. Me mum, she says good things, they come in threes. There was a slide in th' mine, ye see, and it broke me mum's leg, save she wasn't me mum then, and she met me da when she was healing and had me oldest brother, and she didn't never have to go back to the mine again. The lord, he'll be right proud of ye when he gits back."

Elaine feebly fought to rise above the despondency that had turned her brain to haggis. Hattie—a snake? Good things coming in threes—breaking a leg, getting married, and having a kid? The lord coming back?

What's wrong with your left hand? Is this putrid thing spreading?

Oh, yes, the lord would be proud, all right. So proud he'd have her committed, not for general, all-purpose lunacy, but for criminal violence.

Why had she lost control like that? She had never so much as lost her temper in the twentieth century.

Katie gracefully jumped up, unhampered by either a crippled leg or a crippling conscience. "Up ye go, marm! The water, it be gitting cold. We don't want yer throat to worsen, now do we?"

Elaine dutifully stood up and allowed Katie to wrap her in a bath towel.

The maid briskly rubbed her hands down the bulky cotton. "His lordship, he be worried 'bout ye, m' lady. 'Katie,' he says to me when I gave him yer note after ye got yerself boskey. 'Was milady still afl-aflicked with the putrid throat when ye woke her?' He was right stricken when I said ye was, marm."

Right. Stricken that she hadn't died, perhaps.

Why had he married Morrigan when he so obviously disliked her?

"Now ye just step out of here."

Katie held Elaine's arm to help her over the rim of the tub onto the towel lying on the floor. Elaine felt it absorb the water on her feet, assisted then by efficient hands. The maid led "m' lady" around the Japanese screen.

"I'll brush yer hair and then we can tuck ye into bed. A nice, good rest, that be what ye need to git the roses back in yer cheeks. Yer hair be ever so pretty, marm. All thick and curly, it be, hanging down yer back. Ye just sit yerself over here."

Elaine held the towel tucked between her breasts and sat down on the curved wooden bench. Katie leaned over her shoulder and picked up the brush.

"Me middle sister, she's got hair like yers, 'cept hers feels like a horse's tail, marm, not like yers at all."

Elaine ignored the tugging pain shooting through her scalp. Katie was acting as if nothing out of the ordinary had happened, as if Morrigan screaming twentieth-century obscenities happened, if not every other day, at least every other week.

"Katie, I—" She stared in surprise at the full red lips in the mirror. Morrigan's voice was low, husky, alto to Elaine's own soprano. A far cry from the shrill banshee shrieks that had gushed out of her throat such a short time ago. She licked her lips before carefully enunciating, "Did you think I sounded . . . strange?"

That *question* sounded strange.

Aside from the lord's accent, he had not talked so very differently from her twentieth-century contemporaries. He had not used as many contractions, that was all. She licked her lips again. "What I mean is, do you think the putrid throat has, ah, affected my voice?"

Katie plowed through a nest of tangles. "Well, marm, I was a bit surprised to be hearing some of those words ye was shouting. I ain't never heard the half of them before."

Elaine gritted her teeth. She hadn't heard half of them before either. At least, not in spoken format.

"Guess ye learned those when ye lived in that heathen country. Not that old Hattie didn't deserve it, mind ye! But I suppose anybody'd sound strange when they was screaming to wake the dead." She put the brush down on the dressing table and surveyed her handiwork. "It still be mortally damp. I'll stoke up the fire to keep away the chill."

The maid disappeared from the parameters of the mirror. Elaine heard drawers being opened and shut, her mind and adrenals busy at work again. Morrigan had lived in a heathen place—Scotland? Cornwall? What exactly had Katie meant that she supposed anybody would sound strange when they were screaming? Did she mean that a Scottish accent sounded like a British accent when spoken loud enough to shatter glass?

Why hadn't Katie noticed that Elaine wrote with her right hand and not the left that Morrigan used?

"Oh, marm! What pretty underthings ye got. Look here! Why, a body can see right through them! Ye need a bit of rearranging, m' lady. All this pretty stuff should be in the top drawers, not stuffed away like something nasty. Here we be! This'll keep ye warm and feel ever so grand on yer skin."

Katie returned with a long-sleeved white nightgown. She held it up expectantly. Sunlight streamed through the thin silk.

"Ye've got to rest yer throat now, m' lady," Katie said reprovingly. "Ye don't want it to git all putrid again."

"Katie." Elaine's voice cracked. She was almost used to seeing Morrigan's face in the mirror. She doubted if she would ever get used to hearing her voice.

"That old Hattie, she's gone now. Ye don't have to worry 'bout her; ye can sleep anytime ye want."

Hattie was gone.

That was what Katie had been prattling on about earlier.

Hattie was gone, and the lord was gone. Elaine's overworked brain reeled at the possibilities. With both gone . . .

"Katie." Elaine brutally clipped her voice. Morrigan must have an English accent. Heaven knows if she did not, Katie would be the first to ask what was wrong with her. As far as not noticing that Elaine wrote with her right hand . . . well, it was not as if Katie would have nothing to do but observe Morrigan when she had her own cleaning tasks to perform. Quite likely Katie simply did not know that Morrigan was left-handed. "It's"—*no, no, limit the contractions*—"it is too early for bed. I want to get dressed."

Elaine had to curtail a laugh. The relief of being able to talk, to simply open her mouth and *say* what she wanted, was overwhelming.

Euphoria instantly metamorphosed into resoluteness.

The lord would not be gone forever.

"And I want to go to the"—she forced the word out of her mouth, crossing her fingers; a place this size simply had to have one—"library."

Elaine kicked the wall-to-wall-length bookcase, then braced herself against it before she collapsed on top of the leather-bound books strewn about her feet like so much literary carnage.

"Marm?"

Elaine counted to ten before turning around. The maid's mobcap was Cheer white in the fading light.

"Marm!" Katie gasped. "All those books! Hurry, I'll help ye git them back on the shelves before it be time fer yer dinner."

Elaine took a deep breath. It was not Morrigan's fault that she was a run-of-the-mill, nondescript-type person without the foresight to leave an itinerary of her life just in case a twentieth-century woman should someday be transmigrated into her body. She had to retain a proper perspective on things. She was an analyst. Computer people did not indulge in unsubstantiated flights of paranoia.

She glared at the massive ebony desk in front of the wall of French doors at the opposite end of the room. It was, however, entirely logical to put blame where it belonged.

Why did he lock the damn drawers?

Katie knelt down and picked up a book. "John Cle-land. *Memoirs of a Woman of Pleasure.* Oh, marm! Fancy the lord having a book like that!"

The library was unnaturally close and warm for such a large, airy room. Elaine grabbed the slender novel from the maid's hands.

"Just hand me the books and I . . . will put them back."

Katie painstakingly read aloud the author and title of each book she handed up. Charles Dickens, *A Tale of Two Cities;* Nathaniel Hawthorne, *The Scarlet Letter;* George Eliot, *Silas Marner;* Mark Twain, *The Adventures of Tom Sawyer;* Henry David Thoreau, *Civil Disobedience;* Jules Verne, *Journey to the Center of the Earth;* Louisa May Alcott, *Little Women;* Mark Twain, *The Prince and the Pauper;* Jules Verne, *Twenty Thousand*—

"Marm, ye got books here by the same people what wrote the

other ones." Katie sounded disappointed that m' lady showed such a lack of imagination.

Elaine was not concerned about being dubbed unimaginative; she was concerned about copyright dates. She had grabbed books by those authors she could remember from high school and college days.

"Robert Lou-is Stev-en-son. *Treasure Is-land.* D'ye think that be 'bout the man who pleasured that woman's memoirs?"

Elaine's eyes ached from straining to see in the rapidly failing light. "Katie, we will never finish if you read all the titles."

She drew a sigh of relief when the last book had been alphabetically placed. Gold-embossed letters gleamed above her fingers.

"M' lady." A man dressed in the white wig and black-and-red livery stood framed in the library doorway; he held a lighted candle. "M' lady, Cook would like to know in what manner she may best serve you. Will m' lady be dining downstairs tonight, or would she prefer a tray in her chamber?"

Elaine opened her mouth to say a tray would be fine.

"That old Hattie's gone; of course m' lady be dining down here!" Katie jumped up from the floor and fluttered her hands as if she were shooing away a pesky fly. "Now git on with ye!"

The footman bowed. "Very well, m' lady."

Elaine frowned. Her head throbbed, her cheek throbbed, and she was beginning to wonder if she hadn't gotten rid of one keeper only to have a worse one thrust upon her. What kind of servant took orders from a snip of a maid when his mistress was right there to speak for herself?

Blood rushed to her aching head.

Perhaps she should be wondering, instead, what kind of servant took orders from a lady who drank, masturbated, and swore more fluently than the proverbial sailor.

"We got to git ye dressed, m' lady, the dinner gong'll be gonging before ye know it."

Elaine resigned herself to the fact that it was time Morrigan started being a lady of the house, even if all *she* wanted was to go to bed and stay there. Unfortunately, there was a lot of exploring to do.

She reached for the slender book she had tucked high on the shelf, away from Katie's eyes.

Over dinner Elaine turned and twisted the few pieces of information she had thus far garnered, busily trying to fit them into the puzzle that comprised the life and times of Morrigan.

The twin candelabras at either end of the banquet-size table sputtered and flamed. Thomas Edison had introduced electric lighting in the latter part of the 1870s. *Treasure Island* was copyrighted in 1881; *The Prince and the Pauper* in 1882. Surely the lord of the manor could afford modern convenience?

A black-clad arm removed Elaine's empty dinner plate. The arm immediately reappeared, setting before her a dessert plate with a thick sliver of red sponge cake with creamy white frosting.

At least now she knew why the dresses in the armoire were so un-Dickens-like. She was in the latter part of the Victorian era as opposed to the middle. Apparently it amused the lord to have his servants dress in masquerade of times past, the maids in their Dickens costumes and the footmen in their *Dangerous Liaisons* livery.

Elaine looked down in surprise at the bowl of nuts in front of her. Had she already eaten her dessert?

It was palpably clear from the tense silence behind her that she was expected to rise. She hesitated outside the dining room doors. A footman stoically awaited m' lady's pleasure—was she going to stand there like a fool, or was she going to retire so that hardworking men could retire also?

"Would you care for tea in the drawing room, m' lady?"

Elaine smiled in gratitude. "Yes. Please."

She shifted her weight onto her good leg.

The footman remained stiffly at attention beside the library door. Finally: "The butler will bring it forthwith, m' lady."

Elaine straightened her spine. He had accompanied her to her bedroom last night—why couldn't he take her to the drawing room?

Couldn't someone just once volunteer a piece of information? The naked statue beneath the stairs was no help. There was a door on the opposite side of the stairs, though. Upon Elaine's approach, another footman magically appeared and opened it.

The drawing room was all blue and silver. It, too, looked like something out of a movie. Elaine irritably wondered how the gong ringer knew when to announce dinner—she had yet to see a single clock. Idly she picked up a blue vase covered with a lot of gods and goddesses in raised white relief. Her mother had liked stuff like this.

The bottom was imprinted with *Wedgwood, 1786.*

Elaine hastily set it down.

Her mother would have liked the *money* from stuff like that.

Tea was served as impersonally as dinner. The ornate silver pot held enough fluid for a dozen people. Matthew would have insisted upon finishing every drop. Elaine drank half a cupful. It was with relief that she made the long trek back to her room.

Flushed with exertion, Katie lifted a pile of underclothes from the bed and pushed them into the second drawer. "There ye be, marm!" She whisked her hands together in satisfaction. "Ye're all arranged now, with all yer pretties where they ought to be. I took that old wool dress of yers and told Mary—that be me sister; she takes care of yer slops—to burn it. Ye won't be needing the likes of it anymore."

Elaine devoutly hoped Morrigan would appreciate all the changes made on her behalf. She allowed Katie to undress her down to the calf-length slip.

"But marm, ye can't sleep in yer chemise!"

"I—" How could a person talk without using contractions? "I can put my own nightgown on, Katie." Without waiting for an argument, she limped behind the screen and proceeded to do so.

Elaine's aching brain refused to shut off. The loose nightgown aggravated her nipples. She almost grabbed the hairbrush and whacked Katie over the head with it when she insisted upon brushing marm's hair a hundred strokes, yipping about marm's rearrangements like an excited Chihuahua. At last Elaine was allowed to slide between the sheets.

"Oh, marm, I fergot to git ye a nightcap! I'll just—"

"No."

Katie halted mid-pivot. "But marm, ye'll git sick again—"

Good. Maybe she would die and end this whole farce.

"Good night, Katie."

"Well, then, I'll just bank the fire." Sparks flew, settled. The maid bade her a reluctant, "Good night, marm."

The silk-covered canopy glistened in the faint glow of the fireplace. Hattie's parting words reverberated through Elaine's head.

I'll tell, ye 'ear me, I'll tell 'em all an' then we'll see 'oo's so 'igh an' mighty when ye're roastin' in 'ell wi' yer maker!

Elaine turned onto her left side.

That old Hattie's gone; of course m' lady be dining down here!

Elaine flopped onto her back. There was a dull throb in her left side that had nothing to do with the aches accumulated from her fight with Hattie.

Matthew would like Morrigan, Elaine thought peevishly. An ignorant, submissive little girl to mold and protect and who wouldn't make embarrassing sexual demands.

Guess ye learned those when ye lived in that heathen country.

Elaine rolled onto her left side. The pillow pressed against her bruised cheek.

Blue eyes glinted with humor in the darkness. *Does that mean she would allow you to play harlot to a clansman, I wonder?*

Elaine twisted onto her stomach. Her weight pressed flat the aching, tender breasts.

Not tonight, dear, we have a busy day tomorrow. Next week maybe things will slow down.

She flipped onto her side.

The blue eyes gleamed with promise. *I could give you so much. . . .*

How was it that Morrigan had remained a virgin for an entire year of marriage?

Elaine struggled onto her back and methodically extricated herself from the bedspread, the sheet, and the nightgown that threatened to strangle her like a breech-born babe. Perhaps that would conclude Katie's prophesied trio of good things.

She lit a candle from the glowing embers in the fireplace and extricated the slender novel from underneath the mattress, the only place Katie had not turned topsy-turvy. Yet. She moved the occasional table with the candelabra over to the short divan in front of the fireplace and settled down for a relaxing read.

The printed words danced and leaped before her eyes.

There had to be something, someplace that she had failed to look in the library.

She thought of the locked desk. She thought of the hairpins she had stashed away in the vanity drawer after liberating her hair three days ago. She thought of her success at forgery. Why not as a lockpick?

Minutes later, armed with the novel, a hairpin, and a candle, Elaine cautiously opened the door to the hallway.

The windowless corridor was completely dark. Dangerously dark. Her little candle barely provided a shadow.

The little candle was also pray to every hushed breath, every stir of air created by her steps. It was, as nearly as she could estimate, around midnight, the witching hour. Every ghost story she had ever seen or heard replayed in her imagination, causing an entire dynasty of goose bumps to cover her body. Shadows loomed tall and macabre in doorwells, a pointed Ku Klux Clan figure there, a hunchbacked scientist's assistant farther down, farther down yet a tooth-gleaming Cujo.

A tooth-gleaming *Hattie.*

Elaine heaved a sigh of relief, sighting the end of the corridor. Opening the door, her eyes widened with dismay. The staircase disappeared down into a great, black, bottomless cavern.

She fortified herself with another deep breath, not necessarily an easy task when one was hyperventilating. Strangling within the cozy comfort of her sheets suddenly did not seem such a disastrous end, she thought, standing there with nothing but a little candle to hold back the oppressive blackness. If only she had a flashlight . . .

The odor of singed hair permeated the air. Elaine jerked the candle away from her head. A river of hot wax ran into her hand. She was a big girl, she chastised herself, stuffing the book between her legs and transferring the candle to her left hand. And she had *never* been afraid of the dark. She jerked her right hand with the hot-waxed skin back and forth. She refused to start now when there were all kinds of other things to fear. Like setting her hair on fire or receiving second-degree burns.

Elaine maneuvered the stairs without further mishap. She located the appropriate door, down the hall to the right of the dining room. A dull glow reflected off of the ceiling in the center of the library.

A spark of warmth chased away the chill of loneliness. The footman had prepared a fire for her earlier, reduced now to shimmering embers.

Elaine closed the door and stepped further inside the room. It did not look so innocuous in the dark of night with the gold-embossed titles gleaming like a thousand pairs of eyes. She raised the candle higher to shed more light. The couch in front of the banked fireplace was shrouded in darkness. She resisted the temptation to go peek over the back to ascertain that there were no vampires or ghouls napping within its depths.

Elaine deposited the book and the hairpin onto the desk at the far end of the room. She removed the hatbox-shaped shade on the lamp, and lit the five candles from her own. She blew out her candle, then blew on it to more rapidly cool the wax before setting it down on top of the book. Carefully she replaced the shade and stepped back to make sure it didn't start smoldering.

A gleam of gold from the far left corner of the desk immediately attracted her attention. It had not been there earlier that day. Elaine reached out for the box. A scattering of jewels winked and blinked in the inlaid gold.

It was surprisingly heavy. Elaine lifted the gilded wooden box to the center of the desk.

A book was inside. It, too, was inlaid with gold and jewels. Gingerly she lifted it free of the box. She eased down onto the chair and turned the cover.

It was a book of illustrations.

Elaine lightly touched the page.

Hand-painted illustrations.

She studied the small, textured masterpiece.

An Eastern Indian man sat cross-legged on a yellow-and-green rug; a bright orange pillow supported his back. His head was covered by a red turban topped with an exotic white flower. He had a large curled mustache and wore a purple robe with gold print. Elaine gently ran her fingers over the paint, feeling the individual gold flecks.

An Indian maiden lay cross-legged in front of the darker-skinned man, leaning back with both arms over her head and around his neck. She wore strands and strands of pearl necklaces. Her pink skirt and halter top were stitched with pearls, too, also nubby beneath Elaine's fingertips. Her lips were bright red, the same color as the mark on her forehead and the soles of her dainty little feet. Her inky black hair was secured upon her head with intricate strands of pearls. The delicate, shell-shaped ears were outlined with pearl earrings.

The couple's almond-shaped eyes were outlined with kohl. Their red lips were curved in benign, bowlike smiles. The Indian maiden's head was tilted backward, gazing with eternal devotion at the Indian man. A gold tray holding wine and a water pipe sat before them, no doubt the real reason behind their blissful preoccupation, Elaine thought cynically. A variety of bushes strutted above the terrace wall behind the enamored couple. Beyond that a pale blue sky was striated with fluffy white clouds.

Squinting, Elaine bowed her head more closely to the illustration. She impatiently held aside the drape of her hair so that it didn't block the light.

Amazing. The clouds almost seemed like bodies. Naked bodies. Naked, embracing bodies.

Releasing her hair, Elaine sat upright. The detail was incredible, like one of those children's picture puzzles on the back of a box of cereal that have X number of animals hidden in the leaves and sky and water, the object being to find the exact number of hidden wildlife. And almost as irresistible to the eyes.

Grabbing her hair, Elaine leaned over the book again.

Tucked beneath the waterfall of pearl necklaces, the Indian man's hand shaped a round breast.

A smile played about Elaine's lips. Well, perhaps not exactly like a picture puzzle on the back of a box of kids' cereal, she thought, straightening. Though it would certainly ease the passage of bran flakes for adults.

Elaine curiously turned the page.

The little Indian maiden was naked to the waist. Beneath the waterfall of pearl necklaces, the man pinched a red, erect nipple, its length inordinately elongated for the small round breast. Strangely erotic.

Like Morrigan's.

She brought up her hand and touched her—Morrigan's—nipple. A jolt of sensation stabbed through the core of her breast. She quickly brought her hand down.

The bare-breasted Indian maiden held a glass of wine to the man's lips. They both continued smiling benignly, staring down at a book that lay spread open at their feet.

Elaine twisted the illustration upside down.

The artist had depicted a picture within a picture, a simple line drawing, no larger than a postage stamp, of a naked man and woman embracing.

Incredible.

Elaine righted the book and turned the page.

The background had changed. The Indian couple were inside, he sitting in an enveloping red chair, she lying across his lap. A stack of books lay on the green-clothed bed behind them. The little Indian maiden was completely naked. Her kohl-lined eyes were closed in ecstasy, her red lips slightly parted as if in a sigh, curved in the benign smile. The man, still fully clothed, suckled a rouged, elongated nipple. The pearl necklaces cascaded over the unsuckled breast and down over the maiden's side. Her little belly was round, her navel occupied by a large ruby. Beneath the ruby, the man's hand cupped the flesh between the little maiden's splayed legs.

Elaine squirmed. The movement forced the cushion and the silk nightgown up between her own thighs. The dull throb in her side became more centralized. She quickly turned to the next page.

The Indian couple were reclining on the green-covered bed. The man, kohl-lined eyes sparkling with pure male anticipation, lay naked except for the red turban. A strand of gold encircled his lean waist. His ruby-tipped penis thrust up and out from a hairless pubes. The maiden encircled in one hand what she could encompass of the engorged shaft.

Elaine's breath came more quickly. She turned to the next page.

The little Indian maiden lay on her back with her legs spread wide, pearl necklaces spilling around her torso, her ruby-painted mouth curved in a fatuous smile. The turbaned man sat between her legs in guru fashion, gold chain riding the crevice between his buttocks. He plucked one rouged, elongated nipple between the fingers of his left hand. His right hand was poised between the maiden's hairless vulva, all of his fingers save his thumb buried to the hilt between the ruby-rouged nether lips.

A flash of heat shot through Elaine, even as she scoffed at the improbability of the act. A woman simply could not accommodate that many fingers. But fantasy has little bearing in reality, and there was no question that the picture fired the imagination. Elaine gazed at the illustration, mesmerized. A vicarious flow of excitement dampened the silk nightgown pushed up between her thighs.

"Would you like that, Morrigan? Would you like a man's fingers inside your tight little *yoni*, stretching you, opening you . . . ?"

Chapter
13

Elaine gasped, instinctively reaching to close the book. The lord's arms snaked around her body; he grasped her hands within his, flesh every bit as hot and hard as she remembered.

She wriggled frenetically, her body burning up with embarrassment. To be caught viewing such things like a teenager. By *him*, of all people!

"No, don't fight me, Morrigan." His words were warm and moist against her right ear, smelling faintly of brandy. The viselike arms tightened about her body, effectively curtailing even the most minuscule movement.

Sound spewed up in Elaine's throat.

Don't fight him!

She clamped her teeth together to prevent the rising hysteria from spilling out of her mouth. *Damn.* He was not supposed to be here. Katie had said that both Hattie and the lord were gone.

Aside from that, *where* had he come from? The French doors had been closed when she came into the library, and even had he gained entrance there, the cold night air would have alerted her to the invasion. She would have seen him had he come in through the regular library door. So where . . . ?

Light flickered onto the ceiling above the fireplace.

Elaine grimaced.

There had indeed been a ghoul napping on the couch. A nineteenth-century ghoul.

She felt a twinge of betrayal. It had not been *her* buns the fire was intended to warm, but his. The Benedict Arnold.

Double damn. Just when she had been on the verge of discovering, if not about Morrigan, then about this man whose body burned and throbbed through the spindles of the chair.

"That's right; that's my girl," he crooned, the words irrepressibly reminding Elaine of Hattie. Except that she didn't feel very "puir" at the moment. Nor did she gather that he wanted her to be.

How *had* Morrigan remained a virgin for an entire year?

He drew her hands down into her lap and transferred her wrists into his right hand. "I know you don't want to fight me, sweetheart."

Elaine's denial escaped in a hiss as his knuckles pressed into the jointure of her legs.

"I didn't understand before. I know now. . . . I know how hard it is for you."

She futilely tugged to free her hands. Hadn't understood what before? *Knew how hard what was?* Tumbleweed thoughts immediately followed with: how quaint. That's the first time anyone ever called her sweetheart.

"That's right. . . . I know you want, sweetheart. I can feel the heat of you, *here.*" The backs of the imprisoning fingers pressed more deeply into the vee of her legs. "God, you're burning up. I knew you would be. I'll make you burn up. We'll burn up together."

Elaine squirmed back into the chair, succeeding merely in wedging his knuckles and her wrists more firmly between her legs. It was bad enough to be accused of masturbating, worse even to be caught viewing pornographic pictures. But to know that he knew that she had been aroused by said viewing! She wished she would burn up, literally, so that there would only be a heap of ashes left.

Damn, damn, damn!

She threw her head back, hoping to knock one of them senseless, but her hair was trapped between her body and the chair, so that all she succeeded in doing was loosening a scalpful of roots. Tears

welled up in her eyes; dimly she registered the fact that she wasn't
as impervious to mortal pain as she had thought.

"No, no . . . Just relax, Morrigan, don't fight me, don't fight me. . . .
I won't let you fight me, not anymore, not now that I know. That's it,
that's my girl, just relax."

Her spine was fused to the back of the chair and through that, his
chest. The lord's left arm anchored her shoulders, his right hand her
wrists and torso. And he told her to *relax?*

Talk about being stuck between the proverbial rock and a hard
place.

Elaine stared up at the ceiling, at the flickering play of light and
shadow. The lord's breath blew warm and humid, rhythmically filling her ear, retreating, filling.

A sob rose in her throat, unwittingly succumbing to the sultry cadence, the heat of his breath, his arms, his hands, the musky scent of
male flesh. The never-ending ache of female curiosity. Vertebra by
vertebra, the bone-splintering stiffness of her spine dissolved.

The lord pressed his face into the crook of Elaine's neck. His
cheek was scratchy with the sandpaper rasp of unshaven stubble.
He whispered a trail of hot, moist kisses, "That's right, just let me
kiss you, here, yes, it feels good, doesn't it, so good. . . ."

Elaine felt a scalding fleck where her neck joined her shoulders,
resolve further dissolving, shivering at the hot, wet application of
tongue on flesh.

"That's right; relax, relax for me, Morrigan. Relax, sweetheart."

Sharp teeth joined the seduction of slick, papillae-covered
tongue, nibbling lightly on the cord running the length of her neck,
then not so lightly there beneath her ear, soothing the nip with a
melting lick.

"That's right, Morrigan; yes, you taste so good, sweet. Trust me;
relax. Yes, that's right. I won't hurt you; never, never would I hurt
you. Trust me. . . ."

Said the spider to the fly.

Ha! Elaine thought without rancor. She wouldn't trust him if he
cut off both his hands. She wouldn't trust him if he cut out his

tongue. She wouldn't trust him if he was wearing a chastity belt. She certainly was not going to trust him trussed up like Sunday dinner with his hand pressed against that part of her that had been a curse since the day she had reached puberty, and was turning out to be no less of a curse in a different body.

But trust, Elaine found, was an insignificant thing compared to the seduction of sensation. Especially when one was so very ill-equipped to handle it. Twentieth-century mothers warned their daughters not to let a boy touch her "up here" or "down there," an easy enough rule to comply with, as *up here* and *down there* were the only places twentieth-century boys seemed interested in touching. Elaine suspected all the warnings in the world would not work if twentieth-century fathers taught their sons that there were other places to touch first. That there were places to kiss other than the lips.

And yes, it *did* feel good.

Elaine's eyes drifted shut, body throbbing, throbbing in time with the nips, the nibbles, the licks, the hot, moist whispers.

"Now." The lord disentangled his arm from around her left shoulder.

Elaine bit back a whimper of cold abandon. Her eyes opened—when had she closed them?—viewing the book-lined room, the flickering darkness as if through a telescope.

The lord raised his left hand and held it poised at the edge of the illustration. She stared at his long, tanned fingers, at the Indian man, at the Indian maiden whose ruby-rouged nether lips were stretched to accommodate the Indian man's fingers, seeing it all with vivid, crystalline clarity.

"I'm not hurting you, am I?" Sharp teeth encompassed Elaine's right earlobe; he nipped it—yes, that hurt—then suckled it as if it were a nipple.

White-hot sensation pulsed through her breasts. It streamlined directly to that place between her legs where his fingers pressed so tantalizingly close.

His lips broke free with a slight slurping sound. It should have sounded repulsive, that slurp, downright juvenile, even. But it didn't.

It sounded wet. Provocative. Not at all fastidious. Evocative of wet and dirty sex. The substance of fantasies.

"You and I are going to share a little adventure, that's all, nothing to be afraid of. I want to satisfy your curiosity, Morrigan. I want to satisfy *you*. You must trust me in this. I won't let you retreat from me, not now, not now that I know. . . ."

Elaine stiffened. There he went again. Not now that he knew *what?*

"No, don't tense up like that. This is natural; what you see and feel is perfectly normal. The mating act is the most powerful thing on this earth. The most perfect thing on earth. When a man and a woman join, they become one—one body, one mind, one soul. Or that's the way it should be. That's the way it *will* be. With us. If you allow it. Just give it a chance, Morrigan. Give *us* a chance."

Elaine's heart skipped a beat. She had wanted that once upon a time, wanted to become one with a man, one body, one mind, one soul. That was before she had accepted the fact that short, stubby-fingered girls did not become concert pianists. That short, stubby-fingered women did not inspire passion.

The lord's long, tanned fingers turned the page. He could be a concert pianist with hands like that, she thought dispassionately. Morrigan's hands and his hands together could perform beautiful duets.

Elaine's heartbeat quickened at the sight of the illustration, feeling the quickening in that most vulnerable of all places, knowing that he could feel it, too.

The Indian man leaned over the Indian maiden, his red-turbaned head buried between her legs. He held her rounded thighs apart. His pink tongue was frozen in a protruded state, eternally licking her ruby-rouged nether lips. A pearl drop adorned the tip of his tongue.

"The man is doing what the Indians call *auparishtaka*, or 'mouth congress.' That white drop on his tongue, that is her *kama salila*, her 'dew of ecstasy.' A woman gives up her essence, her 'dew of ecstasy,' when she is in a state of arousal. There is nothing sweeter or more precious to a man. It is a woman's ultimate gift of trust and love. I want you to give me that, Morrigan. I want you to trust me. I want you to open up your body and drench me."

A wave of heat swelled from where the lord's knuckles insidiously pressed. Never in Elaine's wildest fantasies had her lover whispered such blatant sexual blandishments. Her body gushed with moisture there where his fingers and her wrists pressed, the valley becoming a veritable river. A red haze seemed to envelop her brain, a ruby red haze matching exactly the two pairs of lips and nipples in the painting. She felt his fingers relax around her wrists. The pressure lightened there at the crux of her thighs. Slowly, ever so slowly, the hard, banding fingers released their grip altogether. Her hips lifted without volition, following their warmth.

He cupped his hand over her stomach, the pressure firm, heavy. Something wild and ominous leaped inside her womb at the proprietary weight, trapped between the heat of his hand and the heat of his body.

"Turn the page, Morrigan."

Elaine sucked in a cooling breath of air. She blindly reached out, right hand, no, *left* hand.

The Indian man lay on his back, turban absent, his hair lying about his head in a pool of blue-black. His lips were curved in a benign smile. The Indian maiden sat in yoga fashion between his legs. Her head was poised between his thighs, pink tongue extended, delicately tasting the ruby red crown of his penis. A pearl drop adorned the tip of her tongue. The Indian maiden's right hand circled the base of the man's thick shaft; the fingers of her left hand teased his round testicles.

The lord soothingly massaged the base of Elaine's stomach. Elaine jerked, far from soothed.

"Again *auparishtaka*, or 'mouth congress.' "

A scalding tongue made a stab into Elaine's ear, wet, so wet, in sound and sensation. She squirmed, a discordant twang of reality briefly flaring. Had she thoroughly cleaned that ear? What if he should lap up a hunk of earwax?

"Note the drop of white on the tip of the woman's tongue." The tip of his tongue delicately lapped the contours of her ear. "That is *kulodaka*, his 'secretions of love.' A man also yields his essence to a woman, even before the act is finished. The women of India greatly value the taste; it is a symbol of passion, of virility, and of pleasures to come." The voice deepened, becoming hotter, huskier. "I have been told it is somewhat salty."

Elaine had no doubt that his sources included whole panels of taste testers. She licked her lips, tasting salt, her saliva thick, slick. The hard, hot fingers more vigorously massaged Elaine's stomach, the callused fingertips rasping against smooth silk.

"A man's *lingam* is made for a woman's *yoni*. There will be no more pain, Morrigan. You were a virgin; that is why you tore and bled. Defloration is accompanied by much ceremony in India. Some of the girls who are to go into the priesthood impale themselves on a large stone phallus."

Elaine stared at the Indian man's *lingam*. The lord's fingers slid lower down onto her stomach. She heard the rasp of his fingertips against the silk, felt the rasp of silk rubbing against her pubic hair. A long finger experimentally probed the closed nether lips between her legs. She gasped at the resulting stab of sensation.

"Some men take a vow to deflower virgins; it has been said up to two thousand," the lord continued, his humid, gravelly voice oiling the descent of rational human being into hot, passionate woman. "They spend their lives traveling from one village to the next that they might find virgins to so bless and fulfill their vow. Before the British came, Indian priests would roam the streets naked, so that women might kiss their *lingam* for fertility."

He covered her ear with his mouth, slowly breathed into the vulnerable orifice. His finger lightly measured the length of those other lips, once, twice.

"It is exquisitely pleasurable for a man to be taken into a woman's mouth, just as pleasurable as it is for a woman when a man takes her with his mouth. Note the abstract expression on the Indian man's face. He has drawn into himself so that he will not ejaculate inside her mouth. So that he might later prolong their pleasure. When he is buried deep inside her. An experienced man can make it last for a woman. Can pleasure her over and over until her little *yoni* flows like a spring. A hot, wet spring that never goes dry. . . ."

The little Indian maiden and her dark-skinned lover wavered beneath the heat radiating throughout Elaine's body. There was just a hint of white peeping from the center of the Indian man's swollen red crown, a drop of pleasure straining to blossom.

"Turn the page, Morrigan."

Elaine turned the page, unable to resist either the lord or herself.

The little Indian maiden perched above the darker-skinned man, her left knee by his right hip, her right hip raised with the leg bent at the knee, supporting foot resting by his left ribcage. The maiden's left hand grasped the root of the man's large penis; the ruby head pierced her rouged nether lips. Several pearl drops lined the thick stalk. The fingers on the Indian man's right hand plucked at the maiden's elongated nipple while the forefinger on the man's left hand teased the top of the maiden's rouged nether lips.

Elaine's left shoulder, which had initially been abandoned so that the lord might turn the page, was again encompassed in his heat; his left hand briefly rested on her upper abdomen before crawling the distance to her right breast. He cupped it through the clinging nightgown.

Her nipple hardened to the point of pain. The long, thick finger of his right hand with which he had measured her again and again found the seam between her legs and plunged in between. A low groan erupted from her throat. She convulsively pinched the edge of thick paper, insensible of the potential damage to the hand-painted illustration.

"Sssh, relax, Morrigan. Relax. . . . God, you're hot down here!"

The finger commenced a gentle seesawing motion, sliding down to her place of entrance, then sliding back up to where sensation crackled and sizzled.

"Hot and wet. *Kama salila*. You flow for me, Morrigan. I can feel it all the way through the silk."

Elaine closed her eyes against the building surge of electricity. *Don't talk anymore*, she thought frantically, *don't disturb the fantasy.*

Her fantasies didn't talk, not at this point; action—all she wanted was action. . . .

The finger rimmed the opening to her body, going round and round.

Elaine remembered a company party when one of the new female junior executives had gotten inebriated. So had the vice president, though whether it had been on alcohol or the pretty young female remained uncertain. The junior executive and the vice president had decided to ascertain the quality of the restaurant's glassware. Dipping a finger into her near-empty glass of wine, the junior executive had proceeded to run the wine-doused finger round and round the glass rim.

The crystal had sung.

As Elaine's body sang now. She could feel herself expanding, opening.

The lord released her breast. He bunched up the silk nightgown and grasped Elaine's distended nipple between his thumb and forefinger.

"Oh, God!" The base of Elaine's stomach convulsed. It felt like jolts of electricity were shooting directly from her nipple to her uterus and back up from her uterus to her nipple. He rolled her nipple between his two fingers; with his right hand he continued rimming the core of her, rolling and rimming, rimming and rolling, too much, not enough. "Don't! Oh, God!" She grabbed his hands. "Don't do that!"

Hot, moist air gusted into her ear. "Keep still. Look at the picture, Morrigan."

Elaine strove to focus on the illustration. Every nerve in her body was concentrated on the fingers busily working underneath hers. His tongue rimmed her ear, briefly dipped inside.

"A woman can control how much of the man she wants to take inside her in this position. Also, it is good for a woman because a man can touch her *madanahatra*"—the lord's finger left the rim of Elaine's body and slid to the top of her lips, briefly rubbed so that she had to bite her other lips to prevent herself from screaming with the lightning bolt of pleasure—"her clitoris."

The finger dipped downward, continued rimming her body, soothing, opening.

"The woman is very excited; look at the drops of her love juice running down his *lingam*. I want you to imagine that, Morrigan. I want you to imagine being on top of me, with me deep inside you, here"—his finger slid an infinitesimal inch inside her opening; internally the silk felt both rough and smooth, shaping to the contours of his callused flesh—"and my finger here." His finger slipped out and back up to the top, where Elaine could feel herself swollen and throbbing. He rubbed the silk-protected nub more vigorously than he had earlier. "Isn't that what you want, too, Morrigan? To feel—*me*—inside *you*?"

The illustration blurred, obtained motion. The Indian maiden moved upon the man, her black hair streaming about her back and shoulders in wild abandon, her crippled leg resting comfortably on its knee, the other one supporting her weight, pistoning her weight. Sweat beaded on the maiden's brow, loins churning, heart pumping, heat building, stronger, stronger—

"Tell me, tell me what you want. That's all you have to do, Morrigan, just tell me, let me know what you want, sweetheart, let me pleasure you, let me. . . ."

Elaine gasped for air. Close, she was so close; soon she would be swept up in that moment of release.

Matthew glared up at Elaine from the illustration, horn-rimmed glasses an outline of black kohl, brown eyes accusatory, judge and jury all rolled into one. *Guilty*, the horn-rimmed eyes charged of the middle-aged, dumpy body that swallowed his. *Guilty*, they charged of the passion that gobbled his sex. *Guilty*, they charged of the fantasy that was no fantasy, but adultery, pure and simple.

"Noooo!"

Elaine leaped out of the chair. The edge of the desk caught her in the lower abdomen; she grabbed hold of the wood and used it to fling herself sideways, out of range of those degenerating arms and hands and fingers and voice. So close—*my God*—she had been so close, was still so close. . . .

She raced to the door, nearly falling before she realized the lurching imbalance was caused by a short left leg that could not travel at the same rate as the taller, stronger right leg. Elaine made the necessary physical and mental adjustments, slowing down only fractionally in her need to escape, lurching and swaying like a runaway crab.

The marble statue loomed out of the darkness, stone skin a pale glow.

Elaine found the wooden banister, used it as much for support as for guidance. She tripped several times over the hem of the nightgown—cursed nightgown; she hated nightgowns, hated this world. But most of all she hated herself, hated the passion that could make her forget every vow she had ever believed in. That could make her forget that she had even made a vow. To another man.

To a man who had never been there when she needed him.

Why had Matthew left her unsatisfied all those long years?

Elaine finally stood in her own room, the key securely turned in the lock. In the faint glow of embers she located the desk chair and pushed it to *his* door, securing it beneath the doorknob. Only then did she allow herself to relax, her sides heaving from lack of breath.

She grabbed onto the four-poster bed lest she collapse now in the aftermath. Her body quivered—not from exhaustion, but from lust. Her thighs were slick with the tears of her body crying its frustration. The muscles in her belly jumped and jerked, as did the engorged tissue between her legs. Her breasts ached, regret that he had not kissed them a wrenching pain. She would have liked him to lick them and suckle them as the Indian man had licked the little Indian maiden's plump nether lips and suckled her elongated nipples.

As the lord had licked and suckled her ear.

Elaine closed her eyes in memory. A searing surge of lust traveled from the nipple that he had made of her earlobe down to her breasts and through her loins. It was chased by a searing surge of regret that she had not followed it through to the end. Just once. Just once in her life she would have liked to find satisfaction through another.

He was Morrigan's husband. And for a while, at least, she *was Morrigan. How could it be adultery to lie with one's own husband?* a small voice whispered.

Elaine's eyelids flew open. She was crazy! Damn him, he had made her crazy!

Charles sat back on his haunches. The harsh sound of his breathing filled the room. He imagined the front of her gown, the silk a dark, wet circle where he had used it to rub and penetrate her body, and he almost came in his pants like a randy schoolboy.

For once, Western medicine had been right. And the Eastern remedy had been exactly what the good doctor had ordered.

Who would ever have thought that his pious little wife was as hot as any seasoned mistress?

He slowly stood up from his crouching position behind the chair, grimacing at the crack of bones. He was not getting younger. The left corner of his mouth kicked up. But he could promise her many years yet of long, long nights. Insatiable nights.

Charles looked down. There was a dark, wet circle on the cushion where she had sat, proof of her passion. His manhood strained against his breeches. He forced several deep breaths into his lungs, then sat down, all his efforts to curtail his burgeoning desire dissipating at the feel of the wet warmth left by her body.

To distract himself, he reached out and set aside the candle, then picked up the book that she had laid on the edge of the desk. Something dropped onto the floor. Leaning over, he picked up a hairpin, briefly perused it before turning his attention once again to the slender book.

He threw back his head and laughed.

Memoirs of a Woman of Pleasure!

Perhaps he had not needed the pillow book, after all.

Setting Cleland's book and the hairpin back down onto the desk, he rose and retrieved from behind the couch the half-empty glass of brandy that, tired as he had been from the hours-long ride back from Damon's, had sent his fantasies into a dreamworld.

A glimmer of light had awakened him just when he had been about to rip away the ugly gray wool dress covering his wife's body. When the brighter reflection of light on the ceiling had broken away from the dull gleam cast by the fireplace, Charles had been ready to bag a thief. Seeing his wife, who rose and retired with the sun, had been quite a surprise. Quite a pleasant surprise indeed when she proceeded to examine the pillow book he had laid out in readiness for her seduction on the morrow following Tantric fare of meat, alcohol, fish, and grain.

He had mentally monitored the turn of the pages. When she ran her finger over the Indian couple, Charles had felt the flecks of paint as if he himself were touching them. When she touched her nipple, viewing the Indian woman's own nipple being pinched, he had felt her pleasure all the way down to his groin. He had smiled in pained satisfaction, watching her squirm at her first sight of a man sucking at a woman's breast. The blast of sexual energy his wife had radiated upon viewing the *pasha*'s fingers thrusting inside the Indian consort had drawn Charles as unerringly as a desert moth to an open campfire.

Yes, his wife had expedited the matter of her seduction rather considerably tonight.

Charles transferred the brandy snifter to his left hand and brought the forefinger of his right hand to his lips. Her taste had penetrated the silk nightgown—salty and very, very sweet. His erection grew, impossibly, another inch.

He readjusted his trousers and resumed his position behind the desk. She contained such passion, this emerging Morrigan, a passion to match his own. He had indeed broken through the facade and melted the ice bitch that night of consummation.

Charles turned the page of the pillow book, imagining his wife's response were she still there.

The Indian woman's legs were thrown over the Indian man's shoulders. The *pasha* was ramming his consort long and hard. And deep. The rouged nether lips of the consort clung to the *pasha*'s *lingam*. Charles imagined wrapping himself in silk and teasing Morrigan there, as he had teased her with his finger. Imagined the cool of the silk and the tight, moist heat of her vulva.

His fingers tightened convulsively around the paper.

Morrigan had been so close! How had she mustered the strength to pull away?

The page of expensive illustration crinkled beneath the pressure. Charles forced himself to relax. The pillow book had been a gift from a *maharatbata,* as had many pleasurable memories. He smoothed the page.

How quickly she had overcome her putrid throat in the throes of passion.

His lips quirked sardonically.

Too bad the words she had spoken were the least favorite in his vocabulary: *Don't. No.* Words he had never really understood. Words he didn't have to understand now, titled and rich as he was.

Words he did not intend to accept from his wife, awakened or not. And judging by her response tonight, those were words he would not be hearing too much longer.

Charles smiled. He liked this new Morrigan. *Putrid stomach!* He would never forget the look on her face as she had downed the milk and egg last night. Or the sound of her desire tonight, the low, rumbling groan she had emitted when he broached the barrier of her closed nether lips, her labored breathing when he rubbed her swollen womanhood through the dampened silk.

No, she would not be able to long hold out under siege. But he would not take her until she asked for it.

He took a stiff swallow of brandy.

Until she begged for it.

Pride dictated that price for the year that she had held him in hellish abstinence.

He had a feeling it would not take his wife long to part with her sanctimonious piety.

Perhaps, he thought, reflecting upon his second plan, even as early as tomorrow.

Chapter

14

Sleep pounded and throbbed in Elaine's ears. She pulled the covers over her head, but the pounding and throbbing, though muffled, continued unabated.

"M' lady, be ye ill? Marm, the door be locked, m' lady. Please open the door; I've brung ye tea!"

Pound, throb.

"Go away," Elaine mumbled beneath the covers. "Go away!"

She had spent the better part of the night walking the floor to calm her body; the remainder of the night she had spent lying supine in bed trying to rechannel her frustration in the hope that she could transport herself back into her own time. The room had been bathed in the pink of dawn before sheer exhaustion had overcome the struggle between corporal agony and cerebral mastery.

Elaine reached out a hand and added a pillow to the pile of covers heaped over her head. Needless to say, she had not been able to transport herself through time. That did not mean, however, that she couldn't play Rip Van Winkle and sleep through to the right century.

"Don't ye fret, m' lady; everything's gonna be right as rain—ye just wait and see. I'll go git his lordship, and he—"

Elaine shot out of bed. She twisted the key and threw back the door.

Katie readjusted a small silver tray bearing a steaming pot of tea so that she held it in both hands. "Oh, marm, I be ever so glad to see ye! I was that afraid, I was, thinking maybe ye-know-who had slipped back and did ye a mischief."

It was not Hattie that Elaine was afraid would sneak in and do her a mischief.

Katie's brown eyes twinkled merrily beneath the white cap. "The lord, he be back, m' lady! Ain't that grand?"

"Just dandy." Elaine pivoted. The bedroom that once again must perforce become her prison lurched beneath her feet.

"Oh, marm, ye're hurt!"

Righting herself, Elaine turned a scowling face toward the maid. Fancy Katie noticing she was lame after all this time, she thought caustically. But the maid's eyes, big as the spindle hole in a floppy disk, were fastened onto the back of Elaine's gown, not her leg.

Elaine grasped the right side of her nightgown and pulled it forward until the back slid within visual range.

The white silk was smeared and speckled with blood.

Red blood.

Fresh blood.

But where had it come from?

She twisted the gown this way and that. It was stained only in the back. *What . . . ?*

Elaine's cheeks flamed with sudden knowledge of the blood's origin.

"Oh, marm!"

The knowledge, too, had just occurred to Katie.

"Oh, marm!" the maid repeated, sounding utterly astonished that a lady was subject to the same physical realities as the lower classes.

Elaine looked down at the maid in budding dismay. *Oh, marm, indeed!* In this era that didn't even have toilet paper, what did they use for . . . ?

Katie swallowed. "Don't ye worry none, m' lady. It be no trouble ye're having. I'll have ye clean as a thistle in no time at all. Yer gown, it'll come clean with a little bit of rubbing—it'll be as good as new, the sheets, too, ye just see if they don't!"

"Katie, I—"

The door slammed in Elaine's face.

"Don't need clean sheets. I need a sanitary napkin!" she shouted. Katie had taken the tray with her. "And I don't want tea—I want coffee!"

Damn.

Elaine clenched her fists. What was she going to do now?

She scrubbed her teeth with the white ginger soap—it tasted much better than lye. Remembering the lord's ominous threat should he discover her trying to lock the door on him, she removed the chair barring the connecting door.

"Marm?"

Elaine whirled about, grabbed the back of the chair. Her face a dangerous red, Katie held out a long, thin roll of white cloth.

Elaine gratefully accepted the unexpected solution, carefully turned it over in her hands. It was exactly what it looked like— folded white cloth. Gratitude gave way to perplexity. How was it to adhere . . . ?

Elaine looked up from the roll of cloth in her hands. Katie's brown eyes were as uncertain as her own must surely look.

The thing would fall right through the crotchless drawers. Elaine was quite certain Katie did not mean for her to stuff it up like a tampon. Did she?

Katie cleared her throat.

"Well, marm, I don't know as how ye fancy ladies do these things, but, we, well . . . I suppose we ain't so different underneath, sort of, if ye catch me drift. Ye probably do it the same as we does it, that is, I . . ."

Her face turning an ominous red, Katie dug into her pocket and held out a long, thin strip of cloth. Elaine accepted it as blankly uncomprehendingly as she had inspected the folded cloth.

Katie cleared her throat again. The maid's cheeks turned, impossibly, redder than they had been before. The blush was contagious. Elaine felt her own cheeks radiate heat. She had never blushed in the twentieth century. Here it was as uncontrollable as a rash.

"Well, marm, that be, ah, if ye'll just let me have the towel, like, and I'll tie this 'round yer waist, and then we . . ."

Comprehension dawned. Elaine was not so young a member of the twentieth century that she couldn't remember the sanitary belts that had preceded the self-adhesive napkins.

"That . . ." She paused, carefully thinking out the words, shaping the sounds. The lord had not restricted his use of contractions last night, but perhaps it was permissible when trying to seduce one's wife, like talking dirty in the sack but not at the dinner table. "That is quite all right, Katie." A smile touched the corners of her lips. "I think I can manage."

Katie did not return the smile. She marched stiffly to the opposite side of the four-poster bed and jerked the covers off. Her red face was centered in the yellow silk frame created by the open drapes.

Elaine had a perverse longing for the steaming beverage she had decried but minutes earlier.

"Katie, you are forgetting something."

"Marm?"

"The tea, Katie. And I need a bath."

The young maid's mouth dropped open. "Oh, marm, ye can't be wanting to bathe *now!* Why, 'tis unhealthy! Ye could *die,* m' lady!"

Elaine laughed, her first laugh in six days. The first laugh, in fact, since she had been transported back into this time. It sounded surprisingly good. Young and husky. Not middle-aged and flat.

Her expression mutinous, Katie bundled up the soiled sheets. Elaine sighed, well acquainted with the girl's stubbornness.

As if bathing were any more dangerous that one time of the month than it was at any other!

Acting on impulse, she twisted the back of the gown to the side and limped to the desk for pen, ink, and paper. She wrote longhand in the exaggerated leftward slant:

I hearby relieve Katie from responsibility in the event her mistress should die as a result of taking a bath.

"There." Elaine stifled a grin. "If I die give the lord this note and he will not hold you responsible."

Katie gingerly adjusted the crumpled sheets so that they could safely be held with one hand and accepted the note. The look of mutiny did not abate when the maid stuffed the paper into her apron pocket and marched from the room.

Five minutes later Elaine had her tea. She sipped it standing, lest she stain the chair, while Katie, having undergone a miraculous change of opinion, brought up the obligatory buckets of water. Elaine grabbed a towel, a pair of drawers, a midcalf-length slip that Katie called a chemise, and the makeshift sanitary equipment.

It was while she was drying her breasts that the full implication of last night's excursion slammed home. She looked down at the right brown nipple, now soft and flat as it should be. The cry of her voice when he had grasped that nipple in a hardened state rang out in her head.

Oh, God. Don't. Oh, God. Don't do that.

Elaine felt the warmth drain out of her body.

She had not been thinking to maintain a British accent last night. It stood to reason, therefore, that she had not cried out with a British accent.

Mechanically she tied the string around her hips and positioned the folded cloth. The nineteenth-century underwear stuck to her steam-moistened body. She reached through the open crotch in the drawers and readjusted the bulky cloth.

Katie whisked behind the screen. "Cook, she made a right special breakfast fer ye and the lord."

Elaine jerked the chemise down over her drawers.

Katie scooped up the soiled nightgown and towel. "We got to hurry, marm; his lordship'll be ever so glad ye're over the putrid throat."

Katie might not notice the difference in m' lady's speech, but

Katie had not noticed that Elaine had used her right hand as opposed to Morrigan's left. The lord had. As he had undoubtedly noticed the difference in her accent last night. As he most definitely *would* notice if she ever opened her mouth in front of him again.

"No, I don'— I think breakfast here in my room will be nice. His lordship must be tired—" Elaine remembered his busy fingers. "I imagine he will want to sleep in—" She remembered the feel of his finger penetrating her. "I want a tray brought up to me here," she said firmly.

Katie put a hand between Elaine's shoulder blades and urged her forward. "Well, we got to git ye dressed, marm, the lord be up and about; I saw him meself when I was bringing yer bath."

Elaine reluctantly stepped around the Japanese screen. Katie had built a roaring fire. The flames leaped up past the chimney. Elaine could feel the blast of heat ten feet away.

She thought of that silly note. What if Katie had actually given it to the lord? "Do you have the note I gave you?"

"It be in me pocket, marm, but I don't be needing it. I told Mr. Fritz what ye be wanting, and he asked the lord, and the lord, he told Mr. Fritz that it be all right fer ye to take yer bath this time of the month."

Elaine felt as if her cheeks would burst from the heat flooding them. Was there *no* privacy in the nineteenth century? She silently submitted to the maid's ministrations.

"There ye be, marm. The lord, he said ye was to have what ye wanted, though it do be a bit strange, m' lady, ye taking yer meals in yer room the minute he gits back. I told them they be wrong; it was old Hattie done made ye the way ye were, that *ye* don't spurn the lord, and here ye be—" Katie grabbed the nightgown and towel and tucked them under the tea tray. "I'll be gitting yer breakfast now, an it please ye."

The door closed smartly behind the maid. The fire crackled and popped in the ensuing silence.

Morrigan spurning the lord! How preposterous. Elaine could not imagine the lord being spurned. By anyone.

The heat blasting from the fireplace was unbearable. Steam rose from the damp ends of her hair. She jumped up and threw open the French doors.

The sun was bright and yellow, the sky clear and blue. A dark speck bobbed and danced high above. The silence was palpable.

She twisted the gold band around her finger, unconsciously looking for the twentieth-century engagement diamond that never stayed upright.

Were this Chicago, she thought, the sky would be gray and dirty—what could be seen of it. She would be sitting at a desk piled high with unburst tabulation reports. Five printers would be click-clicking away down the hallway.

The dark, dancing speck made a kamikaze dive.

No. She had awakened in this time six days ago. Mentally she counted from the day she would have awakened in the twentieth century, Monday.

Elaine frowned.

She would be home, doing Saturday cleaning. And Matthew would be . . . where? In his den, poring over accounting logs? At the office?

The tiny dot grew larger and larger; the shapeless lump evolved into the form of a bird. Just before it crashed beak-first into a tree-top, it made a sharp U turn and raced to meet the sky.

What had the lord meant last night when he kept saying he didn't understand?

Thank God she—Morrigan—had gotten her period. And that Katie had told Fritz, who had told the lord. He would not bother her now, surely. Victorians had considered menstruation a perilous business—Katie's reaction verified that. She would pretend to have debilitating cramps. That would buy her a week's reprieve from the threat of Bedlam.

She looked down at the gold ring she had been subconsciously twisting round and round.

Hattie had demanded that Elaine give it to her that first morning, as if it were a crime to wear a wedding band. As if marriage itself were a crime.

Had Morrigan been compelled to spurn the lord?

Had he shown Morrigan the illustrated book before taking her to
bed?

Katie scratched at the door. Elaine's stomach rumbled in anticipation. She looked down at it in disgust. If she did not get back to
her own time soon, Morrigan's body would become as plump as
her own had been—*was*—in the twentieth century. The thought
did not stop her from eagerly sitting down on the bamboo chair.

A voice murmured outside the door; Katie responded, her voice
higher than the other. Elaine smiled. Contrary to her previous as-
sumption, the bathwater was not tipped out over the balcony—it
was carried down the same way it was carried up. Katie had brought
the little chamber-pot maid—her sister Mary—to help her.

The door gently swung open. Elaine leaned forward expectantly.

The lord walked in; he carried the silver breakfast tray.

Elaine's stomach did a somersault. Her hunger died with a brief,
resentful whimper.

He was dressed in tight leather breeches and knee-high boots
similar to the ones he had worn that first disastrous encounter after
her bath. The white shirt that was tucked into the soft brown pants
was not really a shirt at all, but a pullover with three buttons down
the front. All of them were open, exposing a chest covered with
dark, curly hair.

He deposited the tray onto the desk, then walked to where
Elaine sat near the French doors. His chestnut hair blazed with copper fire in the sunlight streaming through the open doors. His hard,
chiseled face was solemn. Hair coiled forward beneath his ears in
two perfect curls.

"Please accept my apologies."

Elaine's gaze flew upward. Whatever her thoughts about their
next meeting after last night, they certainly had not included an
apology. It was strangely anticlimactic.

"I had no idea Hattie would ever do you physical harm, though I
realized she was unbalanced when she came to me."

The heat flared in Elaine's cheeks, recalling verbatim the lord's
account of his last meeting with Hattie.

"I gave her notice to leave then, but it transpired that I myself left instead, without issuing instructions to ensure her departure. For that I most humbly offer my apologies."

The lord stepped closer. Elaine's face was on a level with his—hips. Fleetingly she remembered the grit of dust and the buttery softness of leather against her swollen skin. Remembered the electric surge of—

PMS.

That was why she had been so receptive to the lord last night. Her own body in the twentieth century always experienced an increase in libido just prior to that time of month. Magazine articles claimed that the surge was perfectly natural, that it was the body's recognition of the last chance to reproduce.

That must also be the reason why she had gone off the rocker, so to speak, when Hattie had taken the key to her room. And why she was finding it increasingly difficult to control her temper.

A faint, musky odor emanated from the lord's person. It elicited a tiny stirring in her body, a body that was supposed to be dormant, having passed that last chance to reproduce. The bulge behind the lord's leather breeches seemed to grow larger in response.

On the other hand, she thought, fingering the gold ring, she had had raging hormones in the twentieth century and she had never teetered between extremes there. Cheeks blazing, she threw her head back for a more comfortable view.

The solemn expression on the lord's face lightened, becoming part mocking, part something that Elaine had never before seen in a man's face. The blazing heat in her cheeks spread down her neck and chest, viscerally if not cerebrally recognizing that look. It was the look of knowledge. Carnal knowledge. Of naked skin and silk and hot, wet flesh.

Eyes hooded, he brought up his right hand, forefinger arched. Elaine stared at his hand, at his finger, in her eyes a woman's curiosity. He repositioned his hand, holding it straight out with his middle finger depressed. Recognition shot through the place between Elaine's legs. It looked slender, that finger, not nearly as thick as it had felt going inside her last night. Instantly the color in her cheeks darkened.

The lord gently traced the dark bruise on her left cheek. His finger was callused, slightly abrasive, several degrees cooler than the trail of crimson he followed over the bridge of her nose and down the length of her unmarked cheek.

"Your skin is so smooth, like silk. You remember what the silk felt like last night, don't you? When I rubbed it round and round. When I eased it inside you . . ."

Elaine had read about people bursting into spontaneous combustion. She wondered if it was a mystery of nature or an act of mortification.

"There's no need to be embarrassed." The blue of his eyes warmed to a sultry Mediterranean. "I want you to take pleasure in what I do." He painted intricate little swirls down and around and over the bruised skin. "I want you to want me, Morrigan. As a wife should want her husband."

He outlined the skin beneath her eye, his flesh cool, rough. Elaine forgot to think, forgot to breathe, totally riveted by the Mediterranean eyes and the delicate caress of corporal promise. His fingertip retraced its original path, outlined the skin beneath her left eye.

"Do you?" His voice deepened. "Does it hurt?"

Unbelievably long eyelashes shielded his eyes; jagged shadows brushed his cheeks. Slowly he raised his lids; his irises were thin bands of blue, the pupils unfathomable black holes. "Fritz told me what happened. Show me where else you were hurt."

A burning log dropped in the fireplace. The warmth drained from Elaine's face.

Of course. Fritz would have told him. Told him everything. How she had kicked and hit an old woman. How she had screamed obscenities.

She jerked away from the caressing finger.

Bedlam. How could she ever forget the threat of Bedlam?

The canal expression on the lord's face immediately disappeared.

He dropped his hand and stepped back. His right lip hitched upward toward the ceiling.

"I know you can speak, Morrigan. Fritz waxed quite eloquently over your surprising vocabulary. And in case you have forgotten last night, I have not. You cried out when I squeezed your nipple. You said—let me see; I don't want to misquote you—ah, yes, you said: 'Oh, God. Don't. Oh, God. Don't do that.' Yes, I have quite a sound memory. I even remember that when you grabbed my hands, you pressed harder, my love. There, you remember now, do you not?"

Oh, yes, Elaine remembered it all, not by the flicker of an eyelash revealing her fears. The question was, did *he* remember it all—the words, yes, but what about the accent? Had Fritz remembered to tell *all*, the profanity that had yet to be invented?

"I am tired of having a recluse for a wife. You will change into your riding habit. Now. I know I purchased you several. As you and Hattie did not see fit to dispose of the rest of the clothes"—the blue shards of ice that his eyes had become raked the high-necked mint green dress Katie had chosen for her—"I assume you likewise have not disposed of the riding habits.

"I'll have a horse prepared for you, something gentle, so you need not look at me with those great black sheep eyes. Perhaps some fresh air and sunshine will improve that horrid, pasty complexion of yours."

Elaine glared at the lord. How dare he try to seduce her one second and then belittle her appearance the next? She sat back in the chair and deliberately folded her arms across her chest. Hell would freeze over before she spoke to him.

"I will, of course, be happy to take you riding dressed as you are. I merely thought to preserve your modesty. But if you don't mind flashing your legs at every jackanapes who happens to pass by, why should I?"

Elaine retained her frozen stance, letting her body language demonstrate what she thought. Except that she suddenly could not remember if crossing the arms over the chest was a sign of assertiveness or defensiveness.

"Very well, if that is what you wish, I will be happy to carry you out to the stables and mount you in walking dress. The servants cannot laugh any harder than they are no doubt laughing now over this parody of a marriage and your ridiculous posturing."

Elaine was abruptly hauled to her feet. She dug her heels into the carpet, resisting the pull of his hands.

Spanning a formidable distance, he thrust his face down into hers. "You will ride, by God, or so help me, madam, you will pray for the gentle mount that is now waiting for you in the stables. Do you understand?"

Ride.

A mount?

What was he talking about?

"I believe we have more than once discussed my dislike of ill-mannered dispositions. Do you understand?"

Elaine nodded, not understanding at all.

"Not good enough. I repeat, do you understand?"

In speech, as in everything else, she was not to be given a choice. She matched the clip of her voice to his. "Yes."

The lord released her. Elaine stumbled, grabbed his arm to retain her balance. *Wrong hand.* She immediately snatched it back. The muscles beneath his cotton shirt visibly corded.

"Good. I will meet you in fifteen minutes at the stables. If you've forgotten where they are, I have footmen aplenty with nothing better to do than act as your guide on *your* estate that you have lived on for over a year."

The lord's voice oozed with sarcasm. And bitterness. And pain. It took a moment for his—for their—intended destination to sink in.

Stables.

Oh, my God. He expected her to ride a horse.

Elaine had never ridden a horse in her life. She had been bitten by one, but that was the extent of her experience.

She wouldn't do it.

She *couldn't* do it.

She simply could not maintain the facade of being someone she was not while riding a horse. She would do something if she fell and didn't break her neck—scream, curse. In Morrigan's voice with Elaine's Yankee drawl.

Elaine stared up at the lord's rage-filled face. There must be give in this man. He couldn't make her do this! Well, physically he could, yes, unlike Hattie, but surely he wouldn't. There had been some tenderness there earlier. He could have raped her last night, but he had not. He could have dragged her out of bed when she had been sick with a hangover, but he had not. Surely, surely in this case also he wouldn't . . .

He returned her regard, the cold that radiated from his eyes so intense it practically froze Elaine's eyelashes.

Yes, he would.

She took a deep breath. There was only one avenue left open. "My lord."

She sounded more a lady of the realm than Queen Victoria herself, Elaine thought faintly.

"My lord," she repeated stiffly. "I am . . . I have . . ." The blood that rushed to her face was so hot it was actually painful. How did one tell a Victorian lord that one was suffering from menstrual cramps? "I have a . . . a woman's . . . indisposition."

Charles stared at his wife in disbelief. *A woman's indisposition?*

The hitch in his right lip eased. His wife, he thought, was turning out to be every bit as amusing as her notes. Fritz had uttered similar words when he had apprised his lord of the baroness's desire to take a bath, thereby placing the potential risk to his wife's health in his hands as opposed to the valet's or Katie the maid's. Fritz, too, had turned that same scalding crimson.

"Very nicely put, my dear. I am certain Fritz would quite think you are redeemable. Both of you, it seems, are avid devotees of our dear Vicky. You, however, are of an age to realize you are experiencing a perfectly natural phenomenon. Exercise will do you good."

Charles studied Morrigan's flaming face. She did not at all look like the virago who had blackened Hattie's eye and then proceeded to "cascade" all over poor Fritz. His wife, who had not blushed once in their entire year of marriage, today glowed like a walking billboard. He felt a curious pang of tenderness.

"Fifteen minutes, Morrigan," he said softly.

"My lord." Morrigan nibbled on her lush red lips. He imagined those lips wrapped around his manhood, tasting him as the Indian consort had tasted the *pasha*.

Charles waited expectantly.

"Please," she finally bit out.

He wondered how that would sound under more advantageous circumstances, with her voice husky with passion as it had been last night. *Please, Charles. Please don't stop.*

He stepped closer to her, tantalizing her with the press of hard muscles and soft leather breeches. Her body radiated heat through the thin silk dress. She smelled of moist heat and white ginger. He used a finger to pry up her chin. A shell-like ear peeped from beneath her hair; it, too, was red. "Please what, Morrigan?"

The black eyes were wary, but filled with emotion now. Yes, he must just exercise patience, hard as it might be, but surely worth the effort, judging by her response to the pillow book.

"I can't—I do not want to ride."

Morrigan's breath was scented with white ginger, certainly preferable to the lye soap she had previously used.

Charles cupped her cheek. Her skin was blistering hot.

"I will not let you fall, Morrigan. I know you can't ride. You have to trust me, sweetheart."

Chapter
15

The lord's fingers slid beneath the voluminous skirt of Elaine's riding habit and what she had learned were called not half-slips, but petticoats. He grasped her unshaven right knee. The horse shied, sharing her embarrassment. Elaine concentrated upon retaining her seat rather than mapping the course of the lord's hand on her leg.

"Relax, Morrigan."

An amused grin played about his mouth. It had been there ever since she had taken her life in her hands and uttered that totally ridiculous statement about having a woman's indisposition. At the time it had seemed an apt euphemism for cramps. Now it only seemed incredibly stupid.

I even remember that when you grabbed my hands, you pressed harder, my love.

She looked away from the knowing gleam in those Mediterranean blue eyes. The ground slammed into focus, fifteen feet above the tallest pissant.

She gritted her teeth. The lord had said that he knew she couldn't ride. Knowing Morrigan was as much a novice as Elaine was herself did not in the least comfort her.

"Hook your knee around here."

Beneath the heavy velvet skirt his hand guided her knee over the peculiar horn she had immediately noticed on her saddle and not his. He then slid his hand toward her outer leg, drawing alarmingly close to the gaping crotch of her drawers, veering at the last second, his fingers gliding down her left leg to her boot-clad ankle. Firmly he pushed her foot through the stirrup, forcing her left leg up against the strange, downwardly curved projection near the misplaced horn.

"At all times keep your right knee hooked around the pommel and your left foot in the stirrup, like this. If you should feel yourself slipping, press your left leg up against the leaping pommel. Don't worry about Jasper. She's as gentle as a cow."

Great. Elaine had as much affection for milk cows as she did horses.

She stared down where her legs were concealed underneath the dark blue velvet. Both were draped on the same side of the saddle, as opposed to one on either side. Surely he didn't expect her to ride like this?

The horse looped its neck, for a second flaring equine nostrils, tanned fingers, and booted foot making contact. She scrunched her toes, fully expecting to lose them.

The lord affectionately pushed the mare's head away, then rearranged the drape of Elaine's skirt so that it fell past her boot in the stirrup.

"Hold on while I walk you around the yard for a minute. Here." He took the reins from the stable boy.

The stable boy glared at Elaine.

"Morrigan."

She pried her right— no, she was glad to retain the more secure hold with her right hand on the edge of the saddle where the horn *should* have been, accepting the leather straps with her left hand, as Morrigan would have done. The horse promptly stepped forward. Elaine dropped the reins and clutched the saddle with both hands.

The lord laughed.

Elaine glared.

He laughed!

She'd never heard him laugh before. The crystalline air rang out with the masculine sound, deep and uninhibited.

Still chuckling, he pried Elaine's left hand loose from the saddle and draped the reins through her fingers. She nervously commenced wrapping the leather thongs around her hand.

His bare fingers covered her gloved ones. Heat penetrated the soft leather.

"No, don't ever do that. If the horse should go down or throw you and you have the reins wrapped about your hand like that, you can't jump free. Either the horse will fall on you or he will drag you and trample you."

To death.

The unspoken words hung in the air.

Elaine took a deep breath and slowly released it. Wonderful. Having managed to sit on top of this "gentle cow," she now had to worry about jumping off of it rather than be fallen on or trampled. To death. Just the words to boost her morale. Her heart raced; inside the leather gloves her hands were bathed in hot, sticky perspiration. She smiled grimly. In addition to being a chauvinistic satyr, the lord must also be a diplomat.

His blue eyes twinkled up at her. He squeezed her fingers, then dropped his hand.

Elaine gripped the reins to prevent herself from diving after that hand, to prevent herself from diving into his arms. She really did not want to do this. The fine line she walked trying to balance Morrigan and herself had been abandoned by the wayside: she was all Elaine.

Elaine survived without mishap being led around the stableyard. The tightly laced corset Katie had insisted she wear forced her to remain upright; otherwise she had no doubt she would be doubled over the horse's neck, hanging on for dear life. Her only consolation was that the riding dress, unlike the rest of Morrigan's wardrobe, did not contain any hip or buttock drapery. Had it done so, she would be permanently indented by the end of this ordeal. Katie had also insisted upon skewering Elaine's hair on top of her head and securing there a jaunty little hat with a lethal looking ten-inch-long hat pin.

As a result of that fashion accessory, she was able to resist staring straight down at the ground and the "gentle cow's" hooves for fear of being stabbed. Which was probably a blessing, as it made it seem more like she was balanced on a low, wobbly cloud with perky brown ears than a bovine, toe-mulching horse.

She fought down the urge to cry, *Look, my hair is up; you told me never to wear it like that. Why don't you send me to my room for punishment?*

All too soon the lord released Jasper's bit and mounted—astride—his own horse, a dangerous-looking black that was far too frisky for comfort. They rode away from the stables side by side, matching clip-clop to clip-clop. Elaine had to bite her lips to stem a flow of nervous chatter. Picturing, then, the lord's surprise should he be unable to get his wife to stop babbling when but a scant hour earlier he could barely pry a single word out of her, she bit her tongue to stop the rise of nervous laughter.

The countryside was comprised of the greenest grass she had ever seen in her life. The sun was brilliant. She inhaled air so crisp it hurt her lungs. Her bovine horse maintained a safe, rolling gait, not at all the bucking, rearing action she had anticipated. The monotonous motion was rather pleasant when one forgot the potential consequences.

The lord remained silent, matching the stallion's gait to Jasper's easy plod. Deep blue gleamed in the distance. Elaine disregarded caution and stood a little way up in the stirrup.

Jasper stumbled. Elaine promptly sank back down onto the saddle and squeezed the two pommels between her legs for all she was worth. She cast a quick glance at the lord. He was studying her, not in condemnation or accusation, just looking. As if he liked what he saw. As if he would like more of what he saw.

No man had ever looked at her like that. Not plain, plump, sensible Elaine.

No man had ever said he wanted to satisfy her.

Not even Matthew, and Matthew loved her.

The lord's tanned face turned moody. Elaine scowled. He was as unpredictable as Chicago weather. As if proving her point, he kicked his horse and galloped toward the lake.

Jasper felt abandoned. The mare attempted to follow her equestrian companion, but Elaine pulled back hard on the reins, keeping the horse's gait at a safe, undemanding roll.

The lord waited for her to catch up with him. They rode around the rim of the small lake. Ducks peacefully floated in the water, a reflective blend of blue sky and sparkling sun. Several of the plain brown females trailed a brood of fluffy little ducklings.

To the left of the aquatic family, a shadow edged Elaine's peripheral field of vision. She turned her head. Her breath caught in the back of her throat.

A black swan swam out of a snag of underbrush. It stretched its neck, then doubled it over in a perfect loop. The brilliant scarlet bill ruffled its black chest feathers in a slow, solitary preening.

"It has been coming here for several years now."

The lord brought his stallion up on Jasper's right, so close his shiny black boot brushed the side of her ankle. She sidled away from the physical contact. He seemed impervious to her withdrawal, eyes locked onto the preening black swan.

"It shouldn't be here—black swans are native to Australia, you know—but it is. Perhaps old man Kentleton sent it to England a few years back. He was an odd man. A general. I served under him for a few months in India, until he opted to return to the more predictable outcome of Australia. He used to regularly ship home Australian curiosities so that his wife could experience a bit of that country without inconveniencing him there with her actual person." He glanced at Elaine, blue eyes glinting. "It's a wonder we don't have kangaroos hopping wild all over the countryside."

The stallion jerked its head upright; the lord brought it back down, the slight jingle of metal echoing through the still air. The stallion stepped closer to Jasper; the lord's shiny black boot again pressed against her ankle. Elaine determinedly perused the Australian swan.

"It's beautiful, isn't it?"

She looked at the lord. There was reverence in his voice—and in his eyes, safely trained once more on the black swan.

"Swans mate for life," he said softly, breath a pale wisp in the cool air. "This poor fellow always comes here alone. Always. Alone."

The big black horse snorted, did a fancy and, to Elaine's mind, dangerous sidestep. The lord reined in the animal without effort, without really noticing its waywardness. He turned toward Elaine. His lips curved in what on any other man would have been a wistful smile. "Perhaps this year it will find it's true mate."

Always. Alone.

Yes, that was how she felt—ridiculous, of course, but true. With Matthew she had always been alone.

Would always be alone.

And so, apparently, would this man.

"Come on, enough of this. I don't want you overdoing it on your first day out. Let's go home."

Home.

Elaine immediately became aware of the myriad aches and pains in her legs and arms and back. The folded cloth was metamorphosing into a tampon. Blinding light glared off the lake. Sweat trickled through her scalp beneath the hat. The horse as was rotund as an industrial drum. And it stank, identifying now the animal smell that had clung to the lord's clothes when he had French-kissed her.

The self-pitying aches and pains soon became unpleasant realities. She shifted from discomfort to acute pain. The muscles in her right leg felt as if they were playing Jacob's ladder.

A band of heat enveloped Elaine; the blue sky and green grass whirled.

"Oh, my God!" She dropped the reins, wildly grabbing for a more substantial hold.

"You do have a limited vocabulary," the lord grunted, lifting Elaine off of the horse and onto his lap.

Elaine sat rigid, legs draped over a hard thigh. The right side of her rump pressed against the front of the lord's saddle, her left side against the lord. His arm curved beneath her right breast, rhythmically pushing and rubbing in cadence with the stallion's movements.

She gulped air, forcing her heart back down from her throat, where it had leaped. Elaine had never been more frightened in her entire life. The adrenaline that had nowhere to go surged straight to her head.

Elaine twisted around to stare up into mocking blue eyes, beside herself with rage. "You stupid jer—"

Her teeth snapped shut. This PMS thing would be the death of her.

"Easy, my love." A pained eyebrow elevated. "I merely thought to make you more comfortable. Here." He grabbed her right leg beneath the flurry of velvet and petticoats. "Put your leg over my saddle; straightening it will help take out the cramp."

He relentlessly maneuvered her leg into position. She grabbed for the saddle, for him, for the horse's mane. By the time she was safely astride, the velvet dress, silk petticoats, and chemise had worked up around her hips, leaving as her sole padding the slippery drawers. Heat radiated from between his legs, her silk-clad derriere tucked firmly between there and the edge of the saddle. His upper body conformed to her back. She slid and bounced while he sat at perfect ease.

Elaine squirmed, trying to tuck her dress between her posterior and him. Failing that, she tried to pull it down over her legs, especially her right leg, where his hand still grasped her.

"Whoa!" The lord reared back. The stallion danced a quick disco number beneath him. "Some things first, I see. Starting with this."

He released her leg. The long, lethal hat pin slid through her hair. He neatly stuck it into the crown of the little riding hat and thrust the whole at her lap. Elaine instinctively accepted it. Wrapping an arm about her waist, he kicked the stallion into a gallop.

"But—" Elaine bit her lip. She had said quite enough for one day. She turned her head back to see the mare's fate.

"Jasper will be fine. She could find her way home hobbled and blindfolded. Hold still; I don't want to lose you."

Elaine held still. She didn't want to lose her, either. Really, she was learning to take orders quite nicely, she thought crossly. The perfect little *hausfrau*. Matthew would laugh.

No, he wouldn't.

Matthew had never assumed any differently.

Elaine had never given him any reason to assume differently.

Elaine had never given anybody any reason to assume differently.

The lord flattened his palm against Elaine's midriff. She sucked in her stomach before she remembered that this temporary body she was housed in didn't have anything to suck in. The hand moved an infinitesimal inch upward. She sucked in more deeply.

"Relax, Morrigan." The laughter was back in his voice, along with the carnality. "We have a long ride ahead of us."

Elaine had a feeling the purpose of this ride was about to be disclosed. Something long and hard pressed against her bottom. She squirmed anew, trying to put more distance between their bodies.

"Hold still, else I will begin to think you enjoy riding." His breath came hot and moist in her ear. He nuzzled the side of her neck. Something—his tongue—skimmed the skin between her ear and the collar of her dress. "But then again, maybe you do. You certainly liked last night, didn't you? Even if you did run scared in the end."

Elaine shook her head in denial.

The stallion slowed to a gentle gait.

Her right earlobe was trapped between sharp teeth, effectively curtailing her negation. Elaine heeded the warning. The threatening pain turned into wet flame. It darted inside her ear—no fears there; she had thoroughly cleaned both this morning.

The foraging tongue slurped free. He nibbled the taut cord running up the side of her neck. "When are you going to give up this farce and admit you like this, hmm? Perhaps I shall take your silence as agreement. Shall we test it?"

The hand inching across Elaine's abdomen toward her breast made a giant leap. Elaine's right hand instantly followed.

He located a nipple through the layers of velvet dress, satin corset, and silk chemise.

"There."

The individual cups in the corset were as soft and malleable and unprotective as her padded bras in the twentieth century. He rolled the nub between his thumb and forefinger. It instantly sprang to life.

"You have sinfully erotic breasts, sweetheart. You remember the nipples on the Indian woman last night. Long, full, like ripe figs. Like yours—yes, I saw you touch yourself; there's no need to deny it. You were quite right to make the comparison." He rolled and plucked, plucked and rolled until her nipple felt as if it were a miniature grenade ready to detonate. "Yes, exactly like yours," he said with satisfaction.

Did he have to keep throwing her actions back up into her face? Elaine dug her nails into the marauding hand. When they failed to elicit the desired result, she squirmed.

His breath rushed in and out of his mouth in time to her wriggles. Her ear was bombarded with moist heat. "That's it, Morrigan. Yes."

She stilled.

"Remove your hand, Morrigan. The ground is a long way down."

Elaine reluctantly complied.

He worked her nipple with single-minded intent, using his fingers and thumb to create a pulling motion, as if his digits were a mouth. Elaine repressed a moan as sensation rocketed into the pit of her stomach.

"A woman has three primary *marmas*. Her breasts and nipples are one. A man can bring a woman to ecstasy through the manipulation of her breasts. Would you like that?"

A mammary orgasm? The marriage manuals had never mentioned that. Elaine threw her head back against his shoulder and blindly stared at the wisp of cloud that swayed and bounced. Their bodies, which had been so at odds only moments before, moved as one with the horse's gait.

"There is a field of energy in your chest." He released the engorged nipple and massaged her solar plexus in small, concentric circles. A strange heat grew at the rotating pressure.

"I can make that energy divide so that it goes into each of your breasts"—he cupped her left breast, his fingers firm, his palm alternately flattening and brushing the painfully distended peak—"and flows out of your nipples."

The heat spread from deep inside the base of her breasts and spiraled upward.

He rimmed the tip of her ear with his tongue. "When that happens, sometimes, not always, a woman gives off a secretion, a white fluid that is sweet and is said to have a rejuvenating effect on the man. The Taoists call it 'White Snow.' "

He released her breast and squeezed her nipple. Hard.

Elaine cried out. Her very soul erupted from the sensitized crest.

"That's good, sweetheart," he whispered against her temple, her neck, in her ear. He inserted a finger inside the velvet bodice. She jerked beneath the exploring pressure. "You're not ready. It's all right. We'll practice. Would you like that? Would you like me to suckle from your breasts?"

Elaine quivered and gasped. Before she could comprehend his intent, he pulled his finger from between the buttons and ducked beneath her velvet skirt. His hand slid up her drawers, the rasp an inaudible sensation, toward the gaping crotch.

"What are you doing?" Every sensibility Elaine had ever possessed screamed in outrage. She dove for his wrist—too late; his hand was already there, touching, prodding the thick pad before sliding up and tracing its anchorage in the homemade sanitary belt. The fingers returned to explore the folded cloth that adhered to the cleft of her.

"A woman's *yoni* is also a primary *marmas*."

Elaine didn't care if her *yoni* was bologna. She ground her teeth, frantically tugging him away from that place where no man's hand should be at that time of the month.

"Shh, I know, I know. . . . Just let me touch you a little. Don't be ashamed, there's nothing to be ashamed about, this is perfectly normal, for you, for me. Tantric priests believe the flow from a woman magical, that it is at this time she is most pure. . . ."

Normal! Pure!

This was the nineteenth century. Nothing physiological was normal or pure in the nineteenth century. For heaven's sake, he was a Victorian! Why couldn't he act like one?

The prodding fingers located her beneath the folded cloth. He commenced a rhythmical pushing. Elaine tensed against the flood of unwilling sensation.

"The mixture of a man and a woman's sexual fluids is called *yoni-tattva*, and it is powerful, celebrated in great ceremonies, but only through the mixture of a man's semen with a woman's flow, *yoni-pushpa*, only then and through that can he attain liberation."

Elaine did not want this, Tantric approval or not. She did not want to be rendered this helpless, in this state, with him spouting alien practices. It was perversive, it was dangerous, and it made it all too easy to forget that her desire was hormonal and that the lord was Morrigan's husband and would not so much as glance at Elaine should he see her in the twentieth century.

"I want you to feel, Morrigan; I want you to burn and itch like the fires of hell. I want you to know what it's like to want so badly you feel like you will die if you go without. I want you to feel like that *now*."

The stallion jolted into a gallop. Elaine released his wrist and grasped the hand holding the reins at her waist. Their bodies were no longer synchronized. The lord pressed tight against the folded cloth, forcing her back and forth between his hand and the juncture of his thighs, pummeled with that which he made no effort to hide and his fingers, the horse doing the work, causing her to bounce and slide upon the titillating pressure.

Elaine's breath came harder, then more rapidly, gushing from her mouth. The energy that had dissipated from her nipples built three-fold in that other *marmas*. Straining backward against the hard muscles of his chest and stomach, she again reached out and clamped onto his wrist, to her everlasting shame pressing it harder against the folded cloth, harder, *harder*.

The green fields passed in a blur. The stallion's breath came in snorts.

"Say my name, Morrigan; say my name and I'll give you what you want, what you *need*." The wind whipped at his voice, no longer a hot, moist murmur, but a cool, detached command. "Say it!"

Yes, yes, she would say it, damn him, she would say anything he wanted, but she didn't know it! Elaine's heart felt as if it were going to explode; she couldn't catch adequate breath, she would pass out, he had to finish it, he had to finish it *now*—

"Poor Morrigan."

"Nooo! Don't stop!"

Elaine gripped his wrist harder in an effort to stay it. He brought his hand out from underneath her skirts and proceeded to pull her dress beneath and about her. She had to let go or lose her own hand or fall off of the horse.

Elaine squeezed her eyes shut, white with shock and sizzling arousal. He couldn't leave her like this. God, she was so close; he couldn't just leave her like this! *Not again! Damn him, not again!*

"Smile, Morrigan; the stable boys will think you didn't enjoy your ride."

Elaine opened her eyes, blinked. They were home? But—

The lord lithely dismounted, then lifted Elaine off of the horse, his hands hot and firm around her waist. They nearly met. He immediately released her.

"Give Shiva an extra ration of oats, Mickey. He more than earned it today. Jasper too, when she comes home."

A solitary clip-clop rang out in the crisp silence. Hot, callused fingers cupped her chin, pried it upward. Elaine recoiled at the rage glittering in his eyes.

"You feel it, do you not, Morrigan? A burning, *kama*. Good." He released her chin. "Perhaps next time you'll remember my name. *Charles.* You repeated it after the reverend during our wedding ceremony, but then, why should I expect you to remember a little thing like that when you've spent the entire year doing your damnedest to pretend that the marriage never took place?"

He patted her cheek. "Dress warmly for dinner. The weather is going to turn chill."

Pivoting, he walked away whistling. There was no sign of the anger that had riveted her but a second earlier.

The man was crazy—laughing at her one minute, seducing her the next, ranting with anger the next minute still. And now he whistled as if he had not a care in the world, as if he had not reduced her body to a living coil of electric arousal.

Elaine had not thought it possible to hate anyone more than she hated Hattie. She hated the lord more, hated him with all the passion he had aroused and not satisfied, and which now with her non-Tantric hang-ups she could not satisfy herself, even if she would do *that* to a body that wasn't her own.

A sharp object stabbed her fingers. Elaine looked down.

The little hat was a crumpled mass of velvet and feather. The lethal-looking hat pin stuck out from the wadded material; it was tinged with red. A drop of blood oozed from the palm of her hand.

So he thought the weather was going to turn chill? Elaine thought grimly.

Wrong.

Not chill.

Elaine limped toward the home that was no home but a scaled-down palace.

It was going to turn *arctic*.

Chapter
16

Elaine paced the Oriental carpet in a frenzy. In addition to the aches and pains accumulated from riding, a dull cramping had commenced in her lower abdomen. Menstrual cramping. Elaine had suffered the occasional back pain and bloating, but never really any cramps. And it was all *his* fault. If he hadn't worked her body into such turmoil, her muscles would not have knotted themselves into a carrick bend.

She pressed her hand against her left breast. The nipple felt bruised, swollen. As did that other spot where his fingers had pushed and thrust, knowing full well the purpose of the folded cloth there.

Her cheeks blazed. Somehow knowing his name made the embarrassment that much worse. This was the late nineteenth century, at the height of the Victorian era in which sex was the male or female gender, not what the male and female together performed. Where had the man gotten such peculiar ideas?

The muscles in her lower abdomen clenched.

With remembered desire.

With remembered frustration.

She would show the lord—Charles. He could not order her around and then treat her as if she were a part of a harem. She was his *wife*.

Poor Morrigan. No wonder the girl had locked herself up in her room with devotional transcriptions. If Elaine thought for one moment copying scripture would take her mind off of that ache that shouldn't be there, especially at this time of the month, she would take up the pen right now.

The dinner gong sounded. A second later a familiar scratch came from the door.

Would you like me to suckle from your breasts?

Elaine squeezed her eyes to shut out the image of the lord taking his dinner from her nipple.

The scratching came again.

Elaine opened her eyes, breath bated. After a few seconds she sensed the servant's withdrawal.

Her lungs filled with air.

It was done. Now Charles would know she was not joining him for dinner. Or for anything else.

Sometime later, another scratch sounded on the door.

A second passed, two, three.

The door handle turned.

Elaine's heartbeat revved in dreaded anticipation. The time of reckoning had arrived.

"Marm? Be ye in there, marm? The lord, he said I was to bring ye up yer dinner. He said as how ye wasn't feeling too good about now. Marm?"

"Katie!"

A laugh welled up in Elaine's stomach, chest too constricted to allow it to rise. She opened the door, her relief so great she could have hugged the girl, so great she opened her mouth to tell her what a wonder she was.

And promptly closed her mouth.

Would she ever be able to speak without having to carefully plan and execute her every word?

Would she ever be able to spend a day without fearing detection?

Unbidden, the ride came into mind.

She had not been afraid of detection then.

* * *

Elaine spent another restless night. The menstrual cramps remained a low, nagging discomfort. She tossed and turned in bed, climbed out of bed and walked and turned along the Oriental carpet, time and again repeating the process, in bed, out of bed, like a bizarre game of musical mattress.

Were this Chicago she could go to the medicine cabinet and take two aspirin.

Were this Chicago she wouldn't *need* to take two aspirin.

Were this Chicago she would stay in bed and cuddle up to Matthew's behind, a surefire cure for whatever ailed her.

The black swan.

Always alone.

How could the lord think that his wife did not remember his name?

Elaine crawled back into bed to warm her feet.

It was all his fault: numb toes, menstrual cramps, forbidden desire, *everything*.

Elaine woke to the dull pain of an overcast sun. It took her sleep-fogged mind several seconds to disassociate the pain from the day's gloom and doom. Understanding the true source of the pain did not help it one iota. So much for Nietzsche.

She groaned.

It was like someone's fist was tangled up inside her uterus, rhythmically clutching and twisting. The pressure finally brought her up and out of bed to the chamber pot behind the Japanese screen.

The folded cloth was saturated with blood. If it continued at that rate, she would bleed to death.

The fist clutched and twisted.

She *hoped* she would bleed to death. It would be far more merciful.

Elaine spent an hour doubled over, perched on the cold, hard edge of the porcelain. She had never experienced pain like this. Her left leg gave out, necessitating her removal from the chamber pot. Thirty minutes later she was back behind the screen.

"Marm?" Katie's voice was no less loud for coming from behind the locked door. "Marm, I have yer breakfast, marm."

Elaine gritted her teeth.

"Marm? Be ye awake, marm? Mayhap ye want I should come back later, marm?"

Elaine slowly drew her body up. Her legs felt like wooden slabs. She staggered to the door and turned the key.

Katie breezed inside the room.

" 'Tis a beasty day, marm; that it be. I brung ye a nice pot of hot tea and Cook's best crumpets with strawberry jam and a nice bowl of porridge with honey and cream and— Oh, marm, ye look awful!"

Elaine smiled, a baring of teeth.

"Be it . . ." Katie rubbed her lower stomach. "Ye know?"

Elaine's silence was answer enough. Katie grinned, heartlessly displaying dozens of white, even teeth.

"It sure be a good thing it only comes once a month, ain't it, marm? Me mum, she says there ain't nothing Eve could of done to make us womenfolk suffer the curse like we does. A hearty break-fast, just the thing to git ye back in spirits, and then we'll tuck ye back into bed nice and tight like a bedbug."

Katie set the tray down on the desk and moved the small ebony table to the front of the fireplace. She transferred the tray to the table, keeping up a steady stream of totally useless babble about Mum and Cook and God and womenfolk while she puttered about, rearranging the silverware, refolding the napkin, pouring a cup of tea, adding a dollop of cream to the porridge.

The fist within Elaine's uterus developed claws. Great, long, sharp claws. Freddy Krueger–type claws.

"And me mum says, 'Katie, me girl—' "

Elaine bolted for the screen.

"Marm? Marm, are ye gonna be sick? Ain't ye hungry? Me mum, she says—"

Elaine closed her eyes. She was beyond the precepts of mortal embarrassment. Let the stupid girl think what she would.

"Marm? D' ye need me help, marm? Should I . . . ?"

I will kill her if she comes back here, Elaine thought in that crys-tal clarity that sometimes occurs when the body is overridden with pain.

When Elaine came out from behind the screen, Katie looked like a wilted chrysanthemum.

"Marm? Are ye feeling any better now?"

Elaine was too exhausted and cramped over to even glare.

Katie cleared her throat. "Perhaps, marm, perhaps ye'd like to try a drop of laudanum?"

Elaine would try cyanide at this point.

"I'll be gone just a bit, marm, so's I can git the medicine fer ye. Me mum says as how a good cup of hot tea helps cure 'bout anything under the sun. I poured out the cold cup, marm. The pot, it should still be warm. I'll bring back some fresh with me!"

Katie skipped to the door. "Ye drink a cup of nice tea now while I be gone, marm, that'll help, mark me words; me mum gets the curse something awful, and she always says as how a nice cup of tea is just the thing!"

Elaine forced a swallow of the remedial tea past the knot in her throat. The warmth radiated from her stomach to her lower abdomen, not helping the pain, exactly, rather dispersing it. She finished the remainder and reached to pour another cup.

"You should have had dinner with me last night. I have it on the best of authority that those who follow the Tantrics do not suffer from the type of pain you are now suffering from, Morrigan."

Elaine dropped the teapot.

Long, tanned fingers caught the delicate china, resulting only in a slosh of liquid and not the splintering of glass that seemed even now to be tinkling inside her brain. The lord—Charles—righted the pot, rescued the napkin, and patted dry her resistant hand, then his.

"What a mess you are."

How could he face her with such sangfroid, having felt her menstrual heat?

"Come." He tugged her out of her chair. "Katie said you were in horrible pain and that you looked like you were about to fall over dead, and if something wasn't done you were going to become permanently attached to the chamber pot."

It was a good thing she was beyond mortification, Elaine thought dully; otherwise she would die of it right about now.

"Her words, not mine." The lord put an arm about Elaine's shoulders and led her to the ravaged bed. His body heat that normally sizzled and burned now made a comfortable haven. "At least, her words to Fritz. Of course, Fritz felt it his duty to warn me of my pending widower status. Sit down."

He bent over, grasped Elaine's feet, and swung them up onto the mattress, bending her legs to slide them beneath the twisted sheet. In a methodical, no-nonsense fashion he straightened the bedcovers and smoothed the silk and velvet over her body.

Elaine automatically lay back and allowed the ministration. Pain was debilitating. One should not fight until one had the strength to win. She sighed, slowly allowing her muscles to unclench.

The lord turned and left.

The clawed fist gave another vicious twist. Elaine bit her lips to keep from calling out to him. She blinked back tears of abandonment.

He returned within seconds, bearing her cup. The mattress dipped; Elaine's body slanted in the direction of his.

"I put a few drops of laudanum in your tea. I want you to drink it all. It will make you sleepy, but that is how it dulls the pain. Be a good girl, now, and don't fight it."

He put his left hand behind her neck and raised her head.

Elaine stared up into his face. He didn't look like a lord now. His eyes were dark and solemn, but not angry, or cold, or mocking. Or filled with the knowledge of her weak, traitorous sex. Or even worse, laughing with the knowledge of her weak, traitorous sex. The hand supporting her neck was warm, gentle in its strength.

Would it be so bad if he found out she was not who he thought she was? He had not liked Morrigan. Perhaps he would like Elaine better.

But who in their right mind would believe that she was anything more than a deranged Morrigan? Elaine was not so sure that even she believed it, was still not certain that she wouldn't wake up between permanent-press sheets.

The cup pressed against her lips, the porcelain cool and brittle.

Elaine closed her eyes and drank the tea. Her head was carefully lowered back onto the pillow. Warm fingers lingered infinitesimally against her nape. Almost immediately a pleasant, drifting sensation settled over her.

"That's right, sweetheart."

Why was he being so kind to a wife who supposedly did not even remember his name?

A light, warm caress grazed her cheek. The sweep of a finger? The touch of his lips? Elaine was too sleepy to tell, or care. It just felt so good to be cared for, she who for as long as she could remember had done all the caring.

The covers were pulled up to her face. Elaine stretched her neck, then used her chin to tuck the soft silk under rather than over it. Immediately, sure, warm fingers were there to do the job for her. She smiled, allowing the cocoonlike darkness to swallow the last of the pain.

"Yes. Go to sleep. You'll feel better when you wake up."

A frown marred Elaine's forehead; she suddenly struggled to pull out of the black cocoon. Feel better when she woke up . . . That meant she'd be back in the twentieth century, back between permanent-press sheets.

Back with Matthew.

She forced her eyes open and anxiously looked up, seeing not Matthew, but: "Charles . . ."

Elaine heard her voice as if it came from a long distance. It sounded slurred.

"That's right, love."

Warm, callused fingers smoothed away Elaine's frown, rhythmically stroked her hair back off her forehead. Her eyes drifted shut. The sensation grew lighter, and lighter, until it and her head were floating away, up, up, up. . . .

"Yes, close your eyes and go to sleep. Don't worry. I won't allow you to suffer this again. If the Tantric doesn't help, a baby will. And I plan on filling that little belly of yours just as soon as humanly possible."

Typical male. As if getting pregnant solved anything. What about when the nine months were over? She'd still be having periods.

A soft laugh followed her down into the pain-free abyss.

Damon had once said that women uttered the strangest things when under the influence of anesthesia. Morrigan had proved him right.

Charles stared down at his sleeping wife. She looked deceptively young and defenseless, the color that had glowed in her cheeks yesterday drained from pain and laudanum.

So his little wife was not quite as ignorant as he had thought. She realized that pregnancy was a state of the body, and that a woman's monthly courses temporarily ceased, only to resume nine months later. He wondered where she had picked up the details. As far as he could remember, that part of creation had been excluded from Genesis.

Morrigan had called her monthly course a "period." Succinct. To the point. The end of a cycle.

Charles . . .

He reviewed the surge of pure rage he had felt when she did not cry out his name yesterday, perched on the threshold of release. There had been only one conclusion. In their entire year of marriage she had addressed him solely as "my lord." Morrigan did not cry his name at her moment of need because she did not *know* his name.

It had been a painful slap in the face, realizing his wife had forgotten his name the moment he had pledged all of his worldly goods to her. It had forced home the fact that she had lost even his ring, a symbol of his earthly commitment, the moment she had come to him with nothing more than the wool on her back and a servant that would be better contained in the kennels.

But now she wore his ring.

And whispered his name.

The crescent-shaped marks on the back of his hand belied her defenselessness.

He touched the fading bruise on her cheek. She snuggled against his finger.

Charles felt the hurt dissipate, replaced instead by the memory of her quivering in his arms, experiencing the small climax.

"M' lord?"

Charles turned and brought his finger up to his lips to indicate silence. Carefully he eased off the bed and motioned the maid outside.

Elaine awakened with a gasp. Hazy, nightmarish images clamored inside her brain. Of needles. Coffin-shaped machines. White-gowned people. Sooty air and racing lights. An explosion of sparks. Little aftershocks tingled through her body, as if she had come into contact with a live electrical wire. The dream emotions lingered: a touch of pain, a sweep of depression. And loneliness so vast it brought an ache to her chest.

Gradually she became aware of a presence near the bed. Elaine knew without turning her head that she was not alone, the lord's caressing voice a timeless loop in memory. The loneliness eased.

"There ye be, marm! I was just wondering when ye was gonna join the rest of us."

Silly, Elaine thought, ignoring the sting of pooling tears. Why should Charles sit with an ailing wife? Matthew had been acutely uncomfortable on those few occasions when she had succumbed to the flu. Why would the lord be any different?

Not that she wanted him to be any different. How could she expect sympathy from a man who thought undergoing the pains of childbirth a solution to menstrual pain? *Stupid barbarian.* Stupid *ignorant* barbarian. Fill her with his baby indeed! As if she were some sort of machine in need of spermatic fuel.

Elaine rolled onto her side where Charles had sat and brought her legs up to her stomach. It still hurt there inside her. A dull headache pounded between her eyes. Her mouth felt drier than autumn leaves.

A rustle of cloth sounded beside the bed.

"His lordship, he said as how I was to give ye this if ye woke up and ye was still in pain. Would you like it, marm?"

Elaine blindly stuck out her hand. A warm cup was placed within it. She raised her head high enough to gulp down its contents—too late, it was already halfway down her throat when her eyelids shot open and she sat up in bed.

My God, the stuff was vile! Was he trying to poison her?

"His lordship, he had it sent all the way from Devonshire, he did. Dr. Damon—that be his lordship's friend, but I guess ye know that—said as how it'd be better fer ye than the laudanum. I had an uncle, he got a taste fer laudanum, got struck by lightning one night 'cause he couldn't wait till the storm was over to visit the chemist, he was that stuck on it. Can I get ye some supper, marm? Would ye like to eat something?"

Elaine shook her head and lay back down. No wonder she felt so drained. And depressed. And lonely. She had ingested a narcotic. In addition to which, she was probably bleeding to death. She really should get up and change the folded cloth before ruining the bed-covers.

Good old Elaine, practical to the bitter end.

What did it matter if she ruined the covers; the lord could afford a different set of sheets three hundred and sixty-five days a year. He was not like Matthew. She and Matthew had had to work for what they had. Had had to work to preserve what they had. The lord was rich by dint of birth.

And brutality.

He probably had a factory employed with six-year-old children who worked from morning to night.

Elaine curled up into a fetal ball. She hurt. She shouldn't have to worry about mundane trivia like ruined sheets. He probably *wished* she would worry and suffer.

"Well, ye just rest now, marm. His lordship, he said I should stay with ye tonight, so's anytime ye want something, ye just yell out; I'll be here."

Elaine did not want a sentinel, especially a Katie sentinel. She shook her head and pointed toward the door.

"Oh, no, marm, I couldn't leave ye! Why, he'd let me go fer sure, he would, and I got me mum and da and five young ones to help feed and shoe!"

As if the "young ones" were a passel of horses. No wonder Katie could conveniently forget about them when the task set for her proved to be onerous. Elaine closed her eyes and counted to ten. By the time the last number rolled into her mind, she was halfway asleep. By the time she opened her mouth to tell Katie she didn't care if the whole herd of them starved, "his lordship" included, she *was* asleep.

Chapter

17

"M' lord," Katie spoke from the contortion of a deep curtsy. "M' lord, ye was wanting me to tell ye 'bout m' lady."

Charles sighed, wondering what exaggerated tales Fritz had been telling the comely little maid that she should treat him somewhat like a cross between a *pasha* and a cobra these last few days. Her white mobcap was starkly illuminated in the bright gleam of sunshine, the face beneath a shadow of a nose, the black uniform a crinkled circle upon the library carpet. Fingers softly thrumming the desktop, he idly speculated upon how long she could remain sunk in such an uncomfortable-looking position. Finally, "Katie, I would better understand you if you spoke to me, rather than to the floor. I am not the queen, you know. You may stand upright in my presence."

Katie flushed. "Yes, m' lord." She straightened with some difficulty.

Charles restrained a grin, observing the awkward accent. Had the maid stayed in the curtsy another minute, like as not she would have been unable to straighten up at all, whereupon he would have had to call Fritz to resurrect the crippled beauty, since he himself had a hard-and-fast rule never to . . . resurrect his own servants.

"You have news for me?" he gently asked.

"Yes, m' lord." Katie's flushed face turned a dark crimson, an alarming contrast against the white mobcap. She fixed her gaze on the desk and commenced wringing her apron, then, realizing what she was about, abandoned the starched white cloth for the more resilient texture of her fingers.

Charles allowed the maid to mangle her fingers for several seconds before giving expression to his rapidly rising impatience. "Well?"

"It be m' lady, sir. She . . . she's ended her curse."

Deep satisfaction welled up inside Charles's chest, immediately followed by a lower welling, a welling that had for the last few days been damn nigh intolerable.

He only hoped absence had made Morrigan's—heart—grow fonder, as he had not visited her since that day she had been doubled over with pain. The truth was, he had not trusted himself to be with her until she was over her monthly flow. While he himself was not particularly fastidious, he felt he had subjected his wife to enough trauma in one week. She had almost leaped off the horse when he had touched the cloth between her legs. Though judging by her later reactions, it would not take much to overcome her inhibitions.

Meanwhile, it was not as if he had neglected her entirely. On the contrary, he had carefully chosen reading material to entertain her during her confinement.

His grin widened, part deviltry, pure anticipation.

"Be that all, m' lord?"

Charles frowned. "Until I tell you otherwise, Katie, I want you to sleep in milady's bedchamber."

It had just occurred to him that, with Morrigan's history of masturbation, she might not become as frustrated as he would like unless the opportunity was curtailed. Once he had her in his bed, she could shag to her heart's content—provided, of course, she had the energy. Indeed, there was something highly arousing in watching a woman excite herself.

"But m' lord—"

Katie's pretty little face screwed up in concentration. Charles lazily wondered whether she looked like that when Fritz tupped her. Alack, poker face that Fritz was, he would never know.

"If I should do *that*, what ever shall I tell m' lady? I mean, she didn't like it none when I stayed with her that first night. She tried to get me to go but I didn't 'cause ye told me to stay with her and so I did. But I don't think she's going to like me sleeping there with her every night."

So much for the *pasha* reputation. The *pashas* Charles knew would whack off the maid's head for questioning an order. Then they would cut out her tongue for impertinence.

"Tell milady that if she has any questions regarding my orders that she should speak to me directly."

The little face cleared up. Katie dared meet the lordship's gaze. Divining the speculation in his eyes, she flushed an even darker crimson.

Charles briefly wondered if *all* of her turned that burning red. Morrigan had exhibited the same aptitude. He would be delighted to test the theory on his wife.

"Yes, m' lord," the maid mumbled, fixedly staring at the desk.

"Very well, Katie, you may go."

Katie sank into a clumsy curtsy, rose, and turned.

The bright noonday sun streamed through the open French doors. The back of his head was pleasantly warm from the penetrating rays. Birds chattered in the garden outside the library. The weather this spring was truly exceptional. It would be a shame not to take advantage of it.

Charles reached for writing materials, simultaneously saying, "No, wait! I want you to give this note to your mistress."

Katie returned to the desk and waited patiently while Charles scribbled a message. He sat back; a gleam appeared in his eyes. Signing the note with a flourish, he waved it for a minute to dry it, then folded it and handed it to the maid. Katie accepted the folded paper with another curtsy. She turned and fled the library.

As if afraid of being resurrected.

What *had* Fritz been telling her?

A gleam of gold riveted Charles's attention. His gaze rested thoughtfully on the inlaid box that housed the pillow book. Morrigan had been so very close that night, so incredibly hot and wet and eager for more. His fingers had been soaked with her feminine essence, shielded though they had been by the silk of her nightgown. And if she had been that hot then, she should be a veritable tigress now. More than one mistress had claimed their libidos were especially strong after their monthly flow. What with the books he had delivered to her room, Morrigan should jump into his net as surely as a spawning salmon.

He closed his eyes and drew in a deep breath, striving to control his burgeoning groin, striving to instill some patience. It was not yet time. But it was so *hard*.

His eyes snapped open; a grin hitched up the corners of his mouth. Hard in more ways than one. But if it was hard for him, he would make it very, very wet for her.

And she would beg.

Perhaps . . .

Yes, why not?

He would make her beg *today*.

" 'Dead flies cause the ointment of the apothecary to send forth a stinking savour: so doth a little folly him that is in reputation for wisdom and honour.'

" 'A wise man's heart is at the right hand, but a fool's heart at his left.'

" 'Yea, also, when he that is a fool walketh by the way, his wisdom faileth him, and he saith to every one that he is a fool.' "

Elaine closed the Bible with a disgusted plop. It made very dry reading material.

She moved to stand up. Her right foot slammed into the books piled beneath the desk. The lord had quite nicely supplied her with a whole miniature library. Of erotica. Although she did question whether the Marquis de Sade rightfully belonged in that category. If he considered it such, that Tantric business was the most harmless of his perversions, and reinforced her decision to stay safely locked in her room.

She reached down and restacked the books. Her fingers lingered over a leather-bound manuscript that went under the weighty title of *The Kama Sutra of Vatsyayana, Translated from the Sanscrit. In Seven Parts, with Preface, Introduction and Concluding Remarks*. Dated 1883, it had the most current copyright.

Restlessly she straightened and walked to open the French doors. She had been in Morrigan's body now for twelve days. Twelve days going on a lifetime, and the only thing she knew with any degree of certainty was that the year was no earlier than 1883. And that Morrigan had an English accent, was left-handed, and suffered from severe menstrual cramps. And that her husband's name was Charles. Who could be kind. And persistent. And who had an extensive knowledge of Tantric practices.

At least she was free now of the chains of folded and knotted cloths. Though, strictly speaking, she had been free of those these last three days, due to the box that had been delivered to her room, filled with several satin and elastic sanitary belts and a few dozen sanitary pads made out of wool and lavender-scented cotton.

She stepped out onto the balcony. The morning was passing into noon. It was too quiet. She didn't belong here.

Elaine closed her eyes, picturing herself in the twentieth century at this time of day. But her mind drew a blank. Desperately she counted back the days. She had gone to sleep Sunday night, thereby awakening Monday morning. That would mean that it was Friday, there in the twentieth century.

What upcoming events had she posted on her calendar? For work? For home?

A scratch came from the main door.

Elaine's eyelids flew open. She didn't have any scheduled events, aside from work. Matthew worked from sunup to sundown, Monday through Saturday, those last two months before tax day. Hundreds, perhaps thousands of systems analysts roamed the streets of Chicago, any one of them more than eager and capable of filling her position.

There was no one who would miss her, no one who would more than in passing notice her absence. In the event Morrigan had been transmigrated into Elaine's body, she doubted if Matthew would even notice anything odd.

"Marm, I got something fer ye."

She would be just as alone in the twentieth century as she was here, she thought moodily.

The doorknob rattled. "Can I come in, marm?"

As if she had a choice. Elaine slowly traversed the distance between the balcony and the main door. She turned the key.

Katie burst through the door. Dropping into a curtsy, she held out a folded piece of paper.

My Lady,

Cook has prepared a large picnic hamper. And although Fritz swears that fresh air is bad for the digestion, I believe he would enjoy a little time with your Katie. Meet me in the library. I shall expect you forthwith.

Your Husband

Elaine reread the note. *I shall expect you forthwith.* Then she studied for long seconds the closing. She turned toward the balcony. The sun was warm with the promise of summer. The giant oaks dotting the grounds stretched their limbs toward the cloudless sky. She could almost hear the grass growing, it was so vivid a green.

A picnic.

It had been so many years since she had been on a picnic.

She stared at the wrought-iron bench, sorting through her life in the twentieth century.

Had she ever been on a bona fide picnic? Her mother, deceased now for several years—no, that wasn't true; her mother hadn't even been born yet, certainly a more cheering thought than imagining her cancer-ridden body filled with formaldehyde and buried beneath a pile of mud and slush—had been allergic to bees, and since bees flocked around food, they had always eaten indoors. Matthew preferred his summer meals sitting at a table in air-conditioned comfort.

No, she had never been on a picnic.

Another first.

"Katie, what day is this?"

"Why, it be Tuesday, marm."

Smiling suddenly, feeling absurdly young for a thirty-nine-year-old matron, Elaine pointed to the sun-dappled lawn. "It"—Charles used contractions haphazardly, she had best try to eliminate them altogether—"is a beautiful day. We are going on a picnic."

"It be ever so fine a day, marm!" Katie agreed exuberantly. "An outing! Fancy that!"

Inferring that *outing* was another word for picnic, Elaine murmured, "Yes." She strode toward the door, hardly noticing the limp.

"Ye'll need a shawl, marm! It be mighty fine out, but it do get to be a bit chill in the shade."

Elaine waited impatiently while Katie rummaged in the armoire. How quickly she was becoming used to having someone wait on her hand and foot. She forced a smile when Katie placed a light, woolen shawl over her shoulders. It was dyed a deep rose, a perfect complement to the pale rose dress she wore. Briefly she wondered if she should change into something with a shorter train, but Katie was the lady's maid, and if she didn't find anything amiss, then it must be suitable. Gesturing that Katie follow her, Elaine made her way to the library.

Charles was standing with his back to the door, dressed in leather breeches, knee-high boots, and a faded blue jacket with tails. His hair blazed reddish gold in the sunlight.

A slight misgiving fluttered in Elaine's stomach. He was so very attractive. She really had no business socializing with him. He was, after all, Morrigan's husband. And she was Matthew's wife.

The lord slowly turned away from the French doors, almost as if he felt her unease. Hot color flooded Elaine's cheeks. His eyes positively gleamed with carnality, the firsthand knowledge of her sensuality. She remembered the taste of him, part brandy, all male.

"Thank you, Katie. You may go now."

"But—"

"But m' lady said—"

Elaine and Katie spoke simultaneously, one filled with disappointment, the other with alarm.

"I said you may go, Katie."

"Yes, m' lord."

Elaine turned toward the curtsying maid, reached out to detain her. The long white fingers were enveloped in a large, tanned hand. Pure sensation shot up the flesh that was Elaine's but not Elaine's. How had he crossed the room so quickly? she wondered.

Katie slipped through the door, leaving Elaine and Charles alone. Together.

She knew his name now. Should he start utilizing that Tantric stuff, she also knew she would use it.

Elaine wrenched her hand aside, but the lord's grip remained firm. She stared up at him accusingly. The note had said Fritz and Katie would accompany them! her eyes screamed. But the lord's eyes remained watching, slightly mocking, as if daring her to voice her opinion.

"Come, I have the perfect spot for a picnic. It isn't far, so you should be able to walk it comfortably. By the by, did I tell you how very fetching you look? No? How shameless of me. I promise I shall not further neglect you."

Elaine scowled. She'd look fetching to him until she did something he didn't like; then she'd be back to having a scrawny arse. Elaine allowed her hand to be drawn into the crook of his arm.

Heat traveled up her arm and through her shoulder. She looked up into Charles's eyes; they gleamed that sultry Mediterranean blue. His lips curved; she found herself reciprocating his smile. His right eyelid drooped. Before Elaine could stop herself, she winked back, then almost laughed aloud at the look of surprise on his face.

The butler waited at the massive front door; he diligently offered a large hamper. The lord jovially accepted the woven basket. Shoulders companionably rubbing, Elaine and Charles stepped outside into the waiting sunshine.

A coach rattled up the drive, followed by a plume of dust as long as the eyes could see. Six sweating horses stopped at the foot of the steps with a jingle of harnesses and a belligerent "Whoa, there, whoa, I say!"

The plume of dust enveloped the coach, then the stairs. Elaine coughed. Charles handed her a large white linen handkerchief. She pressed it to her nose.

One of the two men riding in the driver's box hopped down. He disappeared. The dust abruptly dispersed. He reappeared, holding open the door to the coach.

The wooden vehicle heaved. A short, fat, middle-aged lady descended. She was followed by two younger females, though no less fat, each one shorter than the next, like one of those Russian dolls in which a whole family was housed, one inside the other. A fat, middle-aged man carrying a stout cane followed next, shorter yet. He had bristly side whiskers. A disproportionately small bowler hat was perched on top of his head.

"My lord!" The middle aged woman briefly curtsied. Rising, she beckoned behind her. "Mary! Prudence! Make your curtsies!"

The two younger females stepped forward and curtsied. Elaine judged them to be well into their twenties. They straightened together, as if on cue. Mother and daughters stood side by side, three pairs of impressively large chests puffed forward like overgrown pouter pigeons.

Indeed, they were rather colored like pigeons, too, Elaine thought with a spurt of amusement, all gray and white with bows of pale lavender tied beneath their chins. The gathered material with its drapery cords and tassels that limply padded Elaine's hips and derriere was somehow pulled up and back on their dresses, so that their tail ends reared up like bird feathers.

"Madam."

Charles's voice was frigid. Elaine brought the handkerchief down from her face and glanced upward. His face was back to being carved out of stone, the blue eyes gelid.

"My lord," the middle-aged woman said sourly. "We have come to right the great wrong done to you. At the time, it seemed for the best, but in light of recent circumstances, we shall do our Christian duty as we should have done in the beginning and relieve you of your onerous burden."

The large, rather worn-looking coach suddenly gave a massive lurch, swayed back and forth. The six sweating horses nickered, shied. They took a step backward, then forward.

"Whoa—I says whoa there, Gurty, hold there, Bonie!" The coachman holding the reins jerked back on the leather straps, forcefully controlling the startled horses.

The warm, sunny day cooled and dimmed. The open expanse of clear blue sky shrank to claustrophobic dimensions. All in the space of a heartbeat.

Hattie stepped down from the coach, a hungry black crow amid four fat pigeons. Her small, rheumy eyes glared triumphantly beneath the brim of a dust-covered bonnet, promising a thousand retributions.

Chapter
18

Charles felt the inevitable hitch of his lip upward to his right cheek. His anger at having his picnic and seduction ruined focused on the black-clad figure who had been the bane of his existence for the last year. He opened his mouth to tell Morrigan's relatives exactly where and whom they could visit. The press of a warm body forestalled his words. He glanced down at Morrigan.

His wife's face was white; her ripe red lips appeared faintly blue, as if the breath had been squeezed out of her. Her eyes were dull and flat. Charles remembered how they had sparkled moments earlier and wanted to commit murder. He put his arm around her thin shoulders. It was extremely gratifying to feel her burrow more closely against him.

"Come, Morrigan, I see your manners have not improved," Emily Boleigh said. "Give your aunt a kiss."

Charles gave his wife a reassuring squeeze. "Morrigan is recovering from the putrid throat. It would be best for all if contact was avoided."

"I see you have not yet learned my niece's ways, my lord. Never mind. We can discuss that later. Be so kind as to have your servants direct our luggage to our rooms. My coachman and groom will care for the horses, but they, too, will require accommodation. I am sure our rooms are already prepared, but I hope it will not be too much of an inconvenience to place Mr. Boleigh on the ground floor. As you can see, he is not—"

"I do not know what you are talking about, Mrs. Boleigh. I did not know of your visit, so there are no rooms prepared."

He tightened his arm around Morrigan's shoulders. "Perhaps you did not hear me when I told you that Morrigan is recovering from the putrid throat. I would not wish to expose you or your family to the malady. There is an inn some few miles down the road; you may tell the innkeeper that I sent you. When Morrigan is fully recovered, perhaps then you can spare the time to visit us."

Mrs. Boleigh stared insolently at the wicker basket in Charles's right hand, then at Morrigan, lingering on the dress, the limp drape of cloth and the excessive trail of train. Hattie nodded, as if confirming some particularly heinous sin.

His wife, Charles knew, looked like a young girl dressed up in her big sister's clothes. That fact had been forcefully brought home to him when she had met him in the library earlier. His only excuse for not having noticed the lack of bustle necessary for contemporary fashion was that he had seen her in only three of the trousseau dresses prior to today. That second night after he had returned from his property inspections, at which time she had been sitting at the dining room table when he had arrived (and afterward he had been too far gone in his cups to even care, had he noticed), and the day they had gone horseback riding, first that morning, again at which time she had been sitting for the most part, and then in the riding habit, which was not worn with a bustle to begin with. He gritted his teeth at the contempt in Mrs. Boleigh's eyes, vowing to educate Katie in a hurry about a lady's toilette. He would not expose his wife's budding sensitivities to unnecessary provocation.

"I see," Mrs. Boleigh said. "Pray forgive us. We sent word through the post informing you of our impending arrival, but I see that we preceded the letter. We were alarmed at Hattie's report, and wished to ascertain Morrigan's condition for ourselves as soon as possible. I might add that you do no good by championing the girl."

Charles stared at Morrigan's aunt with all of the hauteur inbred in twelve generations of aristocracy. "Mrs. Boleigh, I am going to try to be civil about this, as you are Morrigan's only living relatives. First, I do not take kindly to unexpected visitors. Secondly, I deeply resent the insinuations you are making in regard to my wife. And thirdly, it really is none of your damned business how I treat my wife. Furthermore, I will not allow that malevolent Scottish bitch inside my home. I hope I make myself clear?"

Mrs. Boleigh wrathfully turned to her husband. "I told you it would be useless to attempt to persuade this heathen of his Christian duty. He and Morrigan are one of a kind; good riddance to them, I say!"

"My dear," Mr. Boleigh said placidly, "his lordship speaks in ignorance."

Charles ground his teeth. The basket handle crunched inside his fist.

"When we explain to him the atrocities that Morrigan has committed, he will perforce see what a dangerous, unhinged individual she is," the bewhiskered man said. "Meanwhile—"

"Meanwhile, I would strongly suggest you get in that outdated trap of yours and get the hell off my property before I assist with your departure. Higgins!" Charles called for the butler, who hovered near the door. "Higgins, have a few footmen assist these—"

Morrigan's uncle slumped to his knees, one hand pressing to his heart.

"My lord! My lord, now you've done it! You've killed him!" Mrs. Boleigh screamed.

Charles would have ignored the older man's collapse, except that the face between those ridiculous side whiskers was a most alarming shade of blue. No one, he thought regretfully, could fake a blue face.

Son of a bitch.

"Higgins, call a footman to assist Mr. Boleigh to the green bedchamber. Send a groom for a local physician. Have the—mesdames'—luggage carried upstairs. The housekeeper will assign bedchambers. Hattie may stay in the attic in her old room. Under no circumstances is she to leave that room. Be sure to alert the cook of our guests. And take this."

The stately butler reached for the crushed hamper handle.

Charles sighed. "It would appear that my lady and I will not be going on a picnic after all." Or doing any of the delightful things a picnic *par deux* invited.

Elaine stared dumbly at the wire cage Katie had dragged from the wardrobe. The maid's face was flushed; her eyes shot daggers.

"Ye should of told me, marm. How was I to know ye ladies hid yerselves inside these here 'traptions? Cook, she didn't know 'bout no bustles. Cook said the old mistress—gone and died before me time, bless her soul—she wore starched muslin. Cook always said as what's good enough fer her ladyship be good enough fer us. How was I to know?"

Elaine blinked.

"The lord, he told me I was to get ye properly dressed fer dinner. Ye're to wear the cream silk. Be there something else ye're forgitting to tell me now?"

Elaine found herself seated in front of the dressing table. Katie twisted the mane of long black hair up on top of Elaine's head.

"Be this grand enough fer yer ladyship, or should ye be giving me d'rections fer this, too?"

Elaine submitted to the maid's ministrations, standing, raising her arms, sitting, lifting her feet, standing again, turning, holding her breath, all the while her brain feverishly trying to assimilate the fact that Morrigan had an aunt, an uncle, and two cousins. In this house. Under the same roof. And that they had brought with them Hattie. And that they seemed to have no doubt whatsoever that she—Morrigan—was already unhinged.

"Very good, Katie."

The lord's voice came from behind, near the connecting door. Katie jerked to attention. Elaine half expected her to salute.

"The train is too full. It should hug the shape of milady's figure. There are tapes in the back of the dress. Tie them tighter, Katie."

Katie threw "milady" an indignant glare before disappearing behind her. Elaine felt a stir of cool air, a lightening sensation.

"Well, I'll be!"

The muffled exclamation came from underneath Elaine's dress. She dug her nails into the palms of her hands.

"Do you need help, Katie?"

"Nary a bit, m' lord!" The maid's hollow voice sounded cheerful and distressingly close. "I'll have her tied all nice and tight in just a second."

"Not too tight, Katie," Charles murmured silkily. "We don't want her ladyship to be too tight."

Hot color inundated Elaine's face and neck. She remembered the penetration of his finger, the smooth abrasion of silk, painfully aware that the man who stood behind her knew in intimate detail just exactly how tight she was, hoping the girl tightening the tapes was oblivious of the double entendre.

Katie re-emerged from underneath Elaine's skirts. She pulled and twitched at the back of the dress.

"Excellent. You learn quickly, Katie."

Elaine could hear the rustle of Katie's skirts descend in a curtsy. "Thank ye, m' lord. I remember what ye told me. I'll be here, m' lord."

"I do not doubt it. Morrigan?"

A black-clad arm reached out and around. Elaine's hand was firmly grasped and pulled through the crook of an elbow, the long fingers startlingly white against the black sleeve. Morrigan's fingers. Not Elaine's.

They would know.

How could members of Morrigan's family, who had probably been around the girl off and on all of her life, not know that something was wrong?

Elaine allowed herself to be led from her room, down the hallway, down the red-carpeted stairs, the bustle an unfamiliar weight, Charles's body an all-too-familiar warmth. Elaine fought the craven urge to turn tail and run back to her room. At the bottom of the steps a footman sprang forward and threw open the pair of doors to the drawing room.

". . . living in India surrounded by heathens. Why, the man

spurns Christian progress—" Mrs. Boleigh's voice cannonaded off the high ceiling inside the blue-and-silver room, "—he has no gas!"

Elaine sputtered. The Boleigh females sat neatly aligned on a brocade divan. At the sound, Prudence—or was it Mary?—elbowed her mother.

"My lord!" Undaunted, Mrs. Boleigh swiveled her head in the direction of the double doors. "A word with you—"

"Later," the lord said. His blue eyes danced in the candlelight. "I'm sure you must be famished after your long journey." He gestured toward the hallway behind him. "Ladies?"

Mrs. Boleigh stood. Gone was the pouter pigeon; in its place she jutted forward in a green-and-white-striped dress like the prow of a ship. The two daughters filed behind her. They wore embroidered pink dresses that would have been better suited for a pair of twelve-year-olds. Their bustles made their hips and behinds look three times larger than what they hopefully were.

In the dining room Charles led Elaine to the end of the table. He pulled out her chair. "There is an art to this," he said softly. "Sit on the edge of the seat."

Elaine did as he instructed. The wire rings surrounding the cage collapsed; it was like sitting on a giant Slinky.

Charles seated Mrs. Boleigh on Elaine's left, at the center of the table, directly behind the blazing fireplace. A footman seated the two daughters across from their mother. Charles took his own seat at the far end of the table, thirty feet opposite Elaine. He disappeared behind the candelabras and the two enormous centerpieces of fresh flowers.

Elaine bit her lip. She felt as though she had wandered into a sitcom parodying the habits of English royalty. Elaine automatically draped her napkin across her lap. She need only get through this evening. Please God, don't let her burst into hysterics.

"Morrigan, sit up straight!"

Elaine jumped. Mrs. Boleigh's voice sounded as if it had been shouted through a bullhorn.

"No, no," Mrs. Boleigh waved her spoon at the footman approaching Elaine. "Pass on the soup. Morrigan is not to have rich foods, my lord. Her disposition is too easily agitated."

The footman looked in the direction of the lord.

"Mrs. Boleigh." Charles's disembodied voice was cool and distant. "You are our guest. We are your hosts. Pray let us behave accordingly."

The footman ladled a carrot-colored liquid into Elaine's bowl. She picked up her wineglass—no, she mustn't forget Morrigan was left-handed. Charles suddenly appeared, leaning to the left of the flowers and candelabras. He saluted her with his wineglass.

Fish followed the soup. "Morrigan, do not stuff your mouth; it is most unbecoming!"

A flake of white meat arched through the fifteen feet of air that separated Elaine and Mrs. Boleigh. It landed in Elaine's plate. She put down her fork.

"Morrigan, do not pick at your food! You should thank God for His bountifulness."

Creamed potatoes and peas followed the fish. Elaine raised her wineglass, on her third refill.

"Morrigan, wine is the beverage of the devil!" A round green pellet burst out of Mrs. Boleigh's mouth. It shot into Elaine's glass. "Regard my girls. You would do well to emulate your cousins."

The two girls promptly ceased stuffing their faces and picked up their water goblets. Malicious triumph shone from their eyes—they the cosseted daughters, Morrigan the fostered intruder.

At last the footman placed a bowl of fruit and nuts on the table, signaling the meal had ended. Charles rose above the flowers and candelabras.

"I believe it is time for that talk now, Mrs. Boleigh. Shall we?"

Mrs. Boleigh padded her mouth with her napkin. "Certainly, my lord. Girls."

Mrs. Boleigh led the way to the blue-and-silver drawing room. Elaine and Charles followed behind the two girls. Mrs. Boleigh looked neither left nor right when she passed the alcove with the nude statue. The two daughters openly goggled, as if they had never before seen the body of a naked female.

Once in the blue-and-silver room, Mrs. Boleigh turned her nose up at Elaine. "In private, if you please, my lord!"

Charles lazily strode toward a glass cabinet. "What is said in the presence of man and wife *is* private, Mrs. Boleigh. Therefore, I would suggest that you send your daughters to their rooms. An after-dinner drink, ladies?"

Mrs. Boleigh's lips compressed. Her spine rigid, she sat down; her two daughters, their eyes shining, lined up on the divan beside her. "No, thank you, my lord."

Elaine perched on the edge of the love seat opposite the divan. Charles, holding two glasses, sat down beside her, his leg pressing warmly against her hip. He leaned forward. She gratefully accepted the stemmed glass that he placed in her hand.

He relaxed against the back of the love seat. "You may speak now, Mrs. Boleigh."

"My lord!"

Elaine instinctively moved to protect her drink. Charles lifted her left hand, which had covered the top of her glass, and placed it onto his thigh. He played with the wedding band, his fingers warm and hard, the muscles beneath the tight black pants equally warm and hard.

Elaine tensed, too late realizing her mistake—she had accepted the glass with her right hand. Morrigan's aunt, who had been glaring at the lord's brandy snifter, glared at the lord's thigh. Ignoring the warning bells that told her to remove her hand, Elaine raised her glass to her lips. Mrs. Boleigh's glare riveted on to the cordial.

"Humph!"

The woman was as predictable as a high school play. Elaine bit her lip to hold back the laughter welling up inside her chest. There was nothing remotely funny about Morrigan's relatives.

Elaine remembered reading once that the body produced a morphinelike chemical under stress. She was probably higher than a kite—had been since awakening in this time, and just hadn't known it.

She glanced at the lord. His gaze locked upon her mouth, where she bit down. Parting her lips, she licked away the sticky sweet drop of cordial.

The blue eyes narrowed, the blaze in them leaping to a roaring conflagration. His hand crushed her fingers into his thigh.

"Well, I never! Girls, you will leave this room at once, do you hear? At once, I say!"

The two girls—tittered, there was no other word for it—and stood. They curtsied prettily, faces demurely downcast. "I want to thank you for a most enjoyable evening, Lord Arlcotte," Prudence—or was it Mary?—simpered. "We want you to know that you will be in our prayers tonight. You, too, Cousin Morrigan. We know that you suffer from an affliction and cannot help being what you are."

The lord looked every bit as taken aback as Elaine felt. She didn't know which she objected to the most: being in the prayers of stupid little hypocrites or being talked down to as if she were retarded.

Elaine grabbed at the only sane piece of information either of the girls, up until then silent, or their mother—not blessed with the same reticence—had uttered. Arlcotte. Morrigan's husband's name was Charles Arlcotte.

"My lord," Mrs. Boleigh said after the door had closed behind the two girls. "I feel it is my Christian duty to inform you of Morrigan's misdeeds. Mr. Boleigh and I were horrified at what Hattie had to tell us. And even though Mr. Boleigh was still quite unrecovered from a seizure of the heart, he felt it his duty to make this trip to set right a great wrong that had been done to you by allowing you to marry this . . . this girl, and since Mr. Boleigh is now unable to do so, I feel it to be my duty—"

"Madam, it is obvious that your duty is a painful thing; therefore I will spare you the consequences. And I will remind you that Morrigan is my wife, and that my relationship with your niece is none of your damned business. Morrigan, my love, I see you are finished." He relieved Elaine of the still-full cordial and set it beside his snifter on the side table. "We will bid you good night, Mrs. Boleigh. If your husband should worsen before morning, send one of my servants for the physician. Come, Morrigan."

Katie sat napping before the fire. At the close of the bedroom door, she jumped upright and beamed.

The lord leaned down and kissed Elaine lightly on the lips. "I'll join you in a few minutes," he whispered.

Elaine's heart jumped up into her throat.

"Never ye fear, m' lord; I'll take care of m' lady."

"Thank you, Katie. Prepare her ladyship for bed. In the white lace, I believe."

"Very good, m' lord."

Katie undressed Elaine, then slipped a white lace nightgown over her head. She diligently brushed the long black hair Elaine saw in the mirror.

"Aye, ye be right beautiful, marm," Katie said, backing off to admire her handiwork. "We'll just get ye all tucked in so's I can make me own bed. The lord, he says as how I should sleep with ye now. I'll just sleep on this little couch over here by the fire; that way I can keep it going during the night so's ye won't git chilled and get the putrid throat back again."

Elaine slipped beneath the covers. Another man was going to be joining her there, a man who called himself her husband. What would he do when she refused him?

How could she refuse him without appearing every bit as crazy as Morrigan's relatives believed her to be?

What would Morrigan do in these circumstances?

A small tap sounded on the connecting door. She opened her mouth to tell Charles to go away—she had a headache. Heaven knew Matthew had used the excuse often enough. The door opened before her lips could more than part.

Elaine's mouth snapped shut.

Charles was dressed in a robe.

And nothing else.

Thick curly chest hair showed between the lapels. Equally hairy legs plunged from beneath the three-quarter-length hem.

"I'll only be a second, m' lord. I just have to make me bed and then we can all get some shut-eye."

Charles paused as if arrested. Elaine's eyes widened.

"Ah, Katie, I don't think—"

"I remember what ye told me today, m' lord, and I done told her ladyship, and she don't mind at all that I'll be sleeping with her now. I brung me own pillow. I'll just sleep on the little couch here; it be plenty big fer the likes of me. Don't ye worry none, m' lord. Everything's just fine here."

Charles's tanned face darkened. "Katie, there's no need for you to sleep with her ladyship tonight. I—"

"But m'lord, ye told me to! I done told the others and everything!"

A bubble of laughter tickled the back of Elaine's throat. They were mad. Every last one of them.

"Katie, get your pretty little arse out of here right this minute!"

Well! Elaine thought indignantly. So Katie has a pretty little arse; all Elaine had was a scrawny one!

Katie flounced toward the couch and grabbed the folded blankets and pillow. "Fine!" the little maid sniffed. "I try to do me duty, and this be the thanks I get! It don't matter none what the others be thinking; it don't matter none that I ain't a real lady's maid and never will be without proper training—I'll just get me things and be gone!"

Charles was not impressed with Katie's impending fall from servant's grace. His lip was hitched up at the right corner, a sure sign of lordly disfavor.

Katie, her arms filled with the pillow and blankets, stiffly delivered a curtsy. The voluminous black skirt dipped into the fire.

"Katie, the fire!" Elaine yelled. She threw the covers back and bounded out of bed. The lace nightgown wrapped around her legs. By the time she had wrestled free, Charles had pulled Katie safely out of the fireplace and was beating out the flaming skirt.

Elaine jerked the blankets out of Katie's hands and used them to help snuff the flammable material. Within seconds she and Charles had successfully combated the flames. A sobbing Katie promptly collapsed into Elaine's arms.

"Katie, Katie, are you all right?" Elaine ran her hands over the back of the maid's clothes, looking for smoldering patches but finding none. "Katie, are you burned?" She held the maid out by the shoulders and shook her. "Katie, talk to me; did the fire burn through your clothes? Katie, for God's sake, say something!"

It slowly dawned on Elaine that the sobs had ceased. Katie and the lord were both staring at her as if she had lost her mind.

Katie, for God's sake, say something! echoed from one corner of the bedroom to the other. Morrigan's voice. With Elaine's Yankee accent.

Elaine watched the long white hands drop from Katie's black-clothed shoulders, felt the muscles of her jaw snap together, the resulting sound sharp in the frozen silence. An ember popped free of the fireplace. The lord stomped out the glowing fissure. Katie's gaping mouth creased, her small face growing round and merry.

"Oh, m' lady! I didn't think you could move so quickly! It be a miracle!"

"Yes. A veritable miracle," the lord said in that voice that said nothing at all.

Elaine reluctantly tore her eyes away from Katie's glowing face. The lord's countenance was as unreadable as had been his voice.

"M' lady, it be grand to have ye jumping about, just like normal folk! Me mum, she that got her leg broke, ye remember—"

"Katie, that will be enough. Go and see to yourself. Tell the housekeeper tomorrow that you should have a dress to replace the one you've burned."

Katie's face suffused with pink. "Oh, m' lord, thank ye! Thank ye!" She dropped another curtsy, rising only to drop another. "Thank ye, m' lord, and thank ye fer saving me. I would've roasted fer sure if ye hadn't of fished me out of the fireplace."

Cretin. It had been Elaine who had saved her, at Elaine's own expense, as it turned out. The least Katie could do was to thank the proper person.

A devil-may-care giddiness swelled inside Elaine's head. A feeling of intense relief intermingled with intense dread. It was over. At last. She would be sent to Bedlam.

Katie curtsied all the way to the door. Charles stood with his back to the fire. The housecoat had come loose. A long, hairy thigh peeped through the wraparound closure.

Katie turned, quite a sight viewed from the posterior. The back of her dress was charred all the way to the waist. A straggly strip of petticoat trailed beneath the gnawed-looking material. Facing Elaine and the lord to make a final curtsy, she turned back around and opened the door. A footman, who had been perched to scratch for entry, scratched instead at Katie's face. The maid fell back into the room, squealing.

She was already in Bedlam. Elaine controlled a hysterical giggle. "What is it?"

There was no question about Charles's mood now. It was all impatience.

Katie swung around. "M' lord," she said indignantly, "this here—"

"Quiet! You." Charles's gaze pinned the hapless footman. "What do you want?"

"The sick man, he wants to see her ladyship, my lord."

"Give Mr. Boleigh his medication and tell him he may see her tomorrow when he is feeling more the thing."

"Mr. Boleigh insisted upon seeing her ladyship, my lord. He seems to be very ill."

"Send for the doctor, then," Charles said testily. He seemed to become aware of the looseness of his robe for the first time and roughly pulled it about his hips. "Her ladyship is not available for house calls."

The footman licked his bottom lip. "My lord, he seemed vastly upset. He said he would not take his medication until he could see his niece. He believes he is dying, sir. He said he wanted to make atonement."

"Very well, tell him we will be with him directly."

Sweat beaded on the footman's forehead. The man's Adam's apple bobbed convulsively. "He said . . . he said he wanted to see her ladyship alone, my lord. He said . . . he said she would understand."

"Morrigan?"

Elaine swallowed, wondering if her Adam's apple bobbed as ridiculously as did the footman's. Was the lord asking her preference, or telling her to go? She didn't want to go. The Boleighs were a thoroughly unpleasant family. Still, perhaps he was dying. Perhaps there had been some fondness between him and Morrigan. It was not Elaine's right to take away a dying man's last moments of comfort.

She licked lips as dry as computer paper. Perhaps Charles had not noticed her lapse in accent. "Yes. I'll—" She licked her lips again before carefully enunciating, "Yes, I will go."

The hitch in Charles's upper lip dropped down; his mouth tightened into a thin diagonal line. "Very well. I would suggest, however, that you put something over that nightgown. I'm sure John here appreciates the view, but try for a little discretion, won't you?"

Elaine dazedly stared down at the front of her body. Katie gasped. Blazing heat flooded Elaine's cheeks. The lace had more holes than a colander; her nipples spilled right through. She glared at Charles. How dare he stand there and allow her to expose her body to the footman?

But the footman was looking at a point beyond Charles. And Charles . . . he was staring at Elaine. His eyes were lit with that disturbing combination of lust and laughter.

Katie led the way downstairs to Mr. Boleigh's bedroom. Elaine clutched the silk robe across her chest, her body warm with embarrassment. No doubt come morning every servant in the joint would be apprised of the length and breadth of her nipples.

"Here ye be, marm." Katie gently scratched on the door. "I'll stay and wait fer ye if ye want me to."

The door silently swung open, by, of course, the very knowledgeable John.

His Adam's apple bobbed. "He's been waiting, my lady," the footman said tonelessly.

Elaine relaxed. John was just as embarrassed as she was. Being the grand lady, it was up to her to set the tone. "Thank you, John. Katie, you may go to bed."

The soothing sense of being in control evaporated when Elaine stepped inside and John closed the door from outside. She nervously assessed the room.

A green oil lamp was lit on the nightstand. Forest green drapes were drawn back from a four-poster bed. A pudgy white hand rested on top of a floral spread.

"Morrigan . . . Morrigan, my dear, is that you?"

Elaine reluctantly stepped forward.

Mr. Boleigh beckoned lamely. "Come closer, my dear."

His eyes glittered in the lamplight. They were small and beady, rather like the eyes of a rat. Like Hattie's eyes. His head was covered with a white stockinglike nightcap that made the side-whiskers appear bristlier than they had earlier.

"We have done you a great wrong, have we not, Morrigan? Your aunt, she has always been jealous of you. It was because of her, you know. All these years she has tormented you. Tormented me."

What was this? Elaine wondered. Deathbed confessions? Was Elaine finally to learn the unexpurgated story of Morrigan's past?

He grasped Elaine's left hand. She shivered. It was like holding hands with a dead carp. Elaine suffered the touch, eager to learn about this body that was for a while, at least, her own

"You have not been happy, have you, my child? I should have known that marriage to a godless pagan would only increase your unhappiness. But he would have you. And your aunt . . . She is demented, you know. She wanted you to suffer. I should have been stronger. For you."

His hand tightened about Elaine's fingers, tugging her downward onto the bed. She briefly floundered off balance before plopping onto the mattress. The thick body beneath the covers bounced against her hip. Elaine tried to pull free. Not only was it like holding onto the hand of a dead carp, but the man smelled like one, too. The Boleigh brood had also smelled overly ripe. Were Charles and his servants the only people in this time who bathed with any regularity?

"Oh, my dear, and now he has succeeded in turning you against me. Do you know when he offered for you?"

Elaine inferred "he" to be Charles. And no, she did not know when he had offered for Morrigan. She did not even know *why* he had offered for her, considering his initial dislike. But she wanted to know. She wanted to know anything and everything having to do with the lord—and Morrigan, of course.

"He came to buy my gentleman cow. You remember my gentleman cow, don't you, Morrigan? A good breeder, that. The lord was most impressed."

The uneasiness Elaine had felt upon entering the bedroom grew by leaps and bounds. He caressed her fingers, circled the thick gold wedding band. Elaine forced herself not to jerk her hand away. This was an aging Victorian gentleman. It could very well be that to discuss a bull's breeding abilities was considered quite kosher.

"He wanted you then, when he watched my gentleman cow mounting his fair lady."

Elaine did jerk back at that, all doubts about proper conversation versus improper conversation falling to the wayside. The man was crazy—crazier than Hattie. Morrigan had been raised by a bunch of lunatics.

"No! No, my dear, I haven't finished yet. I haven't told you how the lady cow enjoyed having that big rod rammed into her."

He was amazingly strong for a man on the verge of death.

"And I haven't told you how Arlcotte bought you so that he could ram his big rod into you. Or how I promised him you would like it. How I promised him I had prepared you, just like my gentleman cow. How I had been poking you in the arse, just like my gentleman cow, since you were old enough to bleed."

The struggle between Elaine and Morrigan's uncle became a full-fledged wrestling match. Elaine jerked and pulled her hand; when that failed, she tried to roll her body off the bed, slipping and sliding on the silk spread. He wrapped an arm around her hips; his fingers poked and prodded her buttocks underneath the wrap, through the lace nightgown.

A high-pitched giggle escaped Boleigh. His voice came in rushed gasps. "And I didn't tell you how I told Arlcotte how much you loved it, did I, Morrigan, my hot little niece? How much you love to

sit on your uncle's knee and bounce up and down like my gentleman cow? How much you love to have your uncle play dairy farmer
and milk your little brown-tipped udders?"

He suddenly released Elaine. She gasped, falling backward, only
to be brought up short when those carplike hands seized her breasts
and viciously twisted them. Then, as if nothing had happened, he
lay back, a vacuous smile pasted on his lips. His beady eyes gleamed
with satisfaction.

Elaine scrambled off the bed, her chest heaving for air. Bile rose
in her throat. She felt dirty beyond belief, contaminated in both
mind and body. She had listened to victims of incest on talk shows,
had read about them in magazines. But she had never, ever encountered it in real life. *My God.* To think that this was what Morrigan
had gone through. The bastard deserved to die. She hoped he died
that night.

Morrigan's uncle straightened the bedcovers, then his nightcap
that had slipped to one side, revealing a bald pate, and folded his
hands across his chest. "Call John, my dear. It is time for my medicine. I am a sick man. You should not try to excite me. It is bad for
my heart."

Elaine slowly backed away, fascinated despite herself. The eyes
that only seconds earlier had gleamed with rapacious lewdness were
guiless. Sexless. The nightcap and bed appeared undisturbed, as if
their struggle had never occurred. She briefly wondered if it had all
been a mirage, a momentary dive into another body, another place.

The thin lips curved complacently. "But it is our secret, is it not,
Morrigan? You would only give your husband a disgust if you should
tell him of our little games. Just as you disgusted your aunt and the
reverend."

Elaine whirled around with a cry. She barely remembered to
straighten her robe before flinging open the door.

John stared at her in openmouthed surprise.

Katie, thank heavens, had not waited for her mistress. Elaine
rushed past John, unable to go fast enough to put more distance between herself and that piece of filth that passed for Morrigan's
uncle.

One thing she knew for certain: Charles did not know about Boleigh's history of molestation, else Boleigh would not have warned Elaine that it was their secret.

Morrigan, as twentieth century incest victims often did, by protecting herself had protected her family.

Chapter

19

Elaine dislodged a blueberry from her muffin with the tip of her fork. The Boleigh brood ate like noisy pigs, indiscriminately slurping bacon and sausage and mushrooms and—*ugh,* fish, kippers, Elaine supposed—that was what the English ate, wasn't it?—and disgusting brown things that rather looked like chicken livers but most definitely didn't smell like them. Prudence—no, Mary was the shorter of the two—scooped up the last of a nauseating combination of rice and flaked fish with a crumb of toast; both disappeared inside the landfill that was her mouth. She immediately pushed back from the table. Elaine's cup rattled; tea splashed over the side onto the saucer. Mrs. Boleigh grimly spread butter into the U-shaped bite of a half-eaten muffin.

Bile rose in the back of Elaine's throat. Mrs. Boleigh knew about her husband's niece-molesting proclivities, Elaine thought, yet she chose to bury her knowledge in an orgy of food like a goddamned hippopotamus.

Good God. What had they done to Morrigan throughout the years? Elaine was torn between pity and revulsion. Pity for the girl she had never known, revulsion because what had been done to that poor girl's body was the same body that she, Elaine, occupied, and so had therefore inadvertently been done to her. She felt intense shame, as if she were not quite worthy of being in the presence of so-called decent people. And anger. That so-called decent people had allowed it to happen.

Incest. Sexual abuse. What ugly words. Not for one second did Elaine believe in the consensual relationship that Boleigh had hinted at last night. That a relationship had existed she did not doubt—how else would he have been able to describe her, Morrigan's, nipples?—but no one would willingly tolerate a maggot.

Mary sat back down at the table, her plate again piled high from the buffet. Prudence raced to finish her first serving. Elaine stared at the two girls, then at Mrs. Boleigh, at the straining seams of her skirt and jacket, at the masticating jowls.

Elaine's lips curled. Obviously there was one who had tolerated his touch.

She ceased the mutilation of her muffin and gulped lukewarm tea. She felt so cold. And soiled. Just when she had been feeling clean again this morning, fresh from a bath and dressed in a bright yellow gown, Mrs. Boleigh had strode into Elaine's bedroom and demanded to see her scribing. Then she had demanded that Elaine cease her "dillydallying" and go downstairs for breakfast. Elaine had acquiesced only because the thought of that woman treating her as if she had something to be ashamed of had galled her more than sharing a table with an accomplice to incest.

"Morrigan, if I have told you once, I have told you a hundred times: food is God's bountifulness; it is not to be wasted."

Prudence reached for Elaine's plate. "I'll take it, Mama."

Elaine grabbed her fork, overcome with loathing for this family who had not once expressed concern over Morrigan's putrid throat and who acted as if she were dumb as well as crippled. Boleigh had said that Morrigan had been with them for years. While they had stuffed themselves and dressed in what Elaine assumed was the height of Victorian fashion, Morrigan had been starved and forced to wear dirty wool clothing that had probably been outdated fifty years earlier. Hattie had provided neither candles nor firewood when Elaine had awakened in this time. She doubted if the girl reaching out to take the very food Morrigan would eat had ever suffered a dark, cold evening in her life.

Just as Prudence's pudgy hand—a carbon copy of her father's—came within utensil range, a black-liveried arm deftly removed the plate from the table. The footman discreetly melted back into obscurity. Prudence stared at the empty space in front of Elaine as if she could not believe that the plate had been taken away. Her mouth opened.

The door to the breakfast room flew wide. Charles strolled in. He bowed slightly to the woman and two daughters. "Good morning, ladies. I hope you spent a pleasant night?"

Mrs. Boleigh fastidiously patted her mouth with a napkin before answering. "Tolerably well, my lord, though your beds are a tad too hard for comfort. My girls and I are used to the softer comforts due to females of a more delicate constitution."

The Mediterranean blue eyes gleamed. Charles slowly perused the bodies of the three females in question. Elaine could almost hear his thoughts. The dining room suddenly seemed a little brighter, a little warmer. A little cleaner.

"I trust Mr. Boleigh is feeling better?"

"Quite so, my lord. He seemed vastly improved. The doctor will examine him later this morning. You are fortunate that your uncle is recovering from . . . yesterday's misadventures, Morrigan. You have so much to atone for."

Elaine felt the blood drain from her head at the veiled threat. She understood loud and clear that strategic little pause. Mrs. Boleigh knew about Elaine's visit with Morrigan's uncle last night. Surely she would not tell the lord about the perverted relationship between Morrigan and Boleigh?

"Nonsense," Charles said briskly. "Morrigan is not to blame for Boleigh's weak heart. He should never have undertaken this trip. Morrigan, Jasper is in need of exercise. Run upstairs and change and we will go for a ride. I'm sure these ladies will forgive you for availing yourself of this truly splendid weather."

Elaine tossed her fork and napkin onto the table; simultaneously she scooted back. The chair toppled, Elaine almost going down with it. She cleared the wreckage just as the lord, coming from one direction, and the footman, from another, reached her.

Elaine was paralyzed with embarrassment.

"Careful, niece! You know you are a clumsy oaf with that twisted limb of yours. My lord, I do not know what you are about, allowing her near a horse. My Mary and Prudence can be ready in a trice. Have your carriage brought around to the door and they will join you for a drive. They will be delighted to demonstrate the finer points of carriage etiquette to their cousin, won't you, girls?"

Mary and Prudence tittered, their cheeks puffed with food like squirrels hoarding winter stock.

The lord glanced at the cheeky duo. His right lip curled upward. "I'm sorry. My carriage has a broken axle. Pray excuse us."

The girls' mouths fell open, displaying a quantity of partially chewed food.

The lord averted his eyes and held out his hand. "Morrigan."

Mrs. Boleigh's mouth contorted; her pale eyes glittered with rage. In the span of a blink her face was once again set in cold disdain. She lowered her eyes and calmly buttered another muffin. "As you will, my lord."

Charles grabbed Elaine's hand and pulled her out of the dining room and toward the stairs. "Go and change. Katie's waiting for you. I'll meet you in the library."

Elaine hurried up the stairs. She was undressed and buttoned into the heavy velvet riding habit before she had time to catch her breath. The maid pushed her toward the door.

"I saw that auntie of yers going into yer room when I was taking down yer bathwater. I told Mr. Fritz she was up to no good. Fresh air'll be just the thing. Ye ain't looked right since those relatives of yers came here without a by-yer-leave. Go on and leave everything to me. I ain't afeared of the likes of them."

Elaine remembered the rage on Mrs. Boleigh's face. "Good for you," she muttered as the door closed behind her. "Give 'em hell."

The Boleigh brood met Elaine at the bottom of the stairs. Morrigan's aunt reduced Elaine's finery to shreds with a glance. Elaine uncertainly wondered if Katie had screwed up again, that a lady was expected to sit on both a horse and a bustle.

"Fine clothes do not make a lady, Morrigan. The lord will soon come to realize what a hindrance you are, and then he will be glad to return you to our care. We will do our Christian duty by you, girl. The likes of you belong locked up."

Elaine jerked as if she had been slapped. How dare Mrs. Boleigh speak of Christian duty after allowing her husband to sexually abuse his own niece? She was the one who needed to be locked up. She and that piece of filth that passed for her husband.

Elaine did not care if they detected a difference in her accent. "Get out of my way," she said every bit as coldly as the lord.

Mrs. Boleigh gasped. "Well, I never!"

Elaine sidestepped the human sewage that had surely made Morrigan's life a misery. The shortened leg that had become a natural extension of her own body trembled so badly she almost collapsed by the time she reached the library.

Charles looked cold and formidable, standing in front of the French doors. Where had the carnality gone? Had Morrigan's aunt talked to him in private? Had Mr. Boleigh bragged of his conquest?

Expression unchanging, he lifted a picnic basket from behind the desk. Elaine sighed in relief. Surely he would not be taking her on a picnic if he thought she was guilty of incest.

Charles did not talk during the walk to the stables, nor did he offer assistance beyond hoisting her onto the back of the horse. Instinctively she brought her right leg up over the pommel and jammed her left foot into the stirrup. He adjusted the hem of her skirt before mounting.

The stallion, like his master, was restrained. Elaine leaned over and patted Jasper's neck. Unbidden, Mrs. Boleigh's face came to mind. How could she ever have compared this innocent horse to a dirty, disgusting cow?

Elaine gradually relaxed, lulled by the silence, the warmth of the sun, and Jasper's gentle, rolling gait. They traversed the same territory they had traveled on that first ride. The grass was even greener than it had been a week ago. Her body swayed in the familiar, oddly comforting gait. Warm air tickled the nape of her bare neck.

Blankets of small blue and purple flowers had sprouted along the banks of the lake. Shiva daintily picked his way among them until they came to a grove of oak trees.

Charles dismounted. He reached up for Elaine and lifted her down. The warmth of his hands penetrated the velvet habit. Beyond him, a small butterfly danced and flitted among the blue and purple flowers. The lake glittered in the sunlight, free of human pollution.

Elaine looked up and smiled in gratitude.

Charles looked down, his expression guarded.

"Are you hungry?"

She searched his eyes for a hidden meaning; there was none. "Yes," she finally said, wondering why she was not. Dinner had been ruined by food pellets last night, breakfast by the sight of the Boleigh brood gorging like pigs.

"Then I shall feed my lady."

The velvet felt cool against her skin when he released her. He claimed the hamper that was secured to Shiva's saddle. Taking out a blanket, he spread it on the grass in the shade.

Elaine impulsively picked up the blanket and spread it in the sun. She needed its warmth to take away the chill of Boleigh contamination.

"You'll burn," he warned softly.

"No," Elaine said with conviction.

"Very well," Charles said lightly. He reached for her hands and tugged the leather gloves off of her fingers. "Then we shall picnic in the sun."

Bowing with a flourish and gesturing for her to be seated, he retrieved the hamper and placed it between them. She reached inside the wicker basket and pulled out two glasses. He reached inside and pulled out a bottle of wine.

Elaine sat naturally erect, feeling every inch the lady, her spine trained through years of wearing a corset, delicately holding the wineglass by the stem as she had been taught during that tedious wine tasting, that she not mar the sparkle of wine with fingerprints. Charles sprawled back on one elbow, the quintessential male, a glass cupped in his right hand, unconcerned by finger-prints. His hair was flecked with pure gold in the sunlight, there just a hint of red.

Should she leave her hat on? she wondered, wanting nothing more than to have it off and the pins taken out of her hair to hang free down her back.

Elaine reached inside the hamper and brought out a heavy, thick chunk of—she unwrapped the cloth-covered object—cheddar cheese. She lifted it to her face and inhaled, eye closing, the better to appreciate it. Lowering the cheese, she opened her eyes.

Charles was sitting upright, solemnly watching her. Elaine offered him the cheese. He took it without hesitation, his eyes never leaving hers.

"Have you ever been on a picnic?"

Had Morrigan ever been on a picnic?

She felt a spurt of resentment. She didn't want to think about Morrigan. She wanted to be Elaine.

"No," she said curtly.

She concentrated on spreading out the picnic, her first, she didn't want it spoiled; please just let him remain silent.

"Has a cat stolen your tongue?"

"What?" Elaine looked up from the array of food, ham sliced wafer thin, crusty bread still warm from the oven, dill pickles, stone-ground mustard, honey, a variety of pastries. Laughter lit her eyes. Was that the Victorian equivalent to "the cat got your tongue"?

Charles produced a pocketknife and proceeded to slice the cheese. His lashes, too long for a man, created great shadowed fringes on his cheeks.

"I said, has a cat stolen your tongue?" He raised his eyes. "Or did I?"

Heat flooded her face. Elaine refused to rise to the bait, thank-fully only the memory of a kiss and not more Tantric perversions. This was an innocent picnic. She was going to keep it that way.

"Are you a thief?"

He reached inside the hamper and brought out china and cutlery. "And if I were?"

"Then I would say keep it." Elaine reared up onto her knees that she might reach unhindered and put something of everything onto their plates. "I do—not accept stolen goods." Smiling with satisfaction, she sat back down.

Charles stared at Elaine. She returned his stare for long seconds. A glint of appreciation momentarily overshadowed the seduction. Without thinking, she broke off a piece of pastry and dipped it into mustard. He did not take his eyes off of hers when she held it up. Carefully she brushed his lips with the edge of the pastry that was free of mustard. He obligingly opened his mouth. Keeping her face solemn, she popped the mustard-dipped pastry between his teeth. His mouth closed; his jaw moved in a chewing motion.

Charles's eyes widened in shock. A splutter escaped him. He swallowed convulsively before exploding with a shout of laughter.

The laughter was infectious. Elaine would never forget the look on his face, the transformation of male lord to boy child. Her mirth ended in a series of breathless coughs.

He reached over and pounded her on the back. "Are you all right?"

She nodded her head, inhaling slowly, deeply.

"Good. I'd hate to be deprived of vengeance."

Elaine looked up just in time to see a honeycomb speared on a pickle fast bearing down. "You wouldn—"

Her mouth was flooded with the taste of tangy dill and sweet honey. "Ugh!" She prepared to spit it out.

"Oh, no, you don't!" He held her jaws together, spreading honey and pickle juice from ear to ear.

Elaine pulled at his hands, succeeding only in pulling her cheeks toward the front of her face. "Lemeo!"

Charles chuckled. "What's good for the goose is good for the gander. Or I should say, what's good for the gander is good for the goose. Chew it like a good girl, and swallow."

Her expressions as she chewed, judging by his mirth, were every bit as entertaining as his had been. She brought her tongue out and licked honey from the tip of her nose, a hitherto undiscovered and not necessarily admirable talent, but effective. Charles collapsed onto the blanket and rolled with laughter.

Elaine had never had a sibling, had always been expected to behave like a perfect little lady. She entered the play with gusto. They fed each other imaginative tidbits. Pickle and mustard for him, for her cheese and honey, for him pickle wrapped in ham with honeycomb. And all of it washed down by rich red wine. Elaine had never laughed so much in her entire life.

As if he were a magician pulling a rabbit from a hat, Charles reached down deep into the hamper and pulled out damp cloths. They scrubbed their hands and faces as if they were a couple of grubby school kids, totally graceless, totally uninhibited. By the time they repacked the hamper, Elaine didn't know what she was high off of the most—sun, alcohol, or laughter. Her lord had successfully cleansed away the grime of Boleigh association.

Charles took off his jacket and rolled it into a ball. He lay back on the blanket, using the jacket for a pillow, and put his arm over his face. Elaine watched him until an unchildish restlessness settled in. She pulled off the soft leather boots and stood up, intending to test the springiness of the incredibly green grass. Immediately the lord sprang to life. He knelt in front of Elaine, that solemn look back on his face, a knight errant asking his lady for a boon.

Elaine stared down into his eyes. "Why did you marry M—" She bit her lip too late. The question was out. "Me?"

His lids drooped down over his eyes. He slid a warm hand beneath her dress. "Why did you marry me?"

Elaine remained still, strangely unalarmed by the fingers sliding up the silk stocking, unalarmed at the thought of scars and unshaven legs.

He pushed the legs of her drawers up and released the stockings from the garter belts that were attached to the corset. Next he began the slow, sensuous task of peeling off the silk, his fingertips raspy, sure.

It was the most luxurious thing Elaine had ever felt. The wine and laughter and sun suddenly caught up to her. Her eyelids were so heavy, they closed of their own volition. The sun was a bright, warm ball behind them, his hands a rough, warm caress along the backs of her thighs, the backs of her knees, the sides of her calves.

Strong fingers issued a warning tug. Suddenly her left ankle was raised up from the ground; he pulled the stocking off of her foot. Elaine staggered, fell forward; she grabbed his shoulders to retain her balance. He lifted up her other ankle and stripped the stocking off of her foot.

Charles sat back on his haunches. Elaine straightened. That look was coming back into his eyes. *No, please,* she silently pleaded, *don't let reality intrude. Don't make me give more than I'm capable.*

The blue eyes darkened. Elaine stiffened with dread. *Here it comes,* she thought. *Back to having a scrawny arse.*

He slowly stood up, as lithe as a jungle cat. The hat pin slid through her hair; the hat was sent flying through the air, more a sensation than a sound. Immediately the sun was warm on her bare head. She closed her eyes, unable to bear the intensity in his, time and again rejected by a wife who had been routinely subjected to childhood molestation and who would probably never be able to respond to sexual intimacy. One by one he plucked out the pins holding up her hair, until it hung as she had wanted it earlier, heavy and free.

"Let's dance."

Elaine's eyes snapped open. Dance? Out here in the grass with no music and her a short left leg?

"I can see by the quizzical gleam in milady's eyes that she doubts her lordly husband. Have a little faith, wife."

He grabbed Elaine and swung her around, very loudly humming "The Blue Danube."

At least, Elaine *thought* it was "The Blue Danube."

She bit her lips to hold back the laughter, failed. Her beautiful, seductive lord was tone-deaf.

"Ah, so milady laughs." He twirled her about, holding her steady when she would have stumbled. "I see you are not a devotee of Johann Strauss. A pity. Perhaps you would prefer something more modern."

He whirled her faster and faster, his feet hitting the notes he missed. Elaine became giddy with laughter and motion, the sky a blue blur, his voice an unbelievable cacophony in her ear, the weight of her hair pulling her head back toward the blazing sun.

A sharp rip rent the air. Charles with Elaine in his arms flew forward. Just before impact, he twisted his body.

Elaine landed on hard muscle and even harder bone. Winded, she struggled to free herself from the imprisoning arms. And succeeded. Only to find herself on the bottom and Charles on top.

Her laughter died in a breathless sigh. Charles lifted up on his elbows; his hips settled firmly against hers. He gently smoothed away long tendrils of hair from her mouth and eyes.

His breath was ragged, a steady bombardment of heat and fragrance, spicy mustard, pungent cheese, tangy dill, mellow wine, sweet honey. Flyaway hair created a golden halo around his head. There were fine wrinkles at the corners of his eyes. Those Mediterranean blue eyes.

"You are so beautiful," Charles said.

Imagine her, Elaine, being called beautiful.

"The sun turns your hair molten, like fiery little rays penetrating the black of night."

His lips brushed hers, again, and again, like rough silk.

"Don't fight me. Don't ever fight me. . . ."

The lowering head blocked out the sun. His lips were every bit as hot and wet as she remembered. His tongue every bit as scalding.

Elaine closed her eyes and opened her mouth.

Charles sucked in his breath, feeling Morrigan's mouth open willingly, feeling her body melt bonelessly. She had given him the most precious day in his life, and now she was giving him what he had sought for the last year. A lifetime. She was giving herself.

She tasted of their picnic, spicy mustard, sweet honey. He caressed the roof of her mouth, exultation a sharp, piercing pain, hearing her gasp, experiencing her pleasure. He kissed her for long minutes, forever, wanting so much more, wanting so much that he was afraid. Afraid it was only a dream. Afraid the old Morrigan would return and render the act one of solitary gratification.

Morrigan brought her arms up and put them around his shoulders. Cool fingers slid up his neck, massaged his scalp. The kiss became harder, more intent. He thrust his tongue in and out of her mouth. Her fingers tightened into a fist in his hair and pulled down, not hurting, but not gentle. She adhered his mouth more firmly over hers.

Charles broke the kiss. He raised his head. "Look at me," he whispered.

Morrigan lifted her eyelids. Her black eyes, those that he had only until recently thought empty black pits, glowed with passion. For him.

Charles laughed softly, exultantly. "You feel it, don't you, sweetheart? The *kama*. It's true. You won't fight me, not any more. You're mine."

The lambent eyes flickered, passion still there, but slipping. She was fighting it. *Damn her*. And damn him. He wouldn't make the mistake of giving her time to think again. Charles's desire to make Morrigan beg was forgotten. So were all of his Tantric teachings. He wanted her passion, and he wanted it now.

He reclaimed Morrigan's lips, his own savage with the need to make her submit. She made a small sound of distress in the back of her throat. He eased the pressure, but refused to give succor. She was his. He would not allow her to cheat him, to cheat them. Together, forever together, him and her. Like two swans.

He undid the buttons on the front of her dress. "Don't fight it," he whispered, half pleading, half demanding. It had been too long coming; he could not stop. He *would* not stop. Charles slipped the heavy velvet down over her shoulders, baring the satin corset that had been part of her trousseau.

"No, don't—"

Charles stopped Morrigan's breathless protest with a kiss. He eased the dress down to her waist, then shifted her to her side to unlace the corset.

Morrigan stiffened; she wedged her hands between their chests and pushed with all her might. Mouth covering hers, Charles tossed aside the corset and rolled his wife onto her back. Morrigan retaliated by drawing her legs together—too late, he was already there, planted between those delectable thighs.

He lifted far enough off of Morrigan to capture a nipple between his thumb and forefinger. It was swollen with need. He rolled it through the silk chemise, softly, harder, gently again, pinching sharply. Morrigan gasped into his mouth; her body arched upward into his. Satisfied, he released her mouth and slid his tongue along her jaw. He felt the protest before it escaped her throat. Quick as a mongoose he was there, stoppering the denial with his mouth, rolling the other nipple, pinching, soft, hard, gentle, sharp.

Morrigan's breath came in soft, hot gusts. Tentatively Charles released her mouth and resumed his journey toward her breasts. She made no more protests, her body taut now with sexual tension. When he gulped a silk-covered nipple into his mouth, she curved upward into a perfect bow, beautiful, so beautiful. He suckled hungrily through the chemise, the silk smooth, wet, her nipple hard, hot. His groin swelled to the point of bursting, hearing the long, agonized groan wrenched from her throat.

"Yes," he whispered. "Oh, God, yes, yes, that's it, let me hear you, moan for me, Morrigan, moan, I want to hear you," he groaned, nibbling, suckling, head wildly rooting from one breast to the other.

Morrigan brought her legs up, creating a cradle for his hips, her pelvis tilted, ready, yes, she was ready, no more fighting, she was his, now, now, he must have her. Now.

Charles slipped a hand up under her skirt, the cloth catching on his wrist, rising, rising. "God, you're so hot!" He wrenched at the drawers—damn, they buttoned—fingers too clumsy with passion to maneuver the small, round obstacles. He heard cloth rip, impervious now to anything but her; then he was there, fingers kneading the smooth skin of her belly, dipping, touching her where she flowed like a hot, bottomless spring. He parted the full, slick folds, no time to dally there now, tested her readiness with a trembling finger. Morrigan jerked in his arms, then shivered.

"Shhh," Charles whispered. He could hear his lungs laboring for air; he sounded like Shiva after a long, hard run. His whole body was burning. He would make hers burn just as hotly. They would burn together.

"Hold tight, sweetheart, no pain this time, Christ!" he gasped. His finger was gripped by her internal muscles, milked in hot, wet, raw silk. "No pain, just pleasure. God, you're so tight, you're going to kill me. Hold on, sweetheart." He squeezed another finger inside her, feeling the opening stretch, making small rotating circles to soothe the slight pain.

"Don't tense up—wait, wait till I'm in all the way. There. Now grip my fingers . . . that's it, try to keep me inside you . . . now relax, let me slide back in . . . deeper . . . that's it. Hold me, harder, yes, relax, let me in again. You feel so good, it's going to be so good." He covered Morrigan's gasping mouth with his and matched his tongue to his fingers, *in*, circle, out, *in*, circle, out, *in*, jabbing deep, "God, yes . . ."

Morrigan whimpered underneath him, her eyes squeezed shut, her mouth open, panting. She alternately clutched him to her and ran her hands over his shoulders. Charles would teach her the subtleties later. If she touched his naked flesh now he would explode.

He slipped his hand free of her body. Morrigan moaned in protest, her hips thrusting upward to recapture him. "Soon. Soon, sweetheart, soon," he crooned, tearing his pants open, widening her legs, those long voluptuous legs. He pressed against her. She was so tight. He pressed harder.

Morrigan whimpered, a different whimper, distress mixed with pain. Charles looked up from where he was trying to join her. Her eyes were open. The black pit yawned in the focusing depths.

"No," he growled. "I won't let you destroy it. I won't let you destroy us. Not now." He pushed harder against her resisting flesh. "Damn it, not"—he sank into her, instantly enveloped in living fire— "God, not now!"

She was so tight, it felt like she was squeezing him in two. Charles withdrew the slightest bit, then pushed deeper, repeated the process until he was pressed against her womb.

He rested his weight on top of Morrigan. Sweat beaded on his forehead and dripped down into her pale face. There was the beginning of true pain in her eyes, he saw, but the kindling of something far hotter. She was his, he thought with satisfaction. He could take his time. Take her with him.

"Relax, Morrigan, relax for me, sweetheart, that's right, so good, let me make it good for you," he crooned, slowly, steadily withdrawing, penetrating, circling, short, beguiling penetrations, long, demanding penetrations.

Morrigan arched her hips.

Charles gritted his teeth. "Yes, yes, that's it, love, hold me, come with me, take me inside, all of me, there's more, take it, love, take it. . . ."

He could feel Morrigan's climax coming, the muscles tightening, gripping. She fought it, but he refused to allow her to back down, thrusting harder, deeper, whispering her name, love blandishments, sex words. The frenzied slap of flesh on flesh echoed in the quiet grove.

A bird sang out, a brief, short warble. He could hear as well as feel the flowing wetness he had created. Suddenly her body surged upward, opening completely. She took all of him in her moment of release, her entire body convulsing, every little muscle in her body tightening, squeezing.

"God! Oh, God!" Charles gasped, the world exploding, his body exploding with it. He sagged helplessly on top of his wife, truly his wife now, in body as well as name.

Chapter

20

Elaine stared up at the clear blue sky. The sun had passed from warm to hot. She felt as if she had been hammered into the ground; the grass tickled anatomical parts that were never intended to be exposed. Her nether regions ached and burned. Charles's body was glued to hers with their combined sweat. His chest convulsed in and out, causing the wiry mat of hair there to rasp and rub the chemise against her tender breasts.

Charles mumbled something against her ear, more of a sigh than actual words. He shifted his weight, then lifted himself free of her body. Elaine winced at the fresh spurt of pain, at the sound of wet flesh disengaging from wet flesh. He collapsed beside her onto the grass.

Elaine sat up. She pushed her gown up and down, then methodically refastened the buttons.

Charles stirred, rolled onto his back. "What is it, love?"

A lazy finger trailed up the velvet covering her spine.

He chuckled. "I didn't take you on an anthill, did I?"

Elaine clumsily got to her feet. Male essence oozed down her thighs. She gritted her teeth. Her corset had been pitched some feet away. The drawers gaped obscenely on the grass where he had tossed them, tufts of green sticking through the crotchless seam. There were other rents that the seamstress had not included.

Elaine spotted her boots. She stomped her feet into them. Behind her, she could hear Charles sit up.

"What is it?" he repeated more sharply.

Elaine limped toward the horses. If only she could pull herself up on Jasper's back. Then she could ride home and bury herself inside her bedroom, where she should have stayed in the first place.

Just as she thought she was safe, that the lord would not pursue her, hard hands roughly pulled her around. Elaine squinted into the sun.

"What is it, damn it? Did I hurt you?"

The sun receded, shot forward. He shook her, harder, twice, thrice. The grim features towering over her blurred. Elaine instinctively grabbed hold of his arms to retain her balance, the flesh hard and hot beneath the thin cotton, his shirt torn as her drawers had been torn.

By her. In her lust.

Oh, God.

"Speak to me, damn it; I know you can."

He shook her harder still, until finally Elaine gasped. "Please!"

"Oh, you did," Charles grated. "As I did you. For God's sake, Morrigan, you're my *wife!* If you think I'm going to allow you to act like some penny dreadful heroine, forget it. It's past time you grew up and accepted your responsibilities. Do I make myself clear?"

The sun receded, but instead of shooting forward into empty space, Elaine's body was hauled against the lord's. The front of his pants were open. Elaine could feel the length of him through the velvet dress, impressive even when flaccid.

The muscles in Elaine's stomach coiled. She groaned. Why had the Boleighs come with their pig manners and incestuous family skeletons? Why did the lord have to be the one man to satisfy her when seventeen years of marriage to another had not?

The sun was blocked. A firm, open mouth caught her groan. His tongue neatly slid inside her, wet, reminding her of the seepage between her legs, hot, reminding her of the burning, pulsing ache between her legs. He circled her tongue, stabbed beneath it. She remembered how he had circled between her legs with that other appendage, equally scalding, remembered how he had thrust and teased and thrust until she had not been able to tell where his body ended and hers began.

Charles pulled back. His blue eyes were hard and triumphant. "That is the way it will be, Morrigan. Every time I touch you, you will remember. And ache for more."

Before Elaine could guess his actions, he lifted her and plopped her down on Jasper's back. He slid his hand beneath the heavy velvet skirt and hooked her right leg over the pommel. The position rendered her open where she was most vulnerable. Instantly she felt tender skin invaded.

Elaine squirmed backward as far as she dared. Jasper neighed softly; the horse nervously sidestepped toward the lord. The hard, punishing fingers plunged deeper inside her. Elaine's eyes dilated with pain. The fingers worked harder; his thumb rubbed the sensitive nub at the top of her lips.

Blood rushed up to her head and down to that other little head. The nub swelled and pulsed beneath the insistent pressure. Elaine's breath quickened. The animal smells of horse and sex intensified. Tiny lights glinted in Charles's eyes, blue lights, black lights, plunging lights, deeper, deeper. . . .

Charles slowly eased out of her flesh. Elaine clenched her muscles; he relentlessly slipped free with a wet, sucking sound and wiped his fingers on her thigh, her unshaven thigh, his eyes never leaving hers. They gleamed with carnal knowledge and anger.

"Just a little reminder, my dear, sanctimonious wife." He shoved her left foot up into the stirrup. "The wetness isn't all mine."

They rode back in silence, the same way they had ridden out, but with such a difference. Elaine had never realized there were so many different types of silence. There was a contented silence, a happy silence, a placid silence, an angry silence, a silence filled with scorn and mockery, a silence filled with pain and betrayal. Silences that reached out, silences that built barriers.

Back at the stables, Charles swung Elaine down from the saddle.

Her right leg buckled. He turned away. Elaine grabbed hold of the stirrup, her eyes locked onto his back as he made his way toward the house.

Jasper swung her head around to investigate the weight on the saddle. Elaine absently pushed the mare away and eased her weight fully onto her own legs. Charles disappeared around the corner of the house, never once looking back to see how she fared. For all he knew, she could have fallen and been trampled to death.

Elaine was suddenly suffused with red-hot anger. Male chauvinist pig bastard. How dare he calmly assume that he only had to touch her and she would jump into his bed? She would show him. She would show them all—pigs, every last one of them.

The energetic hustle and bustle invaded the warm sanctity behind the Japanese screen. Elaine covered her breasts and glared at Katie. The maid ignored Elaine and picked up the soiled chemise and petticoats. She looked around for several seconds before exclaiming, "Oh, marm, ye've lost yer corset! And yer drawers!"

Elaine's mouth dropped open. The maid never ceased to amaze her. She didn't know whether she should laugh, cry, or scream.

Katie shrugged. "Oh, well, mayhap the lord, he knows where they be."

"Katie!" Elaine said sharply. "If you *dare* go and ask the lord, I'll . . . I will fire you!"

Katie did not look impressed. It dawned on Elaine that she had made yet another major slip—she had used twentieth-century Yankee slang. Hurriedly she added, "I wo—will not let you be my lady's maid anymore, Katie! I swear!"

Katie shrugged again. "Oh, well, as to that, there ain't no others the lord wants to be yer lady's maid."

Elaine's eyes widened at the maid's impertinence, as thoroughly incensed as any nineteenth-century lady.

"What dress d'ye want to wear to dinner tonight, m' lady? How 'bout the blue? It matches the lord's eyes, don't ye think?" Katie said dreamily.

Elaine gritted her teeth. "No, I do not think!"

"Well, ye got to wear something, marm. The lord, he be expecting ye fer dinner."

Elaine fully intended to dine downstairs tonight. It was time that people realized that she—Morrigan—was not a mindless toy. Starting with Katie.

"Give me something in red. Bright, bright red. And then I want you to bring me a pair of scissors and a sharp razor. Now."

Elaine surveyed the red silk dress in the mirror. She had clipped off the little puffed sleeves and taken out the lace inset that covered the breasts.

Katie put a final pin into the French twist she had fashioned Elaine's hair into and stepped backward. Her eyes grew round. "Oh, marm! D'ye think . . . that be . . . mightn't ye catch a chill?"

The dinner gong vibrated through the walls. "Oh, marm, are ye sure ye wouldn't want to change?"

Elaine's look silenced the maid. "Go on, Katie. Go get your dinner."

After the maid left, Elaine counted to a thousand. She pulled the bodice up to cover the top of a brown areola before slowly crossing the room and opening the door. A folded piece of paper slithered across the carpet, a remnant of Elaine's putrid-throat days. Katie's housekeeping was slipping badly, she thought, relishing the chance to remonstrate the girl.

The air in the hallway was chill. Elaine raised her arms to allow cool air to circulate beneath her mangled armpits. A nineteenth-century razor was not shaped for a lady's body.

At the foot of the stairs, a footman jumped to attention. He threw open the doors to the blue-and-silver room.

Elaine expelled a nervous sigh. The footman stepped back. Elaine raised her chin and stepped forward.

Three pairs of eyes darted upward. Mary and Prudence were decked out in their uncomplimentary pink; they were seated on the divan beside their mother. Charles, dressed in the traditional black tuxedo, leaned against the mantel over the fireplace, a brandy snifter in his hands. At Elaine's entrance, he straightened, eyes slightly widening, and stared.

Elaine determinedly thrust her chest forward, enjoying the shock on the Boleighs' faces. She only hoped her nipples remained tucked inside the dress. No, she hoped they did pop out. Surely such a Christian family would not stand for indecent exposure—they preferred their sins hidden away in a closet. They would leave, and the lord would leave, too, when she demonstrated her indifference. Without the constant distractions she would soon be able to figure out how to return to the twentieth century.

Charles padded across the room. The Mediterranean blue eyes glinted with undiluted carnality, as if he had only to snap his fingers and she would lie down for him. Elaine stiffened with renewed anger.

He offered his arm. "Morrigan, you look lovely." His voice was uncomfortably like a purr. The glinting eyes dipped to the altered neckline of the scarlet dress.

Elaine felt her nipples tighten. *Were* they exposed?

"Indeed, I've never seen so much loveliness in my life. Please." He dragged her hand through his arm. "Sit over here by the fire. The night air is chill, is it not? May I get you a drink? Sherry? Something sweeter, perhaps?"

"Disgraceful!" Mrs. Boleigh spluttered. Her face was purple; her eyeballs looked ready to pop out of their sockets. Mary and Prudence swayed forward, eagerly awaiting their cousin's castigation.

"My lord, please, allow me! Morrigan, you will get upstairs this very minute and change into decent apparel! My apologies, my lord! Really, you must now see how prurient she is! How . . . how she mocks all those qualities a decent Christian espouses! Let me—"

Charles stared down at Mrs. Boleigh. One eyebrow lifted. "Madam, I hope you are not referring to this extremely lovely gown Morrigan is wearing. It was a gift. From myself. Surely you are not implying I would gift my wife with inappropriate wear?"

Morrigan's aunt sputtered. Mary's and Prudence's round faces were studies in disappointment.

"I refuse, my lord! I refuse to submit my innocent chicks to this wanton display of decadence! Why, the girl has only to bend over and . . . well!"

"May I suggest, then—and not, I might mention, for the first time—that you send your daughters away. They may then more comfortably dine in their rooms. As may you, madam. Please, we do not wish to cause you distress, do we, Morrigan?"

"Well, I never!"

Charles's eyes twinkled down at Elaine. She firmly pulled free of his arm. The laughter instantly faded, replaced by—

No, a man such as he was incapable of being hurt by someone such as herself.

Mrs. Boleigh silently savaged her dinner. Safe from flying pellets, Elaine fortified herself with wine. After her third glass, however, it stopped being magically refilled. When Elaine motioned to the footman, he offered her a platter of roast beef, an English staple, she had learned. She mutinously waved him and the food away and glared at the centerpiece of fresh flowers. If she could not have wine, then she would have nothing.

The footman, summoned by an invisible hand, sedately walked to the opposite end of the table. Minutes later a small crystal bowl was placed before her. Elaine stared down at the egg custard. For a second time that day she felt the blood drain from her head.

Good God. She could be pregnant.

Elaine forgot about shocking the Boleighs or freezing the lord, forgot the guilt of having found satisfaction outside her marriage, forgot the fact that she was in a body that was not hers and that her prime directive must at all times be to return to the twentieth century and a husband who had never, ever satisfied her. All those things paled in the face of potential pregnancy.

It didn't matter that she wasn't Morrigan or that the lord wasn't her husband. He could make her pregnant.

"Morrigan! Morrigan, I said it is time to leave the gentlemen!"

Elaine blinked. Morrigan's aunt and two cousins were impatiently standing beside their chairs.

"Morrigan, I said it is time to leave the gentlemen!" Mrs. Boleigh barked.

Stupid cow, Elaine thought sourly. There was only one gentleman at the table. Charles had joined them last night; why should tonight be any different?

Elaine started to scoot away from the table. Her chair was promptly pulled back for her by one of the invisible footmen who were magically there only when needed. Standing, she could see the lord. He remained seated. A decanter of dark red wine sat near his right hand. A mocking, get-even kind of smile curled his lips.

She remembered the first time they had eaten together. After ordering a decanter of port, he had told her there was no need for her to leave the table, that he could get as drunk with her as easily as he could without her. She deduced now that proper etiquette dictated a lady leave a man to his port, and by the smile on his face, that for once he was going to adhere to tradition.

Elaine led the Boleigh brood to the blue-and-silver drawing room. She hoped he got so drunk he had triple vision and stood up on the wrong floor.

"I should expect no less, of course. What a graceless piece of humanity you are, Morrigan. Ring for tea!"

Elaine could think of far more entertaining things she would like to do. Like wrapping the cord around Mrs. Boleigh's neck and watching her hang like a cow wrestler in a Western movie. Smiling, she perched on the edge of the love seat.

"I'm not at all surprised that the servants are lazy. You are incapable of managing a house, as I will soon convince Lord Arlcotte. Then you shall have your comeuppance," Mrs. Boleigh said, averting her eyes from her niece's bosom. "Prudence, ring for tea!"

"Yes, Mama." The taller of the two girls pulled the silver cord hanging by the drapes. Almost immediately the butler appeared, as if he'd been listening at the door.

"Be so good as to bring up a tray of tea, my good man. And include a plate of sweets. Dinner was not at all acceptable. The beef was tough, the vegetables underdone, and the pudding sour." Mrs. Boleigh glared triumphantly at Elaine. "Be off with you now."

Elaine stared at the woman's bulging gown. She could see the outline of the corset where Mrs. Boleigh's flesh swelled around it.

"No," Elaine said clearly. "No sweets. No food of any kind." She smiled graciously at the butler. "Dinner was quite excellent. Thank you."

Mrs. Boleigh's mouth gaped open. She seemed surprised that her niece could talk. Elaine wondered if Morrigan had ever been allowed to speak in their presence.

"Very good, my lady. Thank you. I shall give Cook your compliments." The butler bowed his head and backed out of the room.

Elaine felt a surge of bittersweet power at being acknowledged lady of the house. The lord's lady.

"Have you rid Lord Arlcotte of his cats, Morrigan?"

Elaine looked, somewhat surprised, at—Mary. This was the first time Mary had spoken. Elaine had begun to think the two sisters had but one tongue between them, exercised by Prudence.

Mrs. Boleigh hushed her daughter. "All will be taken care of in due time. Play the piano. Your cousin could do with some Christian influence."

Mary commenced butchering "Onward Christian Soldiers."

Elaine breathed a sigh of relief when the tea tray arrived—Charles's tone-deafness had been endearing; Mary's was insufferable. Mrs. Boleigh grabbed the silver pot, eager to wrest control.

"You are our guest, Mrs. Boleigh." Charles's voice from the doorway arrested the senior woman's movements. It sounded sober. "Morrigan will pour."

Mrs. Boleigh reluctantly relinquished the teapot. She made room for Elaine on the divan. Elaine, equally reluctant, perched beside Mrs. Boleigh. Once down, she forced herself to stay there. It was most peculiar that people would wear clean clothes but would not bother to clean their bodies. Elaine successfully poured a cup of tea without spilling it.

"You stupid girl. I take four sugars and cream."

Elaine wanted to point out that sugar and cream were on the tray. But nineteenth-century etiquette was different from twentieth-century etiquette. She added the ingredients. When she poured a cup of tea for Charles, he quietly instructed her, "Just lemon, please." He added, "Thank you," when she did as he requested and offered him his cup, something that none of the Boleigh brood had said.

Elaine sipped her tea; it was rich and fragrant. She tried to recall the flavor of a tea bag dunked in lukewarm water.

"Mary, play the piano. I'm sure the lord wishes to be entertained. Prudence, you may sing. She has a truly saintly voice, my lord; the church choir would simply be lost without my Prudence."

"Thank you, but no. Perhaps some other time. Morrigan and I had a tiring day. We will retire. But do stay, as you please."

The cup was removed from Elaine's fingers. Her hand was grasped in a firm, implacable grip. She was pulled upward.

Elaine took a deep breath. It was time for round two. She supposed it had been too much to hope that he might pass out in drunken oblivion.

Charles matched his steps to Elaine's. He paused in front of the door most proximate to her own. His eyes gleamed in the lamplight.

"My room tonight, I think," he murmured. He grasped her elbow as if afraid she might bolt, and opened the door.

His bedroom was decorated in black and gold, with the occasional bright crimson accent. Very elegant. Very Eastern. Totally masculine.

The moment the door was closed, Charles pulled Elaine into his arms and kissed her. He licked and prodded the seam of her lips. Elaine stood quiescent. The tip of his tongue forged a pass. Elaine clamped her jaws together. He licked and prodded her teeth, her gums, the soft, slick flesh on the inside of her lips.

Elaine remained unresponsive.

Charles tore his mouth away from hers. "Damn you!"

The blue of his eyes glittered like shards of ice. Elaine smiled, concentrating on making herself as cold as those eyes.

He grabbed Elaine's head in both hands and held it upward. His lips and tongue resumed their play. With the added bonus of teeth. He gently plucked her bottom lip into his mouth and nibbled on it. Then he suckled it as he had her earlobe that night over the pornographic texts. As he had her nipple through the chemise earlier that day.

She had underestimated him. The lord was not going to send her flying against the door in a rage at being rejected. Elaine pushed at his chest, in a sudden panic over the outcome of this skirmish. *This is adultery,* she reminded herself. *He could make you pregnant,* she reminded herself when that failed to squelch the sensations spreading through her body. She jerked her lip free. "Don't!"

Charles gave a bark of laughter. "Oh, I don't think so, milady. You can't fool me now. You may be able to fight me, but you can't fight yourself, can you? I can feel your nipples against my chest. They're swollen and hard, I would imagine—yes, should I prove it? I would imagine that is not the only thing that is swollen, is it?"

He bent and captured Elaine's earlobe between his teeth, issuing a sharp nip before plunging his tongue inside her ear.

"Are you wet, sweetheart?" His words were warm and humid, beguiling as the original serpent. "Does your little *yoni* ache and pulse?"

Elaine desperately shook her head.

He laughed softly. The blue of his eyes glowed, ice giving way to fire. "It does. But not as much as it will. When I'm finished with you, sweetheart, you're going to drip like honey. When I touch you here"—his hand grasped the inside of her thigh through the dress just above her knee—"it's going to be slick and hot. *Kama salila,* remember? Love juice."

Elaine succeeded in jerking free of those debilitating arms. "No!" She backed away from that equally debilitating body, toward the door, toward peace and safety. If she could reach her room she could lock him out, in her panic forgetting about the connecting door.

The soft wetness of the lord's mouth hardened. He stalked her slowly, menacingly.

"Don't touch me!" Elaine yelled, forgetting nineteenth-century speech patterns. He had made her forget who and where she was before; it could not happen again. "I don't want you. I don't want you, damn it!"

No sooner did the words leave Elaine's mouth than Charles pounced. He grabbed the front of her scarlet dress and yanked. Her breasts popped free, unrestrained by either chemise or corset. The air was amazingly cool, considering that not that much more of her was exposed.

"Not want me?" he jeered. "Sweetheart, if you wanted me any more your nipples would split open."

A steely arm anchored Elaine's shoulders against the front left side of his body. Charles's other arm lowered; he wrestled with the hem of her skirt. Cool air traveled upward. Elaine flinched at the intrusion of his hand inside her drawers. Stupid crotchless things. Useless. Totally useless.

Long hard fingers forced their way up inside her. She cried out, partly in anger, partly in pain. She could feel her flesh pulse around him.

"Not want me? You're so wet, I could damn near slide my fist up inside you."

He widened her stance with his feet. Another finger squeezed up inside her. Elaine bit her lip to hold back another cry. She would not show him weakness. She would not, she would not, she would not!

"Only two more to go," he murmured silkily. "Shall we try for a fourth?"

The cry would not be held back then. Elaine felt as if he was rending her apart. The extra pressure instantly eased.

"Not four yet, I think. Later. Later you will beg for that fourth finger."

The pressure eased altogether, accompanied by that telltale slurp of wet suction. He slid his fingers to the top of the slick folds and rubbed the swollen nub there until it pulsed and quivered.

"Not want me?" he whispered, rubbing and rubbing, there, on the right side, where it was ultrasensitive. Air gushed through Elaine's parted lips. "If you didn't want me, Morrigan, your little clit wouldn't be engorged like a fat, ripe pomegranate. Kiss me. Kiss me, Morrigan, and I will make it easier for you."

Elaine blindly raised her head to his. She tried to nuzzle his lips apart, but he kept them closed. His fingers rubbed lighter, less fast. She used her tongue to open his lips. His fingers pressed ever so slightly harder, a little faster, there, exactly where she needed to be touched. She tried to bury her lips inside his. The pressure decreased again. Desperately she fastened her lips over his. The pressure increased just a little. She was so close. Elaine ground her mouth against his. The pressure lightened. She gentled her kiss. The pressure remained too light, too slow.

In a sudden burst of insight, Elaine realized what he wanted. She tentatively thrust her tongue inside his mouth. He sucked on it, hard, so she couldn't have brought it back out if she had wanted. The fingers ceased their work altogether, no sooner the pressure stopping than she felt another pressure, sliding, opening, plunging deep inside.

Elaine tore her mouth free of his. "No! Not there!" she gasped. "You promised! You promised to make it easier!"

"When you beg for this, Morrigan, I will give you what you want. Only when you beg for *this*," his fingers plunged hard inside her; Morrigan was almost lifted off of her feet; then they slid out of her and gently rubbed at the top of the heavy, swollen lips. "Not when you beg for this."

"But you hurt me," Elaine said thickly, throbbing, throbbing, not just where his fingers gently swirled, but deep, deep inside.

"No," he said. Three fingers slid back inside her, increasing the throb. "No, I won't hurt you. Not if you open up to me. Completely. Do you understand?"

He slid free of her. Elaine jerked. Charles smiled. He removed his hand from underneath her dress. Before she could discern his intent, he smeared his fingers on her lips.

She could smell her own arousal. Taste it in that split second before his mouth came down and licked clean her lips, then made thorough love to her mouth, tongue plunging, retreating, circling, gently feathering the roof of her mouth. The ache inside her increased, almost surpassing that of the bud.

When Charles released Elaine, she stood quivering, panting. He stepped back and took a throbbing nipple between each thumb and forefinger. The four fingers gently twisted the elongated nipples back and forth. Elaine almost collapsed at the stab of sensation that slammed directly to the pit of her stomach.

Charles's face flushed with triumph and desire. His mouth curved in a knowing smile, lips shiny from his kisses and her essence. Something Elaine did not recognize shone in the Mediterranean blue eyes, something that wrenched away the last of her resistance.

"You're trembling, did you know that? For me. Come, let me help you undress. We don't need any more barriers, not tonight, not ever."

Undressing became another provocation. First the removal of hairpins, then the slow, sinuous comb of fingers. Her head limply fell back. He unbuttoned the dress and slid it over her hips. Elaine had never realized the back had so many nerve endings. There. She instinctively arched. Charles ran his tongue down her spine to the top of her buttocks, to the crevice there and just beyond. She nervously stepped forward.

Charles sighed, straightened, and turned her around. He was naked. Funny. How could he simultaneously undress both of them? Elaine wondered, carefully keeping her eyes focused upward.

His face was suffused with amused frustration. "I keep forgetting. We still haven't passed the major hurdle yet, have we? No matter. The rest, I think, would be best carried out in bed."

He picked Elaine up in his arms. She didn't have to worry about being dropped, or straining his back. Or of the ultimate indignity—of his not being able to lift her. It was quite a novelty, being worry-free.

The bedspread was turned down, revealing a glimpse of black sheets. With a minor adjustment of Elaine's weight he reached down and yanked the top covers over the foot of the bed. The silk was cool and slick beneath her body. Charles settled down beside Elaine. She ran her hands over his arms, his chest, testing the malleability of flesh, the hardness of bone, the tautness of muscle. He kissed her, his hands gently caressing her sides, her shoulders, her hips, her legs. Elaine squirmed, on fire for him to touch her in less innocuous places. At last she grabbed his hand and placed it on her stomach.

Charles laughed—and promptly moved the hand to her breasts.

He cupped her left breast, then her right. He pinched her nipples, rolled them round and round. Elaine felt a trickle of fluid escape from her body and dampen the silk beneath her. Wordless whimpers escaped her throat.

"Shhh. Not yet. You're not ready yet."

Like hell, Elaine thought miserably. Charles chuckled. Had she said it out loud?

"Hell will be a lot cooler than what you're going to feel tonight, sweetheart."

Charles's mouth joined his hands. A jolt of electricity surged through Elaine's body at the feel of his tongue. Her naked breasts were almost painful in their sensitivity. He raked his teeth along the length of her engorged nipple before greedily sucking on it. The vacuum of his hot, wet mouth sent bolt after bolt of agonizing sensation to her abdomen. The little release he had granted her while horseback riding remained always on the edge. She imagined herself spouting White Snow, imagined him drinking from her. He kissed and suckled her breasts until Elaine could not keep still, until she moaned and groaned a litany of *please, please, please.*

Charles anchored Elaine with his thigh. She stilled beneath the weight. He slipped his leg between hers, opening her until he could settle between her thighs. His hand slid over her stomach, past the soft nest of hair.

"Yes!" she cried, arching and straining for contact *there.* But the fingers slipped past that spot. "No!" she moaned, trying to arch her hips to regain contact.

His fingers slid deep inside her, commencing a gentle, deep rhythm. It felt like he was stroking her insides. She wanted . . . she wanted that—it was so good—but she wanted the other more. She had only once climaxed the other way, earlier that day, and the pleasure had been intermingled with pain. Please let his fingers return to that *other* point.

"I can feel you stretching, widening for me. Feel it? Open for me, yes, you know the rhythm. That doesn't hurt, does it? You're so hot and wet. Your body knows what it wants. *This* is what it was made for, to have a man deep inside you." His movements became stronger—the bed rocked with them, the sound of his slapping hand and her sucking wetness loud over her panting breath.

His fingers slipped completely free of her body. Elaine felt empty—so empty there was an actual hollow feeling inside her. She grabbed for the lord's shoulders, but they were sliding down her body. He left a trail of moisture, scorching hot lips sliding down her chest to her stomach, past the soft nest of hair, to—

Elaine's body arched completely off the bed. *"No!"* She grabbed his hair and pulled with all her might. Fantasizing was one thing. Reality was another thing entirely.

Charles ignored her yanking fingers, sticking to her bucking body like Krazy Glue. His tongue found that spot that she had desperately tried to lead his fingers to.

Elaine again tried to pull his head away, but instead found her hands cupping him closer. His tongue was soft and wet and smooth and driving her out of her mind. She allowed her legs to be pulled up and bent back toward her body. Open. She was completely open. Touch. Sight. Smell. There was nothing she could hide in this position.

She gritted her teeth, feeling the beginnings of the most tremendous climax in her life—only to be balanced on the edge. The lord drew away from the press of her hands. Her desperate, twitching flesh subsided. Leaning forward, he delicately licked her, only to have it start over again, to again be left there hanging while he investigated the slick folds, the opening to her body, always returning to that helpless, quivering piece of flesh that had always been a curse but that now had been made into an instrument of torture.

"Please, please." Elaine sobbed, fighting to hold his head in place. "Please lick me, please, damn you—I can't stand it anymore. Please. Lick it, damn it, *lick it!*"

Charles pulled free of her hands and sat back on his haunches. He leaned forward over her then, using one arm to hold her legs bent back to her body. His breath was rushing in and out of his lungs, as if he had been the one undergoing torture, and not her.

Elaine could feel the gush of hot breaths there where he held her exposed. Deliberately, purposefully, he brought his other hand between her legs. The invading fingers were welcome, the hard, sure rhythm even more so. And then there was the pressure that was more than pressure. A picture of the little Indian maiden and the dark-skinned Indian man flashed into her mind. Of the Indian man's dark fingers buried inside the rouged nether lips of the Indian maid.

Charles's head hung over her. Perspiration glistened on his forehead. His eyes were dark with intent, with purpose. The pressure increased—pain, pleasure, it didn't matter anymore. Elaine opened her body. "Please," she whispered. "All. I want all of them. I want all of you."

And then they were inside her, his fingers, gently fluted to accommodate her passage. Elaine threw her head back, gasping. The black canopy twisted and whirled. When his fingers started a long, slow rhythm she thought she would die. Closing her eyes, she arched her body, pushing upward for more—"Harder, deeper"—not hearing her words, lost completely in what he was doing to her and what he was making her feel.

Charles's fingers slipped free. Elaine opened her eyes. He was leaning over her. His breath overrode hers. They sounded like horses panting at a race, she thought dimly, like at Arlington Park.

"No more play, Morrigan. Hold your legs back to your chest."

Elaine instinctively did as he instructed. With both hands free, he pulled the soft silken flesh apart and then there was no holding back and Elaine cried out, feeling him come inside her far more deeply than had his fingers.

Charles leaned over her and rested his hands along her sides. He commenced a gentle back-and-forth motion, pushing and pulling, circling his hips. It felt as if her insides were being churned, as if he had pierced her all the way to her throat. The gut-churning sensation grew and grew—her body seemed to be suicidal; it opened wider and wider to take more, more, it was coming. *Oh, oh. oh . . .*

The thrusts eased. She clawed at his back and his buttocks.

"Say my name." He grunted.

He thrust harder, then eased just when it seemed as if she were going to fall off the Sears Tower.

"Say my name."

Yes, yes, she would say his name. Just as soon as she caught her breath.

He eased out an inch, circling, circling, but without the necessary depth.

"Say my name." He gasped for breath between the short sentences. "Tell me; I want you to know me. Say . . . my . . . name!"

Elaine grabbed the lord's tight little aristocratic buns in both hands. "Charles!" she screamed, at the same time pulling down with all of her might. She wrapped her knees along his ribs, clinging for dear life. Pride evaporated when the playful circles continued. "Charles, please come inside me, please, harder, I need you, deeper, I have to have you, oh, please f—!"

Charles gave Elaine what she wanted, what she needed as surely as she needed air to breathe. The bed rocked and rolled like a carnival ride. The room echoed with the sound of slapping flesh. Charles grunted and groaned and sweated. Or perhaps it was Elaine who grunted and groaned and sweated. She knew that he spoke, but the words were beyond her comprehension. Every sense was focused on what was happening and what was about to happen. She had never felt anything like it in her entire life. Had never dreamed anything like it existed.

Suddenly his arms caught her behind the knees and forced her legs apart and back, opening her wider, wider, pounding deeper, deeper.

"Charles! Oh, God, Charles. God, oh, God!" Elaine dimly heard the echoes of her cries. It sounded as if she were in agony. In the next instant the breath completely left her body. A whole Fourth of July Grant Park fireworks exploded inside her. And it went on and on until she felt his male flesh lodge impossibly deep inside her body and gush and jerk and gush and jerk.

From somewhere far away Elaine felt her legs slide down onto cool silk. If that didn't make her pregnant, she thought, nothing would. She was asleep before Charles had disengaged their bodies.

Charles looked down at Morrigan. Sweat poured off his body; he felt as though he would never get enough oxygen to his lungs. His blood sang with the most incredible release of his life, stronger even than what he had felt at the lake.

He looked down to where they had been joined.

The black sheet was inundated.

He grinned.

What a woman. He had never had a woman so hot in his entire life. She had damned near crushed his ribs.

And she was still a novice.

He reached for the covers draped over the foot of the bed and dragged them up over their bodies. The candles flickered; they would go out soon. And even if they didn't, he did not have the strength to leave the bed.

Tomorrow he would instruct her in the use of birth control. The kind of sex he envisioned for the future would not be possible if she were pregnant. And much as he wanted an heir—several, in fact— he wanted this passionate little wife of his far, far more. Perhaps in another year he would have had enough of her that he could take it easier with her.

He winced, feeling an ache in his ribs.

Or she could take it easier with him.

He pulled her into his arms. She mumbled in her sleep and half-heartedly tried to roll over onto her side. He followed her, nestling his slack manhood against her delectable little bottom. It surged toward the warmth that lay hidden between her cheeks.

He sighed ruefully. Well, maybe they would wait two years.

Charles went to sleep, dreaming of all the things he would teach Morrigan.

Chapter
21

Elaine awoke reluctantly. She had to fight through fifty layers of cotton. The battle would not have been worth the effort if she had not heard voices.

"Tell Katie to keep an eye on her ladyship, but not to disturb her." There was amusement in the male voice. "Let her sleep as long as she wants to. When she does awaken, I want a large breakfast and a hot bath in readiness. Perhaps not in that order. She'll need the bath more than anything, I imagine. Tell Katie to add a healthy dose of Epsom salts to the bath. And to make sure that the water is very hot."

"Very good, my lord."

The second male voice sounded disproportionately stuffy.

Several things surfaced at once: Elaine ached abominally; the flesh between her thighs felt like it had been rent with a steel beam. There was a peculiar scent to the sheets. Heavy. Musky. Not at all the floral composition that she had become used to. The voices belonged to the lord—Charles—and Fritz, his valet, in that order.

Elaine's eyes flew open. The ache and the scent were sex. And Charles was the perpetrator.

And this was not her room. Either in the twentieth or the nineteenth century.

The door closed softly. Charles leaned over the bed. His eyes were very blue, almost black. The slight hitch in his right lip was gone. He looked totally relaxed, totally at ease.

"I'm sorry; I didn't mean to awaken you." His voice was low, husky with shared pleasure. "How do you feel?"

Elaine bit her lip.

How did she feel? Very strange. Uncertain. A little off-kilter.

"Are you sore?"

Elaine started to shake her head, then thought better of denial. What if he would want a repeat performance? Her cheeks burned, remembering the extent of his and her performance last night. She vigorously nodded her head.

"Let me see."

Elaine stared at him mutely. She did not understand his meaning until a hand with very long, tanned fingers reached out and pulled the covers down. Cool air enveloped her warm body.

Elaine tore her eyes away from those devastating fingers and grabbed at the covers.

"Don't be silly. I've seen and tasted everything you have, Morrigan." His pupils dilated. "Well, almost everything. Lie still now."

Was he crazy? Elaine didn't even allow a gynecologist to see what he proposed seeing. Well, except once a year, for the mandatory Pap smear.

"Amazing. You do blush all over."

Elaine squeezed her eyes shut.

"Even here."

A warm finger touched her toe. Elaine jerked. Which was nothing compared to what she did when he touched her *there*.

"Hold still, sweetheart. I just want to look."

He parted her legs, then gently parted the soft folds in between. Charles sucked in his breath. Elaine felt as though her body would burst into a ball of flame. Did she blush there, too? she wondered.

"Lord, you are so beautiful. Hold still. Let me get a washcloth."

Elaine was immobilized with embarrassment. Seconds later a cool cloth was pressing up against her.

"Feel better?"

Amazingly enough, it did. She rewarded him with a nod.

He gently washed there where he had been. Elaine opened her eyes. Her flesh was very, very raw. His hand prevented her from closing her legs. He wiped her there with the cloth several more times, until he seemed satisfied with his results. Charles laid the cloth on the bed and held her open.

"You're like chocolate and strawberries down here." His eyes were totally intent upon the inspection. Elaine felt a different heat join that of embarrassment. "Here"—a finger gently flecked the outer folds of the flesh he was inspecting—"is a rich mocha chocolate, and here"—Elaine winced when the finger slid the length of the moist inner lips—"is a velvety ripe strawberry."

Charles immediately removed his finger. "Poor baby," he murmured. He leaned down and kissed the sensitive inner skin. His tongue flicked soothing and scalding hot. He kissed her long and leisurely there, rimming over and over the torn, bruised flesh. When he raised his head, the heat from the non-embarrassment had escalated several notches. He pulled the covers back over her.

"I want you to take a long, hot bath. Katie will take care of it. Afterward I want you to use some of the cream I have. It will help inside where the water can't penetrate."

He stood up. "Should I call Katie now, or do you want to sleep more?"

Elaine felt rather like a small child, very vulnerable yet very cared for. "Call Katie now, please," she said, sounding every bit as young as she felt.

The bath did help. Elaine was surprised at the inclusion of Epsom salts. It was a familiar soak. Her mother had lived and breathed the benefits of Epsom salts when Elaine had been a child and practiced overlong at the piano. After bathing, Elaine gingerly applied the cream Charles had supplied. It felt wonderfully cool and soothing. She gently eased her fingertip inside this body that had become more her body within the last twenty-four hours than her own had ever been.

Deliberately shutting her mind to what Katie might or might not think, Elaine fortified her chair with a pillow before she sat and wolfed down a mountain of fluffy scrambled eggs—she paused, fork midway to her mouth. Well, too late to worry about the fertile bene-fits of eggs. Either she was or she wasn't. Several pieces of bacon, toast with marmalade, and a bowl of strawberries—she remembered Charles's comparison—with heavy cream—ah, that would be him—followed the mound of eggs.

Sighing, Elaine sat back and licked a drop of cream from her lips. Just like a Cheshire cat. She remembered her ability to lick the tip of her nose that she had discovered yesterday on the picnic, and grinned. Exactly like a Cheshire cat.

"Marm, ye have a note here. I found it on the floor by the door."

Elaine regarded Katie between lowered lids. Ah, yes, she thought. It was time to issue chastisement for the maid's poor housekeeping.

Katie thrust the note into Elaine's hand, stacked the dishes left over from breakfast, picked up the tray, and marched out into the hallway.

Elaine wryly watched the maid's departure. Shrugging, she opened the note. The writing was slanted leftward. Just as she thought—Katie had dropped one of Elaine's notes and neglected to pick it up. It must have been lying there for over a week—she had only once written a note in longhand for the maid, when Katie had been reluctant to bring her a bath during that time of the month. She started to refold the piece of paper.

A great cold fist clenched inside her stomach. Elaine ripped open the note.

Dear Elaine,

   Yes, I bet you thought you would never hear or see your own name again, did you not? Imagine your surprise and, dare I say it, your pleasure at finding that you were wrong.

   Or perhaps you are not pleased. I think you like my husband just a little too much. Imagine Matthew should he discover what you have done, Elaine. You didn't think he knew about your perverted little sex books, did you? But he knew. He used them as evidence to prove your instability. He would not believe, you see, that I had taken over your old, fat body. So he had me—or should I say you?—yes, I believe I must, because he did believe it you as opposed to me—committed to an insane asylum.

And Matthew loved you. Or so he claimed. One really must wonder what Arlcotte would do should he believe his wife believed she was someone else.

The note was not signed.

Elaine's heart beat time and a half.

The note did not have to be signed. The extreme leftward slant was signature enough. Morrigan was here. Somewhere. Somehow.

But that was impossible.

Did Katie *know?*

Surely not. Katie had been acting peculiarly, but Elaine suspected her behavior stemmed from loss of dignity over her lack of knowledge as a lady's maid.

Morrigan had been in the twentieth century, in Elaine's body. She had, of course, fleetingly considered the possibility, but the reality was staggering.

Elaine felt . . . violated.

Matthew had not recognized that Morrigan was not Elaine. He had had what he thought was Elaine committed.

Elaine felt . . . betrayed.

But this whole thing was impossible. Matthew wouldn't do that to her. Not to Elaine. Not to the woman he had been married to for seventeen years.

The note had mentioned her marriage manuals. How could a prankster in the nineteenth century know about that?

Ugly little memories surfaced. Elaine had once suggested that she and Matthew experiment with oral sex. Matthew had been repulsed, claiming it was unsanitary. Elaine had studied techniques to prolong ejaculation. Matthew had refused to discuss it. Elaine had suggested they visit a marriage counselor. Matthew had said he wasn't the one who needed help.

Elaine's eyes burned. The place between her legs throbbed. Her left leg ached from last night's unaccustomed exercise. Her breasts felt swollen and tender.

I think you like my husband just a little too much. . . . One really must wonder what Arlcotte would do should he believe his wife believed she was someone else.

Morrigan did not sound like a little gray mouse, Elaine thought numbly. She sounded quite threatening, in fact. As though she would be more than a match against Hattie and the Boleighs.

What she needed, Elaine decided, was to have a good cry. Perhaps then she could view things in a clearer perspective. Except that her eyes were painfully dry and all she could think about was that Matthew had had her committed.

Elaine limped to the door to turn the key for the much needed privacy. Self-pity evaporated, to be replaced by the true stirrings of fear.

The key was gone.

Katie, when she returned to empty the bathtub, said she did not have it. Together they searched the surrounding floor, lifting the carpet, crawling beneath furniture. When that proved to be futile, they searched the hallway.

"Perhaps the lord has the key, m' lady."

Elaine did not doubt the lord had the key to the connecting door. Holding that, he had no need for the key she was concerned about.

"Perhaps that old Hattie, perhaps *she* took it, marm. She's been slinking 'bout, giving me and the other servants the creeps something awful."

So much for Hattie's confinement. Elaine grimaced. Just what she needed to hear.

Katie's solemn little face broke into a hopeful smile. "I'll go and tell Mr. Fritz, and he can tell the lord, and *he'll* git to the bottom of things!"

"No, I don't think so, Katie. Let it be."

Katie's face fell. Shoulders slumped, she picked up the two empty buckets and headed for the Japanese screen.

Elaine felt a twinge of remorse. It was obvious Katie was looking for a way to get close to Fritz. Besides, if Katie left, Elaine would be alone, without benefit of a locked door.

Impulsively she put out her hand. What harm could there be in talking to a servant who butchered the English language merely by opening her mouth?

"Sit down, Katie. I don't think you are very happy right now, are you? Did you and Fritz have a . . . an argument?"

The maid put the two buckets aside and sat down where Elaine indicated. Tears rolled down her cheeks.

"Oh, marm, he said I was getting idears above me station, that a girl like me with no schooling ain't *ever* gonna be grand enough to be a lady's maid, and the lord, he only wants me now cause there ain't no one else!"

Elaine wondered what bug had crawled up Fritz's behind. She remembered a song her secretary used to sing, something to the effect that a woman needed a man as much as a fish needed a bicycle.

"And he said as how it ain't seemly fer me to always be coming to him. He don't want me!"

Katie burst into noisy tears. Every mothering instinct Elaine had ever suppressed came to the fore. She pulled Katie into her arms and let the maid cry it out on her shoulder. Making comforting little sounds, she patted the cumbersome mobcap flat to reach the head beneath it, then used the starched white material to mop up a few tears of her own.

Long minutes elapsed, the lady holding the maid. Finally Katie drew back, pulled out the dusting rag from her apron pocket, and blew her nose. A stream of dust enveloped them. Elaine surreptitiously wiped her cheeks before waving her hand to clear the air.

Katie sniffed and put the dusting rag back into her pocket. "I be that sorry, marm, fer the way I been acting. Mr. Fritz, he has the right of it. I know I ain't schooled. But that ain't no reason to be taking it out on ye the way I been doing."

"Absolutely Mr. Fritz is not right," Elaine said bracingly. "Katie, I'm surprised at you. We women have to stick together, you know. You're a wonderful lady's maid. Don't ever let a man put you down. Women will never become liberated if they don't stand up for themselves."

A look of budding determination flowered in Katie's expressive brown eyes. Elaine suppressed a grin. She had probably just planted the first seeds of women's lib.

Katie shyly ducked her head. "Ye know, marm, I didn't half like ye before Hattie left. Ye never spoke to us servants. Ye always treated us like we wasn't there. Not that that ain't proper!" Katie hastily assured Elaine. "It just be that m' lord, he's been ever so kind, and we did—that is, the other servants and me—want him to have a lady that'd be kind to him, too, if ye know what I mean."

Katie reached out and gave Elaine's hand a quick squeeze. "I just want ye to know that we think ye're a grand lady, even with that limp of yers, and we're ever so glad the lord married ye!"

Elaine didn't know if she had been complimented or insulted.

The maid jumped up from the love seat. "Oh, it be time fer lunch! Should I put yer hair up fer ye, m' lady? It looked ever so grand last night."

The Boleighs were already at lunch when Elaine joined them. All four Boleighs. She stopped cold on the threshold of the small breakfast room that was used for informal dining.

Charles looked up, a rare smile lighting up his face. "Morrigan!" Jumping up from the table, he drew her inside the room and seated her at the opposite end of the table.

The chair was much harder than what Elaine had been sitting on in her room. She winced.

Leaning over, Charles brushed his lips against the nape of her neck. "I like this hairstyle. It leaves more to the eye." *And touch*, he did not need to add.

The warm shiver the butterfly light contact elicited died a quick death beneath the four pairs of watching eyes. Mrs. Boleigh. Mary. Prudence. And . . . Mr. Boleigh.

The dark, ratlike eyes regarded Elaine with distinct disapproval, as did all the Boleighs. No, that wasn't true. Prudence's eyes were filled with an entirely different emotion. Malice. Hate. Envy.

Had Morrigan managed to come back in Prudence's body?

It really must be one of the three: Mrs. Boleigh, Mary, or Prudence. The coincidence was too great. Morrigan had not appeared, so to speak, until after they had.

Invisible fingers played the length of Elaine's spine.

It didn't have to be one of the three, she thought with foreboding.

Hattie's eyes had glittered with hateful knowledge when she had stepped out of the coach. Mrs. Boleigh had said that she had told them disturbing things about Morrigan. But Elaine had not done anything so very disturbing. Hattie had accused Elaine of masturbating with no proof. Could it be Hattie? Had Hattie all along been Morrigan?

What appetite had survived the sight of Mr. Boleigh shriveled. Elaine stared at the food the footman was placing on her plate with distaste.

"You are succumbing to bad habits, Morrigan. Sleeping late. Making servants wait on you as if you were a grand lady. I did not raise you so."

Elaine regarded the older woman. She was filled with as much spite as Hattie. What better guise than a proper Christian wife. Could it be Mrs. Boleigh, then? Had Morrigan traded one "old, fat body" for another?

"Perhaps Morrigan is back to her old tricks, Mama," Mary said maliciously. "Perhaps she has been out all night dancing around the mushrooms."

Could it be Mary?

Elaine had come full circle. She shifted in her chair. She really did wish she had a cushion. One faced adversity so much better in comfort.

"How's your bull doing, Boleigh?"

"He misses your heifer, my lord."

The fork dropped from between Elaine's fingers. A footman was there instantly, picking up the old, providing a new. She smiled shakily. One side of the footman's mouth lifted, on that side of the face shielded from the others at the table. Just as quickly the exchange was over, leaving Elaine to wonder if she had imagined that reassuring half-smile.

"Morrigan was ever a clumsy girl," Mr. Boleigh said mildly. He dabbed at his mouth, for a second only his bald pate, ratlike eyes, and side-whiskers visible over the napkin. "As for my gentleman cow, he is quite the beau in Cornwall. Lord Tallery himself recently rode over to see him. I remember you yourself remarked on his accoutrements."

Elaine choked on a swallow of bread. Mary giggled.

"Really, Boleigh," Charles interrupted sharply. "I hardly think such conversation appropriate at the table. I talked to the doctor this morning. He said you would be capable of traveling in another day or so. I'm sure you're looking forward to returning to Cornwall."

"I'm sure my niece is looking forward to it also."

Charles eyes twinkled. "I'm sure of it," he said.

Damn right, Elaine thought. *I can't wait to see the last of you, you child-molesting bastard.*

The rest of the meal passed in silence, Mr. Boleigh quite certain the lord had seen the light and decided to return Morrigan to the bosom of her family. Elaine contemplated the slurping Boleigh females, wondering if Morrigan already resided there.

Elaine spent the day curled up in her bedroom with an original copy of Jane Austen's *Pride and Prejudice*. Her thoughts ran round and round the typed print. How had Morrigan returned when Elaine had not been able to? How was it that the two could be in the same century? Why hadn't Elaine been returned to her own body? Why hadn't Morrigan returned to *her* own body?

Mr. Boleigh did not appear for dinner. Elaine breathed a sigh of relief. Charles did not talk, buried behind the flowers and candelabras, allowing Mrs. Boleigh to bitch in peace. Elaine concentrated on dodging the resulting barrage of food pellets.

After dinner Mrs. Boleigh methodically annihilated Elaine's

manners, her clumsiness, her dress, her hair. Elaine handed her a cup of tea with four sugars and cream. Mrs. Boleigh accused Elaine of using cosmetics. Elaine supposed she was referring to the effects of romping in the sun. She briefly debated telling Mrs. Boleigh how she had gotten that color. Except now more than ever it behooved Elaine to listen and watch.

Prudence interrupted Mrs. Boleigh's recital of Elaine's faults. "Mama, I wonder if Lord Arlcotte has heard Morrigan play the piano?"

"No, I haven't," Charles said, coming up behind Elaine and resting his hands on her shoulders. "Do you play, my dear?"

Elaine glanced from Prudence to Mrs. Boleigh. There was a vicious light in the girl's eyes. The older woman was filled with smug complacence.

Damned if she did, Elaine had a feeling, and damned if she didn't.

"Play for the lord, Morrigan," Mrs. Boleigh said. "You will have him think we did not give you a proper education."

Charles kneaded Elaine's shoulders. "I am not complaining about Morrigan's accomplishments, believe you me, Mrs. Boleigh," he said fervently.

The heat spread from his fingers to Elaine's cheeks.

"But Morrigan plays so beautifully, my lord," Prudence said. "You must insist she play."

"Yes, do, Morrigan!" Mary joined forces with her sister.

Did Elaine detect a threat in the voices of the two sisters? Yes, do Morrigan, or you'll find out that an unloving husband is no different from a loving husband? Or, yes, do, Morrigan, because we want to see you make a fool of yourself and justify our petty little lives?

Elaine stood up. Charles accompanied her to the piano. He lifted the top of the bench. "Shall I get you some music?"

Elaine shook her head. She might as well make a fool of herself and get it over with. She hadn't read music in almost twenty-five years. She only hoped her fingers were not as rusty as her brain was. Besides, Morrigan had apparently not played for a year. Even a virtuoso needed practice.

The bench was painfully hard. Elaine held out her hands and flexed her fingers. The instructors had told her that hands like these would improve her abilities. She only hoped they were right.

Now, what to play?

But her fingers knew what to play: the last song she had played for recital in that other life. Slowly she picked out Beethoven's hauntingly beautiful "Ode to Joy" that Miguel Rios had made popular in 1970. Midway through, she forgot to stumble. By the end she had forgotten why she was even playing. The last chords echoed in the vaulted room.

Charles clapped. "Bravo!"

There was only silence coming from the Boleigh brood. Elaine dared to turn around and look. Prudence looked positively malevolent. Mary looked subdued. Mrs. Boleigh glittered in outrage.

Charles immediately made their excuses. Elaine was relieved when he led her to her own room, she told herself. Katie undressed her and slipped a slinky silk-and-lace nightgown in pale rose over her head. She took down Elaine's hair, talking a mile a minute and administering one hundred strokes. Charles entered just after she had finished, dressed only in his robe that exposed his hairy chest and equally hairy legs. He came over to where Elaine sat and touched her hair.

"You're tired, aren't you?"

"Yes."

"Did you use the cream?"

Elaine threw an agonized look toward Katie. The maid was turning back the bedcovers, avidly listening to their every word.

Charles frowned. "You didn't, did you?"

Elaine squirmed. "Yes!"

"Did you put it inside you?"

"Yes!" she hissed.

"I don't believe you. You've been squirming all day like a cat on a hot plate. Don't worry, I'm not going to violate your sanctimonious little body. Katie, you'll be staying with milady tonight." He pulled Elaine up from the curved bench. "What did you do with that cream?"

Elaine opened the little drawer in the vanity.

He snatched the opaque jar from her hand. "Come with me."

She had little choice in the matter. He dragged her through the connecting door.

"Lie down."

"I don't—"

He silenced her with a look. "I said," he said succinctly, "lie down."

Elaine lay down and closed her eyes. The gown slid up her legs.

"Lift your hips."

Elaine clumsily lifted her hips.

"Spread your legs."

The *F* word rose to her lips. The bed depressed. Elaine's body rolled slightly toward him. He parted her legs, then held them apart when she tried to snap them back together.

"I assure you, I am receiving as little pleasure from this as you are."

Back to the scrawny arse, Elaine thought resentfully. How fickle the male species was. She left her legs as he had spread them.

"I see you did use it."

A creamed finger eased up the narrow, abraded passage. It was cold, and it hurt. She bit her lip. The finger slipped free. Elaine relaxed. The finger returned with more of the cream. He probed as deep as he could reach. Elaine slid back toward the headrest. The finger followed. Tears pricked her closed eyelids.

"There. Be a good girl now, and go back to your room. That is where you want to go, isn't it?"

"Yes," Elaine said spitefully. It smarted where his finger had been. But no sooner had the word gotten out than she wished she could rescind it.

She scrambled off the bed and pulled her gown down. He stood aside.

A black swan. Alone.

Elaine pictured her shell of a body locked in a padded room. Alone.

She rushed through the interconnecting door. Katie waited by the bed, dressed in a voluminous white nightgown and matching cap. The maid looked ready to drop. Elaine crawled beneath the sheets.

Katie held out her hand. "This be fer ye, marm. I found it underneath the door."

A faint trembling commenced in the pit of Elaine's stomach.

Dear Elaine,

You are a whore. Matthew was right to have you committed. First you diddle with your uncle, then with another woman's husband. And, oh, yes, with yourself. Matthew told the doctor you frequently diddled with yourself. The last doesn't bother Arlcotte, but how do you think he would feel knowing that you bedded him only after being excited by your uncle?

Yes, I imagine that surprises you. Who is it? you ask. There is nothing you do that I don't know about, Elaine. I see everywhere.

Arlcotte is almost as big as the "gentleman cow," isn't he? But you probably like that, being the bitch that you are.

"Be everything all right, m' lady? Ye be awful pasty-like."

Elaine crumpled up the note. She forced a smile. "Everything is fine, Katie. Just fine. Toss this into the fireplace. Let's get some sleep."

Elaine laid in the dark listening to Katie's breathing deepen into a soft snore.

Matthew had known. All those years when he had patted her on the rump and told her to go to sleep, he had known that she had needed more, had known that she had sought more, and had held her needs and her solitary satisfaction against her.

She slid out of bed. The interconnecting door opened without a squeak. Charles's bedroom was even darker than hers. Her big toe struck a wooden leg. She slowly crawled into his bed, tears running down her cheeks. Very, very carefully she inched across the slippery sheets until she encountered hard, naked skin. She curled up to a masculine behind.

Almost instantly the hard, naked body turned. Muscled arms

pulled her inward. She wrapped her arms and legs about Charles and buried her face into his chest. Elaine could feel him hot and turgid against her stomach.

Charles buried his face into her hair and kissed the tip of her ear. He sighed. She sighed. They both went to sleep.

Chapter

22

Charles's bed was empty when Elaine awoke quite late the next morning. Reluctantly she rose and returned to her own room. Katie prepared her a hot bath with Epsom salts. The place between her legs no longer burned and throbbed, so she dispensed with the cream.

Katie brought Elaine's breakfast. When the maid lifted the lid she exclaimed, "Look, m' lady, another note! D'ye think one of the footmen has the hots fer ye?"

Elaine grabbed the note. "Don't be silly!"

"Well, someone has to be writing them. I know it ain't me. If it was the lord, he'd have me bringing them to ye. Best I tell Mr. Fritz. He'd know who was doing it!"

"Absolutely not!" Elaine exclaimed. Quickly then, to distract the maid, she asked, "Speaking of Fritz, how are the two of you getting along? Did you kiss and make up?"

Katie hung her head. "Mr. Fritz, he ain't never kissed me. Said as how it ain't proper-like, me being beneath his station and all. Can't never anything come of it, he said."

"You should forget Fritz, Katie." Elaine said severely, irrepressibly reminded of herself and Matthew. "I really don't think the two of you are suited." Heaven knew Elaine knew whereof she spoke. Fritz would never accept the maid's natural exuberance. It would kill the girl if she tried to adjust her nature to that of another. "I think you should find a nice footman. There are certainly enough around to choose from. Don't you find any of them handsome?"

"I think they look awful silly wearing those wigs. And they strut so in the servants' hall. Mr. Fritz, he never struts. And he tells such interesting stories 'bout the times when he and the lord was fighting heathens."

Mr. Fritz never struts because he has nothing to strut, Elaine thought sourly. And he tells such interesting stories about his time with the lord because he has no life worth mentioning of his own. But Elaine wisely refrained from airing her opinions. Charles must like him. And he had gotten rid of Hattie that day. Maybe there was more to the man than what he had thus far revealed to Elaine.

Elaine read the note while Katie straightened up the bedroom.

Dear Elaine,
   Did I forget to tell you that you are dead?

Elaine dropped the note into her tea. Quickly she fished it out. Entire letters dripped down the page.

You have strange transportation in your century. Your trains are not powered by steam. They have three rails instead of two. But you know all that. I escaped from the hospital. People are no smarter in your time than they are in mine. It was simple. I offered to do to one of the male nurses what I did to Uncle John. Have you done it to my husband yet, I wonder? Anyway, I walked out of the hospital. I did not like your time, Elaine. But you wouldn't come back. I tried. When I jumped onto the third rail—yes, I knew what it would do—I tried with all my might to bring you back into your body. But you resisted. So I had to find a different body. Aren't you curious as to whose body it is?

Now you know that unless you give me what I want I will demonstrate to Lord Arlcotte that you are not me. By the by, I must compliment you on your performance last night. I had no time to waste on trivial matters such as playing a piano. I'm sure many people are wondering how you came to be so proficient. You see how easy it would be to prove you insane?

You have something of mine, dear Elaine. Something that was hidden in the bottom chest drawer. I want it back.

Elaine felt a strange sensation building inside her. It was rather like a black whirlwind, she thought dispassionately. It built and built until every nerve in her body was sensitized. The light was too bright. Katie jerked the bed hangings; the metal *clang* clawed inside Elaine. The aroma of eggs and sausage caused her stomach to churn. Her mouth was too dry. Her skin too tight.

There was no way of going back now. Ever. She was trapped. Forever. In a world without indoor plumbing. Without central heating.

I'm dead, she thought numbly, yet with every nerve screaming. The nightmare she had had when drugged with laudanum had not been a nightmare. She had been experiencing her own death. Electrifying, flesh-burning death.

"Marm? Marm, the note, be it bad? Marm?"

Katie's voice echoed shrilly. Elaine looked wildly at the maid. Was there no escape?

The room shriveled and shrank. Sound rushed up to her throat.

Dimly she realized she was going to have a fit of hysterics. She had to get out. Had to get away.

Clutching the note, she rushed from the room. Katie's bewildered "Marm?" trailed after her.

She paused indecisively at the foot of the stairs. Mrs. Boleigh tittered at something in the drawing room. The door opened. Prudence stepped out, her eyes bright and narrow.

Was Morrigan lurking inside Prudence's body?

Elaine ran to the door. The butler rushed to open it. The sun was so bright it almost blinded her. She ran past the stables and headed for a grove of trees. She just wanted someplace to hide, she thought. Just for a while. Until she felt more . . . sane.

She was out of breath by the time she reached the grove of trees. Adrenaline raced through her bloodstream. She walked faster and faster until she came to a small clearing. A stream sparkled in the sunlight. She took her shoes and stockings off and waded in the ice-cold water.

Yes, that was what she needed. She stood in the center of the shallow stream and watched minnows play between her feet. She tore the note into minuscule pieces. The fish eagerly bobbed for the potential food matter.

The stream babbled and gurgled. Numbness invaded her feet and ankles and legs. The sun danced and glittered on the water.

And there was still no place to escape.

"Morrigan?"

Elaine squeezed her eyes shut and turned her head to the sun. *Go away,* she silently begged. *Please. Go away.*

"Morrigan, are you all right?"

Of course I'm all right, she wanted to shout. *My husband had me committed; your wife killed me. What could be more all right than that?*

Hot, thick tears spilled onto her cheeks and ran down her chin and neck.

She heard sounds come from the bank, the creak of leather, a grunt of exertion, a muffled impact, then another. The water splashed, as if a marlin had joined the minnows. Or perhaps the Mad Hatter had come to have his tea.

"Morrigan, sweetheart."

Elaine was gently turned around.

"Ah, Morrigan, don't do this to yourself."

Elaine was enveloped from head to foot. Her numb feet were trapped between the heat of his. Her face was pushed into the abrasive wool of his jacket, the warm softness of his shirt, her nose tucked into the firm, musky skin beneath the shirt collar.

Charles rocked her, gently, slowly, as if she were three instead of thirty-nine. As if she were alive instead of dead.

"Oh, no!" She cringed from the thought—she was dead, had been fried like a catfish—and wrapped her arms about his body, slipping her hands beneath his coat, pulling up the hem of his shirt, seeking his warmth. Finding it.

Hot, he was so hot.

She needed his heat; she needed his body. She needed reaffirmation that she was alive.

The arms tightened around her. "Hush, Morrigan. Sweetheart, don't do this to yourself. Everything will be all right. You'll see. I'll take care of you. Always. Don't do this to yourself. Don't, sweetheart. It's all right. Everything is all right. I promise. I'll make everything all right. You'll see. Shhh . . . It's all right, ah, sweetheart, don't do this, it's all right, it's all right, it's all right. . . ."

The words were warm, moist, there, against her ear, muffled then, against her hair, warm and moist again on her forehead and cheek. Elaine gradually became aware of sobs. Who was crying? They sounded so tormented. Her heart went out to that person who was crying as if the world had ended. *Who . . . ?*

No, it couldn't be Elaine. Not good old Elaine. Elaine never cried; Elaine went placidly on like a mutant species of tortoise. A sexless species of tortoise.

Elaine drew her head away from Charles's neck and shoulder and pulled his head down to hers. She put her soul into that kiss, using lips and teeth and tongue as he had taught her the other night.

Charles groaned deep in his throat and pulled his head back. "No, it's too soon. I don't want to hurt yo—"

Elaine pulled his head back down to hers, burying the words inside her mouth. She didn't want him to pull back. She could not bear it if she should be rejected now.

Another groan emitted from his throat before he opened his mouth and took charge of the kiss, using his lips and teeth and tongue to combat the arsenal that hers had become. Elaine brought her hand between them. She tore open the two middle buttons of his breeches and wrapped her fingers around hot, pulsing flesh. He reached beneath her dress, inside the open crotch of the drawers. She squeezed. He thrust. She pumped. He rotated.

"Jesus, you're killing me," he gasped.

That was the wrong thing to say. Killing. Death. Elaine wanted no part of that. She renewed her assault.

His fingers slipped free of her body. He tried to grab her hand through the layers of dress and chemise and petticoats. She forced his head back down and thrust her tongue inside his mouth, then out, matching the movements of her hand.

Charles allowed her free reign, helpless to stop her. He delved back inside her drawers. Elaine was wet. She forced a drop of ecstasy from him. He used her own passion to rub and tease the ultra-sensitive bud at the top of her lips.

Bringing her left hand down from around his neck, Elaine grabbed the front of his pants and jerked. The three remaining buttons ripped free; she heard them plop into the water. Then she had both hands inside his pants, touching the twin leathery pouches that were tight and ridged with the force of his desire. She explored and played and teased as she had never been allowed to do in the twentieth century.

"Enough."

The marriage manuals had claimed the perineum was an extremely sensitive area. Elaine probed the area directly behind the ridged pouches.

"Dear lord, I can't—" Charles's breath audibly caught in the back of his throat.

His uninhibited response was more potent than an aphrodisiac. Elaine dragged the breeches down past his hips and sank into the water, impervious to the cold, the wet.

Charles stared down at her, his eyes heavily lidded. He did not try to stop her.

Elaine tasted the drop of essence she had excited. It was salty, as he had told her that night when they had viewed the pornographic texts. His flesh here had a musky smell, Charles's scent, not repulsive at all. Hungrily she sucked him inside her mouth, taking in as much of him as she could, as deep as she could. She sucked and licked as if he were a particularly luscious lollipop and she a particularly voracious little girl.

The flesh inside Elaine's mouth grew harder. Charles's breathing became raspy, labored. Something was happening here. Elaine trembled with his excitement. She pulled back to see exactly what was happening, but his hand shot down and clamped around the nape of her neck, holding her head pressed firmly against him. An agonized groan rumbled up from his chest; it erupted into a full-fledged shout. The flesh in her mouth leaped and quivered; a warm, thick fluid spurted against the back of her throat. Elaine convulsively swallowed, once, twice, five times in all.

The hard fingers released her neck. Elaine sat back and looked up. A thin, warm fluid dribbled from the corner of her mouth.

Charles's blue eyes smoldered. He reached down and gathered the pearly essence onto his forefinger, then offered it to her, the last remnant of his passion. She unhesitatingly took the tip of his finger into her mouth.

Elaine was hauled to her feet so quickly the sky rocked. Before she could even begin to guess his intent, Charles hoisted her up in his arms. Water cascaded from the dress.

Elaine shivered, aware now of the icy water, the cool temperature of the spring day. Charles's face was hard, almost cruel, every inch that of a lord. For a second she wondered what she had done, but then it was too late to wonder; he was setting her down on a patch of brilliantly green grass and twirling her around to unbutton her dress. The dress sank like a lodestone onto the ground, followed in rapid succession by the bustle, the petticoats, the corset, the chemise, the drawers. The odd male article interspersed the heap of feminine clothing, a jacket, a shirt, breeches. Elaine stood naked before his nakedness.

As she had done to him, so he did to her. He made love to her mouth, rapaciously, his hands kneading her breasts, rolling her nipples. His lips scorched a trail down her throat and chest. He drew a nipple inside his mouth, hard, then drew as much of her breast inside his mouth as he could. His left hand anchored her buttocks; his right hand slid to her front and teased and thrust, then slipped free to tease and tease.

A sob rose in Elaine's throat. There would be no mercy. Her body yearned for more, to be filled—with fingers, with him—but he played and teased without filling her. As if he read her mind, a finger rimmed her opening, round and round. Elaine's body arched—for fulfillment, in frustration. She didn't want that, to come that way! She wanted him inside her!

"Isn't this what you wanted, my pretty little wife? Isn't that what you prefer, here"—the thumb rubbed—"as opposed to here?" The rimming finger sank a fraction of an inch, not enough, not nearly enough.

"No!" Elaine choked.

Sharp teeth sank around her left nipple. The finger rimmed and rimmed, the thumb rubbing faster, faster.

"Charles . . . Charles, no!" Elaine gasped—too late, her body convulsed, so empty, oh, so empty. He covered her mouth with his and plunged his tongue inside her, catching her breathy whimpers, her aching cries, his rubbing thumb eliciting a series of jerks and throbs from her body as if she were a puppet.

"Beautiful, so beautiful, ah, Morrigan, you are so beautiful like this. There's more, sweetheart, so much more," Charles murmured into her mouth, between her breasts, into her naval.

Elaine drew a shaky breath, unerringly realizing his intent. She whimpered. It was too soon. She wouldn't be able to. But then his mouth was there and it was like being consumed by a wet, slick furnace. She grabbed his hair in both hands and held on for dear life. It felt so good. She could feel herself grow, incredibly, even wetter. Her thighs were slick with it. She would get it in his hair. No, she couldn't do that, not in his beautiful hair, but he wouldn't let her pull away, and then he was going at her as voraciously as she had him and her body was convulsing again and again and her legs couldn't hold her up, only his arms, his hands, fingers digging into her buttocks as he licked and sucked and licked.

She came down only to be forced back up, time and again, two orgasms, four, five. Her whole body trembled. She had hardly the strength to hold on to him. Mercifully he raised his head.

Carefully supporting her with his left hand, he explored the inside of her thigh with his right hand, then lower. "My God," he said, his voice husky, slightly in awe. "You're wet all the way down to your knees."

Charles backed Elaine through the soft grass until rough bark impacted with her skin. He lifted her up by her behind. "Put your legs around me," he rasped.

Concentrating all her energies, she managed to slide her legs around his waist. Her hot, wet body was wide-open. He promptly sank inside her, access easy, accruing only a faint pinching feeling when he first penetrated.

"Oh!" Elaine gasped. Her eyes, nearly closed with exhaustion, opened wide. She would have thought herself unable to feel anything sexual. He proved her wrong. It was as if she had been filled with an electric prod.

Charles smiled, more of a sexual grimace. "Oh?" he teased, his voice rough and gravelly, gently pushing and pulling at her insides. "Is that all you have to say?" He slowly pulled almost all the way out, inch by slow inch. "You were much more voluble a few minutes ago. I daresay if I was less of a gentleman I would be quite shocked at your vocabulary. As it is . . ."

Elaine squirmed, but he remained just inside her. "Charles, please!" she finally begged. If she did not have him, all of him, she would die. "Charles, more, give me more, please, I want to feel you inside me, all of you, oh, please, *please* come inside me!"

The breath whooshed out of Elaine at the force with which he obliged her. She held on to him with all of her strength, unable to do more. She felt as if she could swallow him whole; her body gulped and gobbled at him as if it could. She felt as if he wanted to be swallowed whole, as if he were trying to climb inside her very soul. When the climax came, she had never felt so close to another human being in her life, bone to his bone, breath to his breath.

Charles rested his forehead on top of her shoulder. His fingers explored her where they were still joined. "Beautiful," he whispered. He raised his head. "The joining of a man and a woman is the most beautiful thing on this earth. Don't ever let anyone tell you differently," he said fiercely.

Looking into those beautiful Mediterranean blue eyes, Elaine could believe anything he said.

"Feel it!" Still supporting her buttocks with his left hand, he reached around his neck and grabbed her right hand. He brought their joined hands up beneath her. "Feel us!"

She was hot and wet and slick. His flesh disappeared inside hers. The base of him was hot and wet and slick, from her, from him. He forced their fingers up inside her, alongside his flesh. She was completely open to him, to them. Elaine's nostrils flared.

Charles's face softened. He released his hold on her hand. She felt very forlorn at the expulsion of their fingers. He kissed her lightly on the mouth.

"You're my wife, Morrigan. What we do together is good and right. 'A man shall cleave unto his wife.' Don't ever forget that. Don't ever forget the feel of us. Together. One body. One flesh. If you ever start doubting the sanctity of marriage, I want you to come to me. All right?"

Elaine was gently lowered to the ground. Charles slid out of her. The slickness on her thighs felt cold and slippery. She felt empty again, and so lonely she wanted to bawl.

"Damn, I was going to use something to prevent conception. I find I'm greedy. I want Mama all to myself for a year or so. Pregnancy would definitely hinder our little sexual adventures. And there is so much more to explore. Come over here with me; perhaps we can reduce the chances a little."

Charles pulled Elaine over to the stream and into the water. "What are you doing?" She pulled against his hand. The water was freezing!

He laughed. "Come on; I promise I won't subject you to anything I won't subject myself to."

Before she could prevent it, he had dropped to his knees in the middle of the stream, dragging her down with him. Charles sat back on his haunches so that the water covered his genitals. His eyes widened. "Son of a bitch!"

Elaine giggled.

"I wouldn't laugh if I were you," he warned. He splashed water over her breasts. Elaine gasped.

"Exactly. And its going to be a lot colder where next I splash you," he said enigmatically. He reached over and pulled her legs wide apart.

Her pelvis was plunged beneath the icy water. Elaine yelped.

"Hush." Charles's hand disappeared beneath her. Elaine yelped again and would have shot straight up if his other hand had not grabbed hold of her shoulder. His fingers slid inside her and held her open. Water gushed up deep inside her. Ice-cold water.

"Are you nuts?" she cried, instantly freezing, hearing the echo of twentieth-century slang.

Little flames danced in his eyes. "What odd euphemisms you come up with. I told you, I want you to myself. What sperm I can't wash out, I'll freeze."

By the time he was finished with Elaine's makeshift douche, she was completely numb.

"Don't worry," he said, laughing. "I promise I'll thaw you out tonight."

Elaine had a good laugh on him when he pulled his breeches on and there were only two buttons to fasten. He threw her a comical look. "I'm married to a violent madwoman," he said jokingly.

Elaine's laughter abruptly died. Matthew had had Elaine committed. And as the note had said, Matthew had loved Elaine. What would Charles do under similar circumstances?

Elaine's dress was soaked. Spring had never felt so cold, save for the occasions in Chicago when it had actually snowed. She briskly walked toward the house, gaining a good head start on Charles while he figured out how to keep his pants from falling around his ankles. He caught up with her all too soon.

"Who has been writing the notes? Katie said you've gotten three now."

Elaine's lips tightened. Damn Katie. Couldn't she keep her mouth shut just once? She was going to have to see that the maid married the valet, if ever she was going to have any privacy.

"Morrigan, I asked you a question. Who wrote the notes?"

"No one." She stumbled over a half-buried piece of wood.

Charles caught her. "Don't give me that rot," he snapped. The blue eyes relentlessly bore into hers. "Was it one of those hellish relatives of yours?"

Elaine remained silent.

The blue eyes softened. "Morrigan, you're twenty-one years old. You're a woman now. In every way. My woman. They can't hurt you. You're free. You don't have to listen to their mealymouthed, pious hogwash anymore. What we have is very special. They can't destroy it if you won't let them."

Elaine dully registered this latest piece of information about Morrigan. The notes didn't sound as if they had been written by a twenty-one-year-old. They sounded as if they had been written by someone as old and canny as Medusa.

The Boleigh brood met them in the entranceway. They had a positive genius for showing up at inopportune times. Mrs. Boleigh sniffed disdainfully. Prudence glared. Mary looked enigmatic.

"You've missed lunch," Mrs. Boleigh said. "You always were an unchristian girl. Look at you! You look as if you had been wallowing around with some disreputable character!"

Charles squeezed Elaine's elbow. "That is exactly what we have been doing, Mrs. Boleigh. Though I would not describe my character as disreputable. Please excuse us. We are quite wet and likely to catch a chill if we don't change."

Elaine brooded while she took her second bath for the day. Poor Katie—the girl would be worked to skin and bones carrying all that bathwater up and down. She wondered who carried up Charles's water. Fritz? She hoped so. For Katie's sake she hoped the little tadpole worked himself into a frazzle. She sank down into the water. Katie had added Epsom salts again. She almost wished Charles was with her to warm what he had so thoroughly chilled.

That night at dinner Elaine studied the assembly of diners. The centerpiece flowers had been pruned, so that all around the table were visible.

Mr. Boleigh unfortunately graced the table. He sat between Elaine and Mrs. Boleigh, looking every bit as disdainful as he had the last time. No doubt Mrs. Boleigh was having the time of her life keeping him informed about their niece's scandalous behavior.

Elaine shuddered. Had she and Charles been watched at the stream today? Someone must have watched them the day of the picnic. The note had been beneath her door before she had gone to dinner that night. How horrible!

Neither Mrs. Boleigh nor her brood looked the type to watch someone making love. She doubted Mrs. Boleigh had ever made love. Perhaps the two daughters had been left beneath cabbage leaves. They certainly had retained the overall shape of the vegetable. Elaine took a sip of wine, then hastily concealed a yawn.

Charles threw her a knowing look. Elaine's cheeks burned with the knowledge of the source of her exhaustion. He forked a sausage from the platter the footman offered. Holding the whole sausage to his mouth, he slowly bit off the tip.

Why was it, she wondered, that embarrassment never came when it was supposed to? She would never in a million years have done to him what she had done if she had been as aware then of the act as she and he were now.

Elaine watched Morrigan's uncle cut a sausage into chunks. Morrigan had implied that she had performed oral sex on him.

Elaine fortified herself with another sip of wine to prevent herself from gagging. She took great pleasure in refusing the sausage platter when the footman came to her.

Her wineglass was truly bottomless tonight. After her fifth glass, Charles was enveloped in a warm, cozy aura. What had he meant about a method to prevent conception? Had they had things like that then? She meant now. For better or for worse, it appeared as if this was now her time. The thought added to the glow of the wine.

Charles and Mr. Boleigh lingered after dinner over port. Elaine grimly led the Boleigh brood into the blue-and-silver drawing room. It was time, she decided, to discover who the real Morrigan was.

"More tea, Aunt?" Elaine asked.

Mrs. Boleigh resentfully held out her cup. She had not forgiven Elaine for the humiliation when Charles had ousted her from pourer status. Elaine dutifully added four lumps of sugar and a heavy dollop of cream.

"Quite the lady now, aren't we," sneered Prudence. "We saw you come in with Lord Arlcotte today. How dare you even show yourself after playing the whore for him?"

Plain speaking indeed. How did the saying go? Give a person enough rope, and they will hang themselves?

"More tea, Prudence?" she asked blandly.

"Ill take more," Mary said.

"You would take second helpings of cow dung," Prudence cried.

"Prudence!" Mrs. Boleigh effected shock. Indeed, Elaine was rather shocked.

"It's true!" Prudence protested. "You know what she is!" The youngest daughter pointed to Elaine. "You know what she did! How can we sit here and allow her to serve us as if she is our better?"

Elaine took a fortifying breath. She spoke carefully, slowly, trying to economize her words. "What did I do, Prudence?"

Prudence laughed rather hysterically. "As if you need to be told!"

"Hush, Prudence Anne Boleigh! I'll not hear another word out of you!"

"It's all your fault for not speaking up, Mama! Look at her! She's married to a great lord while Mary and I are courted by local bumpkins! How could you have let her marry? She needs to be locked up! She's a murderer!"

The blood ran cold in Elaine's veins. Her skin crawled as if it were trying to escape association. *Murder! Promiscuity! Incest!*

Mrs. Boleigh stared at Elaine with eyes as cold and heartless as hell itself. "My dear, I assure you your cousin will get everything she deserves."

Elaine felt sick to her stomach. It had to be Mrs. Boleigh. She remembered the look of unmitigated rage on her face when Charles had not taken Mary and Prudence driving.

She jerkily rose to her feet. Her body felt as if it would disintegrate. It was true. How obscene. Elaine's body in the twentieth century had been occupied by a sexual pervert and murderer. And now she occupied the body of a sexual pervert and murderer.

Elaine made it up the stairs and to her room without intervention. Later, she watched the play of moonlight through the French doors. Katie snored gently from the depths of the couch.

Boleigh busily searched through the bowl of nuts.

Charles impatiently watched the lights gleam on top of his bald head. Like a great, giant nut, he thought. Morrigan had used the word at the stream.

Instantly he remembered the cold of the water and the heat of her body. Had Fritz prepared the lemon juice as instructed?

"I see you are well enough to travel," he said abruptly.

"My lord?" The pudgy fingers ceased their ravishing. Beady little eyes shone above folds of puffed flesh. Squirrel eyes, Charles thought with a spurt of amusement, glancing at the nearly empty bowl of nuts. "How so?"

"Your appetite is excellent"—mentally he reviewed the quantity of food consumed that night, enough to feed a party of twelve— "and your color vastly improved. Signs, surely, of good health?"

"The physician warned me of excess."

"Really." Charles raised an ironic brow. "Then it would be best if you returned to Cornwall, where there are fewer temptations."

"That is exactly my purpose, my lord. My niece is a fragile child—"

Charles's left brow rose to join his right. The voracious woman who had met his passion thrust for thrust was neither a child nor fragile.

"—and should be shielded from worldly pleasures. Only consider—"

"You are taxing my courtesy, Boleigh. And you in ill health. I have quite endured enough on the subject. Morrigan is my wife, and she shall remain so. End of discussion. I will personally consult with the physician tomorrow. Together the three of us can decide upon a means to transport you back to Cornwall without further injuring your health. And now, if you will excuse me, I have more pressing matters to attend."

Like furthering his wife's education.

Mrs. Boleigh and her two daughters occupied the salon. They were strangely silent as they drank their tea. He hoped Morrigan had finally given them the comeuppance they deserved. "Where is my wife?"

"Your wife—" Mrs. Boleigh turned rage-filled eyes upon Charles.

"Never mind." Charles surveyed with dislike the woman who had treated his wife with contempt and ridicule ever since her untimely arrival. Her table manners, moreover, had been learned in a pigsty. He had been forced to forsake his dinner due to a barrage of flying food particles, emitted, it seemed, every time she opened her mouth at the table. The growing admiration he felt for his wife increased. Hattie belonged to these self-righteous pigs, but not Morrigan. "I see she had the good sense to retire."

A soft snore permeated Morrigan's bedchamber. Charles smiled; his smile widened, realizing the snore came from the maid and not the lady. Poor wife. She must come to his bed merely to get rest.

Morrigan stared up at him from the shadows of the bed. The silk drapes were open; her loosened hair was midnight black against the white pillow. Her hands lay outside the covers; the gold ring gleamed in the dark.

Charles felt a not altogether pleasant sense of vulnerability. She had turned to him today. What would be her response tonight?

Morrigan held up her arms.

With a smothered exclamation, he pulled the covers down and scooped her up. His room was warm; a candelabra was lit on either side of the bed. The air was redolent with the smell of lemons. A little bowl sat on the left nightstand.

Charles's satisfaction was complete. Fritz had followed his instructions to the letter. He set Morrigan down on her feet and pulled her nightgown over her head. She mutely watched him as he undressed, letting his clothes fall were they would. He felt ridiculously exposed, his turgid flesh as heavy as if it were weighted by an anvil.

Slowly, hesitantly, she reached out. Charles aged ten years waiting for her touch. When it came, he almost dropped to his knees.

Morrigan's head was bent, the dark hair a silken cashe. "What is the third primary *marmas?*"

He squeezed his eyelids shut, the stab of sensation he felt for his wife then so intense it was painful.

"Charles?"

He opened his eyes. His wife's eyes were wary, behind them a hint of loneliness, a tinge of hurt. He cupped her face between his hands. "This," he said.

Gently he took her bottom lip between his. For long moments he nibbled on it, suckled it. She tasted of wine flavored with ginger. Uniquely her own taste.

He released her lip. It was red and swollen and trembling. For him. Only for him.

"And this," he said.

Her mouth was a willing receptacle for his tongue. He stroked her tongue with his, pulled it into his mouth and suckled it as he had her lip. She groaned, the sound deep and wet inside his mouth. When he pulled away, she cried out and tried to pull him back.

"Wait, sweet. Wait a minute."

Charles jerked the covers to the foot of the bed. He laid her down, then reached for the bowl on the nightstand. Moving her legs wide apart, he sat guru-style between them.

"What are you doing?"

Charles smiled. Her voice was hot and husky now, not cold and brittle or cool and indifferent. He fished the sponge out and squeezed it lightly; a stream of liquid splattered into the bowl.

Morrigan watched him in open curiosity. She trusted him, he thought exultantly. She trusted him with her whole body.

"What is it?" she asked softly.

Charles flashed her a devilish grin. "A sponge," he said, "soaked in lemon juice. Vinegar is more commonly used, but lemon juice is preferred in the Far East, and I confess to a partiality to the taste of lemon as opposed to vinegar. Now." He eased closer, perforce widening her legs. "Bring your knees up—no, higher. Keep them apart."

He delicately pulled the folds of flesh apart and introduced a finger-width span of lemon-soaked sponge. She instantly tightened her muscles.

"Don't do that," Charles said. "Once this is in you won't even feel it. Neither will I. Relax for me, sweetheart."

He commenced stuffing the sponge up inside her. In seconds it was inserted, protesting muscles or no protesting muscles.

He sat back on his haunches and surveyed the swollen lips. A thin stream of lemon juice mixed with her own moisture glistened there. "How do you feel?"

"Stuffed," she promptly said, opening her eyes to stare into the murky depths of his. "Like a capon."

Morrigan suddenly looked unsure.

Charles laughed, more and more enjoying her quaint sense of humor. "Imagine how you would feel if it were a lemon stuffed inside you instead of a sponge. In China the fruit rather than a sponge is used."

Her eyes widened.

"Perhaps we will try it someday, when I can more readily curtail my eagerness. Poor Damon would no doubt find it difficult to face either of us over dinner should he be required to fish out a lemon from your womb."

He slid his hands underneath her calves and up, cupping her knees and easing them back against her chest. "We can talk later," he said, nuzzling her. "Did I tell you that you have the most delicious-looking clit I have ever seen? It matches your nipples, ripe and full, made for a man's mouth. Mmm, I love the taste of lemon." He licked the tart juice from her, briefly foraged inside.

Morrigan burst out laughing.

He raised his head, not at all amused. "What?"

"The lemon juice," Morrigan murmured. "You did get out all the seeds, didn't you?"

"Don't worry, my dear," he said, teeth gleaming. "I had Fritz especially strain it."

He burst into laughter at the bright red blush that spread from her ears to her toes. He nibbled on the latter appendages before returning to the alluring tartness of lemon and hot, wet woman.

Chapter
23

The mattress shifted. Elaine rolled with the motion, hand automatically reaching for the anchor of warm, muscled flesh. She found it, only to have it slide away from beneath her fingers. Her eyes popped open.

Charles stood near the bed, stretching. Elaine admired the play of sinew and bone.

"You're the one who is beautiful," she whispered.

He turned. A smile lit his darkly tanned features. "Why, thank you, milady, though I beg to disagree. I tried not to wake you. Go back to sleep." The blue eyes gleamed mischievously. "You had a hard night."

Elaine shook her head. Hair slithered side to side on the silk pillowcase. She didn't want to go back to sleep. Images of burned black flesh and a preaching Matthew had plagued her dreams.

"Then let's take a bath and have breakfast together. Afterward you can ride with me to inspect the repairs on the tenants' houses."

Both of them away from the threat of Mrs. Boleigh! Elaine jumped at the chance, only to grab the covers. Modesty was a little belated, but in the cold light of morning Elaine was mortifyingly aware of minor imperfections such as unshaven legs and uninhibited responses. Charles reached down and retrieved the silk nightgown from the floor. Elaine gratefully accepted it, wriggling and squirming between the silk bedcovers. She squeaked in shock when the bed expelled her.

Charles caught Elaine before she slid to the floor posterior-first in an avalanche of silk and more silk. He kissed her lightly on the lips, a primary *marmas*, she had learned.

"There's no need to fight for what I would willingly give," he murmured.

Elaine attempted to pull back, but Charles merely pulled her closer. The kiss deepened, engaging lips and tongue. She forgot about little things like unshaven legs in another one of those surges of uninhibited response.

Charles caressed her bottom; the pads of his fingertips were rough against her own smooth, firm flesh. The next instant brought a sharp report, the stinging application of that warm, callused hand across the taut skin of her bared buttocks.

Elaine yelped and jumped free. Charles laughed. She wrapped the silk nightgown around her body and marched stiff-legged to the connecting door. The sponge felt . . . there, now that she was upwardly mobile, so to speak.

He reached the door ahead of Elaine and casually leaned against it in all of his naked glory. "Where are you going?"

She averted her eyes. There was no part of her body he did not know, no part she did not know of his. Why was it, then, that he had merely to touch her and she came panting to life, whereas he always appeared cool and controlled? "To take a bath."

His eyes twinkled. "Extraordinary. I was just on the way to a bath myself. Won't you join me?"

Elaine glanced tellingly toward the corner of the room. She knew very well Fritz had not brought up any bathwater. There was no vapor over the gilded Japanese screen.

"I see milady needs persuading."

The silk nightgown was neatly yanked from around her body. The room tilted and turned. Elaine gasped, presented with an entirely different perspective, held high in the lord's arms. She could feel the heavy train of her hair sway back and forth in little aftershocks.

"No, no, fair lady, no trouble at all, even if you do weigh more than my horse."

That was mean. And belittling. No doubt that was exactly what he would think of her twentieth-century body.

Charles gently lowered Elaine to her feet behind the Japanese screen. There was no bathtub. She stared at the door that was hidden there instead. The muscles in her neck corded, straining to prevent him from lifting her chin.

"Hey, I was only teasing. You're light as thistledown. I could carry you all day. I *will* carry you all day. We'll leave the horses in the stables. I'll even deck out in a saddle and bridle, what?"

That was an intriguing thought. Elaine had yet to ride him. A particular illustration rose to mind, that of the fair Indian maiden impaled on top of the dark-skinned Indian man.

Warm lips lightly pressed against hers. Elaine jerked her head back. The look of solicitude on Charles's face quickly changed to one of annoyance.

"I do not kiss my horse," Elaine said haughtily.

Humor sparkled in the blue eyes. "You just tup him, hm?" He opened the hitherto concealed door. "Come on, you little baggage!"

Elaine's eyes widened. She stepped inside. Charles had a bathroom. A bona fide bathroom! With very little variation from its twentieth-century counterpart. The white porcelain toilet varied from its modern antecedent only in the fact that the tank hung from the ceiling. The sink was encased in a wooden cabinet with a mirror above it. The bathtub was very large. It had a faucet. And spout. The sink had a faucet. And spout. The toilet had a chain. And a roll of toilet paper. A fire burned cheerily in a small fireplace opposite the facilities. Steam rose from the filled tub.

Charles pointed to the toilet whose base was formed in the shape of a dolphin. "Need to?"

Elaine did, but not enough to use it in front of him. He suffered no such qualms. Heat spread over her face, watching his tight little buns while he stood with his back to her. He lifted the wooden seat. There was a splash of water on water. A familiar gurgle exploded when he pulled the chain.

He ambled over to the sink and washed his hands. Then, opening a side drawer in the cabinet, he took out a toothbrush and a tin, like the kind that commemorative talc came in. He shook some white powder into the palm of his hand, moistened the toothbrush, and stuck the damp bristles into the powder. He proceeded to vigorously brush his teeth.

With a toothbrush.

Elaine had scrubbed her teeth with a washcloth and soap for the past month. Not only did he have a toothbrush, he had a bathroom. With running water and a toilet that was more than twelve inches off the ground.

Elaine fumed, torn between embarrassment that he would use that bathroom in front of her and outrage that he *had* a bathroom. All this time she had been poisoning herself with soap and crippling herself using a chamber pot, not to mention the rash caused by stationery, while he . . . ! And Katie! The maid had damned near broken her back lugging water up and down for "m' lady's" bath.

Elaine became aware that Charles was watching her in the mirror. He rinsed his mouth out with the glass. Turning toward her, he smiled. Arctic lights glittered in his eyes.

"You could have been sharing with me this year and more, Morrigan. I never expected you to live in that bedchamber of yours."

Charles stepped into the bathtub and lay back, the perfect picture of sybaritic decadence. Without opening his eyes, he imperiously held out his hand. "Come. I'm tired of dealing with your silly repressions. You've cheated us long enough."

Elaine gingerly accepted the hand and stepped into the tub. The water was a little warmer than she would have liked. They would both turn lobster red. She turned and sank down, her back to the faucet so that she faced the man who looked more asleep than awake. Deceivingly so. No sooner had her bottom touched the water than she found herself neatly turned, encountering hairy male flesh instead of smooth porcelain. He wrapped his arms about her waist and breasts and pulled her back against his chest.

They soaked in companionable silence. Elaine had never taken a bath with a man before, had never realized that such a degree of intimacy could exist outside a sexual embrace. Steam rose around her in wavy patterns. The fireplace crackled and popped; the burning wood added a smoky aroma to the thick humidity. She felt herself succumbing to the hot water gently lapping against her sides and belly, to the wiry chest and stomach rhythmically rising and falling against her neck and back. The strands of hair floating around her pleasantly tickled. Her eyelids drooped. Charles's arms became heavier, as if he, too, were being lulled to sleep.

"My lord, I've brought more hot wa— My lord!"

Elaine's eyes flew open. Fritz stood in the doorway, carrying a pail of steaming water. His face was as red as Elaine had predicted her and the lord's bodies would turn.

Elaine struggled up. Charles held her down, one arm blessedly hiding her chest. She cupped her fingers to cover that other strategic place.

"I suppose I'm going to have to get one of those unsightly gas-heated baths now." Charles sighed. "Nevertheless, you would be well off to knock before entering a room, Fritz. Morrigan, quit wriggling. Fritz, close your eyes and come add that water before it cools."

"But—but my lord, how can I tell where I pour with my eyes closed?"

"We'll let you know if you scald us, Fritz," Charles said dryly. "For heaven's sake, man, use your brain! Our feet point south. Pour at that end."

The hot water poured noisily into the tub; Elaine jerked her feet back out of the way. Fritz's face was screwed up to the point that he looked like a Cabbage Patch doll. Elaine followed his example and shut her own eyes. A small, vindictive part of her soul rejoiced that the valet had to carry up hot water for my lord's baths. It was the least he could suffer after the way he had treated Katie.

"Hand me the soap and a cloth; there's a good boy." The arm wrapped around Elaine's waist lifted. Goose bumps rose on her exposed flesh. The distinct odor she had come to associate with Charles surrounded her.

"No, be a little imaginative, Fritz. We don't want her ladyship smelling of sandalwood, now, do we? Give us something a little less scented."

A few seconds later the door closed. Charles heaved a heartfelt sigh. "Pity. I could stay here all day. I daresay Fritz would die rather than supply any more hot water, though. Up we go, milady"

Elaine was propelled into a sitting position.

"Hold up your hair." He lathered her back and shoulders, immediately following the soap with a brisk application of wet cloth. Pulling her around in the tub so that she faced him, he vigorously washed her arms and breasts. "Hold up a leg." Elaine meekly held up an unshaven leg. "Other one."

When she would have reciprocated, he gently scooted her toward the faucet. "Another time. We have a full day ahead of us. By the by, next time you wish to remove any hair, I would suggest you use a depilatory. It is far more effective and a lot safer."

Elaine surpassed the lobster red. So he had noticed. She remembered his wandering tongue. How could he not have noticed? Safer for whom? she wondered, fully cognizant of the hackneyed job the straight razor blade had done with her armpits. For him or for her?

It was rather comical watching Charles scrub under his arms, his chest, sticking out first one hairy leg, then another. He stood on his knees and lathered his genitals. Elaine viewed with interest her first glimpse of an uncircumcised man. Well, she had seen *this* man, more than seen, in a state of arousal, but he looked much the same then as did a circumcised man. He pulled back the foreskin and cleaned beneath the pocket of skin.

Charles sat back down in the water. "Now you."

Elaine stared at him uncomprehendingly.

"Up you go."

Elaine was lifted to her knees for the most thorough washing she had ever received. She squirmed when he insisted upon cleaning absolutely *everywhere*, between both lips and cheeks. When she was rinsed to his satisfaction, she gratefully sank back into the water.

"No." Immediately he grasped her hips, easing her back up onto her knees. "Have you forgotten something?"

He reached between her legs and pulled. The sponge slid out, stretching sensitive skin along the way. It felt as if it had grown to twice the size it had been last night. It lodged at the exit, rather like a tampon, which was why Elaine had never used them. They just were not shaped to come *out*.

His eyes narrowed. He gently tugged on the ribbon. A faint smile curled his lips at the continued resistance. He brought up his other hand and lightly touched that part of her he had praised last night for being ripe and full. "Give up, love," he whispered.

The blue eyes delved into hers, speaking of more sponges, of the pleasures to be had, of the pleasures this sponge had afforded. Elaine melted. The sponge slipped free. The scent of lemon surrounded them. He rinsed her thighs free of the residual sperm that had escaped with the sponge, then leaned over and buried his head in her wet flesh. Charles inhaled deeply before abruptly standing, bringing them both up out of the water.

He was in that state where circumcised and uncircumcised men looked the same. Elaine's mouth went dry.

Charles grinned devilishly. "Won't Cook be surprised next time she serves lemon tart and I ravish you on the dinner table?"

He sent Elaine to her room so that Fritz could shave him. "I don't trust Fritz with a razor when you're around."

Elaine, half-aroused, dreamily allowed Katie to dress her. The menacing fact that a rather belligerent-sounding Morrigan was back had faded. Sexual satiation was more effective than taking Valium. Not that she ever had. But Elaine's secretary had, and nothing had ever seemed to faze her.

Katie laced up Elaine's corset. "Mmm, marm, be that a new perfume from the lord? It smells ever so nice. Like lemons, it does."

Elaine's body turned bright red. It was a relief when Charles entered to escort her to the dining room. Her relief was short-lived. The Boleighs were at the breakfast table.

Mary raised her head at their approach. She scanned the buffet. "Mmm, lemon tarts!" she cried eagerly. She jumped to her feet and ran to the buffet. "I smell lemon tarts!" she cried petulantly. "I know I smell lemon tarts!"

Charles sputtered.

Mr. Boleigh decapitated a kipper; he stuffed the head inside his mouth. "Perhaps they're preparing tarts for tea, dear."

Charles burst into laughter. Elaine glared at him. He laughed until tears ran out of his eyes. The Boleighs stared at him as if he had lost his mind. Then they stared at Elaine as if she had made him lose his mind.

She unfurled her napkin and placed it on her lap. Feeling in dire need of stimulus, she disregarded Morrigan's presumed preference for tea and reached for the coffeepot.

"My lady!" Jamie the footman dropped to his knees beside her chair.

Elaine glanced at the bewigged man in surprise, even though she had been in this century less than a month fully aware that a footman on duty was considered little more than a piece of furniture, and as such, deaf and mute. The Boleighs paused with forks midway from table to mouths. Charles's eyebrows rose.

"My lady, you dropped this." The footman held out a folded piece of paper.

Elaine incongruously remembered Katie's comment about how silly footmen looked in their wigs.

The Boleighs stared at Elaine inquisitively. Charles's face took on the closed, cold expression; the corner of his lip kicked up toward the scar. The footman looked stoic, calmly holding out the note.

Now you know that unless you give me what I want I will demonstrate to Lord Arlcotte that you are not me. . . .

How could she have forgotten that last note? Elaine pasted a smile on her lips. "Thank you." She numbly accepted the damning piece of paper.

The footman effortlessly rose to his feet and resumed his position beside the breakfast buffet, as if the destruction of lives was all in a day's work. Why couldn't the lord's staff be a little less efficient? she wondered bleakly. If the footman hadn't noticed the note, then

Elaine would not have noticed it. Saving that, why could not the footman have adhered to servant etiquette and remained *mute* while doing his duty?

Five pairs of eyes stared at her expectantly. She briefly toyed with the idea of opening the note and reading it aloud. It would be easy to identify Morrigan should she do so. The culprit would be the one who was not surprised. Except that was the exception as opposed to the rule in television shows like *Perry Mason* or *Columbo*. The culprit would be the one who was *most* surprised. In which case Elaine would still have her answer. She wondered if the satisfaction of knowing would end before or after her incarceration in Bedlam.

"What is it?" Charles asked, sounding every bit the lord. It was as if they had not spent endless hours undergoing endless ecstasy.

One must really wonder what dear Charles would do should he believe his wife believed she was someone else.

Elaine's face felt as if it would crack. "Nothing. I made a list of things for . . . for Katie to do. I dropped it, I guess. Excuse me. I have to get some breakfast." She was vaguely aware that that was the longest speech she had made outside of Katie's presence and the lord's arms.

Charles joined Elaine at the buffet. She ignored the cold, questioning eyes, heaping a plate with eggs and sausage and bacon and ham, staring kippers and those ugly dark lumps that looked and smelled like rancid chicken livers. Blindly she topped it off with a couple of rolls.

"Have a little pity on Jasper." Charles took her filled plate and slipped his empty one between her frozen fingers. Transferring a roll onto the empty plate, he grasped her arm and led her back to her chair.

Elaine sat down and methodically ate the roll, alternately sipping coffee and chewing. She looked down at her right hand in surprise. It was empty. She looked at the cup and plate in equal surprise. They too were empty. She looked at her left hand.

Her left hand was also empty.

Her gaze flew to Charles. He was sipping coffee and watching her. The heap of food on his plate was virtually untouched.

The plate.

The note.

Elaine raised up her plate.

She had had the note in her left hand, the same hand she had held the plate in. The filled plate. The plate *he* had taken.

Charles had the note.

Black waves of panic swelled over Elaine with increasing velocity.

How stupid of her, Elaine. How clever of Morrigan.

How clever of the lord.

Elaine stumbled to her feet. If she did not make a rapid exit she would either faint or scream, or with her luck, both. "Please excuse me. I have to . . ." What did she have to do? Pack for Bedlam? "Excuse me."

She would have expected to feel a tinge of relief now that the game was over, but she didn't. She only felt oceans of panic and a ripping sense of loss.

Elaine made it through the hall and up the stairs. By the time she reached the corridor she was running, or as much of a run as that cursed, crippled, unshaven leg would allow. She threw open the bedroom door.

The armoire was open. Dresses were spilled over the floor and bed like dead soldiers on a battlefield. A round black butt backed out of the wardrobe.

Elaine gasped. "You!"

Hattie glared at Elaine.

"It was you!" Elaine said, suddenly uncertain. The old woman's eyes were old, too old. How could those eyes be the mirror of a twenty-one-year-old girl?

"Aye, I be th' one 'oo tol' 'em. Ye're e'il, an' I willna let ye be nae more! Where'd they be, I say?"

No, the old crone was not Morrigan. Did Morrigan exist? Had this whole thing been manufactured by a crazy old woman bent on revenge? Had Elaine ran in terror from Hattie and a bunch of nineteenth-century Christian propaganda?

"Where'd they be, I says." Hattie bristled with righteous anger. "Ye'll gi' me yer tools o' th' de'il, Morrigan, an' then ye'll be mine. Aye, I'll take care o' ye, e'il misguided soul ye be, an' we'll bring ye back t' th' fol'. Repent, Morrigan, repent in th' name o' th' Lord an' gi' up th' tools o' Satan."

Elaine felt laughter bubbling up inside her. It *was* Hattie. This whole fracas had been Hattie's work! So that she could regain dominion over her "puir" little lamb, "e'il" misguided soul that she be.

The old woman whirled around in the familiar sweep of rancid black. Elaine instinctively stepped back. Hattie swept down on the shoes lining the bottom of the armoire. A flurry of yellow, red, black, white, and blue pummeled the air; each shoe shook before being tossed aside like so much flotsam. Elaine watched in growing incredulity and anger.

Hattie turned back toward Elaine in fury. Her rheumy old eyes glowed like live coals.

Elaine instinctively recoiled. Hattie's insanity was far more dangerous than a resurrected Morrigan.

Hattie thrust her face up into Elaine's. "Where'd they be, ye de'il's spawn? I willna leave till I 'ave 'em, ye 'ear? Ye'll not escape ol' Hattie again! Ne'er again! Ye 'ear, Morrigan, m' girl, I willna let ye be bad again!"

Hattie had called her Morrigan. Again.

"You're crazy," Elaine whispered, impervious to the vent of halitosis. *Please*, please *let it be Hattie.* Let the entire thing be the work of a crazy old woman bent on the salvation of a crippled young girl. It could be. Elaine could have spoken in her sleep. She could have called herself Elaine. She *could* have cried out for another time. Another man. *She called me Morrigan.*

The ringing slap of a hand against Elaine's cheek resounded through the morning quiet.

"Ye willna call me crazy, ye ken? I willna 'ave ye callin' yer betters names!"

This was all too familiar. The vituperation. The slap. The fight for dominance.

Elaine thrust her face down into the old woman's. "Get out of here! All of you, go back to where you came from!"

"Aye, ye'd like that, wouldn't ye?" Hattie gloated. "Then ye could practice yer e'il ways an' think t' 'scape th' 'and o' God! Gi' me th' tools an' it'll be th' easier on ye, Morrigan, girl."

Elaine switched tactics. "Who wants them, Hattie? Who wants these tools of mine?"

"Th' rev'ren', 'e wants 'em! Ye'll ne'er be saved till ye gi' up th' ways o' Satan."

"Who wrote the notes, Hattie? It was you who delivered them, wasn't it? Who else wants me to give up my tools?"

"We all be God-fearin' Christians!" Hattie shouted. "We all be wantin' ye t' gi' up yer e'il ways!"

Charles quickly perused the note. He felt as if a giant fist were squeezing his heart.

"Another note, my lord?" A ball of bread shot into his lap.

Charles was suddenly consumed with anger. It was their fault; none of this would have happened if they had not forced their unwanted presence upon him and his wife.

His *wife*.

God.

"Get out of here." His voice rang crystal clear over the chomping quadripartite. They acted as if he and Morrigan were a display at Crystal Palace. "All of you. I want you packed and inside your carriage within the hour."

Boleigh looked pleased. "Of course, my lord."

"Morrigan's up to her tricks again, isn't she, Papa?" Prudence asked gleefully. "Will you lock her away this time?"

"Shut up!" Charles pushed his chair back from the table. "Just shut up and get the hell off my estate." He glared at the two elderly Boleighs. "I wouldn't turn a mad dog over to the likes of you."

Mrs. Boleigh's eyes narrowed. "You—"

"Mrs. Boleigh, please," Boleigh said complacently. "Let this be resolved in a gentlemanly manner. If you would but listen to reason—"

"I have told you that there is nothing to resolve," Charles said icily. "Morrigan remains with me."

Boleigh's little squirrel eyes glittered. "My lord, you know not of what you speak. She is writing notes to herself, is she not? The rev—"

"My wife's actions are none of your concern."

"She is the concern of every God-fearing Christian. Morrigan is mad!" Boleigh shouted. More calmly, he added, "The reverend thought the marriage would suppress those tendencies brought about by virgin fantasies. They have not. Let her return to a life of chastity, where she can purge herself."

Boleigh's lips were turning blue, a visual reminder that the man suffered a heart condition. A footman stood stiffly behind him. This conversation would no doubt provide the servants many days of entertainment.

Charles took a deep breath. "Jamie, summon John to assist Mr. Boleigh to his room. They will be packed and out within the hour. Is that understood?"

"Yes, sir."

He stood. The Boleighs stared at him with various expressions on their faces: Mrs. Boleigh with rage, Mary with apprehension, Prudence with envious spite. Charles supposed he should be gratified. For once they found a situation more interesting than the food on their plates.

"And Jamie, send Katie to milady."

Upon attaining Morrigan's bedchamber, Charles's wrath found a convenient outlet in Hattie. The harridan stood nose-to-nose with his wife, shouting Christian nonsense. Morrigan's trousseau littered the floor.

Hattie's eyes darted past Morrigan. "Ye stay out o' this, ye *Sassenach!* This be fer th' good o' Morrigan's soul! Th' de'il, 'e done made 'er crazy wi' 'is e'il promises!"

"I told you to keep to your room while you were on my premises. Get the bloody hell out of here!"

Hattie threw Charles a malevolent glare before scuttling from the room like a black beetle. The door clicked shut.

Morrigan turned. Her face was white. Five red fingerprints throbbed on her left cheek.

The fist enclosing Charles's heart squeezed harder.

He held out the note.

"I would suggest you explain the meaning of this," Charles said.

Chapter
24

Elaine reached for the note. The paper was cool and crisp, as if freshly creased. The long, tanned fingers that had delved deep inside her body did not easily release possession. Elaine forced her eyes to meet those of the man whose passion she had shared, expecting disgust and she knew not what else. How did one view a mate whom one intended to have committed?

The disgust was there, and more, much more. Intractability. Coldness. Anger. When Charles knew she was aware of how he felt, he released the note.

What shall I do? He has had me again, has forced me down paths of iniquity so that now I am afraid to show my face to God for fear he shall strike down my other limb. I was safe within the care of Hattie and the reverend; they would not abandon me to that sinful side of myself that is best left unnurtured. But he will have me again, and I know that in my weakness I shall not be able to restrain that other side of myself, that base and lewd self that wallows in imprudent habits.

At times I feel as if I were two people, and am left to wonder which shall reign the coming moment, that sick, wanton creature whom in my despair I have named Elaine, that I might more thoroughly disassociate myself, or myself, Morrigan, raised in the strictest of moral and Christian fortitude. Yet I seem to have no control over that other side of myself. I pray each day to God that righteousness and goodness shall triumph over my wickedness.

How am I to conquer this looseness of morals that must bring disgust to all those containing the veriest shred of Christian and human decency? If only my uncle in his regard of my welfare had not forced me into this marriage. Yet it is equally wrong to deny my husband. Oh, I am surely mad! that I must so divide my conscience to appease both my husband's sinful appetites and the moral fiber of my soul.

Elaine bemusedly stared at the note. What a piece of nonsense! . . . *divide my conscience to appease both my husband's sinful appetites and the moral fiber of my soul.* Good grief! It sounded like a scenario from a nineteenth-century soap opera. How could Charles or anyone else take this seriously? Only a crazy person would write . . .

. . . such nonsense.

Elaine drew an unsteady breath. She forced her head up and met those gelid blue eyes. What could she say? That she had been writing a melodrama for the *Christian Monitor*? Whoever had written the note was extremely clever. If Elaine admitted who she was and where she came from, she was damned. If Elaine continued the pretense of Morrigan, she was damned.

"Well?" Charles said softly. "Did you or did you not write this?"

Ah, another case of damned if you do and damned if you don't.

Elaine looked down at the ring on her left finger. The gold glowed faintly red in the morning light. Superimposed over the plain wide band appeared the sparkle of a half-carat diamond mounted on a thin fourteen-carat-gold band.

She had not been there in the twentieth century to defend herself. If she had, perhaps Matthew would have listened to her. She could not do anything about that other life, but she could try in this one.

Elaine threw her head back and stared into the blue shards of ice. "No. No, I didn't write it."

Charles's full lower lip twisted sardonically. "Is this the—let me see, how did the note put it?—the self who submits to her husband's sinful appetites or the self who cringes in Christian horror? Elaine the whore or Morrigan the pure? Which self did not write it?"

Ouch. So much for honesty. A whore, though. Did he have to call her a whore?

Charles grabbed Elaine's shoulders and shook her. "Well?" he demanded. "Tell me! Which self was it who wrote that ridiculous note?"

Betrayal. Each tooth-rattling shake was like the plunge of a knife directly into her heart. The pain she had felt upon learning that Matthew had committed her faded in comparison. She had never given her all to Matthew. Not the way she had to this man who had taken and taken from her until she had nothing left to hold back. She had trusted Charles. Trusted him with her whole body. And he did not believe her. He had called her, Elaine, a whore. The fact that she had not expected him to believe her did not cushion the agony one whit.

Charles thrust Elaine away from him, as if he could not stand the touch of her. Elaine's feet became entangled in a pretty gown of pink muslin. She collapsed in an undignified heap.

He raked his fingers through his hair, suddenly looking like a bewildered boy. "I will not put you back into the hands of those monstrous relatives of yours. Nor will I abide that evil-smelling harridan that goes by the name of Hattie. Damon . . . I will have Damon examine you. He will know best what to do. Meanwhile . . ."

Charles threw his head back, as if seeking the answer to his dilemma on the ceiling. "Meanwhile, you will stay in this room and do whatever it is that makes you feel more"—he lowered his head, blue eyes pinning hers—"more in control of yourself. Copy from the Bible. Pray. Whatever you did before we—before I enacted my conjugal rights."

His right lip curled toward the thin white scar on his cheek. He turned toward the door. "Katie will be here shortly to clean up this mess."

Elaine opened her mouth to call him back. Pride dictated otherwise. She would rot in hell before she ever called upon a man who did not believe in her.

The door clicked shut. At least he did not lock her in, Elaine thought bitterly. Of course, the key had not been in the lock. There were at least two keys that Elaine knew of. Hattie had one. Elaine had taken the second one from Katie. If Hattie had handed hers in—which she probably had done; otherwise there would have been no need to steal the second key—then it was quite likely she would shortly find herself locked inside her bedroom. Wasn't that what people did to those who were mad? Lock them up?

Elaine would be locked in, but Morrigan or whoever had written that note would not be locked out.

Perhaps she was mad. There was no proof Morrigan had come back from the twentieth century. Indeed, there was no proof she had ever been there. There was no proof Elaine was in the nineteenth century. This could all be a hallucination. And even if it wasn't a hallucination, there was always the possibility that Hattie *had* heard Elaine muttering in her sleep and reported it to Morrigan's aunt. Mrs. Boleigh could be acting in what she believed to be the best interests of her niece by convincing Charles that his wife was crazy so that Morrigan could be drawn back to the bosom of moral rectitude.

Good *God*. Elaine *was* crazy if she believed it possible that someone was trying to prove her insane, all in her "best interest."

Elaine collected the shoes and lined them back up in the bottom of the armoire. She had hung up several of the dresses before Katie came flying through the door.

"Oh, marm. I heard it all, and don't ye worry none, we don't believe it, the servants and me! I know ye didn't write those notes to yerself! And Jamie, the footman in the breakfast room, he said as how the note had been tucked up inside the napkin and how it fell out when ye picked it up. I'll just go and tell the lord he ain't right thinking what he's thinking."

Elaine closed her eyes against this latest act of perfidy. The servants knew of the notes and their supposed author, knowledge that they could glean only from the lord. Somehow that little betrayal hurt worse than his rejection.

"No, don't bother, Katie. Just help me hang these clothes up, OK?" Elaine belatedly realized the unlikelihood of "OK" being a nineteenth-century colloquialism. Seeing the maid's eyes widen, she hastily added, "Thank you for your support, Katie, but the lord"—would think her equally insane when he discovered the truth—"the lord and I have to work it out between ourselves."

And when that happened, she had a few other miracles to perform. Like parting the waters or shortening the necks of giraffes.

The maid looked slightly mollified. "But how could he think a thing like that, m' lady? Ye and the lord been sleeping and doing things together. How can a man think bad things of his woman?"

Elaine bit her lip until she tasted blood, remembering in detail all the things she and Charles had done together, the probing caresses, the mutual lemon-flavored kisses. She remembered then that Katie had slept in her bedroom last night. Had Elaine's cries been audible through the walls? Had the maid's statement implied more than general knowledge of what went on between herself and Charles?

Her mortification died a spontaneous death. What difference did it make if the entire household had heard them? She needn't worry about facing anyone if she was locked up.

Elaine and Katie hung up the dresses. Afterward, Elaine restlessly paced the length and width of the bedchamber. She had wished for peace and quiet. She had wanted the lord to stop making impossible demands.

She looked at the flames leaping and crackling in the fireplace. The silk wallpaper and the lacquered furniture gleamed in the candlelight. A distinct odor of burning wood and wax permeated the scent of white ginger.

Her mother had often warned her to think before she wished. Wishes, she had said, sometimes came true.

Elaine did not touch the dinner tray that Katie brought to her. She had never missed a meal in the twentieth century, not even when she had had her tonsils removed. Another wish come true, a carryover from her plump days, when she had wished for something to take away her appetite.

Katie sat on the couch by the fire and made neat little stitches in an apron. A basket of clothes that required mending sat at her feet.

Elaine recognized the chemise that Charles had so hastily removed that day at the creek. Beneath that was the blue velvet riding habit that had ripped during their dance by the lake.

You have something of mine, dear Elaine. Something that was hidden in the bottom chest drawer. I want it back.

Looking at the white silk, Elaine realized what Morrigan wanted. What Hattie had torn the bedchamber asunder to find.

"Katie, when you rearranged the drawers, did you find a . . . a marble and a bundle that was wrapped in white silk?"

Katie sewed busily.

"Well?" Elaine said impatiently.

"I . . . I don't rightly remember, m' lady. It be ever so long ago."

"It wasn't that long ago, Katie." Elaine was suddenly overcome with the need to end this charade that had cost her everything. "Come now, think!"

Elaine cringed at the sharp voice that echoed from one corner of the room to the other. It sounded more lordly than did Charles himself.

She took a deep breath and exhaled to the count of twenty. "Come on, Katie," she said more gently. "There was a small glass ball—very blue—and a bundle of dried mistletoe wrapped in white silk. They were in the bottom drawer in the chest. With the negligees. I had"—Elaine did some quick thinking, thoughts running round and round. Yes? Yes? She had . . . ?—"I had hidden them from Hattie, you see. She didn't want me to have any mementos from when . . . from when I met the lord."

You can do better than that, Elaine old girl, a small voice jeered. Morrigan's a little too old to be playing with or receiving marbles! The lord might make a gift of Ben-Wa balls. . . .

"I found the marble when the lord and I went walking. Before we were married. And he gave me the mistletoe when— What's wrong, Katie?"

Tears ran down the maid's cheeks and dripped onto the apron she was mending. Elaine sat down on the couch beside her.

"Katie, what's wrong? Did you prick yourself on the needle?"

Katie sniffed. "I didn't know, marm; honest, I didn't!"

Elaine had a lowering sense of premonition. "Didn't know what, Katie?"

"I didn't know what ye was keeping them fer, and the mistletoe, it be ever so dry and dirty like so I"—Katie sobbed—"I burned it!"

Strike one.

"What about the marble, Katie?"

Another sob escaped the maid. She stabbed at the apron. "I . . . I took it fer me little brother, he be so small and sickly like, and he can't get out and play like the others, so I thought—I thought it be so pretty and I didn't think ye'd mind none, marm, so I took it fer him!"

You mean you didn't think I'd notice, Elaine thought grimly. Strike two, one more ball to go.

"What about the piece of white silk, Katie? What did you do with that?"

Katie sobbed in earnest, "Oh, marm! Oh, marm!"

Strike three.

"I done made me mum a silk hankerchief from it—she ain't never had any so fine, and I thought . . . I thought—"

"I know." Elaine sighed. "You didn't think I'd notice."

Katie buried her head in the apron. She cried like a Lucille Ball impersonator. Elaine stared at the maid's bowed head in exasperation. The chemise in the sewing basket caught her eye.

"Oh, never mind, Katie." Elaine reached down and plucked the chemise out of the mending basket. Grabbing the torn bodice between her hands, she jerked. The material ripped in half.

Katie raised her head out of the apron.

"Go find me a twig of some sort, about the size of the mistletoe."

Katie dried her face on the apron, then used it to blow her nose on. "Oh, marm, I can't do that! I got to stay with ye!"

Elaine's mouth flattened. Two could play that game.

"Shall I tell the lord that you destroyed her ladyship's property?"

Katie twisted the soiled apron. "Oh, marm! Oh, marm, please don't! The little ones, they got to be fed and—"

"I know. Shoed. I would suggest, then, that you go and find a twig."

Katie dropped the snotty apron into the mending basket. While the maid did Elaine's bidding, Elaine wrote a note, frequently pausing to nibble on the tip of the wooden handle. Katie returned some time later bearing a small tree limb. Elaine eyed it disbelievingly.

Katie smiled sheepishly. "It be the best I could find, marm."

Elaine sent Katie on another errand; this time the maid went without protest. Elaine trimmed the limb down to a manageable size. By the time it approximated a bough of mistletoe, she had lost ten nails and gained enough splinters to use for kindling. She wrapped the newly formed twig inside the white silk, a remnant of the chemise.

Katie returned with a crystal decanter filled with amber liquid. Elaine took out the miniature crystal-ball stopper and looked around for something to break away the stem. The mutilated chemise lay on the floor by the couch. Elaine swooped on the silk and wrapped it about the stopper. She carried the silk-clad crystal stopper over to the desk, placed it on the Bible, and took a brass candleholder to it.

"Marm! Oh, marm, what ye be doing? Ye've broken the crystal, and I took it from the salon! The butler, he saw me do it, and he'll think I done broke it! Oh, marm!"

Elaine carefully separated the silk folds. The miniature ball was chipped, but without a stem. She held it up to the light.

"Shush, Katie! I'll tell the butler that you didn't do it. You won't be held responsible, I promise."

"Oh, but marm, the lord, he did make me respons'ble fer it! Fer ye! Oh, marm, he'll take away me position fer sure!"

Katie's lament fell on deaf ears. The crystal ball was too large—and clear, Elaine thought—but it would have to do.

"Katie, there's a note on the desk over there. I want you to take that note and give it to Hattie."

Katie gasped. Apprehension flared in the maid's eyes.

"You do know where Hattie's room is, don't you?"

A reluctant nod.

Elaine retrieved the note and held it out to the young maid.

Resolve hardened her heart. "Then take it to her, or I'll just have to tell the lord what a clumsy, irresponsible thief you are."

Katie's large brown eyes stared at her like the eyes of a wounded cow. No, like Jasper's eyes. Elaine pointed toward the door.

Katie returned tight-lipped. Elaine forbore questioning the maid, understanding all too well how obnoxious Hattie could be. The maid folded the snotty apron and set it on top of the small stack of mended articles on the couch. Elaine refrained from comment.

Bedtime came and went. The stack of mended clothes had grown. Elaine's leg ached, the increasingly familiar pain of overexertion. Last night Charles had taken it in his hands and kissed and caressed the knotted muscles. She, like some dumb, domesticated animal, had allowed him to do what he would.

It was time for this farce to be over.

But Elaine's note did not elicit the expected results. It must be near midnight, Elaine thought anxiously, and no word of acknowledgment. Katie slept over her mending.

She banked the fire. Katie snorted in her sleep. Elaine gingerly picked up the stack of mended articles and laid them on top of the basket. She shook the maid's shoulder.

"Katie? Katie, are you awake?"

Katie emitted a long, whistling snore. A reluctant grin spread across Elaine's face. She eased the maid along the length of the couch and covered her with a housecoat.

A soft knock sounded on the main door.

Elaine's heartbeat accelerated. Charles? Had he decided to continue his conjugal rights? She was ashamed at how eager she was for him to do so.

A note slid beneath the door, the slip of paper startlingly white in the gloom of shadow. Elaine waited long seconds before picking it up. The handwriting was even more slanted than usual.

Dear Elaine,
I thought you would—how do your people say?—see things my way. You remember that small stream in the woods where you enjoyed

Arlcotte with such zealous appetite, do you not? Meet me there in one hour. I need not remind you to bring my possessions.

Hot color burned in Elaine's cheeks. How did this person know what she had done to Charles that day? No one could possibly know that, save her and, of course, Charles.

She remembered that the Boleigh brood had witnessed their return from the stream. It would not have taken much imagination to have figured out what they had been doing. Their clothes had been wet and dirty. It had been quite evident they had made love, even to someone who had plucked their children from a cabbage patch. The note did not out-and-out state that Elaine had taken Charles in her mouth. It had merely mentioned that she had enjoyed him with "zealous appetite." The fourth note had mentioned something about appetites, too. She deliberately pushed from her thoughts the note that had stated that Morrigan knew everything.

Katie snored happily away on the couch. Elaine debated over waking the girl. The fear that Katie might learn of her transmigration exceeded the fear of facing the person who supposedly was Morrigan returned. She let the maid sleep on in enviable oblivion.

Elaine grabbed a cape from the wardrobe. She tucked the marble in a deep side pocket and hid the silk bundle beneath the folds of the soft wool. Even though the note had given the meeting time as an hour away, Elaine had no watch, and it could very well take her an hour to find the place in the dark.

She eased down the stairs and out of the house without encountering a footman. A pale sliver of moonlight illuminated the skies, which was better than none, she thought bracingly. The air was freezing, or maybe it only seemed so because her bedroom had been so warm and toasty. Or perhaps it was because the blood seemed to be frozen in her veins.

Elaine walked and walked, alternately stumbling, limping, hopping, praying. Most of all praying. Please let this be the right decision. Please let her at least find out who was behind everything. Please let her be able to bring out the culprit and end this blackmail.

Please let her come to some sort of peace and security. *Please let Charles take her back.*

The trees blocked the sky. Elaine wandered at random, panic rising with every stumble, when she saw a ball of light dancing and shimmering in the distance. A whole army of fingers walked up her back. She remembered her grandmother telling her about jack-o'-lanterns, ghostly balls of light that mischievously followed unsuspecting victims. Which, supernatural or not, would make a more pleasant companion than the person who had been writing those notes. Elaine made her way toward the flickering ball as unobtrusively as she could. The light remained stationary: it was a campfire.

Icy water seeped through the soles of her shoes. The wool cape pressed down on her shoulders, the tail acting as a giant sponge. She staggered backward out of the stream, tripping over a log that she did not remember having been there.

Elaine scrambled to her feet, grimacing. It was a very soft, rotten log, still warm from the sun. A perfect haven for night critters. She immediately felt thousands of tiny pronged feet tromping over her body, imagining every type of insect that could possibly inhabit decayed wood. Ants. Termites. Beetles. Spiders. It was pure imagination, of course, but that did not decrease the imaginary footsteps. When she moved to distance herself from the log, she found it and her cape fast friends.

Shuddering, Elaine traced the cape to the point where it had snagged on the log. A piece of wire protruded upward. Beneath the wire, the log was flaccid and wet. Sticky wet. A mane of coarse weeds surrounded the thin, flaccid wood.

Elaine peered more closely at this strange log. It was very pale at the end where the wire protruded. There was a suspicious gleam beneath the mop of weeds.

Elaine stooped closer, finding that she was blocking what little light there was from the campfire. She stooped closer still.

"Ahh!"

Elaine jumped as far back as momentum would allow. The cape rent, a slice of sound in the silent night.

She landed with a splash in the icy stream. A small rock ground up into her tailbone. But Elaine was impervious to pain. Impervious to the permeation of icy water through wool, silk, bustle, and more silk.

That was no log. And the mane was not a clump of weeds. And what glimmered in the dark was an eye.

A human eye.

Chapter
25

Hysteria rose in Elaine's throat.

A body!

A human body!

A dead human body!

And she had touched it!

Elaine compulsively rubbed her hand on the wool cape. Her fingers were sticky with blood.

"Oh, God, oh, God," she whimpered, rubbing and rubbing. "It won't come off! Oh, God!"

"Come now, Elaine, don't be so missish. I bet you didn't act this way when you woke up and found *my* blood smeared between your thighs. My virgin blood, I might add. And Lord Arlcotte's seed, of course. I bet you quite liked that, in fact. It had been many years since you were a virgin, though of course that mealymouthed husband of yours was not nearly as well endowed as Charles. Quite like a bull, is our lord. And how long, I wonder, had it been since you had been inundated with a man's seed? We do not have to ask how long it's been now. Do you like fornicating with another woman's husband? Do you like committing adultery, Elaine?"

The voice seemed disembodied, neither male nor female, yet frighteningly familiar all the same. A section of wood separated from the forest, darker than the other trees, shorter, fuller. It stepped closer and closer, an inch at a time, playing cat to her mouse.

Elaine clumsily scooted across the stream, away from that figure of death and that other figure of life. "Who are you?" Her voice was high, as if she had swallowed helium. "What do you want?" And then, as that other figure came closer, "Stay away from me!"

Pale flesh emerged from the sides of the dark figure, dimly recognizable as hands. The wraithlike hands pushed back what Elaine now realized must be a hood. More pale flesh was revealed, a head. "Don't you want to know who you so rudely trampled, my dear?" The voice was clear now, unmuffled by cloth. "Don't you want to know who I really am?"

Oh, God. Oh, God. Oh, God.

Elaine knew who it was. Nausea rose in her throat, choking the hysteria.

"Come, my dear. Come give your uncle a kiss."

"You're crazy! Oh, my God, you're crazy!" Elaine stumbled to her feet. She felt as if her lungs had collapsed. Air would not penetrate. She almost hoped she would faint.

Mr. Boleigh—Morrigan's uncle—stepped closer, into the stream. His rotund figure was draped from top to bottom in a flowing dark garment, like that of a monk. The water-laden robe pulled taut over his bulbous stomach.

The soft laughter ensuing from those horrid, perverted lips was an obscenity. "Now, now, puss. You like it with Charles. I can hear you caterwauling a mile away when you're with him. I assure you I can perform better than Matthew. Why not give me a chance? I bet I could show you things that would simply amaze you."

As if from nowhere, a soft, clammy hand reached out and grabbed Elaine by the neck. Those pudgy, uncallused fingers contained incredible strength. Elaine choked for real.

"Yes, let me show you what my life was like, Elaine Metcliffe, at the mercy of a monster and a Methodist aunt who was jealous of any attention that was not lavished upon her or her daughters. Do you know what it was like to tremble for fear of going to bed, knowing that your body would be violated and there was nothing"—the fingers squeezed—"absolutely nothing you could do to stop it?

"Do you know what it was like facing that monster every morning over breakfast, sick and hurting from his abuse, and being told that I was evil because I had a twisted leg? And being forced to do daily penance while subsisting on the meanest of food and physical comforts?"

Elaine was shook back and forth.

"Do you?"

"No," Elaine croaked. She clawed at the hand that held her with superhuman strength. She couldn't breathe. The dim light cast by the campfire was growing speckled.

The squeezing fingers released Elaine's throat. Her body flew through the air. She landed with an audible thump and a whoosh, considerably closer to the campfire than before. A piece of burning wood popped in the silence.

The silence.

Woods were supposed to come alive at night with crickets, tree frogs, and a whole host of noisy, sinister-sounding creatures. City slicker that Elaine was, she knew that much. Yet it was totally silent. Like the trees outside her bedroom.

"No, of course not," Boleigh sneered. "All you ever had to worry about was satisfying those insatiable appetites of yours. Matthew was right to put you away. You deserved to die. I'm glad I killed Hattie. She knew. All those years my uncle crept up to my little iron bed in the attic, she *knew*. And now I want you to know. I want to experience what my uncle experienced. I want you to know what it is like to have your body ripped in half by an ugly old geezer who makes your stomach roil just to look at him."

"You . . ." Elaine's voice cracked. She rubbed her bruised throat. The darkly robed figure towering over her looked ten feet tall and just as wide. "You don't mean that."

Boleigh cackled with laughter. "Don't I? Well, we will see, will we not? Where are my tools?" The oily voice sharpened. "What have you done with them?"

"I . . ." Elaine peered around her. Where was the silk bundle? It had been in her left hand just before she had stumbled in the water and fallen over the . . . log. Not seeing it, she frantically thrust her hand into the side pocket of her cape. Jagged glass bit into her fingers. "I—the mistletoe, I dropped it. It's over there." Elaine pointed toward the log that wasn't a log at all.

"So you know what it is." Boleigh visibly preened. "Shall I tell you what it's used for? Would you like to know how it is that you came here into my century inside my body?"

Actually, Elaine *would* like to know.

"Do you even know what time you are in?"

"No. I don't know. Not exactly."

Elaine could more feel the condescending smile that her admission brought than see it. Boleigh turned, unconcerned that his quarry might fight or flee. He waded across the narrow stream.

"It is 1883. May . . . Ah!" The dark, shroudlike figure bent over the . . . log. When Boleigh raised up, Elaine could see the stark white of the silk bundle. "You clumsy girl. I will have to punish you; you know that, do you not? You dropped my Silver Branch."

Elaine breathed a sigh of relief. He had not noticed that the flora wrapped inside the silk was not mistletoe.

"Where is my *Glain-nan-Druidhe*?"

"I . . ." His *what?* Had Elaine missed something that day she had discovered what she had thought were Morrigan's mementos from a happier past? Had Katie taken another item and been too afraid of losing her job to volunteer the information?

Boleigh materialized in front of Elaine, carrying a white silk bundle as if it were a scepter. He could move at incredible speed. Or perhaps it was a trick of the night, with the spill of the moon and the waving tree tops and the flickering campfire. Like strobe light. A pale hand extended between one blink and another.

"My *Glain-nan-Druidhe*. My serpent's egg. The sperm of mating snakes, which I managed to steal while they writhed and hissed in sexual union. They chased me mightily, but I crossed a stream that I had diverted and escaped with their essence."

Dear me. Elaine wondered what young Katie would say at giving her little brother snake leavings. She stared at Morrigan's uncle, light-headed with relief. Morrigan's *uncle*. Not Morrigan. A person who was crazier than a proverbial loon. Not a transmigrated soul. A person who had murdered, but could not harm her, Elaine, if she could distract him and get the hell out of here.

There was no warning of violence. One minute the pale, wraith-like hand was extended in front of Elaine; the next it slammed into her face. "Where is it?"

Elaine had lived her entire life—thirty-nine years—without once being subjected to corporal punishment. Yet in the last few weeks she had been slapped four times, twice that day. She had endured all the physical abuse she was going to, murderer or no murderer. "I have it on me, but if you touch me again, I'll throw it so far you'll need a troop of marines to find it."

That demonic laugh. Elaine winced. She really wished he would not laugh like that. It was unnerving.

Elaine quickly forgot about the laugh. The dark, round figure commenced circling her counterclockwise. A chill ran from her frozen feet all the way up her spine. She turned, following his movements, Hattie the log a clear reminder of what happened to the unwary.

"*Fith-fath*, Elaine, *fith-fath*."

Elaine suppressed a nervous giggle. It sounded like he was saying "fee-fa." She half expected him to follow it with "fee-fi-fo-fum."

"I will make the spell of *fith-fath* on you if you don't give me my *Glain-nan-Druidhe*. How would you like to spend the rest of your life inside the skin of a sheep? Hattie always called me a 'puir' little lamb. Or perhaps you would prefer to be a fox; they're very popular here in merry old England. Arlcotte hunts. Imagine your lover taking your tail for a trophy someday. Or perhaps you would prefer something else. Don't worry, I'll think of something interesting. '*Fith-fath*, / Will I make on thee, / By Mary of the augury—' "

"You're crazy!" Elaine stumbled on the hem of her dripping dress, righted herself, slowly turning, turning, the sky and trees turning with her. "Do you think you can scare me?" No need to let on that he was doing a damn fine job.

" '. . . By bride of the corslet, / From sheep, from ram—' "

"I can recite nursery rhymes, too! You're nothing but a sick old man who preys on children!" And old women. And young women.

" '. . . From goat, from buck, / From fox, from—' "

"Well, I'm not! I'm not some poor child you can bully and molest!"

" '. . . from wolf, / From sow, from boar . . .' "

The silk clad bundle extended to touch Elaine on the head. It felt like thousands of ants crawled over her skin.

Elaine jerked back out of reach. "Damn you, I told you not to touch me!" She dug the makeshift serpent's egg out of her cape pocket and held it poised above her head for one second.

The chanting stopped. A pudgy hand grabbed for the stopper.

Elaine threw the crystal as hard as she could.

The veins bulged in Boleigh's forehead; his skin turned an unhealthy-looking puce, visible even in the flickering light. The grasping hand reached for Elaine.

Elaine stared at the rage-contorted face, at the short, stubby fingers curved for capture. He should have scrambled after the crystal ball, not her. She instinctively turned to flee.

Elaine felt herself caught, felt the heavy, wet cape peel off her shoulders like the skin off a snake's back. A snort of laughter escaped the constriction of her throat. Did snakes shed their skin before or after they released their sperm?

"You whore!" The pudgy hands grabbed the back of Elaine's dress. "You adulterous tart!"

Whore. Tart. Lemon. No wonder Charles had gone into hysterics at the breakfast table.

"You pox-riddled sailor's doxy!"

Tart. Doxy. Elaine was receiving a course on nineteenth-century slang. The problem was, she didn't think she could afford the tuition. Her legs cycled forward, making about as much progress as she had made on her exerciser in that other time.

Elaine was reeled backward. Two hands wrapped around her throat.

"I can find the *Glain-nan-Druidhe* come daylight, you stupid fat whore. Long, long after you're dead. But first I'll see for myself what interests my body held for dear old uncle. It's only fitting, don't you think?"

Boleigh's breath was hot and fetid, coming just below her ear. That combined with his body odor would have made Elaine gag, if only she had enough breath to do so.

"You think I am some demented old satyr. Oh, yes, you can't hide your thoughts from me. What proof do you want, Elaine Metcliffe? Do you want to know the names of the books you kept hidden in your bottom drawer? Does the title *Joy of Sex* mean anything to you?"

Indeed it did. Elaine had gotten the set, *Joy of Sex* and *More Joy of Sex*, on special at Kroch's and Brentano's for under seventeen dollars. She had purchased it as a sort of dual anniversary present for herself and Matthew. That had been the last time she had attempted to share her sexuality with Matthew.

"Should I continue?"

Elaine shook her head. No, she had heard quite enough to convince her that Boleigh was Morrigan from the twentieth century. That did not, however, make him . . . her—how did Elaine refer to Morrigan now?—any saner.

"Should I tell you about the strange clothing I woke up in? The big blue top and the matching breeches that were held up with elastic at the waist? Should I tell you how revolting it was to wake up in clothes that are polluted by another woman's excitation?"

Polluted by another woman's . . . ?

Not another woman's excitation.

Elaine's excitation.

"No, I can see you wouldn't know what it was like. After all, you like earthy pleasures, do you not, Elaine Metcliffe?"

The fingers tightened around Elaine's throat. She felt her eyeballs bulge from the pressure.

"Do you not?"

A garbled sound snagged inside her throat. Those Herculean fingers loosened ever so little, but enough that Elaine was able to replenish her starving lungs. She noisily gulped air.

"Shall I tell you what happened after I woke up? I convinced your dearly beloved Matthew that I was sick. He left me alone then."

Yes, Elaine thought dully, Matthew would have.

"I was quite fascinated with your home. It surpassed anything I had ever dreamed. Iceboxes that produce ice, electrical boxes that captured human lives and voices. Heat came out of the floor. Hot water poured from the sinks and bathtub. . . ."

Elaine remembered her first nineteenth-century bath. She had wondered if Morrigan was bathing in the modern enameled bathtub even while Elaine bathed in the primitive metal one. She wanted to laugh, realizing how shocked she would have been if she had really thought her speculations were correct. She wanted to cry, knowing now how close they had been.

"It was what I had wanted, to escape into another time and body, what I had long labored to do, but I became frightened, stupidly now, I realize. Of what use was my magic, I thought, when all around me everyone else was capable of creating magic simply by turning a knob or pressing a button? And your land. Your people have no land, no trees, no sacred oak groves, no magical streams of water. How could I communicate with my gods? I need the tools of my magic."

The body behind her hummed with malevolent energy. It showed no signs of tiring. The fingers wrapped around her throat had loosened enough to allow small trickles of oxygen, but showed no signs of further loosening. Elaine knew with heart-stopping certainty that if she did not gain release she would pass out. And if she passed out, she would die. Here, alone, in 1883 May. . . . *Ah.*

Desperately she strove to organize the thoughts that seemed to be shrinking smaller and smaller. Seconds collapsed into eons. She felt her hands drift behind her.

"And your husband!" The fingers tightened ominously. "Bah! He questioned me and questioned me until I thought I would go mad. When I told him what he wanted to know, he thought you were insane. My uncle's *love* was more enduring than that of your husband. You will find that Arlcotte's lust will wither just as quickly.

You see, I wrote him a note. He will find Hattie, your first victim, then he will find you. I will tell him you killed Hattie in some Druid sacrificial ritual, and had planned to do the same with me, that you had written me a note to meet you here and that when you attacked me I defended myself. I will say you used me in a Druid orgy. After I've finished with you, I will partake of the sacred berries so that I will be in a drugged state, proof of your perfidy. Tomorrow I will find my *Glain-nan-Druidhe*. Uncle's fat old body cannot tolerate the strain much longer. He's sick; that was why I was able to take him without my tools of magic.

"I will find another body, one that is young and whole and healthy. Perhaps Mickey, the stable boy. He saw me one night, dancing in the moonlight. I told him I would turn his tongue into cow dung should he tell anyone. Or perhaps it will be Arlcotte's body I take, fitting punishment, do you not think? And then . . .

"But the rest doesn't matter to you, does it, my dear? You will be quite dead. After I have had the pleasure of taking myself."

Elaine's fingers floated into contact. The robe was coarse, the stomach beneath rotund. The flesh she sought was much lower, too low for her to grab without bending.

As if by magic, the hands released Elaine. A crack resounded through the darkness. Elaine's head exploded.

She dropped to her knees. A blazing kaleidoscope twirled in front of her eyes.

"The mighty blow of Taranis. Were you worthy of sacrifice, you would receive three blows. With an ax. Then I would garrote you. In the name of Esus. Just at the point of death I would drain your blood into the sacred vessel. Teutates would embrace you in the shallow depths of the stream over there. But you are not worthy—you are crippled and licentious—so I will use my hands."

The soft fingers deftly undid the buttons lining the back of Elaine's dress.

"Filidh was my mentor. She thought Druidism was to foster peace and harmony. I learned all she had to teach, but she was only one of my sources. Prudence could never understand why her kittens kept disappearing until she saw me perform *Taghairn*. You wouldn't know what that is, though, ignorant bumpkin that you are. It is also known as 'giving his supper to the devil.' First you find a cat, or a kitten, as the case may be, then impale it and roast it alive. The spirits are obliged to give you whatever you ask. I asked for knowledge.

"Filidh was frightened when she saw how powerful I had become, but unlike you, Elaine, she was smart enough to recognize me, even in this gross body I now have. She threatened to expose me. That could have been awkward. I took a garrote to her, too. She struggled more than Hattie. Filidh was another waste. She was not worthy of sacrifice. Someday I will gather together Druids such as myself, and we will follow the old traditions.

"I shall be their queen. Their 'Great Queen,' and fly high over the battles as I did thousands of years ago, disguised in my feathers of black. I was not meant to be locked in that crippled body. But I really don't want you having it, either."

The night air was biting. The kaleidoscopic flashes whirling in Elaine's brain dimmed. She looked up. A short, fat man stood over her. He struggled to get a robe over his head.

Elaine became aware of a painful stabbing sensation. She looked down. Something was jabbing into her naked hip. A stick. Damp, cold grass tickled her bare back.

A heavy drape of cloth swished to the ground. Elaine looked up. The short, fat man was naked. He looked like the Pillsbury Doughboy with bushy side-whiskers. She wondered if he would giggle if she stuck her finger into his stomach.

The bewhiskered Doughboy squatted down. He had little doughy genitals between his legs. Elaine's forehead wrinkled. No, that wasn't right. The children of America would have their growth permanently stunted if the Doughboy appeared with genitals.

The night was strangely silent save for the somewhat labored breathing of a man who is woefully out of condition. The Doughboy's belly moved in time with the rhythmic sounds.

The touch of soft, flabby skin brought Elaine out of the stupor. She writhed, bringing tooth and nail to her defense. And screamed. The screams were muted from the crush of protuberant weight.

* * *

Charles cupped the glass of brandy between his palms. He brought the snifter to his lips. The glass was warm and brittle. Not warm and pliable, like Morrigan's flesh.

He slammed the snifter down onto the marble-topped table. Warm brandy inundated his fingers. He watched the glistening trail. Her warmth had inundated those same fingers last night, the warm, thick passion of a woman.

The knife of betrayal twisted. He picked up the snifter and consigned it to the fireplace. Glass tinkled. Flames burst up the chimney.

Passion.

Charles felt the muscles in his face pull.

No, Morrigan had no passion. Elaine was the passionate one. Morrigan was the sanctimonious one.

Damn her. Damn her soul to the deepest depths of purgatory.

Mad. His wife was madder than the proverbial Hatter, a character from Lewis Carroll's *Alice's Adventures in Wonderland*, which he had previously thought merely quaint.

The flames in the fireplace flickered blue, then returned to their normal burn.

Normal.

God.

Charles rested his head against the back of the chair and closed his eyes. He should thank her rather than curse her. If she had not revealed her madness now, he would eventually have begotten children on her. Mad little Charleses and Morrigans.

He jerked his head up and glared at the flickering flames.

Why couldn't she have stayed Elaine? Why did the sanctimonious Morrigan have to step in and ruin everything?

Society was right. Marriage had nothing to do with caring. He had not cared for his wife the entire year she had been a silent, invisible lodger. Why should he start now, just because for the first time in his life a woman had given him everything, every little bit of herself?

How could she be mad? She had laughed and frolicked; she had cried her passion. Were those the actions of a madwoman?

Yet he had read the note with his own eyes. It had been her writing, Morrigan's. No one could imitate that writing without breaking their wrist.

Charles thought and brooded until the fire dimmed. The bed would be cold. Unwarmed by the flesh of a woman. By the flesh of Morrigan.

They had drenched the sheets with their heat last night. Again. She had opened herself like the petals of a rare exotic flower. And it had all been *lies!*

A scurrying movement came from behind the main door, the door that did not connect with Morrigan's. Rodents. He would have to call in the exterminators. His house would be out of order for an entire week.

Damn!

Old man Boleigh had suffered a relapse, a temporary setback, the physician had assured him. They would leave on the morrow, he thought grimly, if he had to pay for the doctor to accompany him all the way to Cornwall. He could feel them, sighing and whispering through the walls of their bedchambers where he had confined them.

If Charles did not know for a fact that Morrigan had come to him with literally nothing but the clothes on her back and that decrepit Scottish hag, he would consider the possibility that perhaps her relatives were trying to prove her insane to gain her inheritance. But he did know differently. Morrigan had not a farthing to her name. Everything her parents had owned—land, money, jewels—was confiscated upon their death to pay the duns.

Charles sighed. Misguided as the Boleighs were, they were convinced they were doing their Christian duty by taking Morrigan back with them.

The fire shot up a weak flame. Charles gritted his teeth with the fortitude that was born and bred in a gentleman. There was no sense in delaying the inevitable. To bed. Alone.

He banked the fire. A piece of blackened log smoldered in the ashes. Black. Warm. The color of Morrigan's eyes as she had lain naked in his bed last night.

Charles shot to his feet. Traitorous legs carried him to the connecting door. Behind the wood was bleak silence.

Without direction his body turned to the main door. He would find the most boring book he possibly could, he decided grimly; with any luck, he would soon doze in the library. One thing was for certain: he could not sleep here in this room, next to her, with only a door, to which he had the key, to separate them.

The folded slip of paper immediately caught his eye. It had been slid under the door. Charles picked it up with trembling fingers. His gentlemanly fortitude balked at reading another one of Morrigan's mad messages.

He squeezed his eyes shut. Not another one, he prayed, please don't let it be another one.

When he opened his eyes, the paper was still there. Gentlemanly fortitude prevailed once again. Charles unfolded the white stationery.

Dear Charles,

How I miss you, my darling! How I miss having you deep inside me. I have tried to keep her away. Morrigan pretends to be so pious. If you only knew the things she does! She has seduced her uncle, her own uncle, to acts that would make you sick if you only knew. He has no choice but to do as she wishes. She drugs him with berries so that he is insensible. Afterward she threatens to destroy his reputation should he tell anyone.

Oh, Charles! I am so frightened! So alone! Please don't spurn me! There is no one else I can turn to. No one else I want to turn to. You have brought me the only love I have ever known. And now she is going to destroy that, just as she has destroyed everything else.

Morrigan is evil, Charles! She believes she is a powerful Druid, exempt from the morals and conscience of mortal men. Tonight she is going to do something so sick, so evil, that I cannot bring myself to write it. Please, darling, please! For our sake, come to the grove tonight, there where I first tasted you and you took me against the tree with my legs wrapped around your waist.

Help me! Please!

No signature was needed; it was Morrigan's handwriting, the slant more painfully leftward than ever before.

Groaning with agony, Charles crushed the note into a ball and threw it with all of his strength.

She *was* mad.

Charles felt violated that she should refer to that moment at the stream. That had been special. That had been the first time Morrigan had taken the initiative. That she had indicated that she really, truly wanted him.

And she had not even been sane.

The sense of violation became fury. Charles scrambled for the note and smoothed it out. The right corner of his lip hitched up to the scar.

That bastard. That pompous, twat-faced hypocrite.

Morrigan had been molested by her own uncle. No wonder she was insane. He would kill Boleigh with his own two hands.

How do you know this note isn't a fabrication, like Morrigan's belief that she is compelled to lust by an arch personality? the insidious voice of logic reasoned.

The rage inside Charles cooled. Without hesitation he unlocked the connecting door.

Morrigan's bedchamber was dark save for the dim light that filtered through the French doors. Charles knew without looking at the bed that it was empty. He spotted a patch of white on the small couch in front of the nearly dead fire.

A gentle snore wafted through the still air. Anger simmering just below boiling point, Charles stalked the couch and grabbed a handful of shoulders. He shook it for all he was worth.

"Here now!" Katie came up struggling. "Just what d'ye think ye're doing here— M' lord!" Katie straightened her mobcap. "M' lord! I . . . I . . . be there something I can do fer ye, m' lord?"

"Where is she?"

"Who, m' lord? Where be—"

"I gave Fritz explicit instructions that you were not to let your mistress out of your sight. Now where is she, damn you?"

Katie shrank into the couch. "Why . . . Why, m-m' lady," Katie stammered, "she was ... she was ... I ... I—" Katie burst into tears.

Charles grimaced in disgust. "Stop that bawling! Fetch Fritz and tell him to send a message to Damon posthaste that he is needed here without delay. Tell Fritz to have laudanum on hand for when I return with her ladyship. She will need something to calm her."

Katie's "Y-ye-yes, m' lord" was lost in the slam of the door.

Charles quickly traversed the dark corridor. He missed the first step at the top of the stairs. Had he been a less agile man, he would have tumbled to the bottom of the stairs and broken his neck. And maybe that was exactly what his little wife planned. She would be quite a rich, titled lady, able to enjoy all the benefits of position without a nasty husband who insisted upon conjugal rights. He grabbed the banister on the third step down, resulting in a bruised tailbone instead of a broken neck.

The night was cooler than usual. There was rain in the air; it would probably come before morning. He hoped Morrigan had thought to grab a cloak, then roundly cursed himself at the thought that he might still care, *if* he had cared at all. It would be best all around, particularly for Morrigan, if she caught a chill and died from pneumonia. Being locked up for the rest of one's life could not be a very pleasant prospect. And Morrigan, by her actions tonight, had proven the necessity.

Charles could not believe the sight that met his eyes when he gained the grove where he had known Morrigan in every sense of the word.

Chapter

26

Elaine kicked and clawed. Skin scaled beneath her nails. Her fingers slid on slippery blood.

Boleigh cursed in an unknown language. A soft, clammy hand wrapped about Elaine's throat and squeezed. She writhed desperately, but her fingers could find no purchase, and he—*she*—Elaine felt the rising giddiness that preceded unconsciousness. She didn't even know what gender to call her rapist/murderer. A male body inhabited by a female presence. Did Elaine refer to Boleigh as Morrigan, or Morrigan as Boleigh? Did she refer to Boleigh as *her*, or Morrigan as *him?*

A flabby knee managed to insert itself between Elaine's legs. The Doughboy-size genitals pressed against her abdomen, hard as the body they belonged to was not. She would die, she would simply die if that thing succeeded in penetrating her, but Elaine seemed to be fighting a losing battle. What little breath that had not been crushed from her lungs by the weight of the corpulent body on top of her was being trapped by the fingers wrapped around her throat.

To be raped by Morrigan. To be raped by the person Elaine had thought was a poor little gray mouse. To be raped by the rightful owner of Elaine's borrowed body!

It surpassed farce. It surpassed horror.

A sound like that of a trapped animal erupted from Elaine's throat. She rammed her face as hard as she could against that of her attacker.

Only to butt open space.

Air rushed into Elaine's lungs.

Boleigh was sprawled on the ground some five feet away. Charles stood over the prone body. Elaine could feel the rage emanating from him. He jerked Boleigh upright and slammed a fist into his nose. Again. And again. And again.

There was bone under all that flab. Elaine distinctly heard it crunch several times. Boleigh's eyes were wide with horror. Blood spouted from his mouth and nose.

"Lord Arlcotte!" Boleigh grabbed at a descending fist. "Lord Arlcotte, I beg of you!"

The two figures looked so incongruous Elaine could only lie on the ground and stare. Charles, the image of health—young, handsome, sublimely elegant in his dinner tux—and Boleigh, dressed in pale, rotund skin with bushy side-whiskers and rosebud genitals.

"My lord, I beg of you! 'Twas not I! 'Twas her!" A pudgy finger pointed to Elaine's prone body. "She violates every human decency; she's a harlot, born to the devil and his ways! She forced herself upon me. She—"

The crack of bone against bone effectively stopped Boleigh's outburst. The naked, flabby body staggered, flailed wildly to regain balance, stomach jiggling and rolling. What had been filled with menace only seconds earlier now only appeared old and pathetic.

Elaine felt a spark of pity. It seemed so unreal, the fact that Morrigan was Boleigh and Boleigh was Morrigan. All that was evident was that Charles was beating up a naked old man twice his age and weight.

Boleigh tripped and fell to his knees. Blood and tears streamed down the whisker-framed face.

"You disgusting piece of shit!" Charles growled. "I didn't want to believe it, to think that my wife had been molested by her own uncle. And she only a child. You deserve to be castrated and fed piecemeal your own flesh. Though from the looks of it, it wouldn't be much of a mouthful. Get up, you worthless turd, and fight like a man."

"No, no, you don't understand," Boleigh blubbered. "It was she. She lured me here tonight. She put poison in my medicine, and I could not resist her. Look! Look there! You will see! She murdered her nu— Oh, please don't hit me anymore, please! I'm an old man, my heart, please don't hurt me!"

Charles hauled Boleigh to his feet. There was no mercy in his eyes or in his voice. "You should have thought of that precious heart of yours before you met with my wife."

"Oh, no, oh, no, I have proof!" Boleigh wriggled from Charles's hold and scampered toward the silk bundle lying beside the black robe.

Elaine shrank against the cold damp grass. Boleigh grabbed the mistletoe that was not mistletoe. Once it was in his pudgy little hand, he jumped upright. Laughing, he held the silk bundle as if it were a magic wand.

"You will not have me, my fine lord. I will cast a spell, and you will not be able to see me."

Grinning ignominiously through the streaks of blood, Boleigh chanted, " 'A magic cloud I put on me, / From dog, from cat, / From cow, from horse, / From man, from woman, / From young man, from maiden, / And from little child. / Till I return again.' "

A peal of laughter rang through the night. Elaine's blood ran cold.

Charles looked at Boleigh in disgust. "You are as mad as my wife." He walked over to the robe. Bending down, he swooped it up and tossed it at the naked old man. "Get dressed! I've had all of your face—and other parts—I can stomach."

A look of supreme surprise suffused Boleigh's face. He reflexively caught the robe. "But . . . but I'm invisible! You can't see me!"

Charles ignored Boleigh and collected Elaine's scattered clothes. He dropped them beside her with a heavy, wet plop. "You, too, madam. Damon will be here come tomorrow morning. I will let him decide what is to be done with you. There are asylums that are capable of caring for people with your affliction, I'm sure.

"As for you!" Charles swung toward the confused gnome of a

man that Boleigh had been reduced to. "I don't care if you have to walk back to Cornwall; I want you and yours out of my house tonight. Do I make myself clear?"

"But . . . but you don't understand! 'Tis your wife, 'tis Morrigan who's at fault! She drugged me! See!"

Boleigh avidly unwrapped the silk bundle. "The mistletoe, it has berries—"

The silk fell away from the twig, bare of all but spindly leaves.

"You bitch! You fornicating whore from a diseased future! You tricked me! *You tricked me!*"

The twig, the size of a switch, slashed down viciously. Elaine gasped at the cut of thin, pliable wood on bare skin. The twig came down again, across her breasts, eliciting a cry of pain. She jumped up into a crouch, but the crippled left leg was not up to holding her weight in such a position. Elaine fell back onto her backside. She used her feet to scoot out of range of the raining switch, one arm raised to protect her face.

"You thought to steal my husband! I will not allow it! Arlcotte is mine! Go back to your own husband! Go back to your own godless time! I will not let you have what is mine!"

Several more welts were added to the first before Charles lunged forward and grabbed the flaying switch. The young man and the old man struggled for endless seconds, one holding one end of the switch, the other clinging to the opposite end. Charles raised an elegantly shod foot and kicked the dough-belly.

Boleigh toppled over onto his posterior. The round, bewhiskered face contorted. He grabbed his heart.

Charles hurriedly kneeled beside Elaine. He pulled her hands away from her body.

"Are you all right?" he asked softly.

Elaine nodded. Relief coursed through her. It was out. Morrigan had revealed herself.

Charles took off his jacket and wrapped it about her naked shoulders, a shield of warmth.

"So cozy," Boleigh sneered. The curled lips were blue. "You'll never know who she is, will you, my lord? Elaine the whore, or Morrigan the witch?" That insane cackle splintered the night. "I taught her everything she knows. Everything they both know. Elaine the whore and Morrigan the witch. You'll lie awake many a night, I wager, wondering at that. Bad blood runs in the family. Morrigan's father was quite mad. How do you think Morrigan gained her crippled leg? Edward knew that she had inherited his madness, so he ran them all off the cliff—himself, his pregnant wife, and, of course, his mad daughter. But Morrigan survived."

"Bad blood does. Best to destroy her now, tonight, where they'll be no witnesses. You must have heirs. Can you trust yourself not to touch Morrigan should you allow her to live? Will you have your line end in madness?"

Elaine could feel Charles withdraw further and further with each word. "Shut up!" The words burst out of her mouth in pure desperation. Surely Charles had seen that Boleigh . . . that Morrigan—oh, God, she sounded mad even to herself—surely he had seen that things were not as they appeared!

Elaine tried again. "Charles, don't listen to her—"

His lip curled in disgust.

"Charles, you must know, you must see! Oh, I can't explain, I don't know how— Listen to me! For God's sake, do I sound like Morrigan?"

Charles stood up. "Enough," he said curtly. "Enough has been said. Come back to the house with me." He turned and stared dispassionately at the old, naked man. "I'll send footmen with something to carry you on, though I don't think you'll need it. You're dying."

How could she have allowed this man to touch her? Elaine wondered woodenly. How could she have given him everything she had to give? He calmly commanded that she meekly rise and follow him to the house so that his friend could assign her to an asylum, and then in the same breath informed a man he was dying. Even Matthew would have displayed more sensitivity.

Boleigh smiled. "How astute you are, my lord. Yes, Morrigan—or is it Elaine?—accompany the lord. Perhaps he is right. An asylum is where you belong, locked behind iron bars where there will be no temptation."

"Damn you!" Elaine hissed.

Charles put out a restraining hand. Elaine shrugged it off her shoulder.

"And damn you! How can you believe her—yes, that is Morrigan, I don't know how, but that is Morrigan in that pitiful dying body— how can you believe I'm crazy after what we had together? I touched you, *me*, Elaine. I touched you in the most intimate way a woman can! I let you touch me; I let you do things to my body that I had never even thought a man could do! I trusted you, damn you! I trusted you and all you did was use me! Well, damn you both to hell! You deserve each other!"

Elaine became aware of the pulsing throb on her left hand. She looked down at the gold wedding ring. Representative of another world. Another life. Another man.

Without giving herself time to think, she twisted the ring off of her finger.

It was loath to come off. No doubt a result of all the fattening food she had consumed. A matter that she need not worry anymore, corrupting a body that was not hers to corrupt. It would soon belong to its rightful owner.

A sob rose in Elaine's throat. Just when she thought the ring would win, it came off of her finger with the skin of her knuckle. She threw the gold wedding band at the stone-faced man who wasn't worthy of her love.

"Take it! Take it and find some other poor sucker! I don't want you! I don't need you!"

Charles felt as if a knife stabbed through his heart. Morrigan had never looked so magnificent. Her tangled hair hung down over the lapels of his coat, black caressing black. Her delectable little breasts heaved beneath the masculine cloth. Doubt, true doubt, proving that he was as crazy as she was, assailed him. How could she say things like that? How could she believe that he had used her? He had given her *his* all, too, damn it.

He caught the gold band in disbelief. She had taken it off. His offering. She had thrown his ring at his face.

"Take it! Take it and find some other poor sucker! I don't want you! I don't need you!"

A gasp came from Boleigh. He was dying; Charles knew that—he had seen enough men die in India to know when a man had only minutes. He tore his eyes away from the agonized fury in his wife's face.

Boleigh's face was transformed. A look of almost sexual ecstasy had taken away the pinched look of death. The eyes looked so familiar with that wild, otherworldly light.

He remembered suddenly where he had seen that look: in Morrigan's eyes, when he had observed her in the forest that day before inspecting Boleigh's bull. He had thought then that the look designated a woman of rare spirit and passion.

Boleigh concentrated totally on Morrigan. Charles could feel a surge of energy. The night crackled with it. Strange. Alien. He pulled at his shirt collar. The air was suddenly leaden.

Boleigh's berry-round eyes grew brighter and brighter, even as his lips and face darkened in death. That was not natural. The eyes grew dim near death. Charles could not count the times that he had literally watched the light fade from mortally wounded men, men dehydrated to mere shells of their former bodies from dysentery, men rotted alive with gangrene, men filled with balls of lead. In all cases, in all manner of death, the eyes grew dim.

Charles instinctively moved to protect his wife. He knew not from what, only that there was danger. He licked lips that felt drier than the sands of India. His limbs were paralyzed.

What was happening to him?

He forced his eyes away from Boleigh, an almost impossible task. It was as if the man were hypnotizing him. Morrigan had turned to face Boleigh. She, too, seemed mesmerized by the dying man. At seeing his wife, the invisible menace that Charles felt increased.

The pain and fury had been wiped clean of Morrigan's face, as if she were a blank slate. And her eyes . . . Those beautiful, expressive black eyes of hers . . . it was as if all the warmth were being drained from them. They were changing back to the cold snake eyes he had once compared . . . Morrigan's to.

It was true. It couldn't be true, but it was true. She was going away from him. Dying, somehow. Becoming the old Morrigan, like the old man.

No, it couldn't be true. It was insane.

The light grew dimmer and dimmer within her eyes, while the light within the dying man's eyes grew brighter and brighter.

She was leaving. His wife, his *true* wife, was leaving him.

He couldn't let her go. She couldn't leave him. He wouldn't let her leave him.

A cry ripped through his throat. "No! Don't leave me!"

The moment the ring left Elaine's finger she knew what would happen. She faced Morrigan proudly, willing her to take back this body of hers, wanting only to be gone from this world and the other. Matthew had not believed her. She could forgive Matthew. He had been a small, unimaginative man incapable of caring beyond his concept of what people should be. She could not forgive Charles. He was so much more than that. Yet he had no more faith in her than had Matthew.

Coldness seeped through her body. She had once had a gallbladder test; they had given her an IV solution of dye. It had felt like ice water dripping into her vein. She had become colder and colder, more and more numb until she had felt nothing but a cold void where her body should have been.

Just at the point where she should now feel nothing but a cold void, however, Elaine felt as if she were being flooded with sewage. How could a person live with such a filthy soul?

Elaine tried to draw back—too late, she could feel the erratic beat of Boleigh's heart, the pull of gravity on excess pounds. There was filth there, too, in that other body, filth and smallness.

"—*leave me!*"

So much filth. Elaine remembered how clean she had felt after she and Charles had made love.

"Don't leave me! Damn you, woman, don't leave me, don't you dare leave me!"

Someone was calling out.

"Come to me, damn you! Fight! Damn you! Goddamn you! Don't you leave me alone!"

Alone.

Black swan.

Not right. Not right that he should be alone. That she should be alone.

"Charles," Elaine mumbled. But from whose lips?

"That's right. Fight. Come to me. You have to come to me!"

But it was too late to fight. Death was already there, like an anvil that smashed and smashed at her heart. It was frightening not to be able to draw air into her lungs, yet at the same time she wasn't frightened at all.

"Damn you! I won't let you go!"

From the corner of an eye—Boleigh's eye—no, Morrigan's eye—Elaine could see Charles lurching and stumbling as if it were he who had a shortened leg. How frail those mortals be. Charles swayed back and forth over Boleigh—no, he was swaying back and forth over Elaine—no, he was swaying back and forth over Boleigh again. Dear God, it was so confusing. A leather shoe appeared as if out of nowhere, directly in front of Elaine's face, aiming at Elaine's, no, Boleigh's, Elaine's—

Stars exploded in Elaine's head, followed by blackness. And numbness. Complete numbness.

So this is death, Elaine thought. It was pleasant not to feel the pain and turmoil and betrayal of the living. Why had she fought it?

"No!" The scream pierced the night, that, too, swallowed by the shrinking blackness.

Epilogue

Elaine stared into the vanity mirror at the pale oval face and the apron-covered midriff behind it. Katie caught up a strand of dark hair and secured it with a sharp pin. Reflexive tears pricked Elaine's eyelids.

"It be a pity 'bout yer uncle's ticker giving out like it did, what with him saving ye from those poaching cutthroats and all."

Sunshine poured through the open sides of the four-poster bed. A bird warbled just off the balcony.

"Imagine, murder and mayhem right here in Dorset. Can't rightly see why they up and stiffed that old Hattie like they did. Mind ye, it couldn't of happened to a more deserving soul. Would of made a fine hanging, watching those cutthroats dancing on the end of a gibbet. Didn't find hide nor hair of them, they didn't."

Katie jabbed another pin into the fat bun. "That auntie of yers done gone back to Cornwall. The lord, he let her have a trap fer the cold meat. She said as how she wouldn't have him—that be yer uncle, marm—buried here on heathen ground. Cook said she ain't ever heard such blasphemy. Yer uncle, he died in the line of duty, and it be proper he be buried here. I had a cousin—that be on me da's side, marm—he got himself full of holes holding up a coach. . . ."

Elaine was not surprised to hear the events those three nights ago passed on as the work of "poaching cutthroats." She merely felt a dismal sense of déjà vu. She had come full circle, confined inside her bedroom with a gibbering, unfeeling maid, awaiting Bedlam.

She closed her eyes to shut out those great black orbs staring at her from the mirror. Instantly her heart started hammering, trying to outpace the anvil smashing down on it. Charles's foot shot out of the darkness, just inches away from her head. She jerked back.

"Here now, marm! I be that sorry, I am. Just a few more pins now and we'll be all done here. That Dr. Damon, he be right dishy, ain't he?"

No, Elaine did not think that the black-haired, black-eyed, Heathcliff-like doctor who had awakened her two days ago by prying open her eyelid was "dishy." He made her uncomfortable. She had caught him looking at her with an expression in his eyes that reminded her of Charles, the look of a man who had hidden beneath a woman's bed and observed things he had no business observing. The only thing she could say to his credit was that he had not put her in a straitjacket. Of course, one couldn't put too much stock in that, because who knew whether straitjackets had been invented in this time?

"There ye be, marm!" Katie stepped back. "Now then . . ."

The maid bounced out of view of the mirror. Elaine could hear her rifling through the dresses in the armoire.

"It be a beautiful morn, marm! Cook, she says she ain't seen a spring this fine since her da's cow dropped a two-headed calf."

Elaine stood up and walked toward the open French doors. Dust motes shimmied in the blaze of light. The sun was warm on her face and neck.

Katie held up a yellow satin dress. "The lord, he's sent fer ye. Dr. Damon says as how yer fit as a fiddle now; he said ye just needed a bit of rest to put the roses back in yer cheeks."

How dark and chill the room was. What a perfectly irritating noise that damn bird was making. Elaine scowled. So after avoiding her these last three days, Charles was finally going to have the decency to tell her her fate. To her face, no less.

Elaine stepped aside when Katie attempted to toss the yellow dress over her head. When the maid persisted, Elaine batted the garment away. "I don't want to get dressed, Katie! And even if I did, I wouldn't want to wear that. It's . . . too young-looking."

"But marm! The lord, he said as how I was to dress ye in the yellow. If I don't, he'll let me go without a farthing to me name, and I have t' help feed and—"

"Shoe the little ones. I've heard the story before," Elaine impatiently interrupted. "We both know the lord is not going to let you go, with or without a farthing. Now be a good girl and go pester Fritz. Though I doubt he wants your attentions any more than I do."

"M' lady!"

Elaine felt lower than a worm with tread tracks. It wasn't Katie's fault the lord was going to send Elaine to Bedlam.

"I'm sorry, Katie. I didn't mean that. I guess I . . . haven't completely recovered from the . . . from those poaching cutthroats yet. I am sorry. Really. Fritz must have a loose screw not to want to marry you."

"Well, marm, I don't know 'bout no loose screws, but Mr. Fritz, he's got a powerfully nice handle."

Blood flooded Elaine's cheeks. Katie surely could not have meant what it sounded like she meant. The last time they had had a friendly mistress-to-maid discussion Fritz had not even kissed Katie.

Elaine meekly submitted to being dressed in the yellow satin. Surreptitiously she studied the maid's glowing face. She had a sneaking suspicion she had just been manipulated by a mastermind. Again.

"There ye be, marm!" Katie stepped behind Elaine and fluffed the dress over the short, ruffled, apron-shaped garment she had tied around Elaine in place of the wire bustle. She then jumped forward and readjusted the pompadour neckline that Elaine had been futilely tugging to stretch over the swell of her breasts. "Don't ye make a right pretty picture, now!"

Elaine pasted a smile across her lips. "Thank you, Katie." It was ridiculous, she knew, to feel embarrassed at the expanse of bare skin. Especially after wearing that red dress. But everyone had thought she was Morrigan then. Now Charles thought she was mad.

Elaine, the mad whore. What if he thought she was trying to seduce him?

"Get me a shawl, Katie. The lord will wish to see me in the library, I'm sure. It tends to get a little cool in that room."

"Pshaw! If ye was to put on any more clothes in this heat, ye'd burn to a crisp! Come along now!"

Elaine meekly followed Katie down the corridor, then the stairs. She felt depressingly old and clumsy being led by the sprightly young maid.

Katie made a right-hand turn at the foot of the stairs instead of the left-hand one that led to the library. When the maid approached the great entranceway, the poker-faced butler threw open the massive doors with all the pomp and ceremony of serving royalty. Or the eagerness extended to a departing visitor who had overstayed her welcome.

"Come *on*, m' lady!" Katie said impatiently. "The coach be waiting!"

Elaine felt her heart plummet through the yellow satin slippers. Charles was wasting no time in ridding himself of his "mad" wife. He had probably already interviewed a whole bevy of girls to fill the marital vacancy. Girls with big bazookas and two straight legs.

A footman waited outside by the coach. He impassively helped Elaine up the steep steps. It was dark and musky inside; Elaine had no more settled onto the plush velvet seat than the door slammed shut. The vehicle abruptly sprang forward. She grabbed for the velvet strap hanging by the window.

Well, Elaine thought grimly. Another first, traveling in a genuine nineteenth-century coach. Soon she would experience yet another first, a real live trip to a nineteenth-century insane asylum. At this rate she would have to start keeping a list of all these firsts.

She wondered how Matthew had arranged her commitment in the twentieth century. Then she imagined the look on the face of the nineteenth-century psychiatrist when she told him how she had awakened in another time and body. Would she be physically restrained before or after she concluded the story and told him that if Charles had not kicked Morrigan—who was in the body of her fat old uncle—in the face, Morrigan would have taken back her rightful body and Elaine would have been the one to die trapped inside the fat old uncle's body?

At any rate, Elaine presumed that was what had happened. Her memory after taking off the ring was comprised of a series of jumbled events and sensations. She remembered the kick because, for one brief second, it had been aimed directly at her head.

Elaine rubbed the skin on her bare ring finger. Tears welled up in her eyes. Charles knew, damn it—he knew that Elaine was not Morrigan and that Morrigan had been inside her uncle's body. Why else would he have kicked Boleigh in the face? How could he send her away, knowing the truth?

How could he send her away in this *coach*? Sweat beaded and ran in rivulets between Elaine's breasts. Her face was sweltering. She felt like Chia plants were sprouting underneath her armpits. She did not have to worry about expiring in a nineteenth-century insane asylum. She would expire in this bone-jarring, teeth-rattling excuse for a means of transportation that was rapidly attaining Fahrenheit-hell temperatures.

Elaine tried the two knobs on either door that were surely meant to lower the glass windows. One of the knobs came off in her hand; the other refused to turn. She didn't know whether to curse or bless the coach when it stopped. Elaine stared for long seconds at the opposite seat, the knob clenched in her hand. She continued staring at the plush blue velvet when the door swung open. "You look like a wilting daisy," an achingly familiar voice said. Elaine's spine stiffened, hearing the timbre of laughter. "Here, come out of there."

Hard, hot hands encompassed her corseted waist. She was deposited onto the ground; her teeth snapped together at the impact. Elaine fortified herself with a deep breath of air before viewing this, her first nineteenth-century asylum. She forced her gaze past a white shirt that was open to expose a mat of dark hair.

Her eyes widened.

The asylum consisted of great leafy trees and a rich green carpet of grass. Blue water glinted beyond his shoulder; bright little flowers waved and danced on the bank of the lake.

Elaine licked her lips. "I . . . I don't understand."

Charles's eyes were hooded. "Don't you?" he asked, not a question at all. "Roger, go on home. Her ladyship and I will make our own way."

"Very good, my lord."

The coach sprang forward. Immediately they were enveloped in a plume of dust.

Thick, gritty, encompassing dust.

It stuck to the sweat and formed great muddy paths on Elaine's face and bosom. She gritted her teeth.

Charles's lips twitched. "Come on, let's get out of this before we both look like street urchins."

He pivoted and strode toward a grove of trees near the lake. Elaine followed, torn between anger that he should see her at such a disadvantage and laughter at the absurdity of it all. Were there no simple emotions in 1883?

Elaine stepped out into a clearing on the other side of the trees. A blanket was spread out on a carpet of tiny blue flowers. A wicker basket sat near the edge of it. Charles flopped down onto the blanket like a big, sleek cat. When Elaine continued standing, he held out a hand to her.

She stared at his long fingers, remembering how they had felt on her flesh, inside her flesh, wondering when they would sign the documents to put her away forever.

He made an impatient sound and grabbed Elaine's hand. "What's this?" he asked when she continued clenching her fist. Slowly, methodically he pried her fingers open and held up the handle to the coach window. "Don't tell me Roger still has not repaired that window!" he exclaimed.

Elaine remained mute. The feel of his skin against hers was unbearable. She withdrew it before she embarrassed both herself and him with a noisy bout of tears. Instantly Charles grabbed her hand and pulled her down onto his lap. He wrapped his arms about her as if afraid she would leap up.

"God, I've wanted you," he said thickly. "You have no idea how hard it was not coming to you. How especially hard it was knowing the only thing that separated us was that little door that wasn't even locked. I'd rather face a thousand warring Indians than to go through what I've been through these last few days keeping away from you."

Elaine stared at his throat. A pulse beat as if working double-time. His heart pounded so hard it shook his whole body. She could feel something harder, she suspected, than had been these last few days, beneath her bottom.

"Why did you, then?" She asked in a tiny voice, afraid to hope, afraid to speculate. Reason told her not to trust another man, that one had used her sexuality against her, that this one might be setting her up to do the same thing.

The world tilted, a maze of blue sky and green leaves. Elaine found herself on her back. Charles leaned over her. His blue eyes were guarded.

"Perhaps because milady needed her rest. Damon said the last thing you needed was a rapacious husband keeping at you all day and night."

Elaine had always thought most doctors were a bunch of incompetent asses. Apparently it was no different in this time.

"Or perhaps . . . perhaps because I was sulking."

That was curious. Why would a lord sulk? she idly wondered, watching the breeze play with a thick chestnut curl beneath his ear.

"You see, you said you didn't want me. That you didn't need me. I didn't want to force myself on you. Again. I wanted you to come to me. But then I realized that it didn't matter. I couldn't stay away. Do you mind?"

The hard, chiseled features were surprisingly uncertain for a man who considered his wife insane. Elaine lifted her hand and tentatively traced the lip that only curled when he was disturbed. An imp of mischief prompted her to say in that low, husky voice that was hers now for better or for worse, "Yes."

The open, uncertain light in those blue eyes dimmed. He drew back, the black swan spurned.

Elaine looped her arms around his neck. "Yes," she repeated. "I mind. I mind that you left me alone for three whole days."

She knew by the sudden gleam in his eyes that payback time was coming. He slipped his head underneath her right arm.

"Where are you going?"

Charles picked up the wicker basket. "It's time for our picnic," he said. And dumped the contents of the basket onto the blanket. A dozen lemons rolled and bounced across the plaid wool.

Elaine sat up in surprise. "This?" she asked. "This is all you brought for our picnic?"

Charles laughed mischievously. Elaine found herself on her back before the words had died on her lips. "This is a lemon-maid picnic."

"No lemon tarts?" she asked tartly.

Charles crowed. "Ah, well, you see, you must take a lemon maid before you can make a lemon tart."

Who would have ever thought lemons could be used so imaginatively? Elaine thought dreamily. If word got around, it could influence the whole commodities market. Instead of recommending an apple a day, doctors would be recommending women all over the world to have a lemon a day. IDs would be required in stores to protect the young and innocent. Young people who reached the age of twenty-one would rush to the grocery stores for their first taste of the forbidden lemon.

Charles lazily nibbled on her ear. "Fritz asked the most amazing question yesterday."

Elaine languidly moved her head to give the nibbling teeth better access. "Mmm . . . ?"

"He asked why he had been required to squeeze lemons when there was a perfectly capable cook to do so."

The slight breeze was suddenly quite cool against her flaming skin. Elaine tried to crawl beneath the cover of his body. Charles wrapped his arm about her more firmly, holding her in position.

"And do you know what I told him?"

Elaine squeezed her eyes shut. "No."

"I told him better lemons than fish."

Outrage surpassed embarrassment. Elaine groaned. *Good grief.* She had known that was an old joke, but over a hundred years old?

"As in schools of fish. Then Fritz asked the most remarkable thing. He asked if he might commandeer a few upon occasion. It appears that he has been reluctant to approach our little Katie because he felt she was too young to be saddled with a school of children."

A smile tugged at Elaine's lips. No wonder Katie had been so smug earlier today. A handle, though? Fritz did indeed have unplumbed depths. She laughed, the sound low, throaty, uninhibitedly carnal.

A hot, wet tongue explored the inner canal of her ear. "What?" he breathed. "Do my amorous attentions amuse milady?"

Elaine took a deep breath. "Charles—"

"No, don't say 'Charles'"—he pronounced his name falsetto—"in that voice. I had a Latin instructor who used to pronounce my name exactly in that manner before sending me to the headmaster. I liked the way you said my name much better when I was straining for seeds."

Heat spread over her skin. "Charles, are we going to ignore what happened three nights ago?"

He sighed. "I don't suppose you can?"

Elaine lay still beneath his exploring lips. He sat up and presented her with a splendid view of twenty-two vertebrae.

"Charles, do you love me?"

Elaine watched the vertebrae fuse together. She didn't know why she had asked that. Perhaps because she had suddenly realized that in all of her seventeen years of marriage to Matthew, he had not said it once.

"Didn't I just demonstrate it?" he asked coldly.

"Charles, would you want me if I were fat?"

Charles turned around and stared at her. A reluctant laugh escaped him. "Sweetheart, you have lemon juice and sweat and dust smeared from one end to the other. What kind of question is that?"

Elaine pulled one end of the blanket over her naked body. "I don't know. All I know is that you haven't once addressed me by name today. I thought when I got into the coach that you were sending me to an asylum."

Charles looked down at the blanket tucked around her torso. Elaine's heart skipped a beat. He was avoiding her eyes. That must mean he was still considering it.

"Charles, if you don't want me, I'll go away—"

"Don't say it!" Charles said harshly. "If you ever talk like that again I'll paddle your little bottom so hard you won't be able to sit for a month of Sundays. My God, woman, I almost lost you once. Do you think I'd ever consent to your leaving me?"

The expression on his face was so forbidding that Elaine forbore answering.

"I believe you. I realize now that you're not the woman I married. Thank God. I just need . . . more time to take it all in. Someday I want to hear all about it, your other life, but for now I just want . . . you."

"I was married, Charles."

His lips tightened. "Did you—do you—love him?"

There was a lingering sense of pain, remembering Matthew's betrayal. "I thought I did. I think I did. I don't know now."

"Did you have children by him?"

"No. He didn't want children."

"I do. Not this minute, but in a year or so I will. I don't know how you prevented conception, unless you abstained altogether. Which I guarantee we will not. But even if I didn't want children, and we took preventive measures every time we came together, there's still a good chance that you would eventually get pregnant."

Elaine felt her heart flutter. He was right, of course. There was no "pill" in the nineteenth century. No Pap smears. No chemotherapy. No penicillin.

The flutter escalated into full-scale fibrillation, realizing how little control she would have over this new body of hers, living in the nineteenth century. What if—

"If you could go back to your other life, would you?"

Elaine looked at the lord's blue eyes, which were now shielded, at the right corner of his lip, which now curled toward the thin white scar.

This was her life now. For better or for worse.

She licked her lip, tasting lemon, tasting him, tasting them together.

For better. *Oh, yes.* Her life now was definitely for the better.

Her heart beat steady and sure. "No."

A smile lit his face. "Do you love me?"

That imp of mischief resurfaced. Besides, he had sidestepped the question when she had raised it. "I never kiss and tell."

He raised an eyebrow. "Oh?"

"But I'm not above show and tell."

Charles laughed. "I do love you, you minx. I love your sense of humor. I love the way you laugh. I love the way your breath always smells like white ginger. I love the way you cry out when I give you pleasure. But most of all . . ."

"Yes?" Elaine found she was not above begging for compliments or anything else from this man. She would even continue cleaning her teeth with soap, if it would please him.

"I loved it when you never talked back!"

Elaine squealed with twentieth-century feminist affront. He jerked the blanket off her. She wrestled free of arms that became amazingly octopuslike when they were bent on amorous conquest.

"Ouch!"

Elaine sat up and reached for the place on her spine that felt as if it had been permanently indented. Charles leaned over, then held out his hand. A thick red-gold ring gleamed in his palm.

"There it is! I was going to present it to you rather in a different manner, but I suppose it's just as well I forgot in the heat of the moment, so to speak. I might have forgotten to remove it in time. Or swallowed it. Here."

Charles grabbed Elaine's hand. The band was warm from the heat of their bodies. It glowed around the long, pale piano finger. Her finger, Elaine's, not Morrigan's. Morrigan had not wanted anything to do with this body that had brought Elaine pure ecstasy.

"Charles, don't you ever wonder why it happened? Why I'm here? Do you think she really was a Druid?"

Charles brought Elaine's hand up to his lips. He planted a warm, lingering kiss on her knuckle, which showed faint scratches from where she had forced the ring over it.

"No, I don't think she was a Druid. Quite a few of the old practices still exist. Like Beltane. But none of them are enacted to hurt anyone. And as far as your being here . . ."

Charles played with the ring, turning it around and around on her finger. "I think I am incredibly lucky, and I shall spend every night and what other time I can arrange in convincing you that you are equally lucky. And though some might trace certain events to this ring, I am not of a superstitious nature. However, if you ever, *ever* take it off again, I will paddle your bottom. In fact, I think I will anyhow, for scaring the hell out of me."

"Charles!"

Elaine found herself face down across Charles's hairy thighs. She turned her head. Their clothes were scattered about the carpet of flowers. Sunlight glinted off of the lake. She felt a brief caress before a hard hand came down on her behind, not enough to hurt, really, but enough to sting.

She jackknifed her body backward. "Charles! Charles, don't! Charles, I love you! Charles—look!"

Charles paused midstroke. The black swan glided across the lake. Behind him trailed a white swan. Some feet away from the shore, the female swan gracefully ducked her head into the water. The black swan slowly circled his feeding mate. He resumed lead position. His long black neck stretched, then doubled over in a loop. The brilliant scarlet bill commenced a self-congratulatory preening.

"Charles, they're beautiful!"

Charles glanced down at Elaine's lightly tinted cheeks. "Indeed they are."

ROBERT FLANAGAN was born in Toledo, Ohio, in 1941. He served in the Marine Corps Reserve, and graduated from the Universities of Toledo and Chicago. He has received a National Endowment for the Arts fellowship and three Ohio Arts Council grants, and has published a novel, *Maggot*. Mr. Flanagan lives in Delaware, Ohio, with his wife and two daughters, and teaches writing at Ohio Wesleyan University.